"By the end of this fascinating and deliciously creepy mystery, all sorts of strange behavior past and present comes to life. . . . The plot includes religious inquisitions, missing medieval manuscripts, and a well-drawn group of alienated Icelandic goths. The most appealing aspect of this mystery is the author's ability to convey to readers her country's unique history, culture, and starkly beautiful landscape."   —*USA Today*

"Top-notch crime fiction . . . steeped in witch hunts and medieval ritual. . . . The investigation takes plenty of wrong turns on the way to a particularly satisfying solution. . . . This is a fascinating excursion into the macabre that keeps its feet firmly planted in reality."

—*Boston Globe*

"An academic detective story, with a bright young lawyer . . . doing the snooping. Thóra undertakes a historical survey course in Icelandic black magic after a German exchange student . . . is ritualistically murdered. History is more fun when it's horrid."

—*New York Times Book Review*

"[A] chilly tale. . . . *Last Rituals* shows . . . confident pacing. Chapter by chapter, the book passes what might be called the velocity test: it moves with sufficient speed to hold even the most jaded reader's attention. And there's something satisfyingly true to Iceland . . . when Ms. Sigurdardóttir's mystery ultimately turns on a battle over rare medieval manuscripts. We pick [mysteries] up in order to ask 'What next?' *Last Rituals* keeps the reader asking."   —*Wall Street Journal*

"[Yrsa Sigurdardóttir] has the storytelling art down pat. . . . [A] straightforward, nicely paced narrative. . . . *Last Rituals* proceeds at just the right tempo. . . . A good, old-fashioned whodunit. The most winning characteristic of *Last Rituals* [is its] charm. Thóra and Matthew are quite different in many ways. He is punctilious and methodical . . . while her method is more, shall we say, improvisational. But the two have in common a sense of drollery that enables their relationship to develop in a bantering manner that seems more natural than fictional. . . . They are well on their way to becoming a Nordic-Germanic Nick and Nora Charles."   —*Philadelphia Inquirer*

entertaining, well plotted. . . . [*Last Rituals*] cleverly combines the historical and macabre."
—*The Times* (London)

"Casts a wide net full of clues, suspects, and tidbits of Icelandic history and magic. . . . The tension is electric. . . . The crime novels of Arnaldur Indridason showed that this small northern country had the potential to produce first-rate mysteries, and Yrsa Sigurdardóttir proves that it was no fluke."
—*Winnipeg Free Press*

"This [is] a fascinating read. . . . It is a well-told story about mistakes, compassion, and forgiveness. I loved how the author took me somewhere I'd never been before, so I highly recommend *Last Rituals*."
—*Romance Reviews Today*

"One of the very appealing aspects of this mystery is the setting. . . . It's an unusual, exotic background. This well-told story is very readable and has a surprising ending. Definitely recommended."
—*Deadly Pleasures*

"A surprisingly light and playful novel. . . . Lawyer Thóra Gudmundsdóttir is an engaging detective."
—*The Daily Telegraph* (London)

"Another excellent Icelandic crime writer. . . . [Thóra Gudmundsdóttir is] a lot funnier than the dour Scandinavian cops crime readers have gotten used to. . . . Thóra is a smart, resourceful amateur detective. *Last Rituals* is less gloomy than the usual northern European crime novel, and hopefully this is the beginning of a series."
—*Mystery Scene*

"Excellent. . . . [Sigurdardóttir] grabs readers' attention from the very beginning with an intriguing storyline, takes them through all the pieces of the puzzle with a tremendous amount of detail, and concludes the novel in a way that will not be predictable. If you are looking for a novel that starts off with suspense and keeps right on going, *Last Rituals* is the one for you. I highly recommend this book."
—Bestsellersworld.com

"If you're looking for something very unusual in mysteries—and don't mind plenty of horror along with touches of humor—then don't miss *Last Rituals*."
—BookLoons.com

"*Last Rituals* pairs a fascinating history of witchcraft and an inquisition with the dynamic interest of a modern murder mystery. . . . Thóra is presented as a well-rounded character as she struggles to balance her personal and professional lives, and we see how her growing compassion for the victim affects her interactions with her son. Tempered with wry humor and a sprinkling of romantic interest."

—TCM Reviews

"The plot twists and turns in the historical search—and the unraveling of the motives for the murder are spellbinding. . . . A delight. Fortunately for mystery lovers, this is the first of a series."

—ArmchairInterviews.com

"Completely engrossing, exciting, and very macabre. . . . This is a spooky read. The malevolence of this novel becomes a tangible presence as the story builds, fairly throbbing off the pages. . . . The imagery was truly lovely and atmospheric, really a terrific background for the subject. . . . This is a wonderful, atmospheric thriller that is not to be missed."

—RomanceJunkies.com

"A skillfully plotted book that will keep you reading from the first page to the end."   —ILoveAMystery.com

Atli Már Hafsteinsson

About the Author

YRSA SIGURDARDÓTTIR is an internationally bestselling author and one of the directors of Verkís, one of Iceland's largest engineering firms. She lives with her family in Reykjavík. Her second novel featuring Thóra Gudmundsdóttir, *My Soul to Take*, is available from William Morrow. To learn more about her, please visit www.verold.is/yrsa.asp.

LAST RITUALS

A Novel of Suspense

YRSA SIGURDARDÓTTIR

TRANSLATED FROM THE ICELANDIC BY BERNARD SCUDDER

HARPER

NEW YORK • LONDON • TORONTO • SYDNEY

This book is dedicated to my dear Óli.

Special thanks to Harald Schmitt,

who lent me his name—

and allowed me to kill him.

—Yrsa

HARPER

This book was originally published in Iceland in 2005 by Veröld Publishing.

A hardcover edition of this book was published in 2007 by William Morrow, an imprint of HarperCollins Publishers.

FIRST HARPER PAPERBACK PUBLISHED 2009.

Designed by Jennifer Ann Daddio

Library of Congress Cataloging-in-Publication Data has been applied for.

ISBN 978-0-06-114337-3

17 18 19 20 ID/LSC 18 17 16 15 14 13 12 11 10 9

PROLOGUE

OCTOBER 31, 2005

The head caretaker, Tryggvi, stood by the coffeemaker. The water dripping through the machine was the only sound in the empty building, which housed the university's history department. Soon the bustling cleaners would arrive, chatting and giggling, dragging their carts and vacuums out of the housekeeping room. The caretaker reveled in the silence and the aroma of brewing coffee. He had been employed by the university for over thirty years and had seen his share of changes, not the least of which was the complete turnaround in the nationality of the cleaners who worked under his supervision. When he started they had all been Icelandic and understood his every word; now his interactions with his subordinates consisted of hand gestures and loudly spoken one-word orders. The women were all recent arrivals from Southeast Asia, except for one woman of African descent. Until the faculty members and students arrived for the day, he might as well have been working in Bangkok.

Taking his steaming cup, Tryggvi walked to the window. He lifted the blinds and looked out, taking an appreciative sip of the strong brew.

The campus was covered with snow. The temperature was unusually low, causing the white blanket to shimmer as if someone had strewn glitter over the ground during the night. The muffling effect of the snow added to the sense of utter stillness. Tryggvi was reminded of the upcoming Christmas season and felt oddly content.

He watched as a car entered the parking lot. *So much for my Christmas spirit,* he thought. The car was carefully maneuvered into an empty space, unusual considering there were no other vehicles present and no obvious reason to take such care. Tryggvi looked on as the driver emerged from the car and shut the door. Through the closed window he heard the indistinct beep of a remote control engaging the locks of the vehicle. The man walked toward the building.

Tryggvi dropped the blinds and finished his coffee. From within the building he heard the faculty entrance door open as the driver came inside. Of all the staff, professors, lecturers, secretaries, and others whom Tryggvi had to deal with, this man Gunnar was by far the most unpleasant. He was uptight, constantly complained about the janitorial services, and had a superior air about him that always made Tryggvi feel small and uncomfortable. At the beginning of the term the man had accused the cleaning women of stealing a paper he had written about Irish monks in Iceland before the Viking settlement. Luckily the article had resurfaced and the issue had died down. Ever since, Tryggvi did not merely dislike him; he detested him. Why would Asian cleaning women who couldn't even read their own names in Icelandic be tempted to steal some highbrow article about Irish monks? In his eyes this was a cheap attack on people who were unable to defend themselves.

Tryggvi was appalled when Gunnar was appointed head of department. He had already spoken to Tryggvi about various improvements that he expected, one of which was that the cleaning women were to conduct their work in silence. Tryggvi had wanted to tell him that their chatter did not disturb anyone, as the bulk of their work was carried out either before or after anyone else was in the building. Except for Gunnar, of course. Why the man had to show up every morning before the buses even began to run was beyond Tryggvi.

A flutter of voices marked the women's arrival. They gathered in the little coffee room and said their accented hellos, followed by the usual giggling. Tryggvi could not help but smile. Then through their noisy bustle he heard a strange sound from within the building. It was a guttural moan, soft at first but growing louder. Tryggvi shushed the women and listened. The cleaners picked up on the sound, their eyes widening. Two of them made the sign of the cross. Tryggvi put down his coffee and hurried out of the lounge with the women in hot pursuit.

In the corridor, Tryggvi listened as the wailing became a scream. He could not distinguish whether the voice was male or female; he was not even sure it was human. Could an animal have gotten into the building and been injured somehow? The primal howl was suddenly joined by the sound of something falling over and breaking. Tryggvi quickened his pace down the corridor. The sounds seemed to come from the upper story. He took the stairs two at a time. The women were still following, and to Tryggvi's annoyance they now began to scream as well.

The staircase took him to the floor housing the department offices. Despite the wailing from behind him, Tryggvi could tell that the scream definitely came from this level. He broke into a run, followed closely by the cleaners. He opened the fire door to the office corridor and stopped so abruptly that the bevy of howling women crashed into him.

It was not the overturned bookcase or the frantic head of department, crawling on all fours over the books that had spilled across the corridor, that held Tryggvi mesmerized. It was the body lying faceup farther down the hallway, protruding from the alcove where the floor's printer was housed. Tryggvi felt his stomach lurch. What in God's name were those patches on its eyes? And the hands, what was wrong with the hands? The women peeked past Tryggvi and their screams intensified. He felt them pulling anxiously at his shirt, which came untucked. He tried to twist his body free from their grip, but to no avail. The head of department raised his hands in a plea for help, desperate to escape from the repulsive scene behind him. Tryggvi braced himself, suppressing the urge to grab the women and run. He took a step forward and the women let out another chorus of piercing screams. They tried to pull him back but he managed to shake them off. He approached the sobbing Gunnar.

He could make no sense of the mutterings coming from the professor's drooling mouth. On a hunch Tryggvi assumed that the body—it had to be a body, nothing living could look like that—had fallen onto Gunnar when he opened the door of the printer alcove. Against his will he gazed down at the appalling human remains. The black patches on the eyes were not patches at all. Tryggvi's stomach clenched. *God help us all,* he thought. The knot in his stomach tightened, and Tryggvi threw up.

CHAPTER 1

DECEMBER 6, 2005

Thóra Gudmundsdóttir brushed a stray Cheerio from her trousers and quickly tidied herself before entering the lawyers' office. Not so bad. The morning's challenges of getting her six-year-old daughter and sixteen-year-old son to school on time were over. Recently, Thóra's daughter had started refusing to wear pink, which would not have been a problem if her clothes had not been more or less all in that color. Her son, on the other hand, would gladly have worn the same tattered clothes year in and year out provided there was a skull and crossbones on them somewhere. His great achievement was to wake up in the morning in the first place. Thóra sighed at the thought. It was not easy bringing up two children alone. Then again, it hadn't been easy while she was still married either. The only difference then was that, coupled with the morning chores, she and her husband had constantly bickered. The thought that this was a thing of the past cheered her up, and a smile crept over her lips as she opened the door.

"Good morning," she chimed.

Instead of returning her greeting, the secretary grimaced. She did not look up from her computer screen or stop thumping at the mouse. *As much fun as ever,* Thóra thought. Deep down inside she never stopped cursing their secretarial problems. They had doubtless cost their firm business. Thóra could not think of one client who had not complained about the girl. She was not only rude but also exceptionally unattractive. It was not being in the super-heavyweight bracket that was the big issue, but her general carelessness about her appearance. Plus, she was invariably angry at every-thing and everyone. And, to top things off, her parents had named her Bella. If only she would quit on her own initiative. She seemed far from happy at the firm and showed no signs of improving. Not that Thóra could imagine any job that would cheer her up. The trouble was, it was impossi-ble to sack her.

When Thóra and her business partner, the older and more experi-enced Bragi, teamed up to open a legal firm together, they were so taken with the premises that they let the landlord add a proviso to the rental agreement: the firm would employ his daughter as a secretary. In their defense, they had no way of knowing what they were getting themselves into. The girl had a glowing recommendation from the estate agents who had rented there before them. Now, however, Thóra was convinced that the previous tenants had moved from the ideal location on Skólavör-dustígur solely to rid themselves of the secretary from hell. They were surely still howling with laughter at how gullible Thóra and Bragi had been about those references. Thóra was equally convinced that if they took the matter to court they could have the proviso overturned on the grounds that the references were dubious. But that would cost the firm the small reputation Thóra and Bragi had built up so far. Who would con-sult a legal firm that specializes in contractual law yet messes up its own contracts? And even if they could get rid of Bella, it was not as if good secretaries were lining up at the door.

"Someone phoned," Bella mumbled, glued to her computer screen.

Thóra looked up in surprise from hanging up her coat. "Really?" she said. "Do you have any idea who it was?"

"No. Spoke German, I think. I couldn't understand him anyway."

"Is he going to call back?"

"I don't know. I cut him off. By accident."

"In the unlikely event that he does ring back, would you mind putting the call through to me? I studied in Germany and I speak German."

"Hmph," Bella grunted. She shrugged. "Maybe it wasn't German. It could have been Russian. And it was a woman. I think. Or a man."

"Bella, whoever calls—a woman from Russia or a man from Germany, even a dog from Greece that speaks in tongues—put them through to me. Okay?" Thóra did not wait for a reply—didn't expect one—but walked straight into her modest office.

She sat down and switched on the computer. Her desk was not quite as chaotic as usual. The day before she had spent an hour sorting the papers that had piled up over the past month. She logged on to her e-mail and began deleting junk mail and jokes from friends. All that was left were three e-mails from clients, one from her friend Laufey with the subject line *Let's get wasted this weekend,* and one from the bank. She had probably exceeded her credit card limit. And she was bound to be overdrawn as well. She decided not to open the e-mail, to be on the safe side.

Her telephone rang.

"Central Lawyers, can I help you?"

"Guten Tag, Frau Gudmundsdóttir?"

"Guten Tag." Thóra searched for a pen and paper. High German. She made a mental note to address the woman with the formal *"Sie."*

Thóra squeezed her eyes shut and hoped she could rely on the good command of German she had gained while getting her law degree at the University of Berlin. She put on her best pronunciation. "How can I be of assistance?"

"My name is Amelia Guntlieb. I was given your name by Professor Anderheiss."

"Yes, he taught me in Berlin." Thóra hoped her phrasing was right. She could tell how rusty her pronunciation had become. There were not many opportunities to practice German in Iceland.

"Yes." After an uncomfortable silence the woman continued: "My son was murdered. My husband and I need assistance."

Thóra tried to think fast. Guntlieb? Wasn't Guntlieb the name of the German student who was found dead at the university?

"Hello?" The woman seemed unsure whether Thóra was still on the line.

Thóra hurried to reply: "Yes, sorry. Your son. Did it happen here in Iceland?"

"Yes."

"I think I know the case you're referring to, but I must admit I've only heard about it on the news. Are you sure you're talking to the right person?"

"I hope so. We're not happy with the police investigation."

"Really?" Thóra was surprised. She thought the police had solved the case admirably. The murderer was arrested within three days of the terrible crime. "You know they're keeping someone in custody?"

"We're well aware of that. But we're not convinced that he's the guilty party."

"Why not?" asked Thóra.

"We're just not convinced. There's no more to it than that." The woman cleared her throat politely. "We want someone else, someone impartial, to go over the case. Someone who speaks German." Silence. "You surely understand how difficult it is for us." Silence again. "Harald was our son."

Thóra tried to convey her sympathy by lowering her voice and speaking slowly. "Yes, I do understand that. I have a son of my own. It's impossible for me to imagine the grief you must feel, but you have my deepest condolences. However, I'm not sure I can help you."

"Thank you for your kind words." The voice was cold as ice. "Professor Anderheiss claims you have the qualities we are looking for. He said you were obstinate, firm, and tough." Thóra had the feeling her ex-professor could not quite bring himself to say "bossy." The woman continued: "But sympathetic too. He's a good friend of our family and we trust him. Are you prepared to take on the case? We shall reward you generously." She mentioned a figure.

It was an incredible amount, before taxes or not. More than twice the regular hourly rate that Thóra charged. On top of it the woman offered a bonus if the investigation led to the arrest of someone other than the man currently in custody. The bonus was higher than Thóra's salary for a whole year. "What do you expect to get for that money? I'm not a private detective."

"We're looking for someone who can go over the case again, examine the evidence and appraise the police findings." Again the woman paused before continuing. "The police refuse to talk to us. It's rather annoying."

Their son has been murdered and dealing with the police is rather annoying, Thóra thought. "I'll think about it. Do you have a number I can call?"

"Yes." The woman recited the number. "I ask you not to take too long to consider the offer. I shall look elsewhere if I don't hear from you later today."

"Don't worry. I'll let you know soon."

"Frau Gudmundsdóttir, one more thing."

"Yes?"

"We have one condition."

"Which is?"

She cleared her throat. "We want to be the first people to hear of anything you uncover. Important or otherwise."

"Let's see if I can help you in the first place before discussing the details."

They exchanged good-byes and Thóra put the telephone down. A great start to the day, being treated like a maidservant. And over the limit on her credit card. And overdrawn. The telephone rang again. Thóra picked up the receiver.

"Hello, I'm calling from the garage. Listen, it looks a bit worse than we thought."

"What's the prognosis? Will the car live?" Thóra snapped back. Her car had refused to start when she wanted to run some lunchtime errands the day before. She had tried the ignition again and again, but to no avail. In the end she gave up and had the car towed off to a garage. The garage owner took pity on her and lent her an old clunker while her car was being fixed. It was a heap of junk, marked "Bibbi's Garage" all over, and the floor by the backseats was covered in trash, mainly packaging from spare parts and empty Coca-Cola cans. Thóra had to make do with the car, though, because she couldn't get by without one.

"It doesn't look good." He was cold. "It'll cost a fair bit." A speech followed packed with car repair terminology that Thóra couldn't make head or tail of. But the price needed no explanation.

"Thank you. Just repair it."

Thóra put down the telephone. She stared at it for several minutes, engrossed in her thoughts. Christmas was approaching with all the accompanying expenses: decorations, spending, presents, spending, dinners, spending, family gatherings, spending and—surprise, surprise—even more spending. The law firm was not exactly turning away clients. If she took on the German project it would keep her busy. And it would solve her money problems and much more besides. She could even take the children on vacation. There must be places for a girl of six, a boy of sixteen, and a woman of thirty-six to go. She could even invite along a man of twenty-six to level out the gender and age ratio. She picked up the telephone.

Frau Guntlieb did not answer; it was a servant. Thóra asked for the lady of the household and soon heard footsteps approaching, probably over a tiled floor. A cold voice spoke over the telephone.

"Hello, Frau Guntlieb. This is Thóra Gudmundsdóttir calling from Iceland."

"Yes." After a short silence it was obvious that she was not going to say anything more.

"I've decided to help you."

"Good."

"When do you want me to start?"

"Straightaway. I've ordered a table for lunch so that you can discuss the matter with Matthew Reich. He works for my husband. He's in Iceland and has the investigative experience that you lack. He can brief you on the case in more detail."

The tone to the word "lack" could hardly have been more condescending had Thóra been guilty of turning up dead drunk at a children's birthday party. But she ignored it. "Yes, I understand. But I want to emphasize that I'm not sure I can actually help you."

"We shall see. Matthew will have a contract for you to sign. Give yourself plenty of time to read it over."

Thóra was seized by a sudden urge to tell the woman to go to hell. She hated her haughtiness and arrogance. But when she thought about a vacation with her children and the imaginary man of twenty-six, she swallowed her pride and mumbled a vague assent.

"Be at Hótel Borg at twelve. Matthew can tell you a number of things that did not appear in the papers. Some of them are not fit to print."

Listening to the woman's voice, Thóra gave a shudder. It was tough and devoid of emotion, but broken somehow at the same time. People probably sounded like that under such circumstances. She said nothing.

"Did you get that? You know the hotel?"

Thóra almost laughed. Hótel Borg was the oldest hotel in Reykjavík, a downtown landmark. "Yes, I believe I do. I suppose I'll be there." Although she tried to salvage her pride by striking a note of uncertainty, Thóra knew she would be at Hótel Borg at twelve o'clock. No doubt about it.

CHAPTER 2

Thóra looked at the clock and put down the documents for the case she had been working on. Yet another client who refused to face up to the fact that his position was hopeless. She was glad she had cleared up a few minor matters before meeting Herr Matthew Reich. She phoned through to Bella on the switchboard.

"I'm going out to a meeting. I don't know how long I'll be but don't expect me back before two." A grunt came over the line that Thóra could only interpret as agreement. My God, what's wrong with simply saying "yes"?

Thóra took her handbag and put a notebook in her briefcase. Everything she knew about the case was from the media, and she had not followed it with any particular interest. As far as she recalled, the scenario was something like this: a foreign student had been murdered, the body mutilated in some unspecified way, and a drug dealer, who maintained his innocence, had been arrested. Not much to go on.

While she was putting on her coat, Thóra looked at herself in the large mirror. She knew it was important to make a good impression at the first meeting, especially if the client was well-off. Clothes maketh the man, say those who can afford the best. And by their shoes ye shall know them. She had never understood that, basing her judgment of people on their character and never their footwear. Fortunately her shoes were quite presentable and her dress suit appropriate for a respectable lawyer. She ran her fingers through her long blond hair.

Thóra rummaged in her handbag, eventually found her lipstick, and hurriedly dabbed it on her lips. Normally she did not wear much makeup, making do with moisturizer and mascara in the mornings. She carried lipstick in case of unexpected situations like this. It suited her and made her feel confident. She had the good fortune to take after her mother rather than her father, who had once been asked to model as Winston Churchill's double for an advertisement. While she could probably not be described as beautiful or striking, her high cheekbones and blue almond-shaped eyes meant that she could safely be called pretty. She had also been lucky enough to inherit her mother's build, which made it easy to keep slim.

Thóra said farewell to her colleagues and Bragi called back, "Good luck." She had told him about the telephone conversation with Frau Guntlieb and the meeting arranged with her representative. Bragi found it all very exciting and felt that being contacted from abroad was a clear indication their firm was on the right course. He even suggested tagging "International" or "Group" onto their modest name in order to spruce it up a bit. Thóra hoped that Bragi was joking, but she could not be sure.

Outside, the wind refreshed her. November had been unusually cold, boding a long, harsh winter. Now they were paying for the incredibly warm summer, although temperatures in the low seventies would hardly be considered a heat wave outside Iceland. Thóra felt that the climate was changing, due either to the natural climate cycle or the greenhouse effect. For her children's sake she hoped it was the former, but deep down inside she knew it was not. She covered her cheeks with the hood of her coat so that she did not turn up for the meeting with frozen ears. Hótel Borg was too close to her office for her to consider driving there in the car from the garage. God only knew what the German would think if he saw her parking that heap of junk outside. Her shoes would have little to say in the matter then, that was certain. Parking was sparse downtown so she would probably spend twice the time she saved by circling around hoping for a space to open up. As an added bonus, walking made her feel as if she were doing her bit to fight global warming. A walk that short hardly made her an ecowarrior—even in a country whose inhabitants chose to drive any distance over a few meters—but it was better than nothing.

A full six minutes after leaving the office she walked through the revolving doors of the hotel.

Thóra scanned the elegant restaurant. The Art Deco interior had been restored some ten years ago to its original state. The result was a rather gentrified atmosphere, bringing to mind women with bob cuts, Charleston dresses, and gaudy ropes of pearls, smoking from long ivory holders. Since its construction in the Roaring Twenties it had been the grandest venue in Iceland, always full of bright young things and various government officials showing off to foreign dignitaries. The refurbishment had toned the place down a little, Thóra thought as she scanned the elegant restaurant. She realized that, apart from the large windows facing Parliament House and Austurvöllur Square, there was little to recall from the years when she spent most Saturday nights at Hótel Borg with her friends—all of them invariably drunk. In those days she had no worries apart from how her butt looked in the clothes she was wearing that night. The greenhouse effect would not have been on her mind, except perhaps as the name of a rock band.

The German looked about forty. He sat straight as a beanpole on the upholstered chair, his broad shoulders hiding the smart back of the seat. He was just beginning to go gray, which lent him a certain air of dignity. He looked stiff and formal, dressed in a gray suit and matching tie that did not exactly create a colorful impression. Thóra smiled, hoping it would make her come across as friendly and interested rather than idiotic. The man stood up, removed the napkin from his lap, and put it on the table.

"Frau Gudmundsdóttir?" A harsh, cold pronunciation.

They shook hands. "Herr Reich," Thóra muttered, with the best German pronunciation she could muster. "And do call me Thóra," she added. "It's easier to pronounce too."

"Please have a seat," the man said, sitting down himself. "And please call me Matthew."

She took care to sit down with her back straight and wondered what the other guests in the restaurant thought of this upright duo. Probably that they were meeting up to found a society for people with steel spine braces.

"Can I offer you something to drink?" the man asked Thóra politely in German. The waiter clearly understood what he said, because he turned to Thóra and awaited her answer.

"Sparkling mineral water, please." She recalled how fond the Germans were of mineral water. It was becoming more popular in Iceland as well—ten years before, no one with any sense would have thought of paying for water at a restaurant where it ran straight out of the tap. Buying carbonated water was somehow more acceptable.

"I presume you have talked to my employer, or rather his wife, Frau Guntlieb," Matthew Reich said when the waiter had gone.

"Yes. She told me I'd get more details from you."

He hesitated and sipped a clear liquid from his glass. The bubbles suggested that he had ordered sparkling water too. "I put some documents together in a folder for you. You can take it with you and look at it later, but there are a number of points I want to go over with you now, if that's okay with you."

"Certainly," Thóra replied at once. Before he had the chance to continue, she hurried to say: "But one thing I'd like to know a little more about is these people I'm going to work for. Maybe it makes no difference to the investigation, but it matters to me. Frau Guntlieb mentioned a surprising figure as my fee. I'm not interested in taking advantage of the family's grief if she can't afford this."

"They can afford it." He smiled. "Herr Guntlieb is the president and largest shareholder in the Anlagenbestand Bank of Bavaria. It's not a large bank, but its clientele includes corporations and wealthy individuals. Don't worry. The Guntliebs are very, very well-off."

"I see," Thóra said, thinking that this explained the servant answering the telephone at their home.

"However, the Guntliebs have not been so fortunate with their children. They had four children, two sons and two daughters. The elder son died in a car accident ten years ago and the elder daughter was born severely handicapped. She died as a result of her condition a few years ago. Now their son Harald has been murdered and the youngest daughter, Elisa, is all they have left. It has been an enormous strain on them, as you can imagine."

Thóra nodded, then asked hesitantly: "What was Harald doing here in Iceland? I thought there were plenty of universities in Germany with good history faculties."

Judging from Matthew's otherwise expressionless face this was a difficult question. "I really don't know. He was interested in the seventeenth century and I'm told he was doing some kind of research comparing continental Europe to Iceland. He came here as part of a student exchange program between the University of Munich and the University of Iceland."

"What kind of comparative research was it? Was it political, something like that?"

"No, it was more in the field of religion." He took a sip of water. "Maybe we should order before we go any further." He waved to the waiter, who approached holding two menus.

Thóra had the feeling that there was more behind his haste than hunger. "Religion, you say." She looked at the menu. "Could you be more specific?"

He put the open menu down on the table. "It's not really the sort of thing you talk about while you're eating, though I expect we'll have to sooner or later. But I'm not sure that his area of academic interest had anything to do with the murder."

Thóra frowned. "Was it related to the plague?" she asked. This was the only idea that occurred to her that fit the time bracket and was too distasteful for table talk.

"No, not the plague." He looked her in the eye. "Witch hunts. Torture and executions. Not particularly appealing. Unfortunately Harald was deeply interested in it. Actually this interest runs in the family."

Thóra nodded. "I understand." She did not understand in the slightest. "Maybe we should save this until after the meal."

"That's unnecessary. The main points are in the folder I'll give you." He picked up the menu again. "You'll also be getting some boxes of his belongings from the police. There are documents connected with his thesis which will provide you with further information. We're also expecting to get his computer and a few other things that may provide some clues."

They looked at the menu in silence.

"Fish," Matthew said without looking up. "You eat a lot of fish here."

"Yes, we do," was the only reply Thóra could think of. "After all, we are a fishing nation. Probably the only one that has managed to regulate its fishing sustainably." She forced a smile. "Actually, fish is no longer the mainstay of our economy."

"I don't like fish," he said.

"Seriously?" Thóra closed the menu. "I do, and I'm thinking of having the fried plaice."

In the end he settled for the quiche. When the waiter had gone, Thóra asked why the family thought the police had the wrong man in custody.

"There are several reasons. First, Harald would not have wasted his time arguing with some dope dealer." He stared at her. "He used drugs now and again; that was known. He drank alcohol too. He was young. But he was no more a drug addict than he was an alcoholic."

"That depends on your definition of addict," Thóra said. "As far as I'm concerned, repeated drug use is addiction."

"I know a few things about drug abuse." He paused, then hurried to add: "Not from personal experience, but through my work. Harald was not an addict—he was doubtless on his way to becoming one, but he wasn't one when he was murdered."

It dawned on Thóra that she had absolutely no idea why this man had been sent to Iceland. She doubted it was to invite her out to lunch and moan about Icelandic fish. "What is it exactly that you do for this family? Frau Guntlieb said you worked for her husband."

"I'm in charge of security at the bank. That includes background checks for prospective recruits, managing security procedures in the company, and money transportation."

"That doesn't involve drugs very much, surely?"

"No. I was referring to my previous job. I spent twelve years with the Munich CID." His eyes fixed on hers. "I know a thing or two about murders and I don't have the slightest doubt that the investigation into Harald's murder was badly handled. I didn't need to see very much of the man in charge to realize he doesn't have the faintest idea what he's doing."

"What's his name?"

Thóra understood who he meant, despite the awkward pronunciation. Árni Bjarnason. She sighed. "I know him from other cases. He's an idiot. A stroke of bad luck having him assigned to the investigation."

"There are other reasons the family doesn't think the drug dealer is connected with the murder."

Thóra looked up. "Such as what?"

"Just before his death, Harald withdrew a lot of money from a fund set up in his name. It's proved impossible so far to establish where the money went. It was a lot more than Harald would have needed to buy drugs. Even if he had planned on staying stoned for years."

"Couldn't he have been investing in drugs?" asked Thóra, adding: "Financing smuggling or something like that?"

Matthew snorted. "Out of the question. Harald didn't need the money. He was independently wealthy. He inherited a fortune from his grandfather."

"I understand." Thóra did not want to press him on this point, but wondered whether there may have been another reason for him to get involved in drug smuggling; maybe for kicks, or just sheer stupidity.

"There's no evidence that the dealer took the money. The only link the police have found between Harald and the drug scene is that he bought dope every now and then."

The food arrived and they ate in silence. Thóra felt a little awkward. This man was clearly not the type with whom silence was comfortable. However, she had never been good at making idle chatter even if the silence was oppressive, so she decided to restrain herself.

They ordered coffee and two hot cups soon arrived with a sugar bowl and silver milk jug.

"This is a very strange country, is it not?" said Matthew suddenly, his eyes following the retreating waiter.

"Well, no. Not really," replied Thóra, suppressing the instinct to jump to the defense of her beloved homeland. "It's just small. There are only three hundred thousand people living here. Why do you find it strange?"

Matthew shrugged. "Oh, I don't know. Maybe it's the cleanliness of the city, or the feeling of being surrounded by dolls' houses, but I think it has more to do with the people. Most locals I have spoken to seem to live by a different logic from the one I'm used to. They answer questions with questions, for example. Maybe it's just a language thing." He went quiet and shifted his gaze to a woman hurrying across the square outside. Thóra sipped her coffee, then broke the silence: "Did you bring a contract for me to look at?"

The man reached for the briefcase that lay beside his chair and took out a thin folder. He handed it across the table to Thóra. "Take the contract with you. Tomorrow we can go over what you want to change and I'll inform the Guntliebs. It's a fair deal and I doubt you'll find much fault with it." He bent down again, fetched a thicker folder, and put it on the table between them. "Take this too. It's the folder I mentioned earlier. I'd like you to browse through it before you make up your mind. There are some gruesome elements to this case that I want you to know about beforehand."

"Don't you think I can handle it?" asked Thóra, half insulted.

"To tell you the truth, I don't know. That's why I'm asking you to look through the file. It contains pictures of the crime scene that aren't exactly pleasant, and all kinds of reading material that's hardly any better. I managed to acquire an assortment of documents from the investigation with the assistance of a man whom I'd prefer not to name."

He put his hand on the file.

"It also contains details on Harald's life. They're not widely known and not for the faint of heart. I trust that, if you decide to back out of the whole matter, you will keep these matters confidential. The family does not care to have them spread around."

He took his hand off the folder and looked Thóra in the eye. "I don't wish to add to their tragedy."

"I understand," Thóra said. "I can assure you that I don't gossip about my work." She stared back and added, firmly: "Ever."

"Good."

"But since you've collected all this material—why do you need me? You seem able to acquire information I'm not sure I could get hold of."

"Do you want to know why we need you?"

"I think that's what I said," Thóra answered.

He inhaled quickly through his nose. "I'll tell you why. I'm a foreigner in this country and a German as well. We need to discuss things with certain people who will never tell me anything of importance. I gathered the bulk of the details about Harald's personal life in Germany, but I've really just scratched the surface. I'm not the sort of person that people find it pleasant to discuss uncomfortable and difficult personal matters with."

"I've realized that," Thóra blurted out.

The man smiled for the first time. Thóra was surprised to see that his smile was beautiful, somehow genuine, even though his teeth were unnaturally white and straight. She could not help returning the smile, then added in embarrassment: "What uncomfortable matters am I supposed to discuss with these people?"

His smile vanished as quickly as it had appeared. "Erotic asphyxiation, masochism, sorcery, self-mutilation, and other kinds of perverted behavior by seriously disturbed people."

Thóra was taken aback. "I'm not sure I know what all that involves." Erotic asphyxiation, for example; she had never heard of that. If it meant having sex while suffocating, she would actually prefer her current situation: not having sex, but at least being able to breathe.

When his smile returned it was not as friendly as before. "Oh, you'll find out. Don't worry about that."

They finished their coffee without saying a word, after which Thóra picked up the folder and made ready to leave for her office. They agreed to meet again the following day and exchanged good-byes.

As Thóra headed toward the exit, he put his hand on her shoulder. "One final thing, Frau Gudmundsdóttir."

She turned round.

"I forgot to tell you why *I'm* convinced that the man in police custody is not the murderer."

"Why?"

"He did not have Harald's eyes in his possession. They had been cut out."

CHAPTER 3

Thóra was not usually afraid of thieves, but on her way from the meeting with Matthew she made sure to clutch her handbag tightly. She could not bear the thought of having to phone him to announce that the documents had been stolen. It was therefore with immense relief that she stepped inside the office.

She was greeted by the stench of tobacco smoke. "Bella, you know smoking's not allowed in here."

Bella jumped away from the window and threw something out in a fluster. "I wasn't." A thin strip of smoke curled up out of one side of her mouth.

Thóra groaned to herself. "Oh, in that case, your mouth's caught fire." Then she added: "Close the window and smoke in the coffee room. Surely you'll feel more comfortable there than hanging over the side of the building."

"I wasn't smoking. I was shooing pigeons off the windowsill," Bella retorted indignantly. Experience had taught Thóra that it was not worth arguing with the girl. She went into her office and closed the door.

The file Matthew had given her was crammed full. It was black, which was somehow appropriate in light of its contents. The spine was unlabeled; no doubt it had been difficult to find an appropriate title. "Harald Guntlieb in life and death," Thóra muttered as she opened the file and examined the neatly arranged table of contents. The file was divided into seven sections, apparently in chronological order: Germany, Military Service, the University of Munich, the University of Iceland, Bank Accounts, Police Investigation. The seventh and final section was called Autopsy. She decided to go through the file in the order in which it had been arranged.

Looking at her watch, she saw it was almost two o'clock. She would hardly have time to read it all before having to fetch her daughter Sóley from after-school day care—unless she hurried. Thóra set her mobile phone alarm to a quarter to five. She was determined to get through most of the file by that time. She preferred not to have to take the documents home with her, although this was not uncommon when she was busy. What it contained was surely not the type of material to be left lying around in the presence of children. She turned over the first separator and started reading.

At the front was a stamped photocopy of a birth certificate. It stated that Frau Amelia Guntlieb had given birth to a healthy baby boy in Munich on June 18, 1978. The father's name was given as Herr Johannes Guntlieb, bank director. Thóra did not recognize the hospital. Judging by the name it was not one of the large state hospitals. She assumed it was either an exorbitant private hospital or a clinic for the wealthy. The space for recording the baby's religion had been filled in with "Roman Catholic." If her memory did not deceive her, Thóra recalled that around one in every three Germans was of that denomination, with a higher percentage in the south of the country. As a student in Germany, Thóra had been surprised by how many Catholics there were. She had always associated Germans with Lutheranism and believed that Catholics were found mainly in more southerly countries such as Italy, Spain, and France.

Thóra read on.

The next few pages were plastic photo album sheets, filled mostly with photographs of the Guntliebs on various occasions. Accompanying each photograph was a strip of white paper with the names of the people it showed. Quickly flicking through the pictures, she saw that Harald was in every one. Besides family shots there were school photos of him at various ages, with the obligatory smartly combed look. Thóra wondered why the photographs were in the folder. The only logical reason was to remind the reader that the murder victim had once been a living person. It worked.

The first photographs, which were the oldest, showed a small and chubby boy, with either his brother—who appeared to be two or three years older—or his mother. Thóra was struck by how beautiful Amelia Guntlieb was. Although some of the photographs were rather grainy, she was obviously one of those women who always seem effortlessly elegant. Thóra was captivated by one shot in particular in which the mother was helping her son practice walking. Taken outside in the garden, it showed Frau Guntlieb holding Harald's hands as he stumbled forward with the clumsy gait of a one-year-old, one foot in the air, leg bent firmly at the knee. Frau Guntlieb was smiling into the camera and her beautiful face radiated joy. The cold voice that Thóra had heard over the telephone did not seem to fit that expression. The boy was young enough that his features were still hidden behind baby fat and a stubby nose, but the resemblance between mother and son could nevertheless be seen.

The next photographs showed Harald at around two or three. Now he bore an even closer resemblance to his mother, although without appearing girlish. His mother was in the photographs too, pregnant first, then smiling as she held a baby wrapped in a thick blanket in her arms. In that particular shot Harald was beside the chair she was sitting in, standing on his tiptoes to peep at the bundled-up baby, his sister. His mother had her hand around his shoulders. From the label under the photograph Thóra saw that the girl had been named Amelia after her mother. Amelia Maria. This was the girl who had died from a congenital disease. Judging from the photograph, the family had not realized at first that she was ill. The mother, at least, looked ecstatic and free from worry. In the next scenes, however, something had changed. Where before she had been smiling in every photo, Frau Guntlieb now seemed distant and sad. In one pose she wore a smile for form's sake, but it did not reach her eyes. Nor was there any of the physical contact between her and Harald that had characterized the earlier photographs. The little boy seemed subdued and confused as well. The baby girl was nowhere to be seen.

Part of the family history seemed to have been omitted, because the next series took Thóra at least five years forward in time. It began with a posed family photograph, the first to feature Herr Guntlieb. He was a respectable-looking man, clearly a bit older than his wife. All the people in the photograph were dressed up smartly and a baby had joined the group, lying in her mother's arms. This must have been the youngest child, the only one alive today. The little sick girl was back, in a wheelchair this time. It did not take a doctor to realize how seriously handicapped she was, strapped into the wheelchair with her head thrown back and mouth hanging open. Her lower jaw hung to one side, indicating that she had little control over it. This seemed to be the case with her limbs too: one arm was bent at the elbow and the hand was abnormally close to it. The fingers of that hand were curled into a claw. Her other hand lay powerless in her lap. Behind the wheelchair stood Harald, eight years old at a guess. His expression was unlike anything Thóra had seen her own son produce at that age; the child seemed devastated. Although the other family members—Herr and Frau Guntlieb and Harald's elder brother— were not exactly the picture of happiness, the boy looked tragically miserable. Something had clearly happened and Thóra wondered whether such a young child could be so affected by his younger sister's illness. Perhaps he simply had psychological problems, which was not unknown among children. He may have been depressed as a child and competing for attention with his younger siblings proved too much for him. If so, it was obvious from the following photographs that the parents did not know how to respond. None of them showed any physical affection for the boy, who always stood apart from the family except in a few instances when his elder brother was by his side. It was as if his mother had simply forgotten him or was deliberately ignoring him. Thóra reminded herself not to draw too many conclusions from the photographs. They captured only moments from these people's lives and could never give a complete picture of what they did or thought.

There was a knock on the door and Bragi, Thóra's partner in the law firm and its founder, peeped inside. "Got a minute?"

Thóra nodded and Bragi stepped inside. He was approaching sixty, stout and hefty, one of those men who are not just tall but simply huge. Thóra thought the best way to describe him was that he was two sizes too large in every respect—fingers, ears, nose and all. He slammed himself down in the chair facing her desk and pulled over the folder Thóra was looking at. "How did it go?"

"The meeting? Fine, I think," Thóra answered, watching Bragi as he flicked casually through the family photographs she had just been examining.

"This lad looks awfully morose," said Bragi, pointing to a photograph of Harald. "Is he the one who was murdered?"

"Yes," Thóra replied. "They're rather strange photos."

"Well, I don't know. You should see my childhood photos. I was a hopeless kid. Miserable, a total loser. As clearly shown by any photos from that time."

Thóra read nothing into this. She was used to all manner of peculiar remarks from Bragi. He was bound to be exaggerating in calling himself a hopeless loser as a boy, just as he did when he talked about how he had to work full-time as a night watchman weighing fish at the harbor and on a fishing boat over the weekends just to pay his way through law school. Nonetheless, she liked him. He had never been anything but kind to her, from the day three years ago when he invited her into a law partnership with him, which she gratefully accepted. At that time she was working with a medium-sized law firm and was relieved to get out; she did not miss the conversations beside the coffee machine about salmon fishing and neckties.

Bragi pushed the folder back to Thóra. "Are you going to take it on?"

"Yes, I think so," she replied. "It's a change. Besides, it's always fun to tackle something new."

Bragi grunted. "That's not always the case, I'll tell you that. I didn't find it exciting having to deal with colon cancer a few years back even though that was quite new to me."

Not wanting to pursue that line, Thóra hurried to say: "You know what I mean."

Bragi stood up. "Yes, sure. I just wanted to warn you not to expect too much." He walked over to the door, then turned round and added: "Tell me, do you think you can use Thór on this case at all?"

Thór had just graduated from law school and had been working for them for a little over half a year. He was something of a loner, unsociable, but all his work was exemplary and Thóra saw nothing wrong with having his help if she needed it. "I'd been thinking more about using him to take over other cases for me so that I could focus on this one. I have plenty of projects that he can easily keep afloat."

"No problem, just do as you think best."

Thóra picked up the folder again and flipped through the remaining photographs, watching Harald grow up into a handsome young man with his mother's fair complexion. His father was much darker and not quite as memorable as his mother. The last page held only two photographs: one from a graduation ceremony, presumably at the University of Munich, and the other showing either the beginning or the end of his military service—at least, Harald was wearing a German army uniform. Thóra was not knowledgeable enough to be able to tell which regiment he belonged to. She assumed that this would come to light in the chapter on military service referred to on the contents page.

The next pages contained photocopies of Harald's certificates for completing various stages of his education, and it was obvious that he had been extraordinarily clever. He always earned top grades, which Thóra knew from her own experience was not easy to achieve in the German educational system. The last account, from the University of Munich where Harald earned a B.A. in history, was in the same vein. In fact, he had graduated *cum laude*. The chronology of the documents revealed that Harald had taken a gap year before enrolling in college, presumably because of military service.

Thóra was surprised that this young man had chosen to join the army, given his splendid academic record. Although Germany had national service, it was simple to avoid, especially for the son of such rich parents. They could easily have had him relieved of that duty.

Thóra flicked through to another part of the folder, marked "Military Service." It was a slender chapter, only a couple of pages. The first contained a photocopy of Harald Guntlieb's induction into the Bundeswehr in 1999. Apparently he enlisted for *das deutsche Heer,* the regular army. It puzzled her that he had not opted for the air force or navy. With his father's influence, she was certain he could have had his pick of the regiments. On the next page was a document stating that Harald's regiment was to be sent to Kosovo, and the third and final page was his discharge paper, dated seven months later. No explanation was given apart from a barely legible *"medizinische Gründe"*—on medical grounds. In the margin of the photocopy, a neat question mark had been made. Thóra assumed this was Matthew's writing; to the best of her knowledge, he had gathered all the information alone. Thóra jotted down a memo to herself to ask about the exact reason for Harald's discharge. She moved on to the next section.

Like the chapter on military service, this one opened with a photocopy. It was his enrollment letter from the University of Munich. Thóra noticed that it was dated only one month after his discharge from the army. So Harald appeared to have recovered quite quickly after leaving the army, if illness was indeed the reason his duty ended. Next came several pages that Thóra could not completely understand. One was a photocopy of the founding agenda of a historical society named Malleus Maleficarum. Another was a reference from a certain Professor Chamiel, singing Harald's praises, and others seemed to be descriptions of courses in fifteenth-, sixteenth-, and seventeenth-century history. Thóra was not entirely sure what she would gain from this information.

At the end of this section were clippings from German newspapers describing the deaths of several young men as a result of peculiar sex acts. Reading them, Thóra gathered that the acts involved constricting the breathing with a noose during masturbation. This must have been the erotic asphyxiation Matthew had mentioned. If the article was anything to go by, this was not an uncommon practice among people who have trouble achieving orgasm due to drug abuse, alcohol, and the like. There was no explanatory note linking the story to Harald, apart from the fact that one of the young men had studied at the same university. The student was not named, nor was any date given. However, there must have been some connection since this article was included in the folder.

Thóra flicked back to Harald's graduation photograph at the end of the first section. Scrutinizing it, she thought she could see a red mark on his neck above the shirt. She removed the photograph from its sheath to take a better look. It was slightly sharper outside the plastic, but not clear enough for Thóra to be certain that the mark was a bruise. She made a mental note to ask Matthew about this matter as well.

The last page of this peculiar collage from Harald's undergraduate years in Munich was the title page of his dissertation. Its topic was witch hunts in Germany, focusing on the execution of children suspected of sorcery. A shiver ran down Thóra's spine. Of course she had heard about witch hunts in history lessons at school, but did not recall any mention of children. That would hardly have escaped her attention, even though history bored her stiff at that time. Since there was nothing apart from the title page, Thóra tried to console herself by hoping that the essay included no evidence of children being burned at the stake. Deep down inside, however, she knew otherwise. She started reading the section on the University of Iceland.

It contained a letter stating that Harald's application for admission to a master's course in history had been approved and welcoming him to the university in autumn 2004. Next came a printout of Harald's grades in the courses he had completed. From the date on the paper, Thóra saw that the printout was made after his death. Presumably Matthew had obtained it. Although Harald had not managed to complete many courses in the year or so that he was a student, the grades were all very high. Thóra suspected that he must have been allowed to take his examinations in English, since as far as she knew he did not speak Icelandic. It appeared he had ten credits left to take, as well as the completion of his master's dissertation.

On the next page was a list of five names. They were all Icelanders and after each name came an academic discipline and what could have been a date of birth. Since nothing else was mentioned, Thóra assumed they were Harald's friends; most were of a similar age. The names were: Marta Mist Eyjólfsdóttir, Gender Studies, b. 1981; Brjánn Karlsson, History, b. 1981; Halldór Kristinsson, Medicine, b. 1982; Andri Thórsson, Chemistry, b. 1979; and Bríet Einarsdóttir, History, b. 1983. Thóra read on in the hope of finding more information about the students, but in vain because the next page was a printout of the campus and its main buildings. Circles had been drawn around the history department and Manuscript Institute, as well as the main building. Once again Thóra had to assume that this was an addition from Matthew. It was followed by another printout from the university's Web site. Thóra glanced through the text, which was in English and described the history department. This was followed by a similar page on study for international students. She could glean nothing from that.

The last document in the section was a printed-out e-mail sent from hguntlieb@hi.is, obviously Harald's address at the university. It was to his father, dated shortly after he began his studies in autumn 2004. Reading the e-mail, Thóra was struck by how cold it was for a letter from a son to his father. Essentially it said how happy Harald was in Iceland, that he had secured a place to live, and so forth. Harald ended by saying that he had found a professor to supervise his dissertation: Professor Thorbjörn Ólafsson.

According to the e-mail, his dissertation would compare the burning of witches in Iceland and Germany, stemming from the fact that most convicted sorcerers in Iceland had been males, whereas in Germany females had been in the majority. It ended formally, but Thóra noticed a PS under Harald's name: "If you care to make contact, you have my e-mail address now." This did not imply much affection. Perhaps his discharge from the army was in some way connected with their poor relationship. Judging from the photographs, his father did not seem to be the most understanding of people, and he was bound to be unhappy about a child who failed to live up to expectations.

On the next page was a curt reply from his father, also an e-mail. It said: "Dear Harald, I suggest that you stay clear of that essay topic. It is ill-chosen and not conducive to building character. Take care of your money. Regards," followed by an automatic e-mail signature with his father's full name, position, and address. *Well, well,* Thóra thought, *what an old bastard!* Not a word about being pleased to hear from his son or missing him, let alone signing it "Dad" or the like. Their relationship was obviously chilly, if not in permafrost. And it was also strange that neither had mentioned Harald's mother, or his younger sister for that matter. Thóra did not know about any other e-mail exchanges between the father and son; there were none in the folder.

The final document in this section was a printout from the university listing student societies and student publications in various departments. Scanning the list, Thóra noticed nothing interesting until the bottom of the page: "Malleus Maleficarum—History and Folklore Society." Thóra looked up from the folder. This was the same name that was on the photocopy of the agenda from the founding meeting during Harald's student days in Munich. She flicked back through the pages to check. Beneath the name of the society on the Icelandic list was written in pencil: *"errichtet 2004"*—founded 2004. This was after Harald enrolled at the university in Iceland. Could its establishment have been his idea? This was not unlikely, unless Malleus Maleficarum was particularly symbolic for history and folklore. Of course, it could mean anything; Thóra knew no Latin to speak of. She moved on to section five, his bank accounts.

This was a thick pile of statements from a foreign bank account. Harald Guntlieb was listed as the holder and his turnover looked enormous at first glance, although little was left in the account at the end of the last period. Several entries had been highlighted with a marker pen: pink for large withdrawals and yellow for large deposits. Thóra quickly noticed that the yellow entries were always the same amount, deposited at the beginning of each month. It was a hefty sum, more than she made in half a year—even a busy one. These must be payments from the trust Matthew said Harald had inherited from his grandfather. It was likely that the inheritance was allocated as regular payments to Harald rather than as a lump sum. This was the most common arrangement for young heirs until a certain age was reached, depending on their reliability. Harald Guntlieb had clearly not been considered very responsible, since, according to Thóra's calculations, he was twenty-seven when he died but still had not been entrusted with the principal. However, considerable sums had accumulated in the account, and Harald's basic living expenses were obviously way below his monthly allowance.

The highlighted withdrawals were a completely different matter. They varied in amount and were made at irregular intervals as far as Thóra could see. Notes had been written beside most of them, and since there were not so many, Thóra browsed them all. She understood some of the remarks immediately, such as "BMW" beside a large withdrawal in the beginning of August 2004, when she assumed he had bought a car in Iceland. Others she could not make head or tail of. *"Urteil G.G.,"* for example, was written alongside a hefty withdrawal from Harald's student days in Munich. Since *Urteil* means "ruling," she had a hunch that Harald had needed to pay someone to conceal the reason for his dismissal from the army. However, the date did not fit and she could not imagine what G.G. meant. In another place was *Schädel,* "skull," and elsewhere *Gestell,* which stumped her. She found more withdrawals with no context and decided not to waste her time on them.

Two entries caught her attention, however. The first, several years old and amounting to 42,000 euros, was yet again designated by the Latin term *"Malleus Maleficarum,"* while the much more recent one had a question mark beside it. This was presumably the money Matthew said had gone missing, just over 310,000 euros. Thóra calculated this to be more than twenty-five million Icelandic krónur. No wonder Matthew doubted the money had been spent on drugs. If it had, Harald would have had his work cut out for him, even if Keith Richards had been around to help. And judging from the bank statements it also appeared that Harald was not short of money, in spite of such large withdrawals.

She moved on to the next page, which showed Harald's credit card use in the months before his death. Scanning through them, she saw that the majority of the charges were to restaurants and bars, with the occasional purchase in clothing stores. The restaurants could all be categorized as what Thóra's friend Laufey would call "trendy." Noticeably few transactions were made in grocery stores. A large sum spent at Hótel Rangá in mid-September caught Thóra's eye, as did another marked "School of Aviation" and a much smaller charge from the Reykjavík family zoo—of all places—dated at the end of September. There were also a number of small purchases in a pet shop on the outskirts of the capital. Maybe Harald liked animals or had even been trying to impress a single mother by gaining her children's approval. Yet another point to ask Matthew about. The section on Harald's finances ended with these statements. Thóra looked at her watch and saw that she was making good progress.

Thóra decided to take a rest from the folder. She turned to her computer and Googled "Malleus Maleficarum." More than fifty-five thousand results came back. She soon found one that looked promising, with a page description saying that the phrase meant "Witches' Hammer" and was the title of a book from 1846. Thóra clicked the link and a site came up in English. The only graphics on the page were an ancient drawing of a woman in a cowl, apparently tied to a ladder. Two men were struggling to lift up the ladder and roll it, along with the woman, into a great fire blazing in front of them. She was clearly being burned alive. The woman looked heavenward, her mouth open. Thóra could not tell whether the artist intended to depict her beseeching God or cursing him. But her desperation was obvious. Thóra printed out the page and went to fetch it before Bella removed it from the printer. That girl was capable of anything.

CHAPTER 4

There turned out to be five sheets of paper in the printer, not one as Thóra had expected. The Web site actually contained much more than just a single screen's worth, and Thóra began reading the pages on her way back to her office.

The brief introductory paragraph stated that *Malleus Maleficarum* was undoubtedly one of the most notorious books ever written. First published in 1486, it was intended as a manual to teach inquisitors how to recognize, prosecute, and execute witches. It emphasized that black magic and various customs of the common people were now considered blasphemy, which was punishable by death at that time—practitioners were burned at the stake. The book was divided into three parts, according to the article. The first was aimed at making people realize that magic and witchcraft were real phenomena, and also that these were considered evil and unnatural. It stated that the mere act of believing in the existence of the black arts was blasphemous, which was a new ruling. Section two was a compendium of lurid tales about witches' practices, dominated by sex with demonic beings. The third and final section laid down the foundation for prosecuting witches. It underlined that torture was a permissible means of extracting confessions and everyone was allowed to testify against those accused of such crimes, irrespective of reputation or other normal standards for deeming witnesses unfit or partial.

The authors of the text were said to be two Dominican Black Friars: Jakob Sprenger, at that time chancellor of the University of Cologne, and Heinrich Kramer, professor of divinity at the University of Salzburg and chief inquisitor in Tyrol. The latter was credited with authoring the majority of the text, as he had been extensively involved in prosecuting witches ever since 1476. The work was reputedly written at the urging of Pope Innocent VIII, who did not appear to be a particularly attractive character according to this account. He was attributed with starting the witch hunts in Europe by issuing the papal bull of December 5, 1484, titled *Summus desiderantes affectibus,* authorizing the Inquisition to prosecute witches and equating sorcery with blasphemy.

It also enumerated this pope's attempts, in old age, to ward off death by drinking milk from women's breasts and having his blood changed. While this did not grant him a renewed life span, it did cause the death of three ten-year-old boys from loss of blood.

Thóra learned that the book soon gained widespread circulation with the advent of printing, and also because its authors were known and respected scholars. Catholics and Protestants alike drew on it in their battles against witchcraft. Part of the book found its way into the law of the Holy Roman Empire, now Germany, Austria, the Czech Republic, Switzerland, eastern France, the Low Countries, and part of Italy. Thóra was astonished to read that the book was still regularly published.

She put down the printout. Interesting as it was, a six-hundred-year-old book hardly shed much light on the death of Harald Guntlieb. Looking at her watch, she saw that she had only an hour left. She stapled the pages together, put them to one side, and turned back to the folder on Harald. She turned to section six, the police investigation.

At first glance the summary did not look thick enough to contain the case documents in their entirety. Perhaps Matthew had only managed to procure some of them; in fact, Thóra was shocked that he could have obtained them at all without a formal request. She flicked through the contents, which turned out to be a photocopy of the police interrogation reports. A stamp indicated that they had been handed over two weeks before.

Here she was on home ground. It was all in Icelandic, which was possibly the reason that the Guntliebs had decided to enlist an Icelander. The pages were heavily annotated in an untidy hand, obviously because Matthew had tried to puzzle his way through them. In the upper right-hand corner of most reports he had written a brief note stating who was being interviewed and his or her connection with Harald. Most of the reports were from interrogations of Hugi Thórisson, who was still detained in custody awaiting charges. Thóra was interested to note that throughout the interrogations he had always had the status of suspect rather than witness—something had surely indicated his guilt immediately. Unlike a witness, he was therefore not obliged to tell the truth, the whole truth, and nothing but the truth. So he could say virtually anything, although it would hardly serve his interests before the court—judges tended to turn grumpy if the accused said they had been out for dinner with Donald Duck or something equally as likely at the time of their alleged crime.

It suddenly dawned on Thóra how Matthew had obtained the documents. The lawyer appointed to defend a suspect was entitled access to police records. Hugi Thórisson's lawyer had therefore had access to them all. Thóra quickly flicked through the reports, looking for one in which Hugi had had a lawyer with him, to see who it was. In the first interrogations Hugi was alone. This was only to be expected; people generally do not ask to have a lawyer present at the start of an investigation, presumably because they think it makes them look more suspicious. When the going gets tougher they begin to hesitate and more often than not refuse to speak without one. This had clearly happened in Hugi's case, because at the very end of the investigation Thóra saw that he had finally had the sense to ask for a lawyer.

Finnur Bogason had been assigned to him. Thóra recognized the name. Finnur was one of those lawyers who generally handle cases in which they are appointed to the defense. In other words, no one approaches them of their own accord. Thóra was convinced that, for the right sum, he would have given Matthew the documents. Pleased with her powers of deduction, she started reading through the interrogations.

The reports were not arranged chronologically, but according to the person being interviewed. Several witnesses were only interrogated once. These included the university porter, the cleaners, Harald's landlady, a taxi driver who had given him and Hugi a lift on that fateful evening, and several of his fellow students and teachers. The head of the history department, who discovered the body, had been interviewed twice because he was in such a state of shock the first time that he had not spoken a word of sense. Thóra pitied the poor man; it must have been a terrible experience, and the horror of finding a corpse in his arms oozed from every sentence of the interrogation.

Next came those who were under suspicion, at least temporarily. Among them—of course—was Hugi Thórisson, who continuously asserted his innocence. Thóra hurriedly read the main body of his interrogation. Hugi said he had met Harald on the evening in question at a party in Skerjafjördur. They left it for a while and then split up when Harald expressed an interest in going back to the party and Hugi had wanted to head downtown. In the first interviews Hugi revealed little of where they had gone together, only vaguely mentioning a stroll through the cemetery. Later on, when he realized that he was going to be charged with murder, he said they had gone back to his flat on Hringbraut to fetch some drugs that Harald wanted to buy from him. He swore blindly that he not seen Harald after that; he could not be bothered to go out again so he stayed at home. He was unable to give precise times for any of these events, claiming he was drunk and stoned that evening.

Given how often Hugi was asked whether he could provide more detail about his movements around one o'clock on the morning of Sunday, October 30, Thóra was convinced that an autopsy had revealed this to be the time of Harald's death. Hugi was repeatedly asked why he had removed Harald's eyes and where he had put them. Hugi consistently replied that he had not taken his eyes. He had no eyes, apart from his own, of course. Thóra could only pity the poor man if he was telling the truth. She suspected that he was. Although she had only leafed through the case, the feeling remained that it would be highly unlikely for a weak-willed person, as Hugi appeared to be, to tell anything but the truth after such long isolation and intense interrogation.

Harald's friends and acquaintances who were at the party in Skerjafjördur were suspects at first, but then they were interrogated as witnesses. There were ten of them in all, including four of the five names on the list Thóra had noticed at the front of the folder. The only name missing was the medical student Halldór Kristinsson.

All the partygoers told the same story. The party had begun at nine and ended at two when they went into town. Harald had left around midnight with Hugi, but no one knew why. The pair had said they were just popping out and had driven off in a taxi Hugi had ordered. Two hours later the others had given up waiting and gone barhopping. Asked whether they had tried to phone Hugi or Harald, they all gave the same answer: Harald's battery had died earlier that evening and Hugi did not answer their repeated calls to his mobile or home phone. Nor had anyone answered Harald's home phone when they rang there. They were also asked about what time they eventually went home from town, but, given the time frame, these questions were more for the sake of form. It turned out that the group had departed at different times, some not leaving until five in the morning. The student friends from the list of names went last, by which time the fifth, the medical student, Halldór, had joined them downtown. Thóra continued browsing in the hope that he had been called in for questioning. He seemed to be the only one who had not been at the party around the time of the murder. *Where had he been?* Thóra wondered.

The answer was at the end of the section. Halldór had been interviewed, and it turned out that he had been working until midnight at the City Hospital, where he had a part-time job. That was why he was not at the party. It involved only a handful of shifts a month, Halldór had said; he came in as a substitute when someone was ill or for other reasons. He had taken a change of clothes with him, and after showering at the hospital and getting ready, he took the bus into town. By his own account his car was not working and he gave the name of the garage where it was being mended over the period in question. Halldór said he originally planned to change buses and take another to Skerjafjördur, but he had just missed the last one and decided to go into town to wait for the partygoers at a café instead of forking out for a taxi or walking there. He claimed he had telephoned them and they said they were just on their way. It was around one when he arrived at a bar called Kaffibrennslan, and he bought a beer while he waited, he said. Around two he finally met the people from the party when they arrived in a taxi.

A series of witness statements followed, interviews with teachers from the history department. These mostly involved how well they knew Harald, and they all said the same—they did not know him outside the university and had little to say about him. There was another question mark over a meeting at the faculty building the night Harald was murdered. It was held to celebrate a cooperative project with a Norwegian university involving a large Erasmus grant. Reading between the lines, Thóra inferred that this "meeting" was more of a cocktail party that lasted well into the evening. The last guests left around midnight. None of the names were familiar to her apart from Gunnar Gestvík, the head of department, and Thorbjörn Ólafsson, the professor supervising Harald's dissertation.

The final statements were taken from a barman at Kaffibrennslan and the bus driver who drove Halldór from the hospital into town.

The waiter, whose name was Björn Jónsson, said he had first served Halldór around one o'clock that night, then several times again within the hour and finally around two when his friends had joined him. He said he remembered Halldór well because of how fast and furiously he drank that night.

The bus driver also remembered Halldór as a passenger on his last journey. There were very few people on the bus and the two of them had struck up a conversation, discussing the state of the health system and how poorly old people were treated. As far as Thóra could see, Halldór had a fairly watertight alibi. As did all Harald's friends, except Hugi.

The reports were followed by several pages of photocopied photographs taken at the scene of the murder. Although blurred and in black-and-white, they were clear enough to give a good idea of the horrific scene. Now Thóra understood even better the shock of the man who found the body, and she doubted he would ever recover.

The alarm on Thóra's mobile reminded her that it was a quarter to five. She hurriedly flipped through to the final section, on the autopsy. *How strange,* she thought, and stood up. There was nothing behind the seventh divider. The section was empty.

CHAPTER 5

Thóra reached the day care on time. She met the mother of one of her daughter's classmates outside in the parking lot. The woman looked at the car with its garage logo and smiled, clearly convinced that Thóra had started going out with some grease monkey. Thóra itched to chase after her and explain that her relationship with the mechanic was strictly business, but instead she walked straight across the school grounds. Sóley went to Mýrarhúsaskóli in Seltjarnarnes, which was not far from where Thóra worked on Skólavördustígur—less than ten minutes' drive. When she divorced Hannes just over two years before, Thóra had made a firm stand about keeping their house in Seltjarnarnes, even though she had had great difficulty paying for his half.

Seltjarnarnes was a small town on a peninsula off Reykjavík's western coast. The surrounding sea was the town's most distinctive feature and somehow managed to make the residents feel they were surrounded by nature, despite the closeness of downtown. It was perfect for families with children, so property there was in high demand. Thóra was thankful that their house had been appraised before the surge in real estate prices started. Were she getting divorced now, she would not have had a prayer of keeping the house. Of course, this was unspeakably irritating to Hannes, who had nightmares about how much she must have made on the deal. Although she regarded the house as a home rather than an investment, Thóra was pleased about the profit she made on it, really only because of how much it annoyed her ex. The divorce had not exactly been on good terms, although they tried to keep their relationship polite for the children's sake. A geographical analogy would be India and Pakistan—trouble was always brewing, although it rarely boiled over.

Thóra went inside and looked around the hall. Most of the children had already gone home. This did not really surprise her, and she had the guilty thought that she was not a good mother. She had followed the Icelandic tradition—have your baby, take six months off, and then reenter the rat race. Nobody stayed at home after having kids, so Thóra knew that she was no better or worse than other mothers. This did not stop her from feeling bad from time to time, though. Mother, woman, maiden: the line from the old poem ran through her mind before she realized that the word "woman" hardly suited her. She had not made a single male acquaintance in the two years since her divorce. Suddenly she was seized by a great yearning to make love to a man. She gave herself a gentle shake; it was difficult to imagine a less appropriate place to think about sex. What was wrong with her?

"Sóley!" the supervisor called out, noticing Thóra. "Your mother's here."

The little girl, sitting with her back to her mother, looked up from the beads she was putting together. She gave a tired smile and swept a blond lock out of her eyes. "Hi, Mum. Look, I've made a heart out of beads." Thóra felt a pang in her own heart and promised herself that she would pick her daughter up earlier tomorrow.

After a quick stop at the supermarket Thóra and Sóley finally reached home. Gylfi, her son, was already there. His sneakers had been tossed carelessly in the middle of the hallway, and his coat had been hung up on a peg beside the door so hurriedly that it had slid to the floor.

"Gylfi!" yelled Thóra, bending down to put the shoes on the rack and hang the coat up securely. "How often do I have to tell you to take your shoes and coat off in an orderly fashion?"

"Can't hear you," a voice called from inside the house.

Thóra rolled her eyes. He could not be expected to hear; the sounds from a computer game were overwhelming. "Turn it down, then!" she yelled back. "You'll make yourself deaf!"

"Come here! I can't hear you!" came the shouted reply.

"Oh, God," Thóra muttered as she hung up her coat. Her daughter neatly arranged her own shoes and coat and Thóra was dumbfounded for the hundredth time at how different her children were. Her daughter was a model of tidiness, hardly even dribbled as a baby, while her son would have preferred to live in a heap of clothes where he could throw himself down contentedly at night. But they did have one thing in common: they were both extraordinarily focused when it came to school and home-work. Somehow it suited Sóley's character, but Thóra always found it rather funny when Gylfi, with his long, unkempt hair and clothes with skeletons on them, turned almost hysterical about something like leaving his spelling exercise at school.

Thóra stepped into the doorway of her son's room. Gylfi was sitting glued to the screen of his computer, clicking furiously with the mouse. "For God's sake turn that down, Gylfi," she said, having to raise her voice even though she was standing right beside her son. "I can't hear myself think."

Without even glancing away from the screen or slowing down his clicking of the mouse, her son stretched out his left hand for a knob on the loudspeakers and turned them down. "Better?" he said, still without looking up.

"Yes, that's better," replied Thóra. "Now switch this off and come and have dinner. I bought some pasta; it only takes a minute to fix."

"Just let me finish this level," the answer came. "Takes two minutes."

"Just two," she said, and turned round. "Let me remind you that it goes like this: one. Then two. Not one, two, three, four, five, six, two."

"Okay, okay," her son replied irritably, carrying on with his game.

When the food was served fifteen minutes later Gylfi appeared and slammed himself down in his usual chair. Sóley was already seated and yawning in front of her plate. Thóra could not be bothered to start the meal by nagging Gylfi for taking more than two minutes to finish "the level." She was about to remind him of the importance of this occasion for the family when her mobile started ringing. She stood up to answer it. "You two start eating, and don't argue. You're both much more likable when you're friends." She reached out for the mobile on the kitchen side-board and looked at the caller ID, but there was none. She pressed the talk button as she left the kitchen. "Thóra."

"Guten Abend, Frau Gudmundsdóttir," said Matthew's dry voice. He asked if it was an inconvenient time.

"No, it's okay," Thóra lied. She thought Matthew would be upset if he knew the truth, namely that she was sitting down to dinner. He seemed a polite man, somehow.

"Have you had time to look at the documents I gave you?" he asked.

"Yes, I have, but not in any great detail," Thóra replied. "Actually, I did notice that the police investigation documents were incomplete. I suggest a formal request to obtain them. It's a terrible drawback having only part of them."

"Definitely." An uncomfortable silence ensued. Just as Thóra was about to add something, Matthew began speaking again.

"So you've made your mind up?"

"About the case, you mean?"

"Yes," he said curtly. "Are you going to take it on?"

Thóra hesitated for a moment before agreeing. She had a feeling that when she said those words, Matthew heaved a deep sigh of relief. "Sehr gut," he said in an exceptionally perky tone.

"Actually, I still have to study the contract. I brought it home to read tonight. If it's true that it's 'fair and normal,' I can't see any objections to signing it tomorrow."

"Great."

"Listen, one thing made me curious: why wasn't the section about the autopsy in the folder?" Although Thóra knew this could wait until morning, she wanted to know the answer now.

"We had to make a special application to obtain the documents and I didn't get them all—just a summary of the main points. I thought it was rather sparse, so I've insisted on seeing the entire report," Matthew replied.

After a moment's pause he added by way of explanation: "It complicated the matter a little, me being a representative and not a relative, but fortunately it's been settled now. In fact, that's why I rang now instead of waiting to hear from you tomorrow as we had discussed."

"Sorry?" Thóra said, not quite grasping the context.

"I have an appointment at nine tomorrow morning with the pathologist who performed the autopsy on Harald. He's going to present me with the documents and go through various aspects of them with me. I'd like you to come along."

"Well," Thóra said in surprise. "Okay, that's fine. I'm game."

"Good, I'll pick you up from the office at half past eight."

Thóra bit her tongue to stop herself saying that she generally did not turn up that early. "Half past eight. I'll see you then."

"Frau Gudmundsdóttir—" said Matthew.

"Do call me Thóra, it's much simpler," Thóra interrupted him. She felt like a ninety-year-old widow every time he called her Frau Gudmundsdóttir.

"Okay, Thóra," Matthew said. "Just one more thing."

"What?" asked Thóra.

"I'd resist having a heavy breakfast. It's not going to be a pleasant conversation."

CHAPTER 6

DECEMBER 7, 2005

Finding a parking space at the national hospital was definitely not the easiest task in the world. Matthew eventually found one some distance from the building where the pathology lab was located. Thóra had turned up at her office early and drafted a letter to the police, demanding access to the documents as the representative of the family. The letter was in its envelope and waiting in Bella's tray; hopefully it would be posted today, but Thóra still decided to up the odds by labeling the envelope with the words: "Must *not* be posted before the weekend."

Thóra had also called the aviation school to inquire about a debit from Harald's card in September. She was told that Harald had hired a small private plane and pilot to fly up to Hólmavík and back the same day. After checking Hólmavík on the Internet, Thóra soon realized what had attracted Harald there—its museum of witchcraft and sorcery. She had also telephoned Hótel Rangá to investigate Harald's trips there, and she was told that he had booked and paid for two rooms for two nights—the names in the guest book were Harald Guntlieb and Harry Potter. As a pseudonym, the latter displayed a singular lack of imagination. She told Matthew about this and Harald's trip to Hólmavík as they circled the parking lot.

"At last," Matthew said, slipping his rental car into a newly abandoned parking space.

They walked in the direction of the laboratory, which was located behind the main building. It had snowed during the night and Matthew walked ahead of Thóra, stomping through the piles of slush and ice. The weather was blustery and the bracing north wind tugged at Thóra's hair. That morning she had decided to wear her hair down but regretted that decision now as the wind swept it in all directions. *I'll look really good by the time I get inside,* she thought. She stopped for a moment, turned her back to the wind, and tried to protect her hair by wrapping a scarf over her head. It was hardly fashionable but earned her hair a respite from the gusts. After this ceremony, she hurried after Matthew.

When they finally reached the building he looked around for the first time since they had left the car. He stared at her with the scarf over her head. She could just imagine how elegant she looked, which she confirmed when he raised his eyebrows and said: "There's bound to be a bathroom you can pop into when we get inside."

Thóra yearned to fire a retort at him, but restrained herself. Instead she gave him a rigid smile and threw open the door. She strode over to a woman pushing an empty steel trolley and asked where they could find the doctor they were supposed to meet. After asking whether he was expecting them, the woman directed them toward an office at the end of one of the corridors. She added that they should wait outside because the doctor was not yet back from a morning meeting.

Thóra and Matthew sat down in two battered chairs by the window in the corridor.

"I didn't mean to offend you. Sorry," Matthew said without looking at her.

Not interested in discussing her appearance, Thóra ignored the remark. She took the scarf off her head with as much dignity as she could muster and put it in her lap. Then she reached over for a pile of tattered magazines that were lying on a little table between the chairs.

"Who could ever be interested in reading this stuff?" she muttered as she flicked through the pile.

"I don't think people come here looking for something to read," Matthew answered. He was sitting up straight, staring ahead.

Thóra put down the magazines, irritated. "No, maybe not." She looked at her watch and said impatiently, "Where is that man, anyway?"

"He'll be here," came the curt reply. "Actually I'm starting to have second thoughts about this meeting."

"What do you mean?" she asked peevishly.

"I think it may be too shocking for you," he replied, turning to face her. "You don't have any experience with this sort of thing and I'm not sure it's a good idea. It would be best if I just tell you what he says."

Thóra glared at him. "I've given birth to two children, with all the accompanying pain, blood, placentas, cervical plugs, and God knows what else. I'll survive." She folded her arms and turned away from him. "So what do you know about gross stuff?"

Matthew did not seem impressed by Thóra's experience. "Lots of things. But I'll spare you the details. Unlike you, I have no need to beat my chest."

Thóra rolled her eyes. This German wasn't exactly a barrel of laughs. She decided to find out what *The Watchtower* had to say rather than try to sustain a conversation with him. She was halfway through an article on the bad influence of television on world youth when a man in a white coat came hurrying along the corridor toward them. He was around sixty, starting to gray at the temples, and very tan. His eyes were flanked by wrinkles from smiling, which led Thóra to conclude that he had had a good time in the sun. He stopped in front of them and Thóra and Matthew both stood up.

"Hello," the man said, offering his hand. "Thráinn Hafsteinsson."

Thóra and Matthew returned his greeting and introduced themselves.

"Do come inside," the doctor said in English so that Matthew would understand, and opened the door to his office. "Excuse me for being late," he added in Icelandic, addressing his words to Thóra.

"That's fine," she replied. "The literature out there is so fascinating, I wouldn't have minded waiting a bit longer." She smiled at him.

The doctor looked at her in surprise. "Yes, quite." They entered the office where there was little in the way of empty space. The walls were covered with bookshelves filled with scientific works and journals of all sizes and descriptions, with the occasional filing cabinet arranged between them. The doctor walked behind a large tidy desk and sat down, inviting them to do the same. "Well, then." He put both hands on the edge of the desk as he said this, as if to emphasize that their meeting was formally beginning now. "I presume we'll be doing this in English."

Thóra and Matthew both nodded.

He went on: "That won't be a problem, I did my doctorate in America. But I haven't spoken a word of German since I walked out of my school oral exam as a teenager, so I'll spare you that."

"As I told you on the phone, English is fine," Matthew said. Thóra tried to suppress a smile at his German accent.

"Good," the doctor said, reaching out for a yellow plastic folder from the top of a pile of papers on his desk. He arranged it in front of himself, poised to open it. "I should start by apologizing for how long it took to get permission to show the autopsy documents in all their glory." He gave them an apologetic smile. "There's far too much bureaucracy surrounding this kind of case and it's not always obvious how to respond when the circumstances are unusual, as in this situation."

"Unusual?" Thóra inquired.

"Yes," replied the doctor. "Unusual insofar as the family chose to appoint a representative to retrieve the autopsy results, and also because a foreign national is involved. For a while I was starting to think we'd need the signature of the deceased to squeeze permission out of the system."

Thóra smiled politely, but could see out of the corner of her eye that Matthew's face was like a fossil.

The doctor looked away and continued. "Anyway, the bureaucracy surrounding it wasn't the only thing that made this case special, as I think you should realize before we begin." The doctor smiled again. "This was the strangest and most extraordinary autopsy I've ever performed, and I saw a thing or two when I was a student abroad."

Thóra and Matthew said nothing and waited for him to continue. Thóra was noticeably more excited than Matthew, who might as well have been a statue.

Clearing his throat, the doctor opened the folder. "Nonetheless, let us begin with what can be called the fairly normal aspects."

"By all means," grunted Matthew, and Thóra tried to conceal her disappointment. She wanted to hear the strange parts.

"Well, the cause of death was asphyxiation by strangulation," the doctor said as he tapped the folder. "When we've finished I'll let you have a copy of the autopsy report and you can read the results in more detail if you want. As far as the cause of death is concerned, the main point is how the deceased was strangled. We think a belt was used, made of some material other than leather. Whoever did it used a lot of force when he or she tightened it; there are pronounced marks on the neck. And it's not unlikely that the pressure was maintained for far longer than was needed to kill him for some reason—presumably in a mad fit of brutality or rage."

"How do you know that?" asked Thóra.

The doctor rummaged through the folder and produced two photographs. He put them on the desk and turned them to face Thóra and Matthew. They showed Harald's badly damaged neck. "You see that at the edge of the strangulation marks the skin was punctured in some places and burned by the friction. That suggests that the surface of the belt was slightly uneven. And notice, too, that whatever it was does not appear to have been regular in shape—it varied in width, judging by the differences in the breadth of the wound." The doctor paused while he pointed to one of the two photographs. "Another interesting thing is that down here at the base of the neck are signs of earlier wounds, not as serious but interesting all the same." He looked at them. "Do you know anything about this?"

Matthew spoke first. "No, nothing." Thóra restrained herself, but she suspected the cause. "I'm sure they have nothing to do with the murder.

But you never know." The doctor seemed satisfied with Matthew's answer; he did not press them further at least. He pointed to the other photograph, which was also of Harald's neck, but enlarged. "This is a close-up, and it shows how a piece of metal, the carved buckle of a belt or some other unknown object on the strap that was used, dug into the deceased's neck. If you look closely you can see it resembles a little dagger—but it could be something quite different. Of course, this is no plaster cast."

Thóra and Matthew stretched over for a better look at the photograph. The doctor was right. A mark left by an indeterminate object was clearly visible on his neck. A scale at the bottom of the photograph showed that the object was eight to ten centimeters long and the outlines up the neck bore a fairly close resemblance to a small dagger or cross. "What's that?" Matthew asked, pointing to abrasions on either side of the mark.

"Something with sharp edges appears to have been behind the small object. These punctured the skin when the strap was tightened. That's the closest I've got."

"What happened to the belt or whatever it was?" Matthew asked. "Was it ever found?"

"No," the doctor replied. "The attacker got rid of it. He doubtless thought that we could have obtained a DNA sample from it."

"Could you?" asked Thóra.

The doctor shrugged. "Who knows? But if it were found now, so long after the incident, the samples wouldn't be reliable." He cleared his throat. "Then there's the estimated time of death. That's a much more technical issue." The doctor flicked through the documents and removed several pages. "I don't know how familiar you are with such procedures, in terms of how we determine it?" He looked at Thóra and Matthew.

"I have no idea," Thóra said quickly. She saw that this annoyed Matthew, who did not say a word, but that didn't bother her.

"I suppose I should explain briefly what it entails so that you realize the results are neither some kind of magic nor irrefutable fact. They only express probability because the accuracy of the result depends on the accuracy of various information or clues that need to be collected."

"Collected?" repeated Thóra.

"Yes, to make such an estimate we need to collect clues that can be found on or near the body itself and in its surroundings. We also make use of clues from the life of the deceased, for example, the last time he was seen before his death, when he last ate, his habits, and the like. This is especially important in the case of violent deaths like this one."

"Of course," said Thóra, smiling at the doctor.

"The information or clues are then applied in various ways to produce the best estimate of the time of death."

"How?" Thóra asked.

The doctor leaned back in his chair, clearly pleased at the interest she was taking. "There are two methods. The first is based on measuring changes in the body that take place at a known rate, such as rigor mortis, body temperature, and decay. The other method involves comparing information with known times: when the deceased ate the food that is in his stomach, how it has been digested, and so on and so forth."

"When did he die?" Matthew got straight to the point.

"That's the big question." The doctor smiled. "To pick up where I left off, I should tell you first about the information that we used to estimate the time of death. I don't remember whether I mentioned it, but the sooner the body is found after death, the more reliable the clues are. In this case the interval was a day and a half, which is not so bad. And because the body was indoors, the ambient temperature is a known value." He opened the yellow folder and glanced at the text on one of the pages. "According to the police investigation, Harald was last seen alive by an impartial witness at 23:42 on the Saturday night when he allegedly paid for and got out of a taxi on Hringbraut. You can call that the *terminus a quo* for the possible time of death. The *terminus ad quem* is of course when the body was found, at 7:20 on the morning of Monday, October thirty-first."

He paused and looked at them both. Thóra nodded to show that she followed and he should continue. Matthew was statuelike, as ever.

"When the police arrived on the scene following the discovery of the corpse, the body temperature was measured immediately and it turned out to be the same as the ambient temperature. That indicated that some time had elapsed since his death. The exact rate depends on various factors; for example, it happens faster for a thin person than a fat person who has a proportionally larger surface area of thermal emission." The doctor gesticulated. "It also depends on the clothing and state of the body, its position, and the air currents, humidity, and various other factors. Information about all of these things adds to the clues I mentioned."

"And what came out of all this?" Matthew asked.

"Nothing really. It merely enabled us to narrow down the time frame a little. This method can obviously only provide us with information about the time of death if the body temperature differs from the ambient temperature." He sighed. "After the body temperature has reached the ambient temperature it remains there, understandably. But we can calculate how long it takes the body to reach that temperature, and infer that as the minimum time since death occurred." He looked down the page. "Here it is. In this case the analysis narrowed down the *terminus ad quem* to more than twenty hours from the time of death."

"This is all very interesting, no question of that," Matthew said. "But I would like to know when Harald is thought to have died and how it happened." He did not look at Thóra.

"Yes, of course, sorry," the doctor said. "Rigor mortis indicated that the death occurred at least twenty-four hours before the body was found, which narrows the time frame even further." He looked at Matthew and Thóra in turn. "Do you want me to go into detail about rigor mortis? I can give a brief explanation if you want."

"Please do," said Thóra, at exactly the same time as Matthew said: "No, there's no need for that."

"Isn't it etiquette to allow the lady to decide?" The doctor smiled at Thóra. She beamed back at him. Matthew gave her a sideways glance, quite a grumpy one as far as Thóra could see. She ignored it.

"As its name suggests, rigor mortis is the stiffening of the body after death. The condition is caused by chemical changes in muscular protein following a reduction in the acidity of muscle cells after death. No oxygen, no glucose, and the pH of the cells drops. Then when the volume of ATP nucleotide falls below a critical threshold, rigor mortis sets in, because ATP prevents the actin and myosin from bonding."

Thóra was about to ask more about this interesting actin and myosin but quickly restrained herself when Matthew deliberately stepped on her foot. Instead, she simply said, "I understand," which of course could not have been further from the truth. Out of the corner of her eye, she saw Matthew the statue smile for the first time that morning.

The doctor continued. "Rigor mortis begins in the muscles that are used most and gradually spreads to the rest. When it reaches a peak the body becomes stiff, remaining in the position it was in when the rigor mortis became dominant. That stage does not last long because rigor mortis wears off and the body relaxes again. Under normal conditions rigor mortis is complete twelve hours after death, then begins to wear off after thirty-six to forty-eight hours. However, in a case like Harald's, where the cause of death is asphyxiation, the process begins somewhat later." The doctor looked through the papers, took out a photograph and showed them. "As you can see, Harald's body was totally stiff when it was found."

Matthew beat Thóra to the photograph. He looked at it without a flicker of emotion, then handed it to her. "It's quite disgusting," he said as she took it.

"Disgusting" was not a strong enough word to describe what Thóra saw. The picture showed the young man whom Thóra knew from family photographs as Harald Guntlieb lying on the floor in a peculiar position she recognized from the photographs in the case file. But those had been so grainy and badly reproduced that they were almost fit to show on children's television compared with what greeted her eyes now. One of Harald's arms stood straight up from the elbow, as if pointing at the ceiling. There was nothing to keep the arm in that position or support it. Nonetheless, it was evident from the photograph that Harald Gottlieb was dead. His face was swollen, bloated, and strangely colored, which Thóra knew was not because the photograph had been poorly developed. Yet what disturbed her most was the eyes; or, more precisely, the eye sockets. She hurriedly returned the photographs to Matthew.

"As you can see, the body was probably resting against something and the hand became stuck in that position. You doubtless know that the murder was not committed in the corridor. He fell out of an alcove when one of the lecturers opened the door that Monday morning. Judging from his account, the body had been hidden there and either fell against the door or was arranged to fall when the door was opened. As the photo shows, the alcove door opens out into the corridor."

Matthew scrutinized the photograph, then nodded without saying a word. Thóra made do with that; she had no desire to see it again. "But you haven't told us when you think he died," Matthew said, handing him back the photograph.

"Yes, sorry," the doctor said, leafing through the papers. He straightened up when he found what he was looking for. "Taking into account the contents of the stomach and the absorption of amphetamine in the blood, the time of death is estimated to have been somewhere between one and one-thirty A.M." He looked up to explain in more detail. "The time of intake of both the pizza and the amphetamine was known. He had eaten a pizza around nine that evening and snorted amphetamine just before leaving the party at around eleven-thirty." He selected another photograph from the stack and handed it to Matthew. "Digestion of pizza is relatively well known and documented."

Matthew looked at the photograph, his face impassive. Then he looked up and handed it to Thóra. He smiled for the second time that morning. "Fancy a pizza?"

Thóra took the photograph, which showed the contents of Harald's stomach. It would be a while before she ordered another pizza. Trying to keep her composure, she returned the photograph to Matthew.

"The amphetamine analysis was made by the Pharmacological Institute. You will receive a copy of their report along with the autopsy results. An ecstasy tablet was also found in his stomach, half-digested. But we don't know when it was taken so it was of no use in determining the time of death."

"Fine," said Matthew.

The doctor continued. "It should be mentioned that the autopsy revealed that the body had been moved after death, a few hours later. We can determine that from bruising that forms in the lowest points of the body as soon as the blood supply stops. When that happens, blood begins to accumulate like puddles due to the force of gravity. We noticed bruising in places that were incompatible, namely, on the back, buttocks, and calves, but also on the soles of the feet, fingers, and chin. The former areas were less pronounced, which might indicate that the body was on its back to begin with, then placed upright some time later. Also, his shoes show signs that the body was dragged some distance; presumably the perpetrator held Harald under the armpits and his feet dragged along. Why this was done, we are not sure. In my view the most likely explanation is that the murderer killed Harald in his own home but was unable to dispose of the body immediately, perhaps due to intoxication. Why he chose to take the body to the faculty building is another mystery. It's not exactly the first place anyone facing this problem would think of."

"What about the eyes?" asked Matthew.

The doctor cleared his throat. "The eyes. That's another riddle I cannot explain. As the family knows, they were removed after Harald's death, which must be some consolation to them in my opinion. But I cannot say why it was done."

"How do you remove the eyes from a dead body anyway?" said Thóra, regretting her question at once.

"There must be lots of ways," said the doctor. "It appears that our murderer used a smooth tool for the job. All the signs, or rather the lack of them, point in that direction." He resumed flicking through the photographs.

Thóra hurried to stop him. "We believe you entirely. We don't need to see any photographs."

Matthew smirked at her. He was clearly amused that she found this repulsive, especially after their exchange in the corridor. This irritated her, so she decided to show him what she was made of. "You began by saying that the autopsy was unusual and strange. What did you mean by that?"

The doctor leaned forward and his face lit up. He had clearly been

looking forward to discussing this. "I don't know how close you were to
Harald Guntlieb; maybe you already know it all." He flicked through his
papers and produced several photographs. "This is what I mean," he said,
placing them on the table in front of Thóra and Matthew.

It took Thóra a moment to realize what she was looking at, but when
it finally dawned on her she could only shudder. "Yuck! What is that,
anyway?" she blurted.

"I'm not surprised you ask," the doctor replied. "Harald Guntlieb obviously practiced body modification, as it is called in the countries where
the habit originated. At first we thought that the state of his tongue was
connected with the disfiguration of the body, but then we noticed it had
healed so much that he must have had it done some time before—it's in a
different league from tongue studs in perversity, I really must say."

Thóra looked at one revolting photograph after another. Gripped by
nausea, she stood up. "Excuse me," she muttered through clenched
teeth, and ran for the door. When she stepped into the corridor she
heard Matthew say to the doctor in mock surprise: "Strange, and she's a
mother of two."

CHAPTER 7

There were few people at the Intercultural Center. Thóra had chosen that particular coffee shop because it was possible to talk in more peace and quiet there than at most other places downtown. She and Matthew could converse without worrying about customers at nearby tables overhearing them. They sat alone in the side room. The yellow folder containing the autopsy records lay in front of them on the mosaic-patterned table.

"You'll feel better after a coffee," said Matthew awkwardly, looking toward the door through which the waitress had just left after taking their order.

"I feel fine," Thóra snapped back. In fact, this was true; the nausea that had come over her in the doctor's room had passed. After leaving his office she found a bathroom down the corridor and refreshed herself by splashing her face with cold water. She had always had a tendency to feel sick and remembered how upset she used to get about the course books her ex-husband had left open everywhere when he was studying medicine. But the photographs in them were nowhere near as bad as what she had seen that morning; perhaps because the illustrations in the textbooks were somehow more impersonal. She added in a milder tone: "I don't know what came over me. I hope I didn't offend the doctor."

"They're not particularly pleasant photos," said Matthew. "Most people would react in exactly the same way. You needn't worry about the doctor. I told him you were recovering from a stomach bug so you weren't in the best shape for looking at that sort of thing."

Thóra nodded. "What on earth was that, anyway? I think I figured out most of the photos but in retrospect I'm not sure that I actually understood what some of them showed."

"After you left, we went over each one," said Matthew. "Harald appears to have had all kinds of disfigurements performed voluntarily on his body. According to the doctor, the oldest ones are several years old, but the newest ones were done only a couple of months ago."

"Why did he do it?" Thóra asked. She could not understand what motivated a young person to mutilate himself.

"God knows," said Matthew. "Harald was never quite normal. Ever since I met the family he was always hanging around with fringe elements. For a while it was the environmentalists, then it was an anti–G-8 protest group. When he finally absorbed himself in history I thought he'd found his bearings." Matthew tapped the yellow folder gently. "Why he started doing this is beyond me."

Thóra said nothing while she pondered the photographs and the pain that Harald must have suffered. "What was that exactly?" she asked, hurriedly adding: "It won't make me sick."

At that moment the waitress arrived with the coffee and snacks they had ordered. They thanked her, and when she had gone Matthew began his answer. "They were the results of all kinds of bizarre operations and surgeries. What struck me most was his tongue. You presumably realized that one of the photos was of Harald's mouth." Thóra nodded and Matthew continued. "He had his tongue cut in two, split lengthways. He must have meant it to resemble a snake's tongue, and I have to admit it was very successful."

"Could he talk properly after that?" Thóra asked.

"According to the doctor, he probably had a lisp afterward, but he couldn't be sure. He also said that such operations were not unheard-of. They are very rare, but Harald wasn't a pioneer in the field."

"Surely he didn't do it himself? Who performs that kind of surgery?" Thóra asked.

"The doctor thought it had been done quite recently because it wasn't fully healed. He had no idea who the surgeon was but added that anyone with anesthetic, tongs, and a surgical knife could do it quite easily. Doctors, surgical nurses, and dentists, for example. And he added that the same person could prescribe antibiotics and painkillers, or at least ensure access to them."

"Jesus Christ, that's all I can say," Thóra said. "But what about all the other stuff, those studs, scars, signs, horns, and God knows what else?"

"According to the doctor, Harald had objects implanted under his skin to produce their outlines in relief. Same thing with those little spikes standing out of his shoulders. The doctor said he removed thirty-two other objects, including little studs like the ones you saw on his genitals." Matthew glanced awkwardly at Thóra. She sipped her coffee and smiled to indicate that she did not find this embarrassing. He continued. "Then there were symbols, all connected with black magic and devil worship. Harald kept himself busy, there weren't many big spaces on his body without some kind of decoration." Matthew paused to eat a small slice of bread. Then he continued. "He doesn't seem to have liked traditional tattoos—he had scars."

"Scars?" said Thóra. "Did he have tattoos removed?"

"No, no. They were tattoos made by cutting the skin or removing it to produce a pattern or symbol from the scar tissue. Quite a decisive step, having that done. I understood from the doctor that you can't get rid of such tattoos except with a skin transplant that would leave an even bigger scar."

"Really?" Thóra said, surprised. When she was young it was considered wild to have more than two piercings in your ear.

"The doctor also said one of the cuts on Harald's body had been made after his death. At first they thought it was just a recent tattoo, but on closer inspection it turned out not to be. It looked like a magic symbol, and it was carved into his chest." Matthew produced a pen from his pocket and reached for a napkin. He sketched the symbol and turned the napkin so that Thóra could see it. Matthew continued. "The meaning of this symbol is unknown, according to the doctor. The police haven't managed to decipher it either, so maybe the murderer invented it on the spot. Another theory is that the murderer was unnerved by the circumstances and didn't make the symbol look the way he had planned. Carving in skin isn't easy."

Thóra picked up the napkin and examined the symbol. It consisted of four lines forming a box, like tic-tac-toe. The ends of the lines outside the box had been struck through and inside it was a circle.

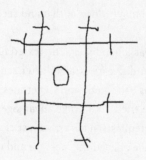

Thóra returned the napkin to Matthew. "Unfortunately I know nothing about magic symbols. I had a runic necklace once but I can't remember what it was supposed to represent."

"We need to talk to someone who knows about these things. Who knows, the police may not have investigated the symbol properly. Perhaps its meaning could help solve the case." Matthew ripped the napkin into four pieces. "The murderer must have had something in mind, anyway, to go to all that trouble. Most people think only about getting as far away as soon as possible after committing a murder."

"Maybe the murderer's a psychopath," Thóra suggested. "It's hardly a sign of a healthy mind to carve runes on a body and pluck out the eyes."

She shuddered. "Or he was stoned out of his mind. Which could in fact apply to that poor guy who's in custody at the moment."

Matthew shrugged. "Maybe." He took a sip of coffee. "And maybe not. Actually we need to visit him in prison as soon as we can."

"I'll contact his lawyer," Thóra said. "He should be able to arrange an interview, and he'll realize the benefits of helping us. It's in our mutual interest. If we manage to find the murderer that the police overlooked, we've cleared his client as well. I've also sent the police a formal request to see the investigation documents. This is very common and as far as I know the family is generally given them without any delay except for unusually sensitive cases."

Matthew took another piece of bread and looked at the clock. "How do you fancy coming to Harald's apartment? I've got the keys and the police have already returned some of what they took when they searched the premises. We could maybe look at that and see if there's anything to gain from it."

Thóra thought it was a good idea. She texted her son and asked him to fetch his sister from day care straight after school. Thóra felt better knowing that Sóley was back home and sometimes asked her son to fetch her early. Although she tried not to take advantage of Gylfi, he generally responded well to her requests. Thóra was just closing her phone when Gylfi's reply came in. She opened the message and read it. "ok when are u coming home?" Thóra texted straight back that it would be about six o'clock, and wondered if she was simply imagining how interested Gylfi had suddenly become in when she got home. Maybe he just wanted to play his computer games in peace, but it didn't escape her attention how often he asked these days.

Before she put her mobile away Thóra rang the office to let them know she would not be back soon. No one answered and the answering machine kicked in after the fifth ring. Thóra announced her absence and hung up. One of Bella's main jobs was answering the telephone, but on the rare occasions that Thóra needed to call the office she only received an answer half the time. She sighed, knowing it was pointless to discuss this with her sad excuse for a secretary yet again. "Okay, I'm ready," she told Matthew, who had used the time to finish his remaining food. Thóra drank the rest of her coffee before standing up and putting on her coat.

Before they left the café they went to the counter and Matthew paid the bill. He emphasized that all this was at the expense of the Guntliebs, but Thóra was uncertain whether this was to make sure she wouldn't think it was at his invitation and therefore a date or whether he said it from a simple obligation to provide information. She nodded casually and thanked him.

They went out into the cold to the parking garage where they had left the rental car. Harald's flat was on Bergstadastraeti, not so far from Hver-fisgata. Thóra had become very familiar with the central Thingholt district after she had started working on Skólavördustígur and could direct Matthew without any problems—although there were not many streets, it could be confusing for strangers to find their way along the narrow one-way lanes. They parked outside a dignified white concrete building on Bergstadastraeti where Matthew said Harald's flat was. It was one of the more desirable properties in the district, clearly well maintained, and Thóra could not begin to imagine the price. At least this explained the astronomical rent that she had noticed on Harald's tenancy agreement.

"Have you been here before?" asked Thóra as they walked up to the side entrance. The front door facing the street led to another apartment on the ground floor, where Matthew said the owners lived.

"Yes, a couple of times in fact," Matthew replied. "But this is only the second time I've been here on my own business, so to speak. The other times I came with the police. They needed a witness when they took away some papers and other items for the investigation, and again when they returned them. I'm sure we'll check the flat much more thoroughly than the police did. They were determined that Hugi was the murderer, so their investigation of the apartment was more of a formality."

"Is the flat as strange as the person who occupied it?"

"No, it's very ordinary," said Matthew, inserting one of the two keys into the lock on the outside door. The keys hung from a ring with an Ice-landic flag on it and Thóra inferred that he had bought it specifically for these keys in one of the tourist shops. She couldn't really imagine Harald in such a store, surrounded by traditional woolen sweaters and stuffed puffins. "After you," said Matthew as he opened the door.

Before Thóra could get one foot inside a young woman came around the corner and called out to them in fairly good English. "Excuse me," she said, fastening her cardigan against the cold. "Are you acting for Harald's family?"

Judging from the way she was dressed, Thóra assumed she must have come out of the other flat. Matthew held out his hand to the woman and said in English: "Yes, we met when I got the keys from you. Matthew."

"Yes, I thought so," the woman said, shaking Matthew's hand with a smile. She was elegant, slender, with her hair and face well cared for, clearly well-off. When she smiled Thóra realized she may not have been as young as she looked at first, because deep wrinkles formed around her mouth and eyes. She held out her hand to Thóra. "Hello, my name's Gudrún," she said, adding: "My husband and I were Harald's landlords."

Thóra gave her name and returned the woman's smile. "We were just going to have a look around. I don't know how long we'll be."

"Oh, that's fine," the woman hurried to say. "I only came to ask if there was any news about when the flat will be vacated." She smiled again, this time apologetically. "We've had a few inquiries, you understand."

In fact Thóra didn't understand, because as far as she knew the Guntliebs were still paying the rent, and it must have been a good arrangement to rent out a flat in that part of town without any of the inconvenience that tenants cause. She turned to Matthew, hoping he might provide an answer.

"Unfortunately it won't be just yet," he answered curtly. "The agreement is still in effect, as I understood the last time we discussed this."

The woman was quick to apologize. "Oh, yes, please don't get me wrong—of course it is. We'd just like to know when the family plans to end it. This is an expensive property and it's always nice to find tenants who can pay the price we ask." She gave Thóra an awkward look. "You see, we've had an offer from an investment company which is difficult to refuse. They need the flat in two months, but it kind of depends on what your plans are. You know what I mean."

Matthew nodded. "I understand your predicament, but, unfortunately, I can't make any promises at the moment," he said. "It all depends on the progress we make going through Harald's belongings. I want to be certain that nothing that could be relevant gets boxed."

The woman, who was beginning to shudder from the cold, nodded fervently. "If I can do anything to speed it up, do let me know." She handed them a business card from an import agency that Thóra did not recognize. It carried the woman's name and telephone numbers, including her mobile.

Thóra produced her own card from her purse and handed it to her in exchange. "Take mine too, and do phone if you or your husband remember anything that could conceivably help us. We're trying to find out who murdered Harald."

The woman's eyes bulged. "What about the man they're detaining?"

"We have our doubts that he's the murderer," Thóra said simply. She noticed that the woman seemed shocked at the news. "I don't think you need have any worries," she hastened to add. "I doubt whoever it is will come around here." She smiled.

"No, that's not the point," the woman babbled. "I just thought it was over."

They exchanged farewells and Thóra and Matthew went into the warmth. In the hallway they found a white varnished staircase leading to the apartment on the upper floor. There was also a door that Matthew said led to the shared laundry room. After they had gone upstairs to the landing, Matthew opened the apartment with the other key on his ring.

The first thing that struck Thóra when she stepped inside was that Matthew had been rather liberal with the truth when he described the flat as "very ordinary." She gazed around her, astonished.

CHAPTER 8

Gunnar Gestvík, head of the department of history at the University of Iceland, strode along the corridor where the director of the Manuscript Institute had her office and absentmindedly nodded a greeting to a young historian on the way. The young man gave an embarrassed smile that again reminded Gunnar of his newly found fame within the university and its institutions. Nobody could seem to forget that it was into his arms that Harald Guntlieb's body fell, to say nothing of the nervous breakdown that he reaped in reward. Never before had he been so popular, if that was the right term, because hardly anyone who now made a detour to talk to him could rightly be classified as a friend.

Of course this business would eventually all blow over, but God alone knew how weary he was of having to answer stupid questions about the incident, which were prompted by nothing but sheer nosiness. He was beginning to feel revolted by the expression people invariably put on their faces while mustering the courage to ask their questions. The expression was supposed to show a combination of sadness at the young man's untimely death and compassion for Gunnar, but almost without exception the outcome was completely different. Their faces radiated only morbid fascination and relief that it had happened to someone else.

Should he perhaps have followed the vice chancellor's advice and taken two months' leave? He couldn't be sure. People might have lost all interest by then, but it would be rekindled when the case went to court. So he would only be postponing the inevitable by taking a rest. Besides, it would merely have spawned endless rumors about him—a nervous breakdown and self-imposed convalescence, binge drinking at home, or even worse. No, he thought it was the right decision to turn down leave and let the storm die down. People would eventually grow bored of the subject and start avoiding him again.

Gunnar tapped on the door where María Einarsdóttir, director of the institute, had her office—more for politeness' sake than anything else, because he immediately opened the door without waiting to be told to enter. She was on the telephone but gestured to Gunnar to take a seat, which he did. He impatiently waited for her to finish the call, which sounded as though it involved an order for printer toner that had not been delivered.

Gunnar tried to conceal how much this irritated him. When María had called him several minutes earlier she said it was a serious matter and demanded that he meet her at once. He had put aside the project he was working on at the moment, an application for an Erasmus program grant for the department of history in cooperation with the University of Bergen. The application was to be submitted in English and Gunnar had just been getting into his groove when María phoned. If this serious matter of hers was about toner, he would certainly give her a piece of his mind. He had begun to arrange a few well-chosen words when she put the telephone down and turned her attention to him.

Before she spoke she gave Gunnar a ruminating look, as if she too were choosing her words carefully. The fingers of her right hand drummed on the desk and she sighed. "Christ," she said in English, finally.

She had clearly not been using her time searching for a phrase from the classics, Gunnar thought, trying not to show how inappropriate he considered it for the director of the Manuscript Institute to use such a word. Times had certainly changed over the forty years since Gunnar was a young man. In those days people took pride in sounding classical—now it was thought cheesy and pretentious. Even a woman like María, well educated and not a youngster anymore, used slang and shoddy grammar. Gunnar cleared his throat. "What is it, María?"

"Christ," she repeated, running both hands through her cropped hair. It was just beginning to turn gray and a few silver strands glittered when she ruffled it. Then she shook her head and got to the point. "One of the old letters is missing." A short pause, and then: "It's been stolen."

Gunnar's head snapped back. He could not conceal his surprise and disapproval. "What do you mean, stolen? From the exhibition?"

María groaned. "No. Not from the exhibition. From here. In-house."

Gunnar sat openmouthed. In-house? "How could that happen?"

"That's a good question. To the best of my knowledge it's the first time something of this kind has happened here." In a sharper tone she added: "Who knows, maybe more than just this letter is missing. As you well know, six hundred manuscripts and fragments from Árni Magnús-son's great collection are preserved here, along with all the old letters he amassed and a hundred and fifty manuscripts from the Royal Library in Denmark. Oh, yes, and seventy other manuscripts and letters from here and there." She paused and stared Gunnar in the eye. "You can bet we'll go through every scrap of paper here to find out whether anything else is missing. But I wanted to talk to you in person before I make it public. As soon as I order a count, it will be obvious what's going on."

"Why do you want to consult me about it?" asked Gunnar, surprised and slightly annoyed. As head of department he did not need to have much contact with the institute and had no particular function in it. "You're not accusing me of taking the letter?"

"For God's sake, Gunnar. I'd better explain the situation to you before you start asking if I suspect the vice chancellor." She handed him a letter that was lying on her table. "Do you remember the documents we had on loan from the Danish national archives?"

Gunnar nodded. The institute often received loans from foreign collections that were in some way connected with its own work. As a rule Gunnar got wind of them but did not commit them to memory unless the documents were related to his own areas of academic interest. The Danish collection was clearly not one. He skimmed the letter, which was written by Karsten Josephsen, a chief of department at the Danish national archive. Written in Danish, it was a reminder that the deadline for returning the documents was approaching. He handed the letter back to María. "I'm completely at a loss."

She took the letter and put it back in its place on the desk in front of her. "That may well be. It was a collection of letters written to the archdeacons of Roskilde Cathedral. They were all from the period 1500 to 1550. I understand they did not arouse very much academic interest here, although the ones dated around the Danish Reformation in 1536 were interesting in their own right. But the missing letter was not one of those."

"What was the letter about?" asked Gunnar, still unsure how this concerned him.

"Naturally I don't know exactly what it said, because it's lost—but I do know that it was from 1510 and written by Stefán Jónsson, then bishop of Skálholt, to the archdeacon of Roskilde Cathedral. I have that information from the register that was sent here with the collection. In fact, that was how I discovered the letter was missing: I used the register as a checklist for packing the collection for its return to Denmark."

"Could it be that it never came here—it's simply always been missing?" asked Gunnar hopefully.

"Out of the question," came the answer. "I was present when the collection was unpacked last year and we took great care in checking it against the register they sent. It was all in perfect order and everything was in its place."

"So perhaps the letter has just been misplaced?" suggested Gunnar. "Couldn't it have accidentally ended up with other documents?"

"You know," María said, "if circumstances were different that might well be a possibility." She paused for a while to emphasize what would follow. "When I discovered the disappearance I went straight to our computer system to examine the letter—you presumably know that we scan every single document we receive, our own or borrowed?" Gunnar nodded and María went on. "Guess what? The file had been deleted—just this one letter."

Gunnar pondered this information for a moment. "Wait a minute. Doesn't that suggest that the letter wasn't in the consignment in the first place? Weren't the letters scanned as soon as they were unwrapped?"

"Yes, that began the following day. But the letter was there and it was scanned. I can tell from the numbering system we use to identify digital files. The collection was given a heading and individual documents a serial number based on their age, with the oldest first." She ran her fingers through her hair again. "One number is missing from the sequence, exactly where the letter would have been."

"What about the computer system backup? They're always going on about how secure we are against data loss. Can't you find the file on one of the backup registries?"

María smiled faintly. "I've looked into that. According to our system administrator, the file cannot be found on any of our daily backups or the latest monthly backup. He says they copy over the daily registries every week; there's a separate Monday registry, Tuesday registry, and so on. So there's never a backup more than a week old on those registries. The same goes for the monthly registries. They're copied over so that the oldest backup we have is a month old. This file was erased more than a month ago. Actually there's a six-month backup kept in the institute's bank vault. I haven't had that fetched yet because I didn't realize the seriousness of the matter until now."

"You still haven't told me where I come into the picture," was all that Gunnar could think to say. Computers and data systems were not his cup of tea.

"Naturally I've checked who was working with the collection. As you know, that's all documented, left, right, and center. According to the register, the last person to have access to it was a student from your department." María's expression hardened. "Harald Guntlieb."

Gunnar put one hand to his forehead and closed his eyes. What next?

Wouldn't this ever stop? Taking a deep breath, he made an effort to talk slowly and calmly and keep control of his voice. "Other people must have looked at the collection. How can you be sure Harald took the letter and not someone before him? There are fifteen full-time positions here plus countless visitors and students doing research."

"Oh, I'm certain," María said firmly. "The person who looked at the collection before him was me, in fact, and everything was in place then. Also, a piece of paper had been inserted into the folder, presumably to prevent having to return it empty. That would have attracted attention. The piece of paper dispels all doubt."

She snatched a piece of paper from her desk in a gesture of irritation.

"I hope you realize that history students are given access to our resources, manuscripts, and documents on the responsibility of the department. You, as head of department, cannot shirk that responsibility. Our institute simply can't afford having a reputation for losing old and valuable documents. Much of our work is based on cooperation with similar facilities in Scandinavia and I can't bear the thought of jeopardizing that cooperation because of your students' dishonesty."

Swallowing, Gunnar looked at the piece of paper María had handed to him. At that moment he would have liked to throw his hands up in the air and storm out. It was a printout of grades and courses from the students' register, clearly marked with the name Harald Guntlieb at the top. Gunnar put the paper down in his lap. "If Harald stole the letter and swapped it for this piece of paper, he was one of the stupidest thieves ever. He must have realized that it would backfire." Gunnar lifted up the printout and waved it.

María shrugged. "How am I supposed to know what he was thinking? I presume he planned to return it. If anyone knows why he can't now, it's you—he only got access to the collection a little over a month before he fell out of the closet and into your arms. Doubtless he saw from the register that the collection hadn't been touched for two months prior to that. Everyone who needed to had already examined it thoroughly. He rightly assumed that he had some time before he would be found out so he'd have a chance to swap it again before then. What he was planning to do with the letter in the meantime is a mystery to me. But he didn't live long enough to bring it back. That's the best explanation I can offer for this incident."

"What do you want me to do?" said Gunnar meekly.

"Do?" María echoed sarcastically. "I didn't call you in for moral support. I want you to find the letter." She waved her arms around. "Look in his place in the reading room and anywhere else he might have stashed it away. You know where to look better than I do. He was your student."

Gunnar gritted his teeth. He cursed the day Harald Guntlieb was admitted to the department and remembered how he alone had opposed his application. It had given him a creepy feeling immediately, especially when he saw that his B.A. dissertation was on witch hunts in Germany. He knew at once that the young man would be trouble. Overruled by a democratic vote in the department, he was now stuck in this mess on top of all the other problems the student had caused. "Who knows about this?"

"Me. You. I haven't discussed it with anyone else apart from the system administrator, and he doesn't know the whole story. He thinks it just involves the electronic document." She hesitated. "I also approached Bogi. He worked with the collection when it arrived and I tried to find out everything he knows. He suspects there's something wrong. I imagine he thinks the letter went astray; I didn't hint at my suspicions that it's been stolen."

Bogi was one of the research fellows at the institute. Gunnar thought someone as easygoing as him was unlikely to make a fuss. "When is the collection due back in Denmark? How long do I get to search for the letter?"

"I can delay it by a week at the most. If the letter hasn't been found by then, I'll have no choice but to notify them of its disappearance. I emphasize that your name will be mentioned again and again. I'll do everything in my power to make sure that you get humiliated by this, not us. Actually a little bird told me this wasn't the first time your department's been connected with missing documents." She looked at him quizzically.

Gunnar stood up, his face flushed. "I see." He did not feel confident about saying anything more at this stage, but turned around in the doorway to ask one final question that had been plaguing him—even though he would have liked to storm out, slamming the door. "Don't you have any idea what this letter was about? You say the collection was examined thoroughly, someone must remember."

María shook her head. "Bogi had a vague recollection. He was researching the establishment of the Zealand diocese in Denmark and its effect on Icelandic ecclesiastical history. That was quite a long time after the letter was written, so he didn't study it closely. But he did remember that it was difficult to make sense of, something to do with hell, plague, and the death of an emissary. That was all I could drag out of him without arousing his suspicions about how things stand."

"I'll be in touch," said Gunnar as he left. He went out and closed the door behind him without waiting for María's farewell.

One thing was certain. He had to find the letter.

CHAPTER 9

Thóra spun around slowly on the shiny parquet floor of the huge living room. It was decorated in the smartest of minimalist styles. The few pieces of furniture in it had certainly cost a fortune. Two large, elegant black leather couches were arranged in the middle of the room, considerably lower than the sofas Thóra was accustomed to. She yearned to sit down on one but did not want to imply to Matthew that this was all new to her. Between the two sofas was an even lower coffee table that looked to Thóra as if it had no legs—the surface almost seemed to be resting on the floor. She tore her eyes away from the furniture and gazed along the walls. Apart from a flat screen in the center of one, all the works of art displayed there looked ancient. A number of old objects had been arranged too, including a clumsy wooden chair that Thóra took to be a replica rather than an original. She wondered whether Harald had taken an active role in the look of the room himself or an interior designer had arranged everything. Such a hybrid of old and new gave the area a very unusual and personal character.

"How do you like it?" asked Matthew casually. His tone suggested that he, unlike Thóra, was accustomed to wealth.

"It really is a very smart place," she answered, walking over to one of the white walls to examine a framed copperplate etching that looked very old. She noticed the theme and stepped back at once. "What in God's name is that?" The copperplate was action-packed and it must have been an enormous effort for the artist to fit all the people into the scene. There were about twenty characters in this pale picture, mainly males, deftly arranged in pairs with one torturing the other or punishing him in some way.

Matthew went over to her and looked at the picture. "Oh, that." With a slight grimace he continued: "This is a picture that Harald inherited from his grandfather. It's German and depicts the situation there in sixteen hundred and something when the religious wars were at their height." Matthew turned away from the picture. "What makes it unique is that it is contemporary. In other words, it's not a later interpretation of the situation. Those works are often less realistic, more exaggerated. Although they may be a little stylized."

"More exaggerated?" Thóra exclaimed. What could be more exaggerated than this?

"Well, sort of." Matthew shrugged. "Through my work for the Guntliebs I've found out a little about this period and, believe me, it's far from the most disgusting piece in their collection." He smiled wryly. "You could almost put this in a child's room compared with some of the other ones."

"My daughter's got a picture of Minnie Mouse on her wall," said Thóra, moving on to the next picture. "You can rest assured a picture like that would never go on her wall, nor any other in my home."

"No, it's not for everyone," Matthew answered, following Thóra to a picture of a man being tortured on a rack in front of men dressed in cowls. The men sat hunched together, intently watching two executioners who seemed to be using all their strength to turn the wheels of the rack. Presumably the idea was to stretch the victim's limbs to increase his suffering. Matthew pointed at the center of the work. "This one shows torture by the Inquisition and it's also from Germany. They put great effort into extracting confessions, as you can see." He looked at Thóra. "I'm sure it's interesting for you as a lawyer to understand the roots of torture because in Europe it can be traced back to law—in the broadest sense, that is."

Thóra prepared for yet another insult to her profession—she had been forced to put up with them ever since she embarked upon her legal degree. "Of course, we lawyers are responsible for all this."

"No, joking aside," replied Matthew. "In the Middle Ages, prosecutions were brought by individuals. Anyone who thought he had been the victim of wrongdoing or criminal conduct had to bring charges himself and prosecute the case. The trials were a joke really. If the accused did not just confess to the court or there was no clear proof of his guilt, it was left to God to decide. Accused people were made to undergo ordeals, walk over burning embers, being thrown into water in a sack, and so on. If their injuries healed after a certain time, or if they sank in the water, they were deemed innocent. Then the accuser was in trouble, because he would face trial. Understandably, people were reluctant to bring charges against others because of the risk that the case would turn against them."

Matthew pointed at the man on the rack. "Eventually that approach was replaced by this system when the authorities and the Church realized there had been a huge increase in secular and religious crimes because the courts were impotent. To cut crime they had to resort to Roman law, which had a different arrangement for bringing charges and prosecuting them. This was based on investigation, which is where the Inquisition comes from. Where the Church led, the secular courts followed, and in this new system the victim no longer needed to bring charges or prosecute the case." Matthew smiled triumphantly. "Ergo—lawyers."

Thóra smiled back. "It's a bit rich to blame lawyers for all this misery." It was her turn to point to the anguished man on the rack. "Excuse me, but I don't quite see the connection between investigation and torture."

"No," said Matthew. "Unfortunately there was a flaw in the new arrangement. In order to find someone guilty, either two witnesses or a confession was needed. Some crimes, such as blasphemy, aren't necessarily witnessed, so everything depended on confessions. Judges needed them, and they could be obtained by torture. That was deemed to be an investigation."

"Disgusting," declared Thóra, turning away from the picture to face Matthew. "How do you know all this?"

"Harald's grandfather was a mine of information about this period and a passionate raconteur. His accounts were great fun to listen to, but I have only a very superficial knowledge of this compared with him."

"Well, well," Thóra said. "Have you seen all these pictures before?"

Matthew looked along the wall. "Most of them, as far as I can see. Actually these are only a fraction of the pictures and other items in the collection. Harald obviously only brought part of it with him. His grandfather spent much of his life collecting it all. And who knows how much money he spent on it. I would imagine it's the most remarkable collection in the world dedicated to torture and executions through the ages. One part is an almost complete set of the different editions of *Malleus Maleficarum*."

Thóra looked around the room. "Was the collection just hanging on the living room walls?"

"No, are you mad?" replied Matthew. "The books and other documents, letters and such, are stored in a bank vault because they are so valuable. And there are two special halls in the Guntlieb home housing the part of the collection that's on exhibit. I don't expect they were particularly upset at losing some of the works. Most of the family hated them; Harald's mother, for example, could never be persuaded to go in there. Harald was the only descendant who shared his grandfather's interest. That was surely the reason his grandfather bequeathed the collection to him."

"So Harald could transport it from one country to another as he pleased?" asked Thóra.

Matthew smiled. "I imagine they would have gladly let him take it even if he hadn't inherited it. I think Harald's parents were simply relieved to get rid of even a small part of it from their household."

Thóra nodded. "Is this chair from the collection?" She pointed to the old wooden chair positioned in a corner of the room.

"Yes," said Matthew. "That's a ducking stool. It's an example of using torture as a punishment, which is quite different from using it in an inquisition. It's from Britain."

Thóra walked over to the ducking stool and ran her fingers across the carvings on its back. She could not read the inscription; the letters had faded badly and she was not familiar with the script anyway. There was a large hole in the middle of the seat and on its arms were rows of twisted and shriveled leather straps that were obviously designed to tie down the arms of the occupant.

"The hole was to let water through so that the seat would sink until the victim was submerged. It was designed as a humiliation but sometimes the person in the stool would drown if the duckers weren't careful."

"I'm glad I wasn't around in those days," Thóra said, letting go of the stool. She generally found it difficult to hold her tongue when she felt strongly about something, so she would have been a prime candidate.

"These are actually some of the milder instruments in the collection," said Matthew. "The originality of some of the inventions defies belief. Pain seems to give the imagination free rein."

"Actually, I'd like to leave this cozy little room. Shouldn't we keep going?"

Matthew agreed. "Come on, I'll show you the other rooms. None of them are much better, but the kitchen is free of all this. Let's start there."

They moved to the kitchen, which led off the hallway. Although not particularly big, it was impressive, fully equipped with the latest gadgetry. Racks of wine bottles were spread along the fitted shelves. Thóra began to doubt that Matthew knew much about "ordinary people." If this was yang, her kitchen was yin. There was a large gas stove with a tall steel ventilation hood overhead, a dishwasher, a cafeteria-standard sink, a wine cooler, and a huge double refrigerator. Thóra went up to it. "I've always wanted to make my ice cubes in one of these."

"So why don't you get one?" Matthew asked.

Thóra turned to face him. "For the same reason I haven't bought other expensive things I fancy. I can't afford them. Difficult as it may be for you to imagine, some households are a bit short of cash."

Matthew shrugged. "A fridge isn't exactly a luxury."

Thóra did not bother to reply. She went to the cupboards and looked inside. In one of the lower ones was a set of steel pots with glass lids that were so clean she doubted they had ever been used. "It doesn't look like Harald did much cooking, even though he had this amazing kitchen," she said, closing the door. She stood up straight.

"No. Knowing him he was probably more one to buy ready meals or dine out."

"His credit card statement gave that impression." She looked all around but saw nothing that could provide further clues. Even the refrigerator door was blank—no magnet and therefore no notes hanging from it. Her refrigerator door was used as a kind of information center for the home. She could hardly remember what color it was; it was covered with timetables, birthday invitations, and other memory joggers. "Shouldn't we look at the rest?" Thóra asked. "I doubt we'll find anything here to move us forward."

"Not unless someone killed him for his fridge," said Matthew, adding teasingly: "Where were you on the night of the murder?"

Thóra made do with a wry smile. "There were a few small transactions in a pet shop on his credit card statement—did Harald keep any pets?"

Matthew shook his head in surprise. "No, there was no animal here nor any signs of one."

"My first thought was that he'd been buying something for a pet." Thóra looked in the kitchen cupboards for cat food or the like. Nothing.

"Call the shop," Matthew said. "Maybe they'll remember him—who knows?"

Thóra did just that. She found the number of the store, dialed, talked to the assistant there, and hung up. "Weird," she said. "They remembered him and said he came in to buy a hamster on several occasions. Are you sure there wasn't a hamster's cage here?"

"Positive," answered Matthew.

"Strange," said Thóra. "The lad I talked to said Harald tried to buy a raven from them too."

"A raven?" said Matthew, shocked. "Why?"

"He had no idea. They don't sell ravens so they didn't go into the reason. He just thought it was odd, which is why he remembered him."

"I wouldn't be surprised if he saw a bird like that as a kind of status symbol in all this magical mumbo jumbo," said Matthew.

"Maybe," Thóra said. "But surely not a hamster."

They left the kitchen and walked down a corridor where the other rooms were. Matthew opened the bathroom door and Thóra popped her head inside—it did not seem to hide any secrets. Like the kitchen it was very modern and stylish, but not particularly interesting in other respects. They went to Harald's bedroom, which turned out to be fascinating.

"Has anyone cleaned up here or did he always keep it so tidy?" Thóra asked, pointing to the neatly made bed. It was unusually low, just like the sofas in the living room.

Matthew sat down on the edge of the bed. His knees almost touched his chin. He rearranged his legs and stretched them out in front of him. "He had a cleaning lady who cleaned everything up the weekend he was murdered, which didn't please the police much. Of course at that time she knew nothing about the murder, any more than anyone else. She just turned up at the appointed time and tidied up. I talked to her and she spoke well of Harald. But she did say there weren't many women where she worked who wanted to take on this apartment."

"I wonder why?" said Thóra sarcastically, indicating the pictures on the walls. They were all in the same vein as those in the living room, but these mainly depicted female torture, punishment, or execution. Most of the women were naked from the waist up, some completely naked. "This is just like any normal man's room."

"You think so? Maybe you've been associating with the wrong type of person," answered Matthew, a smile darting across his face.

"I was joking, actually," said Thóra. "Naturally I've never been in a bedroom with this kind of décor." She walked over to a large flat-screen television that was fixed to the wall facing the bed. "I shudder to think what he had in this," she said, bending down to the DVD player on a low chest of drawers beneath it. She turned on the player and pressed the eject button, but the disk holder came out empty.

"I removed the disk," said Matthew, observing her movements from the bed.

"What was he watching?" Thóra asked, turning to him.

The Lion King," said Matthew, his expression not changing. "Come on, I'll show you the study. That's the most likely place to find something to help us."

Thóra stood up and followed. But she decided to make a slight detour to look at Harald's bedside table. She opened the single drawer and was greeted by a heap of jars and tubes of cream, which had clearly been used for certain personal activities, and a half-full packet of condoms. *So there are women who don't mind the wall decorations,* thought Thóra. She closed the drawer and hurried after Matthew.

CHAPTER 10

Laura Amaming looked at her watch. Fortunately it was only a quarter to three—she had plenty of time to finish her work and still arrive on time for class at four. After years of living in Iceland, she had finally got round to enrolling in a course in Icelandic as a foreign language. She hated being late. Conveniently, the class was in the main building of the university, a stone's throw from the history institute where she worked as a cleaner. It would have been almost impossible for her to attend had it been elsewhere—she did not finish work until half an hour before the class started, and she had no car.

She put the mop in the sink and rinsed it under a jet of hot water. Muttering the Icelandic words for "hot" and "cold" to herself, she mentally cursed the difficult pronunciation.

Laura wrung out the mop and added it to the dirty cloths in the bucket of bleach. She reached for some window spray and three clean dusters. Today she was supposed to clean the insides of all the windows along the north side of the second floor, and she would certainly need more than one duster. She left the broom closet and went up-stairs.

She was in luck; the first three offices were empty. Cleaning was so much easier when no one was around. Especially cleaning windows, as she had to clamber up onto chairs or other furniture to reach the top. She found it so uncomfortable doing this in front of a spectator whom she could not even talk to. It would all be much better when she gained a grasp of the language. Back in the Philippines she had been talkative and outgoing. In Iceland she felt she never came out of her shell except in the company of her compatriots.

At work she often felt more like an object than a human being; everyone spoke and acted as if she weren't there. Everyone except the head of cleaning services, Tryggvi. That man always behaved with absolute decorum and did everything he could to communicate with Laura and her fellow cleaning ladies, although more often than not this boiled down to primitive gestures that could be very amusing at times. Nor did he seem to mind their laughter when they teamed up to guess what he was trying to tell them. He was a true gentleman and Laura looked forward to being able to say something to him in his own language eventually. One thing was certain—she would never be able to pronounce his name after all the Icelandic courses in the world. She said "Tryggvi" in a quiet voice and could only smile when she heard how it came out.

Laura went to the fourth room. It served as the students' common room. She tapped on the door and went inside. On a battered sofa at the far end of the room sat a young girl whom Laura knew belonged to the murdered student's circle of friends. All those young people were easily recognizable, always looking like they were under a thundercloud, both in their demeanor and in how they dressed. The red-haired girl was immersed in a conversation on her mobile, and although she spoke quietly it was obvious that the subject was not pleasant. With a sour expression she looked up and cupped a hand over her mouth and the bottom of the mobile, as if to ensure that Laura did not hear what she was saying. She garbled a good-bye into the phone, crammed it in her camouflage-green shoulder bag, stood up, and strode haughtily past. Laura tried to smile to her and took enormous pains to say good-bye properly. The girl turned round in the doorway, surprised at the gesture, and muttered something before leaving and shutting the door. *What a shame,* Laura thought. She was a pretty girl, could even be called beautiful if she made the slightest effort to improve her appearance, took those awful rings out of her eyebrows and nose, and gave just the occasional smile.

But the windows were waiting and time was racing by. She sprayed the first window and wiped the cloth in successive circles over the glass. Fortunately there was not much dirt. The curtains were usually closed so the windows did not get smudged. She finished the windows one by one, but as she was completing the final one she noticed the first real dirty mark. It was not even on the glass itself, but was a small brown stain on the side of the steel handle used to open the window.

Laura retrieved the used cloth she had put into her overcoat pocket. There was no need to mess up the cloth in her hands—it was perfectly clean. She sprayed the handle and wiped the cloth over and under it. Occasionally the youngest cleaners neglected places that weren't visible, and she could see that this smudge—whatever it was—was under the handle as well. She was pleased at having noticed it; she could just imagine some grumpy student opening the window, grabbing the handle, and then complaining about how badly it had been cleaned.

Laura snorted in disgust at the way they treated that place—the handle was just one of many examples of their sloppiness. Who could have such dirty hands anyway? Whatever it was, it wiped away immediately and Laura rubbed the cloth across a second time for form's sake. She looked at the shiny steel with satisfaction, feeling she had won a minor victory against Gunnar, the head of the department.

As she was slipping the cloth back into her pocket she could not help staring at the stain that was now on it. It was dark red. The brown color had been diluted by the damp cloth. It was blood—there was no question. But how had it come to be on the handle? Laura did not remember any blood on the floor; the person who grabbed the window handle must have bled onto other surfaces. She wondered about a link with the murder, but thought it unlikely. The windows had been cleaned since then.

She wrinkled her brow in thought. Just because she did not recall clean-ing the windows herself did not mean no one else had. She tried to remember—wasn't the east wing cleaned the day after the murder? Yes. Of course it had been. The police had even questioned one of the younger girls, Gloria, who did the weekend shifts.

What on earth was she supposed to do? She balked at the idea of try-ing to explain this incident in Icelandic. It wasn't enough to be able to say "hot" and "cold" for this. Besides, she could end up in trouble with the authorities for erasing the murderer's fingerprints by wiping the handle. It could also be embarrassing if she tried to make an issue out of some-thing that turned out to have a perfectly normal explanation. What a mess! She remembered the fuss Gloria made about the questioning she was subjected to—she'd even shed a few tears when she told the others about how tough the police were. Laura was convinced at the time that they were crocodile tears, but now she was not so sure. She looked all around the floor for any signs of blood. If she could find some it would settle the matter, because she had cleaned here more than once since the murder was committed. Then it would have to be a recent event with a normal explanation.

There was no blood on the floor, not even in the corners where the baseboards met. Laura bit her lip anxiously. She tried to console herself. The police had the murderer in custody. If the blood was connected with the murder it would surely be just one more piece of evidence showing that he was the killer. Laura took a deep breath. She thought about the magazines that were often thrust in her face at the Filipino gatherings, magazines containing interviews with one of the attendees and photographs of them with the most incredible objects that they all seemed to need to hold up against their faces. Laura could not envisage herself holding a window handle up against her cheek on a double-page spread in such a magazine. No, she was being unnecessarily silly—one of the students must have had a nosebleed, felt dizzy, and wanted a breath of fresh air. She breathed more lightly for a minute, until she re-membered her own children getting nosebleeds. They went to a bathroom—not an open window.

All the same. There was nothing to suggest that the German student's murderer had tried to open the window, any more than someone completely unrelated to the murder had been injured and needed some fresh air. Laura took her cloth and decided to see whether there was any blood in the corners—something that could be expected if a major confrontation had taken place in the room. An inexperienced cleaner might not have realized that such traces of evidence could be left. Making the sign of the cross, she decided that if no more blood appeared on the cloth it was a sign from above that she was overreacting. Otherwise she would notify the police even if it meant putting that nice man Tryggvi in a spot of bother. Laura got down on her knees and inched her way along the walls. Nothing. The cloth came up clean apart from some specks of dust and the usual dirt. She felt better and got to her feet, satisfied with the outcome. What silliness—of course there was a normal explanation for that blood. Obviously the fact that it had even crossed her mind was due to her shock when the body was found—a terribly mutilated and ungodly corpse. Once again she made the sign of the cross.

For some reason, on her way out she could not take her eyes off the doorsill. It was much higher from the floor than the baseboards and she bent down to run the cloth along the gap. The cloth became lodged. Laura bent down for a better look at the obstruction. She caught sight of a silver object and looked around for something to dislodge it from the doorsill. She fetched a ruler from one of the desks. Then she tried to ease the object up, finally succeeding after several attempts. Laura picked it up and scrambled to her feet.

It was a little steel star, the size of the nail on her little finger. She placed it in her palm and scrutinized it. The star seemed familiar but Laura could not place it. Where could she have seen it before? But she had no time to wonder because she had to finish the windows or be late for her class. She put the star in her pocket, determined to give it to Tryggvi. He might know where it was from. It could hardly be connected with the murder—any more than the blood on the window handle, for which there was a normal explanation. Or could it? An image of the finger suddenly crossed her mind. She made the sign of the cross to ward off the revolting memory. She decided to confide in Gloria. The girl was bound to be working over the weekend, and Laura would be as well. She might know something more than she had told the others and the police.

Marta Mist was lolling against the wall in the corridor, annoyed at how long the cleaner was taking to finish. It was not as if cleaning that room was a major job—throwing out a few cans of soft drink, washing up some cups, and scrubbing the floor. She looked at the clock on her mobile phone. Damn it—that jerk must be taking a nap on the sofa. Marta Mist called up Bríet's number from her address book with the push of a few buttons. She had better answer; few things got on Marta Mist's nerves more than knowing that someone she called might look at the screen, see who was dialing, and not pick up. Her worries proved unfounded.

"Hi," said Bríet.

Marta Mist skipped the formalities. "I couldn't find it," she said crossly. "Are you sure you put it in the drawer?"

"Shit, shit, shit," moaned Bríet. "I'm positive I put it there. You watched me do it."

Marta Mist gave a sarcastic laugh. "That means nothing, I was seeing double that night."

"I put it there. I know I did," Bríet insisted. "What shall I tell Halldór? He'll go nuts."

"Nothing. Don't tell him a fucking thing."

"But—"

"No buts. It isn't there, so what now? What are you going to do about it?"

"Well . . . I don't know," said Bríet helplessly.

"Consider yourself lucky, then, as I do," Marta Mist retorted. "I talked to Andri and he agrees—we won't say anything or do anything, because there's not much we can do." She left out the fact that it had taken her twenty minutes to talk Andri out of letting Halldór know. Then she added in a gentler voice: "Don't worry about it. If it was a problem, we'd already have found out."

The door opened and the cleaner came out. Judging from the look on her face there was big news in the world of sanitary technology. She looked like she had been force-fed a lemon. *About time too,* Marta Mist thought to herself and lurched off the wall. "Bríet," she said into her mobile. "The cleaner just came out. I'll take a better look. Call you later." She rang off without giving Bríet a chance to say good-bye. Everything was such a bloody hassle.

CHAPTER 11

Thóra was sitting at Harald Guntlieb's desk, browsing through the pile of papers. She looked up, straightened her back, and turned to Matthew. He sat absorbed in the same task in an armchair in one corner of the study. They had decided to start by examining the documents the police took away when they searched the flat, which had just been returned. There were three large cardboard boxes full of papers of all descriptions and after almost an hour's reading Thóra was beginning to lose sight of the point behind all this. The papers were a mixed bag, mostly documents connected with Harald's studies in one way or another along with statements from banks, credit card companies, and other official bodies. Many were in Icelandic so they were little help to Matthew, who had to put a large stack to one side for Thóra to peruse later.

"What are we looking for, anyway?" she asked suddenly.

Matthew put his sheaf of papers on a small side table and rubbed his eyes wearily. "Basically, we're looking for a lead, something the police overlooked. For example, an explanation of what happened to the money Harald had transferred here. We could also come across—"

Thóra interrupted him. "That's no help. What I meant was that we should maybe try to establish who could possibly be connected with the murder or stand to benefit from it. I have absolutely no experience investigating murders and I'd like a better picture before I go through any more papers. I'm not particularly excited by the idea of having to do all this again if we have a bright idea later."

"No, I understand that," said Matthew. "But I'm not quite sure what to say. We're not looking for anything specific we already know about, unfortunately. Maybe we're not looking for anything at all. We're really just trying to figure out what Harald's life was like before the murder so that we have some idea about the circumstances and events that led up to it—if something crops up that points us toward the murderer, that's just a bonus. If it helps you narrow things down, you could say that the main motives for murder are jealousy, anger, financial gain, revenge, madness, self-defense, sexual perversion."

Thóra waited for more but Matthew had completed his tally. "Nothing else?" she asked. "There must be more motives."

"I didn't claim to be an expert," Matthew retorted. "Sure, there are more motives, but that was all I could think of offhand."

Thóra thought before answering him. "All right, let's say those are the main motives. Which of them could apply to Harald's murder? Was he involved with a woman, for example? Could it be a case of jealousy?"

Matthew shrugged. "I think he was unattached. But jealousy could still play a part. Maybe someone loved him and it was unrequited." He paused for a moment, then added: "Actually I think women rarely murder by strangulation, so it's unlikely to have been a crime of passion."

"No," agreed Thóra pensively. "Unless it was a crime of passion committed by another man. Was Harald gay, perhaps?"

Matthew shrugged. "No, he definitely wasn't."

"How do you know?" she asked.

"I just know," he replied. Seeing the dubious expression on Thóra's face, he added: "It's quite remarkable. I can usually tell straightaway if a man bats for the other side. I don't know how, but I'm very intuitive about it."

Thóra decided not to pursue the topic but knew from her own experience that there was an overwhelming probability Matthew was no better than anyone else at identifying people's sexuality. Her ex-husband had the same misconception and Thóra had proved him wrong countless times. She changed the subject: "It doesn't seem to have been rape and there were no signs of recent sexual activity, so we can rule that out."

"So now there are fewer possible motives," Matthew said with a wry grin. "We'll get there soon."

Thóra ignored him. "So why do *you* think he was killed?"

Matthew studied her for a moment before answering. "It was probably something to do with money. But I still can't shake off the feeling that it was somehow connected with his studies of sorcery. What happened to his eyes and the symbol carved on the body clearly suggest that. I can't figure out the motive and that annoys me. Why commit a murder for sorcery or something that happened centuries ago?"

"Isn't that a bit far-fetched? The police found no link between the murder and black magic, in spite of what was done to the corpse. They must have investigated that possibility," Thóra said, hurriedly adding: "And don't say that they're just stupid. That's far too simplistic."

"Actually, you're right," said Matthew. "They checked if there was any link. I think they thought Harald's research was either madness or some kind of mumbo jumbo. They came here, saw what was hanging on the walls, and took Harald for some kind of weirdo. To them, these precious antiques are just plain disgusting, which isn't so different from your reaction." Matthew waited, but when Thóra made no response he went on. "The presence of drugs in his blood didn't help. In the eyes of the police he was a crazy sadistic junkie who was last seen in the company of the same sort of crowd. His companion had no alibi and was stoned out of his mind for good measure. It's not such an unreasonable conclusion to draw but I'm not satisfied with it at all. Too many questions are left unanswered."

"In other words you think Harald's studies of witchcraft and sorcery are linked with the murder?" asked Thóra, hoping that he would say no.

If they were irrelevant to the investigation, she could put more than half the papers to one side immediately.

"Well, I'm by no means certain," said Matthew. "But I've begun to have a strong suspicion that they are. Look at this, for example." He flicked through the pile of papers in his lap and handed Thóra a printout of an e-mail from Harald.

Thóra read it. The heading showed that it had been sent by Harald to a certain malcolm@gruniv.uk and was written in English, dated eight days before the murder.

Hi Mal,

Well, take a seat, buddy. FOUND IT, THANK YOU VERY MUCH.
Call me Your Lordship from now on. I knew it, I knew it, I knew it . . . not that
I want to accuse you of skepticism. Honest.

Just a few tiny details left—some fucking idiot's trying to back out. So—get
ready for the news—totally brilliant, I'm thinking of celebrating, if you know
what I mean. I'll be in touch, you old wanker.

H

When Thóra had finished reading it she looked at Matthew. "Do you think it's a clue?"

"Maybe," said Matthew. "Maybe not."

"The police must have contacted this Malcolm. They would hardly have made do with just printing it out."

"Maybe." Matthew shrugged. "Maybe not."

"Well, at least we can contact him to learn what Harald found."

"And whether he knows anything about the fucking idiot Harald mentioned."

Thóra put down the e-mail. "Where's his computer? He must have had a computer." She pointed to a mouse pad on the desk.

"The police still have it," replied Matthew. "Presumably they'll return it with Harald's other effects."

"Maybe we'll find more e-mails," Thóra said hopefully.

"And maybe not," responded Matthew, smiling. He stood and reached up to a bookshelf above the desk. "Here, take this home to read. It's a good introduction to Harald's mental world." He handed her a paperback of *The Witches' Hammer*.

Thóra took the book and looked up at Matthew, in surprise. "This is a new book. Is it really still in print?"

He nodded. "It is—but I don't think many people buy it except out of curiosity these days. When you read it, though, bear in mind that it wasn't always that way."

Thóra put the book in her bag. She stood up and stretched. "Is it okay to use the bathroom?"

Matthew smiled again. "Maybe. Maybe not." He hurried to add: "Yes, I think that should be all right. If the police burst in to investigate it further, I'll hold them off until you've finished."

"How sweet of you." Thóra went out into the corridor and walked over to the bathroom. She got sidetracked, though, because the walls were adorned with more pictures and antique relics that aroused her curiosity. Actually, they aroused more horror than curiosity. But there was no denying that they were quite fascinating. It was similar to how people slow down when they drive past the scene of an accident. The pictures must have been from the grandfather's collection because the theme was the same as in the living room and the bedroom: death and the Devil.

Unlike the other rooms, there was little in the bathroom to suggest the former tenant's interests. The few movables inside were arranged very systematically in doorless cupboards—all in a matching style. Thóra looked at herself in the impeccably polished mirror above the sink and ran her fingers through her hair to freshen up her appearance a little. She noticed a toothbrush in one of the cupboards. It did not seem to have been used. Then she took a more critical look around. There must have been another bathroom in the apartment that Harald used—this one was far too perfect. No question.

When Thóra went back to the study she lingered in the doorway and said: "There must be another bathroom in the apartment."

Matthew looked up, startled. "What do you mean?"

"The bathroom off the hallway is virtually unused. There's no way Harald would have used dental floss that matched the color scheme."

Matthew grinned. "Top marks. Now don't go claiming you don't know how to investigate." He pointed to the part of the flat they had been through before. "There's a door in the bedroom. The bathroom's in there."

Thóra turned round. She remembered the door, which she had thought led to a closet. She thought about getting back to the papers but decided that she wanted to find out what the bathroom looked like first. A smile came to her face when she looked inside the door. There was a shower compartment instead of a bathtub, but in other respects it was just like any other bathroom in a normal household. All kinds of hygiene products were strewn around the sink, none of them matching anything else. Thóra popped her head inside the shower compartment. On a shelf attached to the wall were two bottles of shampoo, one upside down, a razor, a used bar of soap, and a tube of toothpaste. A bottle hung from the shower control labeled "Shower Power." This all looked more familiar and she felt a slight relief.

But what pleased her most was the magazine rack beside the toilet: if this wasn't typical of people who lived alone, she didn't know what was. Curious to find out what sort of magazines Harald read, she browsed through the rack. It was quite a mixture: several car magazines, one historical journal, two copies of *Der Spiegel,* a tattoo magazine that Thóra quickly flicked past, and one edition of *Bunte.* Thóra looked at it in surprise. *Bunte* was a typical women's magazine, carrying the same kind of celebrity stories as *Hello!* The idea of Harald reading something like this would never have crossed her mind. Tom Cruise and Katie Holmes smiled at her from the cover under the headline "Tom Cruise wird Papa"—"Tom Cruise to Be a Dad!" The Hollywood couple's pregnancy held as much interest for Thóra as an article on cultivating cucumbers, so she returned the magazine to its place.

"I knew it," said Thóra triumphantly when she returned to the study.

"I knew it too," Matthew answered. "I just didn't know you knew."

Thóra was about to cap this retort when her mobile rang. She fished it out of her handbag.

"Mom," said Sóley's little voice. "When will you be back?"

Thóra looked at her watch. It was later than she had realized. "Very soon, darling. Is everything okay?"

Silence, then: "Oh, yes. I'm just bored. Gylfi won't talk to me anymore. It's no fun being alone with him. He's in there jumping on his bed and howling, and he won't let me in."

Although Thóra could not quite picture the scene, Gylfi was clearly not babysitting properly. "Listen, darling," she said gently. "I'll be home soon. Tell your brother to stop playing around and to come out and look after you."

They exchanged good-byes and Thóra put her phone back in her handbag. Inside it, she noticed the note she had written with questions for Matthew about the documents in the file. She took it out and unfolded it. "I'd like to ask you a few things about the documents that were in the file."

"A few?" he said in surprise. "I expected more than 'a few'—quite a few at the very least. But fire away."

Thóra was unsure of herself as she looked at the list. Damn it, had she overlooked so many points? She tried to act nonchalant. "Actually these are the main points, there were too many minor details to write them all down." With a smile, she continued. "For example, the army. Why were those documents in the file when Harald was actually medically unfit for military service?"

"Military service, yes. I just included it to give you the fullest possible picture of Harald's life. It might be irrelevant but you never know where the threads join up."

"Do you think the murder is linked to the army?" Thóra was skeptical.

"No, definitely not," replied Matthew. He shrugged. "But in Harald's case you can never tell."

"But why did he do national service?" Thóra asked. "Judging from his profile he would have been more likely to be against military warfare."

"You're quite right. He was called up, as it happens, but under normal circumstances he would definitely have gone for community service. You know about that option for conscripts?" Thóra nodded. "He didn't opt out of service, however. His sister Amelia had just died and it upset him deeply. I suspect he made the decision in a mental crisis. This was at the beginning of 1999, and in November or December of that year Germany decided to send troops to Kosovo. Harald went there with a smile on his face. I'm not sure about all the details of his military career but I do know that he was a model conscript, steadfast and tough. So the incident in Kosovo took the army completely by surprise."

"What happened?" asked Thóra.

Matthew gave a wry smile. "It's quite a funny story—in a way. Especially bearing in mind that the expedition to Kosovo was the first German mission abroad since the Second World War. Up to then German soldiers had only been involved in peacekeeping work abroad. So it was vital for our troops to be model soldiers."

"Harald wasn't, then?"

"Oh, no. You could call him unlucky. After he'd been there about three months his regiment arrested a Serb who was suspected of having information about a fatal bombing. It cost three German soldiers their lives and many others were injured. The Serb was detained in the basement of the building where the German regiment was stationed. Harald was one of the guards. He was on duty alone when the prisoner had been there for two or three nights and still hadn't confessed a thing. Harald had mentioned to his superior that he knew a thing or two about interrogation techniques and was given permission to try to get some information out of the prisoner that night." Matthew looked at Thóra. "Of course, the man who authorized this had no idea that Harald was well versed in the history of torture. He must have expected Harald to put his head round the door every so often to ask the prisoner a few innocent questions."

Thóra's eyes opened wide. "Did he torture him?"

"Let's just say that the Serb would gladly have swapped places with the men in the naked pyramid at Abu Ghraib. I'm not condoning what happened, but that was like Disneyland compared with what the poor Serb had to put up with that night. When the shift changed the next morning Harald had managed to get the man to tell everything he knew—and a lot more besides. But instead of earning the praise he thought he deserved, Harald was discharged on the spot—as soon as his superiors saw the barely breathing heap of raw meat lying in its own blood on the floor of the cell. Of course the affair was hushed up because it would have tarnished the army's reputation. All the official documents state that Harald left the army for health reasons."

"So how do you know this?" Thóra asked, relieved at being able to ask a reasonably normal question.

"I know people," said Matthew enigmatically. "And I talked to Harald after he got back from Kosovo. He was a changed man, I can tell you. Whether it was his experience of military life or the taste of blood I can't tell. But he became even weirder than before."

"How?" Thóra asked, curious.

"Just weirder," Matthew replied. "In appearance and behavior. He enrolled in college soon after this—he left home so I didn't see him so often. From the few occasions when we ran into each other it was quite obvious that he was caught in a downward spiral. Presumably his grandfather's death shortly afterward didn't help either. They were very close."

Thóra did not know what to say. Harald Guntlieb was clearly no ordinary person. Looking at her notes, she remembered the victim of erotic asphyxiation who was described in the newspaper clipping. But she decided she'd had enough for now. She glanced at her mobile and saw that it was late. "Matthew, I have to go home. My list isn't finished but I have plenty to digest for the time being."

They quickly tidied up the papers they had been rummaging through in the study. They made sure not to mix up the piles of documents they had sorted. The thought of the extra work that would have involved was unbearable.

As she put the final pile neatly to one side Thóra turned to Matthew and asked: "Did Harald make a will—considering all the assets he owned?"

"Actually he did leave a will—quite a recent one in fact," said Matthew. "He'd always had one, but changed it in the middle of September. He made a trip to Germany specifically to meet the Guntliebs' lawyer to draw up a new version. But no one knows what it says."

"Really?" Thóra said, surprised. "Why not?"

"It was in two parts—with instructions to open one before the other. It stated that the second part must not be opened until Harald had been buried—which hasn't been possible because of the investigation."

"Was that all it said?" Thóra asked.

"No, there were also instructions about where he wanted to be buried."

"And where is that?"

"In Iceland—which is strange considering the short time he spent here. The country seems to have captivated him. Another instruction was that his parents have to attend the funeral and stand at the foot of the grave for at least ten minutes after the casket is lowered. If they fail to comply, all his possessions will be bequeathed to a tattoo parlor in Munich."

Thóra asked him to repeat that. "So didn't he expect them to turn up?"

"Evidently not," replied Matthew. "But he made absolutely certain of it with that clause—his parents don't care to be splattered across the tabloids because their son left a small fortune to a tattoo parlor."

"Do you think they'll inherit it, then?" Thóra asked. "That is, if they turn up."

"No," Matthew replied. "They couldn't really care less—they just don't want to end up in the gutter press."

He thought for a moment.

"I think his sister Elisa will probably inherit most of his belongings. But a good share of the money will doubtless go to someone here in Iceland—the lawyer implied that strongly when he was pressed. The second part of the will must be opened here, according to Harald's instructions."

"I wonder who it is," Thóra said, curious.

"I don't have a clue," responded Matthew. "But he or she had ample reason to kill Harald, if they knew about it beforehand."

Thóra was relieved to leave the apartment. She was tired and wanted to go home to her children. Yet she felt somehow uncomfortable. She had the feeling she had overlooked something. But no matter how she tried to recall it after she was alone in her "Bibbi's Garage" car, she could not put her finger on what was eluding her. And when she parked in her drive she forgot it completely.

CHAPTER 12

The effects of divorce are not all positive. Thóra had long been aware that it had its drawbacks too. Previously, two people were running the household, but now Thóra had to stretch a single salary to fill the gap left after the split. The meager amount she received in child support from her husband did little to alleviate her financial problems. It's an easy enough thing to step up one's spending and be comfortable with it; at least Thóra did not recall any particular difficulties in converting from a poor student to a salary-earner. But it's a different matter when it comes to cutting back, as she had found out.

Hannes, her ex, was an ER surgeon—in other words, he was in a stable and well-paid job. After their divorce Thóra had had to relinquish many things she had begun to take for granted. It was no longer a matter of course to go out for a meal, take a weekend break abroad, buy expensive clothes, or do any of the other typical things people who don't need to worry about money do. Although not all the disadvantages involved money—*no sex* flashed through Thóra's mind—what she missed most was the lady who had come to clean their house twice a week. When Thóra and Hannes divorced she had been forced to let her go, simply in order to make ends meet. So Thóra now stood by the broom closet doing her best to shut the door without crushing the vacuum cleaner hose that repeatedly sprang out and prevented it from closing. When she succeeded at last she heaved a sigh of relief. She had vacuumed all the floors in a house of more than two thousand square feet and felt quite pleased with herself.

"Doesn't it make a world of difference?" she asked her daughter, who was sitting in the kitchen absorbed in drawing pictures.

Sóley looked up. "What does?"

"The floors," Thóra answered. "I've vacuumed. Don't they look nice?"

The girl looked at the floor and then back at her mother. "You missed this." She pointed with a green crayon at a ball of fluff under one leg of the chair she was sitting on.

"Oh, sorry, madame," said Thóra, kissing her daughter on the head. "What's that nice picture you're drawing?"

"It's you and me and Gylfi," Sóley replied, pointing to three figures of different sizes on the paper. "You're wearing a pretty dress and so am I and Gylfi's wearing shorts." She looked at her mother. "It's summer in this picture."

"Wow, don't I look smart," Thóra said. "I'll definitely get myself a dress like that next summer." She looked at her watch. "Come along. I'll brush your teeth. It's bedtime."

While Sóley put away her crayons, Thóra went to her son's room. She gave a light rap on the door before opening it. "Isn't this just as good as new?" she asked, again referring to the floors.

Gylfi did not answer immediately. He was lying on the bed talking on his mobile. Seeing her, he said a quick good-bye and in a half whisper promised whoever he was talking to that he would ring later. He half sat up and put down his phone. Thóra thought he looked dazed. "Are you okay? You look so pale."

"What?" Gylfi said. "Sure, everything's okay. Great, really."

"That's nice," she said. "I just came to see if you didn't think the air is fresher since I vacuumed your room. And if I wouldn't get a kiss as a reward."

Gylfi sat up properly. He looked around vacantly. "Eh? Oh, yeah. Cool."

Thóra studied her son closely. Something definitely wasn't right. His normal reaction would have been to shrug or mumble something about not caring what the floors looked like. He darted his eyes and avoided looking at his mother. There was something wrong, and a pang shot through Thóra's stomach. She hadn't been looking after him properly. He had changed from a little boy into a half man since the divorce, and she had been too preoccupied with herself and her own problems to pay enough attention to him. Now she did not know how to act. Most of all she wanted to hug him and run her fingers through his unnecessarily long hair, but that would just look silly—that time had passed, it was long gone. "Hey," she said, putting her hand on his shoulder. She had to crane her neck to look him in the face, because he was looking away. "Something's wrong. You can tell me. I promise not to get angry."

Gylfi gave her a thoughtful look but said nothing. Thóra saw tiny beads of sweat on his forehead and for a moment she thought he might have the flu. "Are you running a temperature?" she asked, stretching out her hand to press the back of it against his brow.

Gylfi dodged her deftly. "No, no. Not at all. I've just heard some bad news."

"Oh?" Thóra said cautiously. "Who was on the phone?"

"Sigga . . . I mean Siggi," Gylfi answered without looking his mother in the eye. He added hastily: "Arsenal lost to Liverpool."

Thóra was not born yesterday and was perfectly aware that he had just cooked up this excuse on the spot. She did not recognize the name Siggi from Gylfi's circle—although of course he had countless acquaintances whose names and faces she did not know. But she did know her son well enough to realize that he was not so into soccer that he'd get depressed over the English league results. She wondered whether to press him further or let it go. Given the situation she judged the latter option more appropriate—for the time being. "Oh, dear. Rotten. Bloody Liverpool." She looked him straight in the eye. "If you want or need to talk to me, Gylfi, then promise me you won't hesitate to do just that." Seeing his flustered expression, she swiftly added: "About the game, I mean. Arsenal. You know you can come to me, dear. I can't solve all the problems in the world but I can try to tackle the ones that end up on our table."

Gylfi looked at her without saying a word. With a wan smile he mumbled something about an essay he needed to finish. Thóra muttered something back, left the room and closed his door. She could not imagine what kind of setback could upset a sixteen-year-old boy—she had never been one, nor could she remember her own adolescence clearly. All that occurred to her was girl problems. Maybe he had a crush on someone. Thóra decided to find out diplomatically—she could pop a few subtle questions to him over breakfast the next morning. This crisis might even have blown over by then. It could all be a storm in a teacup—hormone shock.

After brushing Sóley's teeth and reading her a story, Thóra settled down on the sofa in front of the television. She called her mother, who was on vacation for a month with her father in the Canary Islands. Constant bickering greeted her whenever she phoned. The last time it was not being able to buy curds for breakfast that was killing her parents. Now it was the Discovery Channel, which her father had become addicted to, on the hotel television—if her mother was to be believed, that is. As they exchanged good-byes, her mother said wearily that she was going to flop down beside her husband and hear all about the mating habits of insects. Smiling to herself, Thóra put down the phone and returned to watching TV herself. Just as she was dozing off in front of a banal reality show the telephone rang. She sat up in the sofa and reached for the phone.

"Thóra speaking," she answered, carefully choosing a voice that did not betray the fact she had just nodded off.

"Hello, it's Hannes," said the voice on the other end.

"Hello." Thóra wondered whether she would ever stop feeling uncomfortable talking to her ex. These excruciating exchanges surely sprang from the transition from intimacy to forced politeness, like when she met old boyfriends or men she had slept with when she was younger—an unavoidable hazard when living in a small country like Iceland.

"Listen, about the weekend, I was wondering if I could just call round to collect the kids a bit later on Friday. I'm taking Gylfi out for a driving lesson and I think it's better to do that after rush hour, around eight o'clock."

Thóra said yes, although she knew quite well that the delay had nothing to do with driving lessons. Undoubtedly Hannes had to work later or planned to go to the gym after work. One of the reasons for their endless quarrels after the divorce had been that Hannes never seemed able to take any responsibility; it was always the fault of someone else or fictional circumstances beyond his control. This was not her problem anymore, but his new partner Klara's. "What are you doing over the weekend?" Thóra asked for the sake of saying something. "Should I pack them any special clothes?"

"We might go horseback riding so it would be good if they have outfits for that," Hannes replied.

Klara was a horse lover and had dragged Hannes into the sport. It was a source of endless torment for Sóley and Gylfi, who had inherited Thóra's nervous disposition—if anything, the fear genes had doubled from mother to child. Thóra had trouble driving on icy roads, climbing mountains, taking elevators, eating raw food—in fact, she didn't do well with any activity that could conceivably end in disaster. For some incomprehensible reason, however, flying was the one exception. So she understood perfectly her children's horror at the prospect of horseback riding, convinced as they were that each ride would be their last moment on earth. Hannes refused to admit that this condition was permanent and constantly tried to persuade his children that they would get used to it in the end. "Are you sure that's a good idea?" she asked, although she knew full well that she had little sway over Hannes's plans. "Gylfi's a bit down at the moment and I'm not sure that a riding trip is exactly what he needs now."

"Rubbish," Hannes snapped back. "He's turning into quite a horseman."

"You reckon? Try to talk to him, anyway. I suspect he's having girl trouble and you know more about those things than I do."

"Girl trouble? What do I know about those things?" yelled Hannes. "He's just turned sixteen. You can't be serious."

"No, maybe not. But keep it in the back of your mind and try to deliver some words of wisdom."

"Wisdom? What sort of wisdom? What do you mean?" Hannes was floundering, and Thóra smiled.

"You know, to help him deal with life's challenges." Her smile widened.

"You're joking," Hannes said hopefully.

"Actually, I'm not," replied Thóra. "I trust you'll find a way. I'll do the same for your daughter when her boy problems start. You can try taking him aside on the riding trip and having a quiet chat from the saddle."

They ended the conversation and Thóra had a hunch she had just lowered the odds that they would go riding. She tried once again to reimmerse herself in televised unreality. In vain, though, because the phone rang again.

"Sorry to call so late, but it occurred to me that you might be thinking about me," Matthew said calmly after they'd said hello. "I decided to let you hear my voice."

Thóra was flabbergasted—she could not tell whether Matthew was mad, drunk, or joking. "I can't say you caught me doing that." She stretched over for the remote to turn down the television volume so that he would not hear the trash she was watching. "I was reading."

"What are you reading?" he asked.

"*War and Peace*. Dostoevsky," Thóra lied.

"Really," said Matthew. "Is that anything like *War and Peace* by Tolstoy?"

Thóra clenched her fist, annoyed that she hadn't chosen Halldór Laxness or another Icelandic author he would not know. She had always been a hopeless liar. "I mean Tolstoy. So was there anything special? I'm sure you didn't call to discuss literature."

"Just as well, because I'd have got the wrong number," rejoined Matthew. When Thóra said nothing he added: "No. Sorry. I called because the lawyer of the man in police custody phoned me just now."

"Finnur Bogason?" asked Thóra.

"That's just what I would have said if I could pronounce Icelandic," said Matthew. "He wanted to let me know that we can meet the lad to-morrow if we want."

"Have we got permission?" asked Thóra, amazed. Remand prisoners were not normally allowed visits from strangers.

"This Finnur," Matthew said, pronouncing the name as Fie-neur, al-most with a French accent, "managed to persuade the police that we were working with him on the defense. Which, of course, we are, indirectly."

"What made him do that?"

"Shall we say I gave him a small incentive?"

Thóra asked no more, not wanting to be party to anything under-hand. She doubted that Matthew had threatened the lawyer, and thought it more likely he had promised a fee for arranging the interview—which would have been unethical at best. She felt better imagining they would be assisting the defense counsel.

But to hell with ethics. She had to meet Hugi. Maybe he was guilty after all. Nothing could match talking to people in person, looking the speaker in the eye and watching his movements and body language. "Shouldn't we get a move on, then? We need to see this guy."

"I agree. I just need to let Fie-neur know."

"Why did he phone you so late?" asked Thóra. "Surely he hasn't just got permission tonight?"

"No, no. He left a message for me at the hotel but I've only just got back. I don't like handing my phone number around."

Thóra hated herself for wanting to know where Matthew had been after they parted ways—although the most likely explanation was that he had simply gone into town for something to eat.

They decided that Matthew would fetch Thóra from her office at nine to drive from the city to Litla-Hraun prison. She looked out the window at the snow tumbling down and hoped with all her heart that he knew how to drive on winter roads. If not, they were in trouble.

CHAPTER 13

Thóra was sitting at her computer in her office when Matthew showed up at nine o'clock. She was just finishing replying to e-mails that had arrived the previous day, most of which she had passed on to Thór. Bragi was all smiles when he greeted her that morning. He was still toying with the idea that this German job would be their passport to the world—a source of endless business for their practice. Thóra made no attempt to bring him back to earth, relieved at being able to concentrate on the murder riddle without being torn between petty jobs as well.

She e-mailed Harald's mysterious friend Mal with a brief account of Harald's death and how she and Matthew were involved in the case on the Guntliebs' behalf. She ended her message with a polite request for Mal to contact her, since he might have crucial information. When Bella phoned to announce Matthew's arrival, Thóra said she needed five minutes to finish and asked the girl to tell him to take a seat and wait in the reception area. She was determined to clear her desk so that she would not have to return to the office in the afternoon. She managed to finish in just over five minutes and switched off her computer, pleased with her morning's achievements. She wondered if she should start coming in earlier. Although it would be tough at home, this hour was exceptionally productive, free from the harassment of the telephone before normal office opening hours.

She took a small tape recorder from one of her desk drawers to record their interview with Hugi. While she was checking if the batteries worked her thoughts returned to her son, who had been terribly down in the dumps that morning. Whatever the problem was, it had not gone away overnight as Thóra had hoped. The boy had sat there vacantly with no appetite and she managed to drag only a few words out of him. Sóley, on the other hand, talked nonstop as she always did in the mornings, so Thóra had no time alone with her son. She decided to probe the matter calmly that evening after Sóley had gone to bed. Then she drove these thoughts out of her mind, put the recorder in her handbag, and left the office.

Thóra was taken aback when she entered reception. Matthew was sitting on the edge of Bella's desk talking excitedly to the secretary, who glowed like the midday sun. They did not even notice Thóra's presence and she had to clear her throat to get their attention.

Matthew looked around. "Oh, you, I was hoping you'd be busy a bit longer." He smiled at Thóra and gave her a wink.

Thóra could hardly take her eyes off Bella's face, which had been transformed by simply smiling. She looked almost pretty. "Well, shouldn't we get a move on?" Thóra said, fetching her coat. "Nice to see you so cheerful, Bella," she added, beaming at the secretary.

Bella's smile vanished instantly. Matthew's charm offensive clearly benefited him alone. "When are you coming back?" she asked grumpily.

Thóra tried not to sound disappointed at being cut out. "I don't expect to be back today but I'll phone if anything changes."

"Right, whatever," Bella said huffily, her tone implying that Thóra made a habit of not letting people know her whereabouts, which was absurd.

"You heard what I said." Thóra could not let it pass without comment although she immediately regretted it. "Come on, Matthew."

"Yes, madam," Matthew said with a smile at Bella. Much to Thóra's chagrin, it was reciprocated.

When they got into the car Thóra fastened her belt and turned to Matthew. "Do you know how to drive on icy roads?"

"We'll find out," said Matthew as they left the parking spot. Seeing Thóra's expression he added: "Don't worry, I'm a good driver."

"Just don't slam on the brakes if the car goes into a skid," Thóra said, by no means convinced that Matthew was aware of this.

"Do you want to drive?"

"No, thanks," she answered. "I can't handle that no-brakes rule, if I start to skid I instinctively put my foot down—against my better judgment. I'm very limited when it comes to driving."

They headed straight out of the city and were up on the moor when Thóra's curiosity about Matthew's conversation with Bella finally got the best of her. "What were you two talking about?"

"Us two?" Matthew repeated, all innocence.

"Yes, you and Bella, my secretary. She's normally such a sourpuss."

"Oh, her. We were talking about horses. I'd like to try horse riding while I'm here; you hear so much about Icelandic horses. She was giving me some tips."

"What does she know about horses?" Thóra was flabbergasted.

"She's a horse lover, didn't you know?"

"No, actually I didn't." She could only pity the horse that had to bear Bella's weight. "What kind of horses does she have? Cart horses?"

Matthew took his eyes off the road and looked at Thóra. "Are you jealous?" he asked, smirking.

"Are you drunk?" she fired back.

They drove in silence across the lava field toward the mountain pass. Thóra admired the landscape through the car window—perhaps few people would agree with her, but she thought this was one of the most beautiful places in Iceland, especially in summer when the moss blazed green, its soft outlines in total contrast with the rough and jagged lava. Now the land was covered with snow and seemed two-dimensional. It lacked the majesty of summer. Still, a calmness reigned that appealed to Thóra. She broke the silence. "Don't you think the scenery's beautiful?"

Matthew flicked his eyes off the road to admire the surroundings. There was hardly any traffic. "Well." He smiled at her as if declaring a truce. "It is different, I'll give it that much, but 'bleak' is the word that springs to mind." He pointed at two thick pillars of smoke that stretched up into the sky ahead of them. "What's that?" he asked. "An eruption?"

"Oh, that's steam from boreholes," Thóra replied. "Up ahead there's a geothermal power plant, which produces electricity from steam piped from underground. It also supplies hot water to heat houses in Reykja-vík."

Matthew nodded, impressed. "Lucky you, no pollution."

"Yup," said Thóra. "Clean air, clean water. Not bad."

"Your offices could actually be cleaner, as long as we're on the subject of hygiene," said Matthew.

"Oh, please," snapped Thóra. "They're clean enough. We're lawyers, not surgeons." She turned to look at Matthew. "We don't exactly make a good team," she said, referring to their repeated skirmishes. "Maybe we should change tactics."

He smiled at her again. "You think so? I'm delighted. You're much more fun than my normal company at work. All the old men and the few women I deal with are so poker-faced they'd fall apart if they took off their frowns."

Now it was Thóra's turn to smile. "Actually, you're not half as bad as Bella. I'll give you that." She paused for a while. "Tell me one thing. In the folder was a German newspaper clipping about a young man who died performing that erotic asphyxiation stuff. What was that included for?"

"Ahhh." Matthew drew out the exclamation. "That bloody thing. One of the people in the article was a good friend of Harald's. They met at university in Munich and must have been the same kind of searching souls, so they made a good pair in all the outrageous stunts they got up to. I don't know which of them introduced the other to that peculiar prac-tice but Harald swore it was his friend who started. Harald was present when the man died, so he ended up being interrogated and got into a nasty mess. It's a shameful thing to say, but I think he bought his way out of the situation—you noticed the large bank withdrawal I marked from then?" Thóra said she had. "I included it because Harald was strangled. It may be important. Who knows—possibly he met the same death as his friend, although it seems very doubtful."

They parked in the lot outside the fence of Litla-Hraun prison and walked over to the visitors' gate. A warden showed them into a small lounge on the second floor. "We thought you could stay in here; you should be quite comfortable, it's much nicer than the interrogation room," he said. "Hugi's calm and shouldn't cause any trouble. He'll be here any minute."

"Thank you, that's fine," Thóra said, and walked inside. She perched herself on the edge of a brown sofa and Matthew sat down close by her side. She was surprised by his choice of seat, because there were plenty of chairs.

He looked at her. "If Hugi sits facing us it's better for us to sit like this. I want to look him straight in the face." He raised his eyebrows quickly, twice. "And it's so terribly nice to sit close to you."

Before Thóra could answer, the door opened again and Hugi Thórisson appeared accompanied by a guard, whose hand was on his shoulder. The young man's head was bowed as he was steered through the door. Hugi was handcuffed but he looked so helpless that Thóra couldn't believe it was necessary. When the guard spoke his name he looked up. He swept his waxy hair out of his eyes with both hands and Thóra saw that he was very handsome, completely different from what she had imagined. She found it hard to believe that he was twenty-five—seventeen would have seemed a closer guess. He had dark brows and big eyes, but his most prominent feature was his bony cheeks, probably caused by his thinness. If he did murder Harald, it must have taken every ounce of his strength. He did not look capable of lugging a one-hundred-ninety-pound corpse very far.

"You going to behave yourself, pal?" the guard asked Hugi in a friendly tone. When Hugi nodded, the guard lifted his arms and took off the cuffs. Then he put his hand back on Hugi's shoulder and guided him over to the chair directly opposite Thóra and Matthew. The young man sat down, or rather slumped, into the chair. He avoided looking Thóra and Matthew straight in the eye, turned his face away from them and gaped down at the floor beside the chair where he sat sprawled.

"We're in the room next door if you need us. He shouldn't cause any trouble." The guard addressed his words to Thóra.

"Fine," Thóra said. "We won't keep him any longer than necessary." She looked at her watch. "We should be done by noon."

The guard left and when he had closed the door the only sound in the room came from Hugi as he rhythmically scratched at the knee of his camouflage trousers. He had not looked at the visitors yet.

Prisoners were clearly allowed to wear their own clothes—unlike in the American jails Thóra knew from television and films, whose inmates pranced around in jumpsuits that seemed to be made from orange peel.

"Hugi," said Thóra in the gentlest voice she could muster. She went on in Icelandic, thinking it was silly to begin the interview in English. They would find out later whether that was possible. They couldn't afford to get bogged down in language difficulties; if he didn't speak reasonable English she would have to handle this alone. "Presumably you know who we are. My name's Thóra Gudmundsdóttir and I'm a lawyer, and this is Matthew Reich from Germany. We're here in connection with the murder of Harald Guntlieb, which we're investigating independently from the police."

No reaction. Thóra continued. "We wanted to see you because we're not convinced you had any part in the murder." She took a deep breath to emphasize what she was about to say. "We're looking for Harald's murderer and we think it's quite conceivable that it wasn't you. Our aim is to find the person who killed Harald and if it wasn't you, then it's in your interests to help us." Hugi looked up at Thóra. When he did not open his mouth or show any other desire to express himself, she continued. "You presumably understand that if we manage to prove that someone other than you killed Harald, then you're more or less off the hook."

"I didn't kill him," Hugi said in a weak voice. "Nobody believes me, but I didn't kill him."

Thóra went on. "Hugi, Matthew here is from Germany. He knows all about investigations but he doesn't speak Icelandic. Do you feel up to speaking English with us so that he can understand? If not, that's fine. We want you to understand our questions and be able to answer them without any language problems."

"I can speak English," came the reply, half muttered.

"Good," said Thóra. "If you don't understand anything we say or have trouble answering, we can simply switch back to Icelandic."

Thóra turned to Matthew and told him they could continue in English. Without a moment's hesitation he leaned forward and spoke. "Hugi, you can start by sitting up straight and facing us. Get rid of that whining voice and act like a man, if only for the short while that we're here."

Thóra sighed: what macho bullshit! She almost expected the young man to stand up, burst into tears, and demand to leave, which they would have to accept, since he was here of his own free will. But she had no chance to interrupt because Matthew marched straight on. "You're in big trouble, I don't need to rub your nose in that. You're sitting in front of your only hope of getting out of that trouble, so you should do all you can to help us and answer honestly. Self-pity's easy in your position so it's vital to act like a grown-up, not a kid. Do as I say, sit up straight, look me in the face, and give a conscientious answer to all our questions. You'll feel better if you act like a man. Just try it."

Thóra watched in surprise as Hugi obeyed Matthew's words. He shifted out of his fetal position and did his best to put on a manly show. His teenage looks made it hard for him, but there was some transformation. When he spoke his voice was clearer and more mature. "It's hard for me to look you in the eye all the time. I'm on some medication that makes me confused." Thóra could tell from his eyes; they fluttered and had a dull look most likely produced by tranquilizers. "But I'll try to answer your questions."

"How did you and Harald meet?" Thóra asked.

"I met him partying in town. Talked to him and he turned out to be a fun guy. I introduced him to Dóri just after that."

"Who's Dóri?" Thóra asked.

"Halldór Kristinsson. He's a medical student," replied Hugi, almost with a hint of pride in his voice. "We've been friends since we were little kids. We lived next door to each other in Grafavogur. He's incredibly bright but not a scholarly type, always up for partying."

Thóra scribbled notes; although she had turned on her Dictaphone she was worried that the device would not record properly. Halldór was the young man who missed the party Harald had attended the night of his murder—the one who decided to wait for the partygoers in the downtown bar. "Were you good friends, you and Harald?"

Hugi shrugged. "Sure. Not as close as Harald and Dóri, though. I sometimes sold Harald—" Hugi suddenly stopped in midsentence with a worried look on his face.

"Nobody gives a damn about your dealing now. Go on," said Matthew sharply.

Hugi's Adam's apple bobbed up and down before he decided to resume. "Okay. Sometimes he called me his best friend; but that was just a joke when he wanted to score dope off me. He was fun, though, completely different from everyone else I know."

"In what way?" asked Thóra.

"For a start, he was rolling in money and never minded buying you a drink and stuff. And he had this awesome flat and car." He thought for a moment before proceeding. "But that wasn't the issue. He was so much cooler than other people. He wasn't afraid of anything, always found crazy stuff to do and swept everyone else along with him somehow. He was megacool with all that body art—none of us dared try to copy him. Not even Dóri, who really wanted to. He thought it would ruin his career prospects and really regretted the one little tattoo he had on his arm. But Harald didn't give a shit about the future."

"And it turned out that he didn't have to," said Matthew. "What did you do, what did you talk about?"

"I can't remember what we talked about."

"Did he ever talk about his studies or burning witches at the stake?" Thóra asked hopefully.

"Witchcraft." Hugi snorted. "No one talked about anything else to begin with. When I started hanging out with them Harald invited me to join their witchcraft society."

Matthew butted in. "Witchcraft society? What witchcraft society?"

"Malleus something. It was supposed to be a society for people interested in witch hunts and historical stuff." He avoided Thóra's glare, blushed slightly, and addressed Matthew. "But it was totally different. It wasn't Harry Potter, believe me. It involved four things. Sex, black magic, drugs, and more sex." He smiled. "That's why I liked going around with them. I couldn't care less about history or witchcraft or those magic symbols and incantations they did. I just wanted to have fun. The chicks were pretty." Hugi lost his thread for a moment—presumably reminiscing about an adventure with the "pretty chicks." "But some of the witchcraft stories were actually pretty cool. I remember one where this pregnant woman got thrown into a fire and she gave birth in the flames. The priests got the baby out alive but decided it might be infected with the mother's magic, so they threw it back in. Harald said that was absolutely true."

Thóra pulled a face to bring Hugi back to earth. "Who was in this society? What were the 'pretty chicks' called?"

"Harald was the boss, then Dóri, who was his right-hand man really; me; Bríet, who was studying history at the university—she was the only one who was seriously interested in all this, I think; Brjánsi, or Brjánn, who did history too; Andri, who was studying chemistry; and Marta Mist, who was in gender studies. She was awful, always moaning about injustice against women. Sometimes she'd ruin the fun with her bitching. Harald was always messing with her, always calling her 'Nebel,' which really got on her nerves. It's German for 'mist,' get it?" Thóra indicated that she understood but Matthew sat poker-faced. "That was the core of the group. Occasionally new members joined but we were the only ones who stuck it out. I didn't really follow what they did that closely—as I said I wasn't interested in black magic, just in what went with it."

"You say Dóri was his right-hand man. What do you mean by that?" asked Thóra.

"Those two were always up to things. I think Dóri helped him with translations and stuff. And it was obvious Dóri would take over when Harald went back to Germany. Dóri was well pleased with that; he was infatuated with Harald."

"Is Dóri gay?" Matthew asked.

Hugi shook his head. "No, no way. He was just starstruck, you know. Dóri comes from a poor family, like me actually. Harald threw money at him, expensive presents and praise, so Dóri worshipped him. You could tell Harald enjoyed that. Actually he wasn't always nice to Dóri; sometimes he humiliated him in front of us. But he always made sure to make up for it so that Dóri wouldn't get fed up and bail out on him. It was quite a weird relationship."

"You said Dóri was your childhood friend. How did you feel seeing him so infatuated with Harald? Weren't you jealous?" asked Thóra.

Hugi smiled. "No, no way. We stayed friends. Harald was just in Iceland temporarily and I knew it would pass. If anything I found it quite funny seeing Dóri in the role of the admirer. Up to then he'd always been the one I looked up to; it was sort of a change, seeing him in my role, you know. Not that Dóri ever treated me the way Harald treated him, not so kind and not such a bastard either." Suddenly Hugi's expression turned anxious. "I didn't kill him to get my friend back. It wasn't like that."

"No, perhaps not," said Matthew. "But tell me one thing. If you didn't kill him, who did? You must have some theories. You know it can't have been suicide or an accident."

Hugi's eyes dropped back to the floor. "I don't know. If I knew, I'd say. I don't want to be here."

"Do you think your friend Dóri killed him?" Thóra asked. "Are you covering for him?"

Hugi shook his head. "Dóri would never kill anyone. Least of all Harald. I told you he worshipped him."

"Yes, but you also said Harald was nasty to him, humiliated him in front of the others. Maybe he had got fed up and attacked in a fit of rage. That happens," said Thóra.

Hugi looked up, firmer than before. "No. Dóri's not like that. He's studying to be a doctor. He wants to help people live, not kill them."

"Hugi, I'm sorry to have to tell you this, but doctors have killed people for centuries. All professions have their rotten apples," said Matthew sarcastically. "But if it wasn't Dóri—who was it?"

"Maybe Marta Mist," muttered Hugi unconvincingly. She clearly wasn't his number one. "Maybe Harald called her 'Nebel' once too often."

"Marta Mist, yes," Matthew said. "That's a great theory apart from the fact that she has a watertight alibi. Like everyone else in this little witches' coven of yours. Except Dóri perhaps. His alibi is the shakiest. It's quite conceivable that he could have popped out of the bar, killed Harald, and gone back in without anyone noticing."

"And got the same seat? At Kaffibrennslan on a Saturday night? I don't think so." Hugi sneered.

"No one else springs to mind?" Thóra asked.

Hugi puffed up his cheeks and then exhaled. "Maybe someone from the university. I don't know. Or someone from Germany." He made sure not to look at Matthew when he said this, as if he expected him to be hypersensitive about his countrymen. "I know Harald was celebrating something that evening. He told me he wanted to buy some dope from me to mark some occasion or something."

"What kind of 'something'?" snapped Matthew. "You must be clearer. What exactly did he say?"

Hugi looked affronted. "Exactly? I can't remember exactly but it was something to do with something he'd found at last. He shouted something in German and clenched his fist. Then he put his arms around me and squeezed me really hard and said I'd have to fix up some Es because he was in a really good mood and wanted to party like hell."

"Was that when you left the party?" Thóra asked. "After he squeezed you and asked for some Es?"

"Yes, soon after. I was so out of it. I'd drunk too much and tried to sober up with some speed. It didn't work. I was way too drunk. Anyway, we took a taxi back to my place and all I remember was that I couldn't find any Es. I was so hammered I couldn't even have found the milk in the fridge. I remember Harald was pretty pissed off with me and said it was a fucking waste of time. And I remember lying down on the sofa because my head suddenly started spinning."

Thóra interrupted Hugi. "Did you say you didn't let him have any ecstasy?"

"I couldn't find them," Hugi replied. "I was out of it, like I said."

Thóra looked at Matthew without saying a word. The autopsy report stated that the active substance from ecstasy had been found in Harald's blood, so at some stage he had got hold of some. "Could he have taken some earlier that evening? Or found them at your place when you passed out?"

"He hadn't done any at the party, that's for sure. He wasn't acting that way and I know the effects. And there's no way he found them at my place because the police dug them out from the storage room in the basement when they searched my flat. I'd stashed them there and had the key in my pocket. Harald couldn't have looked in the storage room; I doubt he even knew about it. Maybe he went home to get some. I know he had a few that he said weren't much good. Why are you so interested in this?"

"Are you sure Harald didn't look in your pockets and find the key? You might not remember now, but maybe you told him at the time," said Matthew. "Try to remember. You were lying on the sofa with your head spinning, and then what?"

Hugi squeezed his eyes shut and did everything he could to recall the incident. Suddenly he opened his eyes and looked at them in astonishment. "Yes, I remember. I didn't say anything, but Harald said something to me. He bent down and whispered something to me. I remember I really wanted to answer him and ask him to wait for me but I couldn't."

"What? What did he say?" Matthew asked impatiently.

Hugi looked unsure of himself. "Maybe this is bullshit but I think he said: *Sweet dreams. We'll celebrate later. I came to Iceland looking for hell, and guess what? I've found it.*"

CHAPTER 14

"Don't be a jerk." Marta Mist pursed her lips and blew out a long stream of smoke. She tipped the ash from her half-smoked cigarette and then stubbed it out. "You're just making things worse, so don't think you're doing anyone a favor." She narrowed her green almond-shaped eyes at the young man who was sitting, or rather lounging, on a chair on the other side of the table. He glared back but said nothing. Marta Mist sat up straight and ran her slender fingers through her curly red hair.

"Come on, don't give me that look. You got us into this, so don't imagine you can suddenly turn into a model citizen with a guilty conscience." For support she looked at her girlfriend who was sitting beside her. The best she got out of the young blond girl was a wide-eyed nod. The girl had a crew cut and was boyish-looking, but she could never be mistaken for a boy. She was buxom but petite. From the rear she must have looked like a child sitting beside willowy Marta Mist, who had more to say. "That's typical male crap and it makes me puke. Chickening out when the shit hits the fan." She leaned back in her chair, contented.

Her friend, not daring to look at either of them, concentrated on her soda.

"For God's sake," Dóri replied, pretending to ram his finger down his throat. "How about dropping those fucking clichés just for once?" Annoyance crept over his features and as he stared at Marta Mist his upper lip curled involuntarily, revealing his white teeth. He looked the other way and took a drag off his cigarette. When he exhaled his anger was waning and he added in a slightly calmer tone: "You ought to be glad if I went to the police. Don't you think the women's prison would be utopia? Nothing but women there." He gave her a sarcastic grin.

Marta Mist gave as good as she got. "Then we could phone each other and swap happy tales. You'd be popular in prison too, sweetie, a pretty little boy like you." She returned his nasty grin.

"Aw, cut it out." Bríet spoke up at last. The others only looked at her in mute surprise, so she went back to peering into her glass, blushing now. Then she muttered into her cleavage: "I'm not interested in going to the women's prison, and I don't want you going to prison either." She looked up and stared at Dóri. "I'm terrified."

Dóri smiled at her, genuinely. He liked her. In fact, he realized he was really very fond of her—although he had still not decided whether it was anything more than sexual. "No one's going to prison." He looked up at Marta Mist. "Look what you've done, scaring Bríet out of her wits with all this bullshit."

Marta Mist affected shock. "Me? Hello? You started talking about prison—not me." She looked at Bríet, rolled her eyes, and groaned. "Whose bright idea was it to come here anyway?"

They were at Hótel 101 on Hverfisgata, sitting in the lounge in front of the smokers' bar. Harald's other friends had frequented the place while he ran that strange group. Without him the bar seemed to lose its charm.

Dóri bowed his head and shook it in confusion. "For God's sake, Marta. I'm cracking up. Can't we talk like friends? I thought you'd be able to help me. I think it's terrible that Hugi's inside. Surely you realize that." He looked up but avoided her eyes and reached over for the packet of cigarettes lying in the middle of the table. "And that snake's driving me crazy. When's the fucking funeral anyway?"

Bríet glanced anxiously at Marta Mist, clearly hoping her friend would change tactics. Her wish was granted. Marta Mist heaved a deep sigh but dropped the haughty attitude she had assumed for the fifteen minutes they had been there. "Oh, Dóri." She leaned across the table and took hold of his chin, forcing him to look her in the eye. "Aren't we friends?" He nodded meekly. "Then listen to me. If you go mixing yourself up in this, it won't help Hugi." He studied her face as she went on: "Think about it. Nothing that you're worried about can alter his situation. All it will achieve is to implicate us. This happened long after he was killed. The police aren't interested. They're wondering about who killed Harald. Nothing else." She smiled at him. "The funeral must be just around the corner, and then you're home free." Dóri lowered his eyes and she had to lift his head up to get him to look at her before she continued. "I didn't kill him, Dóri. I'm not going to sacrifice myself on the altar of your guilty conscience. Going to the police is the worst idea you've ever had. The moment you mention weed and being stoned, we're in deep shit. Right?"

Dóri looked deep into her eyes and nodded. "But maybe—"

He did not have a chance to finish the sentence. Marta Mist shushed him. "No buts, no maybes. Listen to me now. You're a bright guy, Dóri. Do you think the medical faculty would take you with open arms once they knew you smoked weed, even if it went no further than that?" She shook her head and turned away from him to Bríet, who had watched the proceedings in fascination, ready as always to agree with the last speaker. Marta Mist turned back to Dóri and said slowly: "Don't do anything stupid. Like I say, the cops are only interested in who killed Harald. Nothing else." She spoke her last words emphatically, then repeated them to be on the safe side. "Nothing else."

Dóri was entranced. He stared straight into the green eyes that looked at him without flinching from beneath pierced brows. Then he gave a tiny nod—the best he could manage with Marta Mist's hand still gripping his chin. It occurred to him that this was precisely why he had told them he was going to the police: he knew that Marta Mist would be able to talk him out of it. He drove the thought out of his mind: "Okay, okay."

"Brilliant," Bríet mumbled, smiling at Dóri. Clearly relieved, she clenched Marta's arm in delight. Marta Mist showed no sign of even noticing this—her attention did not waver from Dóri and she kept his chin locked in her hand.

"What's the time?" she asked, without releasing her grip.

Bríet hurriedly retrieved a pink mobile phone from the bag hanging on the back of her chair. She unlocked the keypad and announced: "Almost one-thirty."

"What are you doing tonight?" Marta Mist asked Dóri. Her voice suggested nothing, her eyes rather more.

"Nothing," came the curt reply.

"Come and see me—I haven't got any plans either," Marta replied. "It's a long time since we've been together and I can see you need a bit of company." She drew out the last word.

Bríet fidgeted in her chair. "Should we go and see a movie?" She stared expectantly at Marta Mist, who ignored her. Bríet felt her foot being stamped on and when she looked down she saw Marta Mist's leather boot completely covering her neat little shoe. She blushed as she realized that her presence was not required that evening.

"Do you want to see a movie?" Marta Mist asked Dóri. "Or do you want to drop by my place for something a bit cozier?" She leaned back.

Dóri nodded.

Marta smiled. "Which? That's no answer."

"Drop by your place." Dóri's voice was hoarse and heavy. None of the three had any misconceptions about what was on the agenda.

"I can hardly wait." Marta released Dóri's chin and clapped her hands. She waved to a passing waiter and asked for the bill. Dóri and Bríet said nothing. She was a little offended, and he had nothing else to say. He fished a thousand-króna note out of his pocket, placed it on the table, and stood up.

"I'm late for class. See you." As he walked away they both turned round to watch him leave.

When he had gone, Marta turned round again and said: "He's got a really nice bum, that guy. He ought to leave us more often."

She looked at her girlfriend who was watching her, hurt. "For God's sake. Don't sulk. He's in pieces at the moment. There's too much at stake." She slapped Bríet on the arm. "He fancies you, that hasn't changed."

Bríet forced a faint smile. "No, maybe not. But it looked to me like he was pretty into you."

"Come on. It's nothing to do with fancying people. You're the one everyone fancies. I'm—well—I'm good in bed." She stood up and observed Bríet coldly. "You know what?" No answer. "I live for the moment. You could try that too. Stop waiting for people to rescue you—enjoy life."

Bríet fumbled for her purse. There was no answer to that. She had taken part in all kinds of escapades with that crowd—she blushed just thinking about it. Wasn't that enjoying life? Had she ever implied that she wanted to be rescued? What crap! On the way out she consoled herself with the thought that boys went after her. Not after Marta. But the stakes were still too high to provoke her into trying to make a statement and competing over who was more desirable. Marta Mist behaved like a female Harald. She controlled Dóri. Bríet did not want to go to prison. No, thanks—forget Dóri. She could get him later. Bríet straightened her back to show off her bust. As they walked toward the door she enjoyed the fact that the three men in suits who were sitting by the window were ogling her—not Marta. Bríet smiled to herself. The little triumphs were often the sweetest.

CHAPTER 15

"Nothing," said Thóra, looking up in frustration from her computer screen. She and Matthew had dropped by her office after visiting Hugi to check for a reply to her e-mail to the mysterious Mal.

Matthew shrugged. "Who knows? Maybe you'll never get a reply."

Thóra refused to give up as easily as Matthew. "Harald might have some information about him on his computer."

Matthew raised his eyebrows. "Do you keep information about your friends on your computer?"

"Oh, you know what I mean, a contact list, address book."

Matthew shrugged again. "Yes, I know exactly what you mean. Maybe Harald had one. You never know."

Thóra turned her computer screen back to its normal position. "Why don't you give the police a quick call to ask about Harald's computer?" She looked at the clock on the screen. "It's only just past two so the office is open." The letter requesting the case documents was not in Bella's tray that morning, so everything suggested it had been posted the day before. It had probably arrived, but that didn't mean it had been dealt with. It would be sensible to wait a day or two and then phone about the computer and the documents at the same time. But Thóra's curiosity outweighed her common sense at the moment. She could see little else to do in the situation. In the Internet directory, Thóra had already checked Harald's friends' mobile phone numbers and managed to find Marta Mist, Bríet, and Brjánn. They had all refused to talk to her—Bríet half hysterically—and pointed out that they had all made statements to the police. So Thóra and Matthew had little to work on for the time being. "Phone," she insisted.

Matthew gave in, and it turned out they could indeed collect the computer from the police. An officer by the name of Markús Helgason would be there to meet them.

At the police station Markús greeted Thóra in Icelandic, then addressed Matthew in English with a strong Icelandic accent: "We've met twice before. Once when we searched the flat and then when you went to see my boss, Árni Bjarnason." The officer smiled awkwardly. "You didn't exactly hit it off, so they decided to send me this time. I hope you don't mind."

He was a youngish man, wearing the blue shirt and black trousers of the police uniform. Markús was fairly short; he must have joined the force after the minimum height requirement was abolished. In other respects he was very ordinary-looking, neither handsome nor ugly, blond with unremarkable gray eyes. When he smiled as he shook their hands, Thóra's initial impression of him changed completely. He had beautiful white teeth and Thóra hoped for his sake that he always had plenty to smile about.

When Matthew and Thóra assured him that they didn't mind not meeting his superior, the young officer gladly carried on. "I'd like to have a chat with you. We understand you're looking into the circumstances of the murder, and since our investigation isn't formally over it would be normal for us to have a little talk." He hesitated, embarrassed, then added: "The computer's being packed in a box now with some other evidence we were supposed to return. So you'll have to wait a while anyway. We can sit down in my office."

Thóra darted a sideways glance at Matthew, who shrugged to indicate that he did not mind. She knew that the explanation about packing
the computer was mere pretense—a one-handed man could do the job in
no more than three minutes. But with a smile she played along and said it
was fine. Visibly relieved, Markús showed them into his office.

There were no personal articles apart from a coffee mug with a Manchester United logo. Markús invited Thóra and Matthew to take a seat
and waited until they were comfortable before sitting down himself. No
one said anything while they went through these motions, and the silence had become uncomfortable by the time they eventually got themselves settled.

"Well, that's that," the police officer said, pretending to sound jolly.
Thóra and Matthew just smiled but neither said a word. Thóra wanted
Markús to speak first, and judging by the tight line of Matthew's mouth
he felt the same. The officer got straight to the point. "We understand
that you went to the prison this morning and met Hugi Thórisson."

"Yes, that's right," said Thóra curtly.

"Quite," said Markús. "What came out of this meeting?" He looked
expectantly at each of them in turn. "It's a rather strange position to
claim to represent the family as you do here and also to assist the prime
suspect—which I understand you did this morning at the prison."

Thóra looked at Matthew, who waved his hand to indicate that she
should answer. "Let's just say that the situation is strange and unconventional and we're simply acting on that. But we're obviously still working
for Harald's family; Hugi Thórisson's interests just happen to coincide
with theirs." She paused briefly to allow the officer to protest, which he
did not. She continued: "We're not at all convinced that he's guilty. If anything, our talk with him this morning reinforced that belief."

Markús raised his eyebrows. "I must admit, I don't understand how
you can be quite so certain. Everything that our investigation has revealed points in the opposite direction."

"We feel there are many questions unanswered, I suppose that's the
main reason," replied Thóra.

The officer nodded, apparently in agreement. "Actually that's quite true, but as I say, our investigation is not entirely over. But I'd be surprised if anything was found to overturn the theory that Hugi Thórisson murdered Harald." He counted on his fingers. "First, he was with the victim just before the murder was committed. Second, Harald's blood was found on the clothes he was wearing that evening. Third, we found a T-shirt hidden in his closet that had been used to wipe up a considerable amount of blood, which also came from the victim. Fourth, he was a member of the murdered man's black magic cult, so he was familiar with the magic symbols carved on the body. And fifth, he was stoned enough to be able to gouge out the eyes. Believe me—no one in their right mind does that. He was a dealer and presumably planned to smuggle drugs into the country. The murdered man had plenty of money to finance that and a sizable sum vanished from his account shortly before the murder was committed. Without a trace. That doesn't happen in normal business transactions. You can always trace them somehow." The officer looked down. He was gripping his left hand tightly with his right. "In all honesty, most convictions are made on a lot fewer counts. All we lack is a confession, which I readily admit would normally have been made under such circumstances."

Thóra tried to look nonchalant. The blood on Hugi's clothes had caught her off guard. She had seen nothing about it in the police reports or the other documents in her possession. She spoke quickly so Markús would not notice that he had unnerved her. "Doesn't it bother you that he hasn't confessed to the murder?"

The officer looked at her candidly. "No, not at all. You know why?" When Thóra did not seem likely to answer him, he carried on. "He can't remember. So he clings to the hope that he didn't do it. Why should he confess to an act that he can't even remember when there's so much at stake?"

"How do you explain the body being transported to the university?" asked Matthew. "This dope dealer hardly had access to the facilities there. It was a weekend, and presumably everything was locked."

"He stole Harald's key. Very simple. We found a bunch of keys on the body—including a key to the department, or rather an access key, because there's a security system. From the system we could see that the key was used to enter the building just after the murder."

Matthew cleared his throat. "What do you mean, just after the murder? Couldn't it just as easily have been before the murder? The timing in this case isn't that precise."

"In fact it isn't, but that's not the point," answered Markús, more dryly than before.

Matthew went on, not willing to let him off the hook so easily. "Let's assume that Hugi stole the key and transported the body from his home, which is in the neighborhood, to the university building. What sort of transport do you suppose was used? You can't put the body of an adult male in your pocket—or take it with you in a taxi."

Now the police officer smiled. "He transported the body on his bike. It was found outside the Manuscript Institute, and, what's more, Harald's DNA was found on it. His blood was on the handlebars. Fortunately it had been thrown aside into the shelter so that it didn't get snowed on."

Matthew said nothing, so Thóra spoke up. "How do you know it was Hugi's bike?" She quickly added: "And even if it was, how do you know it was left there on the night in question?"

The officer smiled, even more pleased than before. "The bike was thrown away over by the trash cans. The garbage was collected on Friday and the local garbagemen are adamant that there was no bike there at that time. Hugi recognized the bike himself and admitted it had been lying untouched in the bicycle storage in his apartment complex on that Saturday—and a woman who lives there stated that the bike was in its place when she took her stroller out of the storage around dinnertime to go shopping with her child."

"How on earth can a witness remember what was in a certain place and what wasn't? I've lived in an apartment complex before and I don't think I could have said what was in the bicycle room, although I often walked through it," said Thóra.

"The bike was noticeable because he used it a lot. Winter, summer, autumn, and spring. He didn't have a driver's license, so he didn't have much choice. And he wasn't the most considerate of people about storing it away—that weekend he'd left it resting on the woman's stroller. She remembers it well because she had to move it to get the stroller out."

Matthew cleared his throat. "If Hugi stole the key for the security system, I presume a code or PIN number went with it. How could Hugi guess that?"

"That's exactly what we wanted to know," Markús replied. "When Harald's friends were questioned it turned out that he had told the number to all of them."

Thóra looked at him in disbelief. "Who do you expect to believe that? Why on earth would he do that?"

"It seems the number amused him. He was allocated 0666, which apparently appealed to him because of his strange obsession with devil worship."

"Actually it was an obsession with magic and has nothing to do with the devil," Matthew said. Then he quickly changed the subject to avoid a long discussion on the nature of magic. "You might be able to tell us one thing. We came across a printout from Harald's e-mail, a short note sent to a certain Mal. Did you find out anything about that?"

The officer looked blank. "I must admit I don't remember that. We went through hundreds of documents. If you want I can look it up and let you know."

Thóra outlined the e-mail to him, even though she did not expect to gain much from the police on this point. Markús would surely have remembered if it had produced anything. He promised to check whether steps had been taken to identify the recipient, but played down the importance of whatever it was that Harald thought he had found at last. "He must mean some girl he was chasing after, that sort of thing," he said. "But to change the subject, are you going to stay on this case much longer?" He looked at Thóra and Matthew in turn.

"As long as is necessary," Matthew said, frowning. "I'm still not convinced you're holding the right man—in spite of what you said. Of course, I might be wrong."

The officer gave a faint smile. "We'd be grateful if you let us keep tabs on you, as the investigation is still ongoing. We don't want any clashes and it would be better if we could cooperate."

Thóra seized her opportunity. "We've received some of the case documents, but by no means all of them. I sent you a letter, which will probably arrive tomorrow, asking to have all the documents handed over on behalf of the family—do you see any objection?"

Markús shrugged. "Not as such, but it's not my decision. It's an unusual request but I still expect a positive answer. It could take some time to gather it all together. Of course, we'll try—" A knock on the door interrupted him. "Come in," he called, and the door opened. A young female officer stood in the doorway with a cardboard box in her arms. A black computer was sticking out of the top.

"Here's the computer you asked for," the young woman said, walking in. She put the box on the desk and took out a transparent folder with a piece of paper inside. "The monitor's down in reception; it's coming straight out of storage because we didn't need it. Actually it was quite stupid to take it along in the first place," she said rather self-importantly to her colleague. "It might be worth pointing out to the teams who search houses that although the documents appear on the monitor, they aren't literally there. They're all in the computer and they come up on any screen." She tapped the top of the computer.

Markús did not appear too pleased at being told off by the young woman in front of Thóra and Matthew. He glared at her. "Thank you for that information." He took the folder from her and took out the piece of paper. "Can you sign this receipt, please?" he said to Matthew. "The other papers that were removed are in there too."

"What papers?" asked Thóra. "Why weren't they returned with the others?"

"They were papers that we felt deserved a close examination. In fact they revealed nothing. I don't know if you'll find anything juicy in there, but I doubt it." He stood up to indicate that the conversation was over.

Thóra and Matthew stood up and Matthew picked up the box after signing the receipt. "Don't forget the monitor," said the female officer, smiling at Thóra. Thóra returned her smile and assured her they would take it.

They walked out to the car, Thóra with the monitor in her arms and Matthew carrying the box. Thóra pulled out the wad of documents before getting into the passenger seat. She flicked through them quickly while Matthew started the car.

"What the hell is this?" she said in amazement, turning to Matthew.

CHAPTER 16

Thóra was holding a small tan leather wallet that she had taken out of the middle of the wad of papers. The wallet was fastened with straps and she had undone them to examine the contents. The leather was still as soft as a glove to the touch, even though it was probably old. It was at least sixty years old, judging from the insignia printed on it: "NHG 1947." But it was the contents rather than the wallet itself that caused her surprise. "What can this be?" she asked, glancing curiously at Matthew. She pointed to some old letters that were revealed when the wallet was opened—ancient letters, in fact, because judging from their appearance and script they were much older than their container.

Matthew regarded the wallet in astonishment. "Was that among the papers in the box?"

"Yes," Thóra said, thumbing through the uppermost letters to count them. She was startled by a wordless howl as Matthew snatched the wallet from her.

"Are you crazy?" he shouted, closing the wallet and flipping the straps back over it in a rush, rather clumsily because of the steering wheel and the cramped seating in the front of the car.

Thóra watched his efforts in bewilderment without saying a word. When Matthew had closed the wallet he placed it carefully in the backseat. Then he wriggled out of his coat and covered the wallet with it, making sure that the lining and not the damp outside touched it. "Shouldn't we move the car?" asked Thóra to break the silence. It was half backed out of the parking space, jutting into the street.

Matthew grabbed the steering wheel with both hands and exhaled heavily. "Excuse my behavior. I didn't expect to see those letters in some crummy cardboard box from the police." He backed out into the street and drove away.

"What are they, if I may ask?" Thóra said.

"They're very old letters from Harald's grandfather's collection, some of the most valuable ones. Actually they're priceless, and I can't understand why Harald sent them to Iceland. I'm certain the insurance company thinks they're still in the bank vault, as they had agreed." Matthew adjusted the rearview mirror to keep an eye on his precious cargo. "A nobleman from Innsbruck wrote them in 1485. They describe Heinrich Kramer's campaign against witches in the city, before witch hunts became widespread."

"Who was Heinrich Kramer again?" Thóra knew she ought to recognize the name but simply drew a blank.

"One of the two authors of *The Witches' Hammer*," Matthew replied. "He was the chief inquisitor in several regions that now mostly belong to Germany—doubtless a warped personality, he had a particular grudge against women. As well as chasing imaginary witches he persecuted Jews and blasphemers, in fact almost any group that was an easy target."

Thóra remembered the article she had read on the Internet. "Yes, right." Then she added in surprise: "So are these letters about him?"

"Yes," Matthew said. "He went to Innsbruck. Maybe he came and saw, but he definitely didn't conquer. It started well for him—he launched an inquisition using extreme violence and torture, and the suspects, fifty-seven women, were not allowed any legal defense. The local clerics and secular authorities were appalled at the trials. Kramer made such a show about the alleged witches' sexual activities that the bishop was outraged and banished him from the city. The women he had detained were released but they were in a sorry state after persistent torture. The letters describe his treatment of the scribe's wife. As you can imagine, it doesn't make particularly pleasant reading."

"Who was he writing to?" Thóra asked.

"All the letters are addressed to the Bishop of Brixen, George II. Gosler. The same bishop who had Kramer expelled from the city. I have a feeling the letters played some part."

"How did Harald's grandfather get hold of them?"

Matthew shrugged. "Lots of things went up for sale in Germany at the end of the war. The Guntliebs invested their assets to hedge the bank against the devaluation of the mark that left most people penniless after the war. It's not a conventional bank—ordinary depositors don't put their money in it and never have. In many ways, it was thanks to Harald's grandfather that his clients didn't lose everything. He was quick to see where things were heading and was able to exchange funds and invest without drawing a lot of attention to himself. So he was in a good position to snap up various things when the economy took a dive."

"So who owned the letters and sold them to him? Letters from the fifteenth century aren't something people keep safe for a rainy day."

Matthew looked puzzled. "I have no idea. These letters aren't in any records or references—they could be forgeries, for that matter. Very good forgeries, though, if that's the case. Harald's grandfather wouldn't go into detail about the purchase. The initials on the wallet are his—Niklas Harald Guntlieb—so they don't give a clue as to the previous owner. I suspect that they were stolen from the Church at some stage." Matthew drove along Snorrabraut and flicked his blinker to change lanes. They had agreed it was best to keep the computer at Bergstadastraeti and were heading there. Soon they would need to make a right turn, and they were in the left lane now. But no one would let Matthew merge—if anything, the other drivers seemed determined to prevent him and force him over the bridge to Fossvogur. "What's wrong with you?" Matthew muttered at them.

"Just change lanes," advised Thóra, accustomed to such behavior. "They're more worried about their own cars than controlling your route."

Matthew took the plunge and slipped into the other lane with no harm done apart from a loud beep from the car he had to squeeze in front of. "I'll never get used to driving in this country," he said in astonishment.

Thóra just smiled. "What do the letters say—what happened to the woman?"

"She was tortured," Matthew replied. "Brutally."

"I didn't suppose you could torture people any other way," Thóra said, hoping for a more detailed description. "What did they do to her?"

"The scribe talked about paralyzed arms and a leg crushed by an iron boot. And both her ears were cut off. There was bound to have been more that wasn't worth putting on paper. Cuts and the like." Matthew glanced away from the road at Thóra. "As far as I remember one of the last letters ended something like this: 'If you are looking for evil, it is not to be found in what is left of my beloved young and innocent wife. It lies in her accuser.'"

"My God," Thóra said, shuddering. "You really remember that well."

"It's not so easy to forget what the letters say," Matthew replied dryly. "Of course it's not all he wrote about. There were endless attempts to have her released, from legal arguments to what you could call outright threats. The man was at his wit's end. He loved his wife with all his heart; she was the most beautiful of maidens, if his words are to be believed. They hadn't been married for long."

"Was he allowed to visit her in prison? Weren't the letters written while she was still detained?"

"Yes and no," Matthew said. "He wasn't allowed to see her, but one of the guards took pity on her and passed on messages which became more and more hopeless and sad, the scribe says. And as regards your second question, all the letters except one were written while she was in prison and the husband was working on her release. That was written after she was let out. It describes a fate that's worth bearing in mind when we complain about our own troubles."

"In what way?" asked Thóra, without really wanting to hear the answer.

"You have to remember that in those days, medicine wasn't anything like what we know today, just nonsense really. You can't begin to imagine how much pain the sick and injured went through, let alone the mental state of a pretty girl who had been much admired for her looks. When she was released, one of her feet and all her fingers were crushed to powder. No ears. Her body covered in knife marks from searching for spots on her that would not bleed. And other things that are only hinted at and not described. What would you do under such circumstances?" Matthew looked at Thóra again.

"Did she have children?" Thóra asked. Instinctively her hand moved up to her ear—she had never thought about how indispensable a part of someone's appearance they were.

"No," said Matthew.

"So she committed suicide," said Thóra, without pausing to think. "You can put up with endless suffering and pain for your children, but not for much else."

"Bingo," Matthew said. "They lived on an estate by a brook and she hobbled over there the night she got home and threw herself in. If she'd been in better shape she could have swum to safety, but wearing a heavy dress, which was the fashion then, with a useless leg and hands, she wasn't capable of much."

"What did he do—is that mentioned in the letter?" asked Thóra, trying to keep the thought of the young woman out of her mind.

"Yes, it is. In the last letter he says he has taken away the most precious thing in Inquisitor Kramer's life, just as Kramer had taken the most precious thing in his life—and now it's on the long path to hell," Matthew said. "It doesn't say who or where the victim of his vengeance was, nor how hell came into the picture. Contemporary records give no further hints. Then he tells the bishop to sleep well—accuses him of failing to answer his appeals in time and says that is a matter for God's servant to answer to his master. Then he quotes from the Old Testament, which as you know is about something quite different from forgiveness. I can't explain it exactly but his last words are some kind of veiled threat, which I don't know whether he carried out—the bishop died a few years later. He may well have got rid of the documents, not wanting them to be preserved in the Church archive."

"That sounds dubious," said Thóra. "If he wanted to get rid of them, why didn't he burn them? They weren't exactly short of fires."

Matthew concentrated on steering into a parking spot near Harald's apartment. The ones directly outside it were full. "I don't know—maybe he visualized Saint Peter and God and didn't want to draw attention to the content of the letters by burning them. Smoke rises up to heaven, after all."

"So you think the letters aren't forgeries?" Thóra asked.

"No, I didn't say that. There are certain points in them that don't fit."

"Such as?"

"Mainly allusions to that awful book of Kramer's. The scribe calls it a flowery account that does little to conceal the diabolical origin of its contents."

"Couldn't he mean *The Witches' Hammer*? After he wrote it, Kramer must have used it in his investigations of these so-called witches. I would assume he practiced what he preached."

"That doesn't fit," Matthew said. "That extraordinary piece of literature is said to have been published in 1486."

"Have the paper and ink from these letters been dated?" Thóra asked.

"Yes, they more or less fit but that's not crucial. Forgers have used old paper and old ink or paint to deceive owners who can afford to have such tests done."

"Old ink?" repeated Thóra doubtfully.

"Yes, or something resembling it. They make ink from old substances or dissolve it from old documents that aren't likely to fetch a high price. It produces the same result."

"What a lot of bother to go to," Thóra said, relieved that she had never decided to become a forger.

"Hmm," said Matthew as they got out of the car.

"But why did Harald have the letters?" she asked. "Did he believe they were genuine or forged?"

Matthew shut the door to the driver's seat and opened the rear door. After carefully wrapping the wallet of letters inside his jacket, he placed it on top of the box and bent over to pick everything up. If he was cold in just his sweater, he didn't show it. "Harald was convinced they were genuine—he was obsessed with the riddle of who or what it was that Kramer lost in the scribe's revenge. He made countless searches to find an allusion to it in documents from all over Germany and even went to the Vatican library for that specific purpose. But he couldn't find a scrap of evidence. Kramer isn't so well known in other respects; he was around more than five hundred years ago."

Thóra noticed footprints in the snow at the corner of the building, leading toward the front door of Harald's apartment. She gestured to Matthew with her chin to indicate these fresh signs of traffic—the footprints only led in one direction so they could hardly have been left when the post or newspapers were delivered. With a finger to his lips, Matthew made his way around the side of the building. Thóra followed quietly.

As they rounded the corner, they saw a man standing a short distance from the front door. He had backed away to look up at the windows on the upper floor. He gave a start when he saw Thóra and Matthew. His mouth moved silently for several seconds before he finally stammered: "Did you know Harald Guntlieb?"

Chapter 17

"How do you do? My name's Gunnar Gestvík, head of the history department at the university."

He shuffled his feet in front of them, unsure of himself. His clothes looked well made; he was wearing a smart winter coat from a label that Thóra recognized from her ex-husband's wardrobe. Beneath it he was dressed in a suit with a loud, carefully knotted tie and light blue shirt collar protruding from it. His whole manner suggested a calm and collected professional man. But at this moment his calm and collectedness were stretched to breaking point. Gunnar had clearly been caught off guard by this encounter and was desperately calculating his next move. Thóra knew this was the man who found Harald's body, or, more accurately, had it thrust upon him. Why he should want to visit his former student's apartment was a mystery to her. Maybe part of the process of acceptance, on the advice of a psychiatrist?

"I was in the neighborhood and decided to see if anyone was here," said Gunnar hesitantly.

"Here? At Harald's flat?" Thóra asked, surprised.

"Of course I didn't expect to meet him in person," Gunnar said quickly. "I meant whether the caretaker or someone else was here."

Matthew could not understand a word and left the talking to Thóra— but the name registered at once. He slipped past her and flashed his eyes to signal that she should invite the man in. He fished the keys out of his pocket and opened the door.

Gunnar watched Matthew with a strange eagerness. "Do you have access to his apartment?" he asked Thóra.

"Yes, Matthew's working for Harald's family and I'm representing them too. We're unloading some of his belongings that we fetched from the police. May I invite you in? We'd be pleased to have a quick word with you."

Gunnar could hardly conceal his glee. He gratefully accepted the offer after glancing at his watch and pretending that he could just squeeze in a visit. He followed Thóra inside. In spite of his elegant appearance he was not quite the perfect gentleman—at least, he did not offer to help her carry the heavy monitor upstairs.

Gunnar's reaction was similar to Thóra's when she had first entered the apartment. Not even bothering to hang up his coat, he walked in a trance into the living room and began studying the objects on the walls. Matthew and Thóra took their time, put down their loads and hung up their coats. When Matthew hung his up he removed the leather wallet containing the letters and took it to the bedroom. Thóra stayed to keep an eye on Gunnar. She walked over to him and stood by his side, although she could hardly bring herself to interrupt his appreciation of the old works of art on the walls.

"This is a remarkable collection of art," she commented. She tried to recall what Matthew had told her about the paintings but was unsure that she could do it justice, so she decided not to try to show off.

"How did he get hold of all this?" Gunnar asked. "Did he steal it?"

Thóra was astonished. How could the man entertain such a notion? "No. He inherited it all from his grandfather." After a moment's hesitation she ventured: "Didn't you like Harald?"

Gunnar was taken aback by the question. "Oh, yes, goodness me. I was extremely fond of him." His tone did not exactly ring true and Gunnar seemed to realize as much. He quickly tried to rectify this. "Harald was an extremely intelligent young man with a good command of history. His approach to his work was exemplary, which is unfortunately becoming rarer these days."

Thóra was still not convinced. "So he was a model student?"

Gunnar forced a smile. "You could say that. Of course his appearance and behavior were rather unconventional, but you mustn't judge young people's fashions. I remember the Beatles and the fashions they started. The older generation didn't think much of them at the time. I'm old enough now to realize that the youthful spirit wears many disguises."

Comparing Harald and the Beatles was pushing it, to say the least. "I'd never thought of it that way." She smiled at Gunnar politely. "But of course I never knew him."

"You said you were a lawyer, so what business are you doing for Harald's family—does it concern the will? The objects on these walls are worth a pretty penny."

"No, it's nothing like that," replied Thóra. "We're double-checking the murder investigation—the family is having trouble accepting the police findings."

Gunnar stared at her, his eyes like saucers. His Adam's apple bobbed up and down. "What do you mean? Haven't they caught the murderer, that drug dealer?"

Thóra shrugged. "We have reason to believe that he isn't the killer." She noticed that Gunnar, for some reason, wasn't particularly pleased by this news. She added: "It'll all come out in the end. Maybe we're wrong—maybe not."

"It might not be any of my business, but what is there to suggest that this man is innocent? The police seem convinced they've got the right man in custody—do you know something the police don't?"

"We're not concealing information from the police, if that's what you're implying," Thóra snapped. "We're simply not satisfied with some of the aspects of their findings."

Gunnar sighed. "Do forgive me for being so pushy; I haven't quite been myself since this happened. To tell you the truth I hoped it was coming to an end. It's been extremely difficult for me personally and it's tarnished the reputation of the department."

"I understand that," said Thóra. "But surely it's not right to convict an innocent man to save the department's reputation, is it?"

Realizing the implication of his words, Gunnar spluttered: "No, no, no. Of course not. One tends to put one's own interests first, but naturally there are limits. Please don't misunderstand me."

"So what brought you here anyway?" asked Thóra. She wondered what was keeping Matthew.

Gunnar turned away from Thóra to examine one of the pictures. "I was hoping to get in touch with someone who is dealing with Harald's affairs. I seem to have found the right person."

"Why?"

"When Harald was murdered he had recently . . . how shall I put it . . . yes, recently borrowed a document from the university, a document that was never returned. I'm looking for it." Gunnar did not take his eyes off the picture.

"What document?" Thóra asked. "There are hundreds here."

"It's an old letter to the Bishop of Roskilde from around the year 1500. We borrowed it from Denmark so it's important that it doesn't go astray."

"That sounds quite serious," Thóra said. "Why didn't you approach the police about it? They could surely have located the document."

"This has only just come to light—I had no idea about it when I was being interviewed, otherwise I would have asked them to let me have it. By coming here I was hoping to avoid having to go to the police and to solve the problem more simply. I don't particularly want to give another statement. That's an experience I've had too much of already. The document is completely unrelated to the murder, I can promise you that."

"Maybe not," said Thóra. "Unfortunately, I haven't come across it. But we haven't gone through all Harald's papers yet. It may well turn up."

Matthew hurried in holding some papers in one hand and sat down on the elegant sofa. With a flamboyant gesture he invited them to do the same. Thóra sat in the armchair and Gunnar went to the sofa directly opposite Matthew. Thóra described Gunnar's business to Matthew, who did little more than repeat almost verbatim what she had said—he had not come across the document, but that didn't necessarily mean it wasn't there. Then he put the papers on the table. He addressed Gunnar in English: "You supervised Harald's research, if I'm not mistaken?"

"Yes and no, sort of," Gunnar said warily in heavily accented English.

"Oh?" snapped Matthew. "Isn't it clear who supervises which students for their dissertations?"

"Yes, yes. Of course," Gunnar said hastily. "He just hadn't got far enough to need supervision by the department staff. That was all I meant. Thorbjörn Ólafsson had agreed to it. I watched from the sidelines, so to speak."

"I see. But I presume he presented an outline or idea for his theme, didn't he?"

"Oh, yes. He submitted an abstract, if I remember correctly, right at the beginning of his first term at the department. We examined the topic and broadly approved it. Thorbjörn followed it up. It was in his field."

"What was the dissertation going to be about?" Thóra asked.

"A comparison between witch burnings in Iceland and elsewhere in Europe, mainly in what today is Germany. Witches were hunted most passionately there, so to speak. Harald had previously researched witch burnings, in connection with his dissertation at the University of Munich."

Matthew nodded thoughtfully. "Am I right in believing that the Icelandic witch hunts took place in the seventeenth century?"

"Yes. Actually, there are records of convictions for sorcery before that time, but the witch hunts proper only commenced in the seventeenth century. The first known burning was in 1625."

"That's what I thought," said Matthew, looking puzzled. He spread out the papers he had put down on the table. "I find it odd how little there is in Harald's papers about Icelandic witches being burned, and I can't understand his fascination with events from a much earlier period. Maybe you could enlighten me; you might be aware of a historical context that escapes us."

"What events are you referring to?" asked Gunnar as he reached over to look at the papers, which were photocopied articles from academic journals.

While Gunnar read, Matthew reeled them off: "An eruption in Mount Hekla in 1510, epidemics in Denmark around 1500, the Reformation in 1550, caves of Irish monks in Iceland before the proper settlement, and more of that nature. I can't see a direct connection, but then I'm not a historian."

Gunnar kept reading. When he had digested the subjects of all the papers he finally spoke: "They don't all necessarily have to be directly connected with his dissertation topic. Harald could have obtained these articles for another course he was enrolled in. Actually, the age of settlement is my specialist field and Harald did not attend my classes, which might have explained the article on Irish monks. But I would still conclude that these documents are connected with courses he took alongside his dissertation."

Matthew regarded Gunnar intently. "No, that's not the point. Most of these are from a file labeled *Malleus*—you're presumably familiar with that name." Matthew pointed to the holes in the margins of the pages. "My conclusion was that he had collected all this in connection with witchcraft, somehow."

"Yes, I know the name—couldn't he simply have put it all in an old file and not got round to relabeling it?"

"Certainly," said Matthew. "But somehow I don't think he did."

Gunnar looked back at the papers. "I must confess it's not immediately apparent. My initial guess would be the link with the Reformation—in a sense that was the precedent for witch hunts, just as in much of Europe. Religion began to change and these developments provoked a kind of spiritual crisis. Regarding the eruption and the epidemics, Harald could have been looking into the connection between the persecutions and the prevailing economic landscape. Natural catastrophes and diseases had a great impact on the economy in those days. Still, other eruptions, such as Hekla in 1636, and other epidemics much closer in time to the witch hunts would have been a more normal avenue of inquiry than the subjects of these articles." He tapped the papers on the desk.

"So he never mentioned this to you or Thorbjörn when you met to discuss his dissertation?" asked Thóra.

"Not to me. Thorbjörn made no mention of it either after he met with Harald on his own," Gunnar said, then added: "As I told you, Harald was still developing his dissertation. His focus seemed to shift—apparently he even implied to Thorbjörn that he was more interested in the impact of the Reformation than in witch burnings, but nothing had been decided when he was murdered."

"Is that normal?" Thóra asked. "Changing his mind like that?"

Gunnar nodded. "Yes, it's very common. Students start off zealously, then discover the topic isn't as exciting as they originally thought and choose a new one. We even have a long list of interesting research topics to let students choose from when they're stuck for ideas."

"Considering Harald's interest in witchcraft in general," Matthew said, gesturing at the artwork on the walls, "which he'd fostered from an early age, I doubt that the Reformation would have pushed it all out of his mind."

"Harald was a Catholic, as you undoubtedly know," Gunnar said, and Thóra and Matthew nodded dutifully. "One of the main aspects of Lutheranism that fascinated him was the general decline in living standards in Iceland around 1550, especially among the poorest sections of the population. The Catholic Church had kept all its property and wealth in Iceland, but with the Reformation this all passed into the hands of the king of Denmark and the country became poorer as a result. Likewise, the Catholic Church acted as an almsgiver, providing food and shelter to those in greatest need. That was cut off with the switch to Lutheranism. Harald thought that was worth looking into because the Catholic Church is seldom seen in that light. He was also impressed that priests and bishops in Iceland were allowed to take mistresses and have children by them—this wasn't tolerated in other Catholic sees in Europe at that time, and still isn't, in fact."

Matthew seemed unconvinced. "Yes, maybe. But could it be that his meetings with Thorbjörn weren't very detailed—perhaps Harald was cooking something up in his research that Thorbjörn, and presumably you, knew nothing about?"

"I wouldn't know about that, obviously," Gunnar replied. "But I didn't get that from my contact with him, at least. That's all I know. Of course he could have examined all kinds of topics without my knowledge—I didn't follow his every move, nor was I supposed to. M.A. students decide most things for themselves and work very independently. But I recommend that you discuss this with Thorbjörn if you want more information. I can arrange a meeting if you like."

Matthew looked at Thóra, who nodded assent. "Yes, thank you, we'll accept that," he said. "As soon as you find out when Thorbjörn's free, you can give me a call. Also if anything occurs to you that might be important." He handed Gunnar his card.

Thóra produced her card from her bag as well, handing it to Gunnar. "We'll see if the letter you're looking for is among the papers we have."

"I would appreciate that—it's rather embarrassing for the university and I'd prefer not to have to declare the letter lost. Unfortunately I don't have a card on me but you can usually get hold of me by just phoning my office." He stood up.

"About Harald's friends," said Matthew. "Can you put them in touch with us? We'd like to have a few words with the ones who knew him best; maybe they could shed light on what Harald was up to. We tried to contact some of them this morning, but none of them want to talk to us."

"You presumably mean the young people in that society of his," Gunnar said. "Yes, I should be able to. The society is based at our department so I bump into them from time to time. Actually I was hoping that society would fold without Harald. I didn't consider it a great credit to the university and certainly saw no reason to support them by providing facilities. But I don't control everything myself so I'm stuck with the decision. I can arrange a meeting with the two students who are at our department. They should be able to put you in touch with others that Harald associated with."

"That would be much appreciated." Thóra smiled gratefully at him. "Why do you think the society is so awful?"

Gunnar seemed to mull over his reply. "There was a minor incident about six months back. I was and still am convinced that it had something to do with that society, but I can't prove it. Unfortunately."

"What happened?" asked Matthew.

"I don't know whether I should say much about it," Gunnar said, clearly wishing he hadn't mentioned it. "It was hushed up and not reported through the proper channels."

"What?" said Matthew and Thóra in unison.

Gunnar hesitated. "We found a finger."

"A finger?" Matthew and Thóra spoke together again, this time in shock.

"Yes, one of the cleaners found a finger outside their staff room. I can still hear that poor woman howling. The finger was sent for tests at the university's forensic science department and it turned out to belong to an old person—a proper sex test wasn't done, but it was probably male. It was gangrenous."

"Were the police notified?" Thóra asked, astounded.

Gunnar blushed. "I wish I could say they were, but after our own investigation into the origin of the finger and the reason for its being on our premises, we felt it was inappropriate to notify them—such a long time after it was found, you know. It was the start of the summer break, as well."

Thóra did not think the summer break was much of an excuse. Maybe they ought to be thankful that no one was on maternity leave when Harald's body was found. Or that the history department hadn't decided to investigate the murder itself. "Well, well."

"So what did you do with the finger?" asked Matthew.

"Um, we . . . er . . . threw it away," Gunnar mumbled. His blush spread up his cheeks and across his scalp. "It was definitely not connected with the murder so there seemed no reason to bring up this dreadful business with the police. They had plenty of other things to think about."

"Well, well," Thóra repeated. Fingers, eyes, a letter about severed ears—what next?

CHAPTER 18

Thóra straightened up and leaned back in her chair. She had just finished plugging the last cable into the computer and all that remained was to switch it on. She and Matthew were in Harald's study—after bidding farewell to the cryptic Gunnar Gestvík. "I must confess that I find this theory of yours and the Guntliebs about a mystery murderer increasingly unlikely." She switched on the computer and a low hum indicated that it was booting up. "The blood on Hugi's clothes, for example—how does that fit in with your theory?" Matthew said nothing, so she continued. "And the papers just now—I don't quite see the link between the murder and a university dissertation, especially because Harald was clearly straying from the subject a little when gathering his material."

"I just know it," Matthew said, without looking directly at her.

Something about his manner struck Thóra as odd. Besides the fact that it was not like him to avoid eye contact, she noticed that he was staring fixedly at the screen of his mobile phone, as if hoping someone would call and extricate him from this conversation. Thóra crossed her arms and scowled. "You're hiding something from me."

Matthew went on gazing hopefully at his phone. "Well, I hope I haven't revealed all my secrets during our short acquaintance," he said with forced joviality.

"Oh, come on—you know exactly what I mean. There's more to it than the missing money and eyes." Thóra still had trouble discussing the gouged-out eyes. She still could not manage to express the idea clearly; words somehow failed to encapsulate it. "Really, that's all there is—oh, yes, and an e-mail that says nothing and now a finger at the university that the professors panicked over and threw away."

Matthew put his mobile in his pocket. "Even if I were hiding something from you—would you still take my word for it that Hugi can't be the murderer, or at least couldn't have done it alone?"

Thóra laughed out loud. "No—not really."

Matthew stood up. "That's a shame. To tell you the truth, I can't make decisions about certain information by myself," he said, quickly adding: "That is, if there *was* anything else."

"Let's imagine that's the case—and that the person who can decide to include me in the picture would allow it—wouldn't it be worth checking?"

Matthew looked at her pensively, then left the room. Thóra noticed his mobile was back in his hand. Hopefully he'd gone out to use it. She cocked her ear and could hear the muffled sound of his voice from the corridor.

A little gray box in the center of the computer screen told her to enter the administrator password. Not knowing it, she had to go by guesswork: Harald, *Malleus,* Windows, *Hexe,* and the like. None of them worked, although Thóra had been very pleased with herself and sure she had clinched it when she thought of the term *Hexe,* which stood for "witch" in German. She leaned back and looked around for inspiration. On a shelf above the desk was a framed photograph that she reached out for. It was of a young disabled girl in a wheelchair. It didn't take a rocket scientist to realize that this was Harald's sister, who had died some years before. What was her name again? Wasn't she named after her mother? Whose name was what? Anna? No, but it began with *A*. Agatha or Angelina. Amelia—her name was Amelia Guntlieb. Thóra tried that. Nothing happened. With a sigh she decided to enter it without the capital: *amelia*.

Bingo! The computer emitted the familiar Windows jingle: *dum-dee-dum-dee,* and Thóra was in. She wondered how long the police had spent trying to find the password, but realized they must have a computer expert who could get in by the back door. They would hardly spend hours on trial and error.

It took a while before it dawned on Thóra what the picture was on the unusual desktop wallpaper. It wasn't every day that she saw the inside of a mouth on a seventeen-inch screen, let alone a mouth with the tongue pinned on either side with two stainless steel tongs and a fiery red slit along it from the tip—or rather, tips. Although she was not well versed in the practice, the photograph had obviously been taken when a tongue was being split down the middle. The operation was either still in progress or just completed. Thóra would have bet money on the identity of the tongue's owner. It must be Harald himself. She shook herself to stave off nausea and opened Explorer, which immediately filled the screen, removing the wretched image from her sight.

A quick search showed that there were almost four hundred Word documents on the computer. She arranged them by date with the most recent at the top. Their names were self-explanatory. A common feature of the file names at the top was that they all contained the word *hexe* somewhere. Since it was so late, Thóra reached over to her handbag and took out a flash memory stick. She copied all the witchcraft files to examine at her leisure at home that evening—if Matthew would reveal what the Guntliebs had been keeping from her. If he didn't, she intended to spend the evening working out whether she could afford to tell them to get lost. She had absolutely no interest in working as some kind of luxury interpreter.

There was still no sign of Matthew, so Thóra decided to search for scanned files. She asked the search function to find all the .pdf extensions and was rewarded with sixty names. She arranged them by date and copied the most recent ones to the memory stick. She had plenty to keep her busy that evening, that was certain. Then it occurred to her to search for Jpegs, and she called them up too. Harald had clearly owned a digital camera, which he had used prolifically. Hundreds of file names appeared, but they told her nothing because they were labeled by a series of numbers automatically generated when the pictures were downloaded from the camera. Harald had not bothered to rename them. Thóra selected "thumbnail view" to see the content immediately. Once again she arranged them by date. She noticed that the most recent ones had been taken inside the flat. The subjects were odd—some showed nothing in particular, most of them taken in the kitchen during preparations for a meal that was photographed in detail. No people were shown but hands could be seen in two of them, which Thóra copied to her memory stick in case they belonged to the murderer. *You never know,* she thought. The other photographs were of a gigantic pasta meal at various stages—these she left alone.

Scrolling down, Thóra noticed that many of the photographs were quite embarrassing for the subjects, taken during an assortment of sex acts. She blushed for the participants as they rolled past in succession on the screen. Much as she would have liked to, she did not feel happy about enlarging them for fear that Matthew would walk in and find her prying. She also came across myriad photographs from the tongue operation, including the one Harald had chosen for his desktop wallpaper. It was impossible to see who was present, but some torsos were visible and Thóra copied those too. Other files contained all manner of scenes from what seemed to be action-packed parties, interspersed with—and these seemed completely out of place—Icelandic landscapes and journeys through them. Several were very dark and featured little more than gray rock faces— Thóra thought she could make out a cross carved on one of them when she enlarged it. A whole series had been taken in a small village that Thóra did not recognize, many of them in a museum where what looked like manuscripts were on exhibit along with a slab of basalt in a showcase. One shot showed a sign that Thóra enlarged to see if she could identify the museum, only to be disappointed—it simply said: No Photographs. Thóra gave up on the pictures for the time being; by now she was down to fairly old ones that could hardly be linked with the case. She opened Harald's e-mail to see what it contained. In the in-box were seven unread messages. More had presumably arrived since Harald was murdered, but the police must have checked them.

Matthew walked in and Thóra looked up from the e-mail. He sat down in his chair again with a twisted smile on his face. "Well?" she said impatiently, wanting to hear what he had to say.

"Well," Matthew echoed, leaning forward in his chair. He rested his elbows on his knees and clenched his hands as if about to pray. "Before I tell you what you think you have to know," he said, emphasizing the word "think," "you must promise me one thing."

"What?" Thóra was quite sure of his reply.

"What I am about to tell you is in absolute confidence and must not go any further. Before I tell you I need confirmation that you'll keep this secret. Understand?"

"How am I supposed to know if I can keep a secret when I don't have a clue what it is?"

Matthew shrugged. "It's a risk you'll just have to take. I can honestly say to you that you will want to tell someone—just so you know I'm not leading you into a trap."

"Who will I want to tell?" asked Thóra. "That seems important to me."

"The police," Matthew replied, without hesitation.

"You, or Harald's family, have information that could be important to the case, but you've decided to keep it secret? Do I understand that correctly?"

"Yep," said Matthew.

"Well, well," said Thóra. She thought about it. Presumably a code of ethics obliged her to inform the authorities of information that could relate to a public prosecution, so she ought to turn down the offer and notify the police that Matthew was concealing evidence connected with the murder. On the other hand, she was well aware that he would deny the allegation and her part in the investigation would then be over. That served no one's interests. So with a rather elastic ethical interpretation she could conclude that she was obliged to swear to keep her mouth shut and, armed with this new information, do her utmost to solve the mystery confronting them. Everyone happy. Thóra mulled all this over in silence. A fairly dubious conclusion, but the best of a bad job—the code of ethics must allow for extenuating circumstances when the end justifies the means. If not, then it was time to change it.

"Okay," Thóra said eventually. "I promise to tell no one—not even the police—whatever it is you are about to tell me." Matthew smiled, pleased, but before he could begin his revelation she added hastily: "But in return you must promise me that if this secret of yours proves Hugi's innocence, and if we can't demonstrate that in any other way, we will pass on the information to the authorities before the trial starts." Matthew opened his mouth, but Thóra hadn't finished: "And the authorities won't be told that I knew. And—"

Matthew cut her short. "No more 'ands'—please." Now it was his turn to think things over. He regarded Thóra steadily. "Agreed. You say nothing and I'll let the police know about the letter if we can't prove Hugi innocent in good time before the trial."

The letter? Yet another letter? Thóra was beginning to think this was one huge farce, but then she remembered the autopsy photographs, which were still vivid in her mind. "What letter are you referring to?" she asked. "I still stand by my promise."

"Harald's mother received a letter shortly after the murder," Matthew replied. "The letter convinced her and her husband that the suspect could not be guilty. It was sent after Hugi had been taken into custody and therefore unable to send things through the post office. I doubt that the police would have done him the favor of posting it for him—especially because I presume they would first have read what it said."

"Which was?" Thóra asked impatiently.

"What it said was nothing special—except that it was quite unpleasant about Harald's mother. But it was written in blood—Harald's blood."

"Yuck!" Thóra said, before she could stop herself. She tried to imagine how it might feel to receive a letter written with her dead son's blood, but could not do it. It was too bizarre. "Who was the letter from—did it say? And how did you know it was Harald's blood?"

"The letter was in Icelandic and signed with Harald's name, but a handwriting expert ruled that it wasn't his hand. He couldn't absolutely confirm this because it was written with a rough instrument. This complicated a comparison with Harald's normal hand, so it was sent for tests, including whether the blood was his. It turned out to be—unquestionably. In fact they also found traces of blood from a passerine bird that had apparently been mixed with Harald's blood."

Thóra's eyes widened. Bird's blood? That repulsed her even more than human blood. "What did the letter say?" Thóra asked. "Do you have it with you?"

"I don't have the original, if that's what you mean," Matthew answered. "His mother wouldn't hand it over, nor a copy of it. She may well have destroyed it. It was quite disgusting."

Thóra looked disappointed. "So what? I have to know what it said. Did you get someone to translate it?"

"Yes, we did. It was a love poem that began sweetly but soon turned rather nasty." He smiled at Thóra. "You're lucky that I managed to copy it out—you see, I was given the job of translating it, with the help of an Icelandic-German dictionary. I probably wouldn't win a prize for the translation but the meaning was obvious." While he spoke, Matthew produced a folded sheet of paper from his jacket pocket. He handed it to Thóra. "I might not have written some of the letters down properly—I didn't recognize all of them, but it ought to be fairly close."

Thóra read the poem. It was long, considering it had been written in blood. She could not imagine how much blood it would have taken to write all those letters. Matthew had written it out in capitals—presumably to match the original. On the sheet of paper was written:

I look at you,
but you bestow on me
love and dearness
with your whole heart.
Sit nowhere,

stay nowhere,
unless you love me.
I ask of Odin
and all those
who can decipher
women's runes
that in this world
you will nowhere rest
or thrive
unless you love me
with all your heart.

Then in your bones
you will burn all over
and in your flesh
half as bad again.
May misfortune befall you
unless you love me,
your legs shall freeze,
may you never earn honor
or happiness.
Sit burning,
may your hair rot,
may your clothes rip,
unless willingly
you wish me yours.

Thóra felt odd reading it—the poem was quite macabre. She looked up at Matthew. "I don't recognize it, unfortunately. Who does that sort of thing?"

"I don't have the faintest idea," Matthew replied. "The original was even more repulsive, it was written on skin—calfskin. It takes a sick man to do something like that to a dead man's mother."

"Why his mother? Wasn't it sent to his father too?"

"There was more with it, in German. I didn't write it down but I more or less remember what it said."

"And what was that?" Thóra asked.

"It was a short text—something along the lines of: 'Mother—I hope you like the poem and the present—your son Harry.' And the word 'son' was double-underlined."

Thóra looked up from the page at Matthew. "What present? Was there a present with the letter?"

"No, not according to his parents, and I believe them. They were out of their minds after it arrived and in no state to lie convincingly."

"Why is it signed 'Harry'? Was the person who wrote it running out of blood?"

"No, his elder brother called him 'Harry' when they were small. Only a handful of people know that nickname—which is one reason why the letter had such an effect on his mother."

Thóra looked at Matthew. "Did she treat him badly? Is that true?" She thought back to that photograph of the lonely little boy.

Matthew did not answer immediately. When he finally spoke he chose his words carefully; it was evidently important to him to express himself properly about the private affairs of employers whom he seemed to respect highly. "I swear that I don't know. It was more as if she avoided him. But I do know that if their relationship had been normal, she would have sent the letter to the Icelandic police. It clearly struck a nerve." He paused for a moment, watching Thóra thoughtfully before continuing. "She asked to talk to you. Mother-to-mother."

"Me?" Thóra gaped. "What does she want from me? To apologize for her bizarre behavior toward her child?"

"She didn't say," Matthew replied. "She just said she wanted to talk to you, but not right now. She wanted time to get over the shock."

Thóra said nothing. Of course she would talk to the woman if she insisted, but it would be a long time before she would console someone who had mistreated her child. "I can't see the motive behind that letter," she said, to change the subject.

"Nor can I," replied Matthew at once. "There's something so crazy about pretending Harald sent it himself that I think the murderer must be a psychopath."

Thóra stared at the sheet of paper. "Could the person who wrote it be implying that Harald was dead and would come back to haunt his mother?"

"Why?" asked Matthew reasonably. "Who could expect to benefit from tormenting her like that?"

"Harald, of course, except that he was dead," Thóra said. "His sister perhaps—maybe their mother mistreated her too?"

"No," Matthew replied. "She wasn't mistreated—I can promise you that. She's the apple of her parents' eye."

"So who can it be?" Thóra asked, floundering.

"Not Hugi anyway. Unless he had an accomplice."

"Pity we didn't know about the blood on his clothes when we spoke to him this morning." Thóra looked at her watch. "Maybe they'll let me talk to him on the phone." She dialed directory assistance and got the number of the prison. The duty sergeant gave her permission to talk to Hugi on condition that they kept the conversation short. She held impatiently for several minutes listening to a digital rendition of *Für Elise*. Finally, a breathless Hugi came on the line.

"Hello."

"Yes, hello, Hugi. This is Thóra Gudmundsdóttir who came to see you this morning. I won't keep you long but unfortunately we forgot to ask you about the blood on your clothes. How do you explain that?"

"That fucking shit." Hugi groaned. "The police asked me about it. I don't know what bloodstained T-shirt they mean, but I explained the blood on my clothes from the night before."

"How?" Thóra asked.

"Harald and I went to the toilet to snort up during the party. He got this huge nosebleed and some of it splashed me. The bathroom was tiny."

"Couldn't you get that corroborated?" Thóra asked. "Didn't any of the other guests remember you coming out of the bathroom covered in blood?"

"I wasn't exactly covered in blood. They were all off their heads too. No one mentioned it. No one noticed, I guess."

Damn, thought Thóra. "But the bloodstained T-shirt in your closet—do you know how it got there?"

"I haven't the foggiest." A short silence followed before he added: "I think the cops planted it. I didn't kill Harald and didn't mop up any blood with a T-shirt. I don't even know if it's my T-shirt or someone else's. They never let me see it."

"Those are serious accusations, Hugi, and to tell you the truth I don't think the police do that sort of thing. There must be another explanation, if you're telling the truth." They ended the call, and Thóra filled Matthew in.

"Well, he has an explanation for half of it," he said. "We have to find out from the other guests at the party if they remember any nosebleeds."

"Yes," Thóra said, hardly expecting it to be worth the hassle. "But even if they do, the T-shirt in the closet still needs to be explained."

A *ping* came from the computer, and they both looked at the screen. "You have new mail" appeared on a tab in the right-hand corner. Thóra grabbed the mouse and clicked the envelope icon.

It was an e-mail—from Mal.

CHAPTER 19

Hey, dead Harald.

What's up, man? I'm getting mail from someone pretending to be the Icelandic police and some scumbag lawyer [Thóra could not help being riled by this—despite having been called much worse in her legal career]. *Those jerks reckon you're dead—as if, eh? Drop me a line, anyway—it's all a bit weird.*

Bye
Mal

"Quick, quick," Matthew said. "Answer while he's still at his computer."

Thóra rushed to click "Reply." "What should I say?" she asked as she typed in the customary: "Dear Mal."

"Just anything," Matthew snapped. Very helpful.

Thóra decided to write:

> *Unfortunately it is true about Harald's death. He was murdered and won't be replying. I'm the "scumbag lawyer" who tried to contact you the other day; Harald's computer is in my safekeeping. I'm working for the Guntliebs—they are desperate to find the killer. A young man is in custody who is probably innocent of this awful deed and I suspect you may have information that could help us. Do you know what it was that Harald claimed to have found and who the "fucking idiot" is he refers to in his last e-mail to you? Please send me a phone number where I can contact you.*
>
> *Regards*
> *Thóra*

Matthew read as she typed and as soon as she had finished—in record time—he gestured impatiently and muttered: "Send it, send it."

Thóra sent the message and they waited in silence for a few minutes. At long last a pop-up announced a new message. Excitedly they looked at each other before Thóra opened it. And they were both equally disappointed.

> *Scumbag lawyer—fuck off. Take the Guntliebs with you. You all suck. I'd rather die than help you.*
>
> *All my hate*
> *Mal*

Thóra slowly breathed out. No mixed messages there. She looked at Matthew. "Could he be joking?"

Matthew caught her eye but could not tell whether she was joking too. He presumed she was. "Sure—I bet he'll send another mail with smileys bouncing all over the screen saying how much he loves the Guntliebs." He groaned. "Screw it. Harald obviously didn't speak highly of his parents to his friends. I think we can forget this guy."

Thóra sighed. "Aren't we wasting our time, then? We could go down to Kaffibrennslan, for instance, and talk to the waiter who gave Halldór his alibi, if he's on duty. I do agree it's a pretty weak testimony. If he isn't working now we can just have a coffee."

Delighted, Matthew stood up. Thóra quickly removed the memory stick, slipped it into her handbag, and switched off the computer.

There were few customers at Kaffibrennslan, so Thóra and Matthew had a choice of seats. They sat at a table close to the bar on the lower floor. While Thóra was struggling to hang her coat over the back of her chair, Matthew tried to catch the attention of the young waitress. Then Matthew turned to Thóra. "Why didn't you wear the coat you were in this morning?" he asked, goggling at the huge padded coat spread out on either side of her chair—the arms were so stuffed with goose down that they almost stood out at ninety degrees.

"I was cold," Thóra said, as surprised by his question as he seemed to be by her coat. "I keep it at the office—I wore the other coat there this morning and I wear this home in the evenings. Don't you think it's nice?"

Matthew's expression spoke volumes about his opinion of the coat. "Lovely—if you were taking core samples from an Antarctic glacier."

Thóra rolled her eyes. "God, you're so uptight," she said, smiling at the waitress who had appeared at their side.

"Can I help you?" the girl asked, returning her smile. She had a short black apron tied around her slender waist and was holding a small notepad, ready to take their order.

"Yes, please," Thóra replied. "I'll have a double espresso." She turned to Matthew. "Don't you just want tea in a china cup?"

"Ha-ha. Very funny," he said, then turned to the waitress and ordered the same as Thóra.

"Okay," she said without writing the order down. "Anything else?"

"Yes and no," Thóra said. "We were wondering if Björn Jónsson is here now. We wanted to have a word with him."

"Bjössi?" said the girl, startled. "Yes, he just got in." She looked at the clock on the wall. "His shift starts now. Should I get him for you?" Thóra thanked her, and the girl went off to fetch Bjössi and their coffee.

Matthew smiled sweetly at Thóra. "Your coat is great. I mean it. It's just so . . . huge."

"You didn't let that stop you flirting with Bella. She's huge too—so huge that she has her own center of gravity. The paper clips at the office go into orbit around her. Maybe you should get yourself one of these coats. They're incredibly comfortable."

"I can't," Matthew said, smiling back at her. "Then you'd have to sit in the back of the car. That wouldn't work. There's no way to fit two of those in the front seat."

Further discussion of coats was put on hold when the waitress arrived with their coffee. A young man was with her. He was good-looking in a slightly feminine way—his dark hair unusually well cut and groomed, and not the faintest hint of a shadow on his cheeks. "Hi, you wanted to talk to me?" he asked in a singsong voice.

"Yes, are you Björn?" said Thóra, taking one of the cups of coffee. The young man said he was and she explained who she and Matthew were. She felt it unnecessary to confuse him by speaking English, and stuck to Icelandic. Matthew said nothing and just sat there sipping his coffee. "We wanted to ask you about the night of the murder, and about Halldór Kristinsson."

Bjössi nodded gravely. "Sure, no problem—I'm allowed to talk to you, aren't I? It's not against the rules?" When Thóra assured him it wasn't, he continued. "I was working here, with some others actually." He looked around the half-empty bar. "It's not like this on weekends. It gets packed."

"But you remember him in particular?" Thóra asked, taking care not to sound as if she doubted his words.

"Dóri? You bet," Bjössi said, a little self-importantly. "I was starting to recognize him—if you know what I mean. Him and that friend of his—the foreign guy who was killed—they came here often and you couldn't help noticing them. That foreigner really stood out. Always called me 'Bear,' like my name means. Dóri came by himself sometimes, too, and I'd chat with him at the bar."

"Did he talk to you that night?"

"No, it wasn't like that. It was crazy in here and I was all over the place. But I said hello to him and we exchanged a few words. He was quite gloomy actually so I didn't hang around."

"Do you know exactly when he arrived?" pressed Thóra. "Given what you've said, you hardly had time to notice that detail—you had no reason to."

"Oh, that," Bjössi said. "He put the bill on a tab so he didn't have to pay every time he ordered another drink. We always make a note of when a customer starts paying on a tab and when he stops and actually pays." Bjössi flashed Thóra a conspiratorial smile. "He did right to pay on a tab that night, because he sure was knocking them back. His credit card would have melted from all the swipes."

"I see," said Thóra. "But are you sure he sat here drinking constantly until his friends arrived around two? Couldn't he have popped out without your noticing?"

Bjössi paused to think before answering. "Well, of course I can't swear he was here the whole time. I was pretty sure and told the police that, but in retrospect I could have been judging from what he ordered from the bar—and of course, I didn't serve him every time. He might have let someone else put a drink on his tab—I don't know." He waved his hands in the air. "But it's not such a big place, and seriously, I would have noticed if he'd left. I reckon so, anyway. I think."

Thóra was stumped. What else could she ask about that night? The waiter didn't seem that sure of himself and her confidence in Halldór's alibi had been severely shaken. After thanking Bjössi she gave him her card in case he remembered anything more, though this seemed unlikely. She turned to Matthew and her now tepid coffee and told him, between sips, what the waiter had said. They finished their coffee and Thóra noticed that it was time to go home, so they paid and left.

It was almost five but the traffic was still light. Few people were out and about in the cold and blustery weather. The handful of pedestrians hurried along without stopping to look around or window-shop. Instead of going to her office, Thóra decided to ask Matthew to drive her to the parking garage, and she'd just make her way home from there. She rang Bella to let her know that she wouldn't be in until the next morning and find out about any business involving her that had come up in her absence.

"Hello," came the answer on the phone—no mention of the company name or who was speaking.

"Bella," Thóra said, attempting to disguise her displeasure. "It's Thóra, I'm not coming back today. But I'll be in at eight tomorrow morning."

"Huh" was the delphic reply.

"Any messages for me?"

"How should I know?" Bella said.

"How? Well, I'm such an optimist I thought the secretary and switchboard operator might have accidentally taken a message. Of course that's absurd of me."

A short silence followed on the other end of the line and Thóra could almost hear Bella softly counting down the seconds. "It's five o'clock—I don't have to say anything more to you. I'm done for the day." Bella rang off.

Thóra stared at her mobile, then said—more to herself than to Matthew: "Do you reckon Bella could be that Mal character?"

"What?" Matthew had reached the parking garage and pulled in.

"Oh, nothing," Thóra said, unfastening her seat belt. "What do you do in the evenings, anyway?"

"This and that," Matthew replied. "Go out for a meal, stroll down to the bars downtown sometimes—now and again I've done some sightseeing, museums and the like."

Thóra felt sorry for him—it must be rather lonely. "It's Friday tomorrow and my children are going to stay with their father. I'll invite you round for a meal this weekend. How would you like that?"

Matthew smiled. "Great, if you promise not to cook fish. If I eat any more fish I'll start growing fins."

"No, I was thinking about something a bit cozier—like ordering a pizza," Thóra said before getting out of the car. She hoped Matthew would drive away before she reached the car she had on loan from the garage. If he thought her coat was cheesy, he'd have a heart attack seeing the vehicle she was driving. But her wish was not granted—Matthew waited to make sure she got into her car and when she unlocked the door she heard him call out to her. She looked around and saw him leaning out of the window.

"You're joking, of course," he called loudly. "Is that your car?"

Ignoring his mocking laugh, Thóra called back: "Want to swap?"

Matthew shook his head and wound up the window. Then he drove away, still chuckling to himself as far as she could tell.

The previous evening, Thóra had arranged for her daughter to go to a friend's house after school. She dropped by there to pick Sóley up and thanked the friend's mother, a young and rather sassy woman, who told her it was nothing—actually it was easier to have the two of them because they could keep each other occupied. Thóra thanked her again and told her that she would hopefully be able to repay the favor sometime soon. Sometime when the sun started rising in the west.

There was a crowd at the front door to her house—Gylfi's friends had been round and were just leaving. The floor was cluttered with a heap of coats, sneakers, and beat-up rucksacks that served as bookbags. The owners, three gangling boys whom Thóra knew well and one girl who was less familiar, were getting ready to leave and trying to identify pairs of shoes.

"Hi," said Thóra cheerily as she squeezed past the group. Her son watched from the hallway door. He seemed just as morose as he had that morning. "Were you doing your homework?" Thóra asked, well aware that this was inconceivable. At that age youngsters did not study together—anyone suggesting such a thing would be ostracized on the spot. But as a parent it was her duty to make such stupid remarks.

"Er, no," answered Patti, Gylfi's best friend for years. He was a good lad and his new thing was being able to say how many months, days, and hours he had left until he could get his driver's license. A few times Thóra had checked the figures, and generally he wasn't far off.

Thóra smiled at the girl, who looked away shyly. She simply could not remember her name, although she had been turning up at their house more and more recently. Gylfi had matured a lot—maybe her son was in love with the girl, or perhaps they were even going out together? She looked sweet enough but hardly stood knee-high to Gylfi and his friends.

Sóley, who had followed Thóra in, had taken off her shoes and coat and arranged them neatly where they belonged. She looked at the teenagers, placed her hands on her hips, and asked them in a housekeeperly voice: "Were you jumping on the bed? You're not allowed to—it ruins the mattress."

Her brother blushed with embarrassment and shrieked: "What did I do to deserve such a family of retards? I hate you both!" He stormed out and slammed the door behind him. His friends were embarrassed as well and left hurriedly.

"Bye-bye," Patti said as he closed the door behind them. Before the door shut completely he seemed to have second thoughts and stuck his head back in to announce: "You're not half as retarded as my family—Gylfi's just going through a moody phase."

Thóra smiled and thanked him. At least this was an effort at courtesy—although the wording could have been more polished. "Well," she said to her daughter, "shall we make some food?" With a conscientious nod the girl lugged one of the shopping bags into the kitchen.

After dinner together—microwave lasagna Thóra had picked up at the store and pitas she had grabbed thinking they were garlic bread—her daughter went off to her room to play while her son tidied up the dishes. He clearly regretted his rash remarks about the mental faculties of his mother and sister but could not bring himself to apologize. Thóra feigned nonchalance and hoped she was taking the right approach—maybe in the end he would tell her what was troubling him. She thought she had made it clear to him that she was there if and when he needed her. After a cautious peck on the cheek to thank him for his help, she was rewarded with a dopey grin. Then he went to his room.

Thóra decided to take advantage of the peace and quiet that had suddenly descended to examine the files she had copied from Harald's computer. She fetched her laptop and settled down on the sofa. First she looked at several shots of cooking and the tongue operation, which was dated September 17. Opening them one after the other, she zoomed in on parts that might be interesting, and this made the photographs slightly less revolting. The main theme was the mouth and the operation itself, but various details could be discerned beyond Harald's jaws. The operation had been performed in someone's house—that was certain—because what was visible of the surroundings could not possibly be a doctor's or dentist's office. She could see a coffee table littered with half-full or empty glasses, beer cans, and other trash—and a huge ashtray filled to the brim. It was also clearly not where Harald lived. This apartment looked much scruffier and cheaper than his pristine modern abode.

One photograph showed part of the body of the person performing or assisting with the operation. He or she was wearing a light brown T-shirt bearing a slogan which was made illegible by the folds in it. She managed to discern the number 100 and "*. . . lico . . .*"

No incision had been made in the first two photographs but the third was taken after the knife had been applied—blood was pouring out of the side of Harald's mouth and an arm that was visible was spattered with bloodstains. The blood must have spurted everywhere when the tongue was cut—if tongue wounds were like ordinary head injuries, it would have bled profusely. Thóra squinted at the arm and zoomed in on what looked like a tattoo. This turned out to be correct—the word "crap" was etched into the arm. No decoration or frills—just "crap." There was nothing else to see in the tongue pictures.

The cookery photographs had caught Thóra's attention because they were dated just before Harald was murdered—at the time when Hugi said he had gone off by himself and broken contact with his friends. The file properties confirmed this—they were taken on a Wednesday, three days before Harald was murdered. Thóra studied the two shots, focusing on the hands making a salad and slicing bread. Anyone could tell that they belonged to two different people. One pair was covered with scars— tattoo scars including a pentacle and a smiley with a downturned mouth and horns. This must have been Harald. The other pair was much more delicate, feminine hands with slim fingers and neatly trimmed short nails. Thóra zoomed in on one finger that had a single ring apparently set with a diamond or some other transparent stone. The ring looked too ordinary to stick in anyone's mind, but she could try showing it to Hugi to find out whether he recognized it.

One thought in particular was preying on Thóra's mind, something which had been plaguing her ever since she first went to Harald's apartment. It was the German magazine *Bunte* in the bathroom. She was absolutely certain that Harald would not read that kind of women's magazine. The Icelanders could be ruled out too. It must have been brought there by a German—and a woman. Tom Cruise and Katie Holmes had been smiling on the cover about the expected addition to their family. If her memory served her well, the baby was born that autumn. Could Harald have had a visitor from Germany—someone who stayed with him so that he did not have time to go out with his friends? Thóra called Matthew, who answered on the third ring.

"Where are you—is this a bad time?" she asked when she heard the noise in the background.

"No, no," said Matthew, his mouth full. He swallowed. "I've gone out for a meal. Had some meat. What's up—do you want to come and have dessert with me?"

"Er, no thanks." Thóra could feel how much she really wanted to. It was nice to go out to dinner, dress up, and drink a toast in glasses that someone else would wash up. "There's school tomorrow and I have to make sure the kids go to bed at a reasonable hour. No, I just called to find out if you have the number of Harald's cleaner. I suspect someone was with him just before the murder—and possibly even stayed there. All the signs are that the guest was a German woman."

"I have the number somewhere on my address list. Do you want me to phone? I've spoken to her before and she speaks good English. That might be easiest—she doesn't know you, but she'll definitely remember me because I paid her last bill."

Thóra agreed and he promised to call back. She used the time to tell her daughter to get ready for bed and was about to brush her teeth for her when Matthew phoned back. Thóra lodged her mobile between her shoulder and cheek so that she could talk while she handled Sóley's dental care.

"Listen, she says that the bed in the spare bedroom was used. And there were things in the bathroom—a disposable razor, a woman's razor—which suggests you're right."

"Did she inform the police?"

"No, she didn't think it mattered because Harald wasn't murdered in his own place. She also said there had often been guests, sometimes more than just one or two at a time. Generally there was more partying when they were around than there was with this particular visitor."

"Could he have had a German girlfriend?"

"Who flew all the way over here and then slept in the spare bed? I doubt it. I never heard any German girlfriend mentioned either."

"They could have quarreled." Thóra thought for a moment. "Or maybe it wasn't a girlfriend, just a friend or relative. His sister maybe?"

Matthew paused. "If that's the case I don't think we should go there."

"Are you crazy?" snapped Thóra. "Why the hell not?"

"She's had problems recently—her brother was murdered, and there's a minor crisis surrounding her own future."

"In what way?" asked Thóra.

"She's a very gifted cellist and wants to make a career of it. Her father wants her to study business and take over the bank. There's no one left—even if Harald were still alive he would have been out of the question. The disagreement over her studies had arisen before he was murdered."

"Does she wear jewelry?" Thóra asked. The hands on the photograph could well have belonged to a cellist—with exceptionally short and well-kept nails.

"No, never. She's not the type," Matthew answered. "She doesn't go in for accessories at all."

"Not even a little diamond ring?"

A short silence and then: "Yes, I think maybe she has. How do you know?"

After Thóra had described the photographs, Matthew promised to consider contacting the girl, and they said good-bye.

"Aren't you done yet?" her daughter said through a mouth full of toothpaste froth. She'd had to put up with having her teeth brushed for the duration of a whole phone call—pearly white, until tomorrow at least. Thóra tucked her in and read to her until she began to grow drowsy. She kissed her half-sleeping child on the forehead, switched off the light, and shut the door. Then she went back to her computer.

After two hours of perusing Harald's other files without finding anything useful, she gave up and switched off the laptop. She decided to get into bed and read the copy of *Malleus Maleficarum* that Matthew had told her to look into. It was bound to be an interesting read.

She opened the book and a folded piece of paper fell out.

"Shut up," Marta Mist growled. "It won't work unless we all concentrate."

"Shut up yourself," retorted Andri. "I can talk if I want."

Bríet thought she saw Marta Mist bare her teeth, but could not be sure because the room was dimly lit—the only light came from a few liquid candles that had been spread around the sitting room. "Oh, stop arguing and let's get this over with." She made herself comfortable on the floor where they were sitting cross-legged in a tight circle.

"Yes, for God's sake," mumbled Dóri, rubbing his eyes. "I was going to have an early night and can't be bothered to carry on with this crap all night."

"Crap?" said Marta Mist, clearly still in a temper. "I thought we all agreed to do this. Did I misunderstand you?"

Dóri groaned. "No, don't twist my words. Just get it over with."

"It's just not the same as it was at Harald's place," Brjánn chipped in. He had made little contribution until then. He scanned their faces. "Harald's gone. I'm not sure it will work without him."

Andri ignored the remark about his apartment. "We can't do much about Harald not being here." He reached for an ashtray. "What was that old cow's name again?"

"Thóra Gudmundsdóttir," answered Bríet. "The lawyer."

"Okay," said Andri. "Let's start. Agreed?" He looked at the others who either nodded or shrugged. "Who wants to start?"

Bríet looked at Marta Mist. "You start," she said, trying to butter up her friend. "You're the best at this by far, and it's important to do it properly."

Marta Mist ignored her attempt at flattery. She looked round the circle. "You know this woman could get us into a hell of a lot of trouble if she starts sticking her nose in the wrong places. It was pure luck that the cops went offtrack."

"We're all aware of that," Brjánn said on their behalf. "One hundred percent."

"Good," said Marta Mist. She placed her hands on her thighs. "Absolute silence, please." No one spoke a word. She picked up the thick pile of papers that was in the middle of the circle and a small bowl of red liquid. She put the papers down in front of her and positioned the bowl by her side. Bríet solemnly handed her a chopstick. Marta Mist dipped it into the viscous liquid and drew a symbol onto the paper with slow strokes. She closed her eyes and began to chant in a low, eerie voice: "If you wish your enemies to fear you . . ."

CHAPTER 20

Thóra had read well into the night and she woke up feeling heavy-headed and tired. She had spent a long time examining the page that fell out of the book, which turned out to contain an assortment of handwritten words and dates. Thóra assumed that the handwriting was Harald's—his name was on the flyleaf of the book. Also, some of the text was in German. He had not written it particularly neatly and Thóra was by no means certain she had read all the words correctly. What she could decipher of the writing said:

"1485 Malleus," the date apparently underlined by Harald several times and the phrase itself double-underlined. Below that, "J. A. 1550??," crossed out. Then came what seemed to be two interlaced *l*s followed by "Loricatus Lupus." Beneath that was some German which Thóra read as: "Where? Where? The ancient cross??" Half of the sheet was a kind of flow-chart with arrows linking points marked by dates and place-names. The arrangement of the points suggested this was a rough map. One point was marked "Innsbruck—1485," above it "Kiel—1486," and above that

"Roskilde." That name was marked with two dates: "1486—dead" and "1505—pardoned." There were two more points above these three. The upper one was marked "Hólar—1535," but this had been crossed out, as had its link with the other point, marked "Skálholt." Two dates accompanied that label, "1505" and "1675." A welter of arrows spread out from the latter date, all ending in question marks. To one side of them the question "The ancient cross??" was repeated. In a different pen, the word *"Gastbuch"* had been added, immediately followed by either a drawing of a small cross or the letter *t*. Thóra pondered the meaning of this. A visitors' book? The visitors' book of the cross? Beneath it was "chimney—stove—3rd symbol!" if her German was to be trusted. In the end Thóra gave up trying to decipher the chart and turned to reading the book itself.

Malleus Maleficarum turned out to be anything but pleasant. Its sheer gruesomeness held Thóra's attention. She did not read it from cover to cover; the first and second chapters were too bizarre for her to take in fully. The book was structured with questions or claims about witchcraft at the beginning of each chapter or paragraph, which were then answered or explained using outrageously flawed theological sophistry.

The stories and descriptions of the witches' deeds and rituals were incredible. Their powers seemed to know no bounds—they could conjure up storms at will, fly, transform men into cattle and other animals, cause impotence and make a man's penis appear to detach from his body. A considerable amount of space was devoted to debating whether the dismemberment was an illusion or a physical detachment. After reading it, Thóra was still not sure what the authors had concluded. Witches had to go to extraordinary lengths to acquire such powers, including cooking and/or eating babies and having sex with the devil himself. Although she was no psychologist, Thóra guessed that the authors were sorely afflicted by the vows of chastity they had sworn as Black Friar monks. This was obvious from their unpleasantly bitter depictions of women. Disgust oozed from every account and it was almost more than Thóra could take. The explanations for women's tainted, demonic character were outlandish, including the claim that the rib taken from Adam to create the first woman was curved inward—which naturally had fateful consequences.

Women would have been perfect if God had used a thighbone. All this evidence was then used to convince the reader that women were easy prey for the devil, which was why most witches were female. The poor took their share of the blame as well—they were more likely than the rich to tell lies and lack character. Thóra could hardly imagine what it was like to be a poor woman in those days.

What intrigued her most was the third and final chapter she read, which dealt with legal aspects of the Inquisition and the prosecution of witches. As a lawyer she abhorred the idea of persuading the accused that a confession would spare their lives and then offering three different ways to break that promise without acknowledging having done so. The proper procedure for arresting witches was described and it was stressed that their feet should not be allowed to touch the ground on the way to prison—they were to be carried on stretchers. Touching the ground could possibly allow the devil to endow them with the power to deny the charges until death. They were to be searched on arrival at prison, because under their clothes witches often wore magic objects made from the limbs of babies. It was also recommended to shave them, since they could conceal such objects in their hair, but there were divided views as to whether the shaving should include pubic hair.

Ways to obstruct the defense were described, for example, presenting defendants with witnesses' testimonies on two pieces of paper—one containing the testimonies and the other the names, making it impossible to know who was claiming what. This applied only when the testimonies were shown to the accused, which was not always allowed; a lengthy passage discussed when this was appropriate and when not. Anyone could give evidence at witches' trials, whereas only the testimony of people of upright character was admitted elsewhere.

The book explained how to practice torture, the interval between sessions, and regular inspections to see whether the victim could weep on the rack in the presence of the judge—which could point to innocence. In fact the tears were not to be trusted, because women would often use their saliva to give the impression of weeping. Presumably, incessant torture would not leave those poor people with many tears to spare when the judge arrived and ordered them to cry; Thóra doubted they could be in their right minds. Crying in the absence of a judge—in cells, on the rack, and the like—did not count. The ultimate goal of all this was to extract false confessions to the acts described in the first two chapters, thereby demonstrating the demonic nature of women. Any normal reader could see that such confessions would have been meaningless, extracted by torture and reeled off to please the executioners and bring the victims' own suffering to an end.

With an effort, Thóra sat up in bed. She glanced at the evil book on her bedside table. She tried to perk herself up by concentrating on the one positive conclusion she had drawn from reading it—humankind has definitely made some progress since 1500. She got up and took a shower. On her way she knocked on her son's door to wake him up. Breakfast, as usual, was a makeshift arrangement and the only one of them with time to sit down and eat was Sóley. On their way out to the car Thóra reminded them that they would be going to stay with their father that evening. They never got excited about going but afterward they were always pleased to have spent time with him. If they could wiggle their way out of horseback riding.

After she dropped off the kids Thóra hurried to the office. She took along the handwritten sheet of paper from inside the book to show to Matthew. No one was there, since there was more than half an hour to go before it opened at nine. There was plenty of time to make coffee and check her mail—to keep up with what was going on outside this bizarre case that now occupied all her time.

Bríet had arrived for her class that began at a quarter past eight but Gunnar had stopped her on her way into the room. A few words from him, and it was out of the question to attend the lesson. Instead of going into the classroom, she rushed out for a smoke on the steps. She had to calm her nerves—and also phone the others to tell them the news. She took a long, deep drag on her slim menthol cigarette—a brand Marta Mist found so weak she said Bríet could claim to be a nonsmoker with a perfectly clear conscience. Marta Mist smoked Marlboros, and while Bríet was finding her number she hoped her friend had plenty of cigarettes—they would need them.

"Hello," said Bríet, flustered, when Marta answered. "It's Bríet."

"Fucking early to call." Marta Mist's voice was hoarse and Bríet had clearly woken her up.

"You've got to get down to the university—Gunnar's gone nuts and says he'll make sure we're all expelled if we don't do what he says."

"That's bull." Marta Mist sounded properly awake now.

"We've got to phone the others and tell them to come here. I'm not going to get expelled. My dad will go ballistic and I won't get my student loan."

Marta Mist interrupted her. "Chill for a minute. How does Gunnar plan to get us expelled? I don't know about you, but my grades are fine."

"He says he's going to complain to the department board about drug-taking—he says he's got things up his sleeve. So he could get Brjánn and me expelled and then make sure the same happened to you and Andri and Dóri. We have to do what he says. I'm not risking it, anyway." Bríet was agitated. What was wrong with Marta Mist—couldn't she ever do what she was told?

"What does he want us to do?" Bríet's agitation had infected Marta Mist.

"He wants us to talk to that lawyer, Thóra. She wants to meet us and Gunnar insists that we cooperate. Actually he said he wasn't stupid enough to believe we always told the truth, but he doesn't care—just wants us to talk to her." She took a drag and exhaled fast. She heard someone at Marta Mist's end, asking what was going on.

"Okay, okay," said Marta Mist. "What about the others—have you phoned them?"

"No, you've got to help me. I want to get it over—let's all meet at ten and finish it. I have classes today."

"I'll talk to Dóri. You call Andri and Brjánn. Let's meet at the book-shop." Marta Mist hung up without another word.

Bríet scowled at her mobile. Of course it was Dóri who was with Marta. So she wasn't planning to phone anyone—just leave all the dirty work to

Bríet as usual. If she had just offered to call Andri or Brjánn it would have been fair. Bríet stubbed out her cigarette against the steps. She walked toward the bookshop, searching for Brjánn's number in her address book.

From his office window, Gunnar watched Bríet walk away. *Fine,* he thought—*I've got them panicking.* When he had met the girl earlier it had been a huge effort to keep on talking. He had nothing on them—except the certainty that they were deeply involved in drugs and God knows what else. His offer to arrange a meeting between them and the lawyer was a shot in the dark—until then they had never done a thing he asked and he did not really expect them to begin now. So he had resorted to threats—the sort of language they might understand—and he seemed to have guessed correctly.

That crowd had always annoyed him. Harald was clearly the worst, but the others were really little better. The only difference was that they had not deformed their outward appearances to match what was inside. In his desperation to rid the university of the abomination they called a history society, he had checked their files and discovered to his astonishment that some of them were outstanding students.

Lowering the blinds again, he picked up the telephone. On the table in front of him was the lawyer's card—he had to stay in her good graces and the German's, too, if he wanted to locate the manuscript that Harald had stolen. STOLEN. It was unbearable to pretend he had liked that repulsive young man and to talk about him respectfully. He was a common thief and a disgrace to himself and everyone who knew him. Gunnar put the telephone down. He had to calm himself—he couldn't phone the lawyer in this mood. Take a deep breath and think about something completely different. The Erasmus program grant, for example. The application had gone in, and there was a good chance it would be approved. Gunnar managed to pull himself together. He picked up the telephone and dialed the number on the card.

"Thóra, hello. Gunnar here," he said in the politest voice he could manage. "It's about Harald's friends—you wanted to meet them?"

CHAPTER 21

Thóra had not seen so much bad posture in one place since her son cele-
brated his sixteenth birthday. Yet the young people in front of her and
Matthew were almost ten years older. They were all sitting as if they had
dropped into the sofa out of the sky—apart from the tall red-haired
girl—and staring at their toes. After Gunnar called that morning, Thóra
had contacted Bríet and arranged for the group to meet her and Matthew.
Bríet did not sound very pleased but reluctantly agreed to round them up
and meet at eleven o'clock—at a place where they could smoke. Strapped
for choices, Thóra had suggested Harald's apartment. Her proposal was
greeted as grumpily as the idea of meeting in the first place, but judging
from the curt exchange that preceded it, Thóra realized that she could
have invited them to Paris and earned the same response. Matthew was
delighted with the venue, which he thought might throw them off balance and make them more likely to tell the truth.

   While they were waiting for the students, Thóra showed Matthew
the handwritten sheet of paper that had been inside *The Witches' Hammer*.

They pored over it for some time without reaching a solid conclusion except that "Innsbruck—1485" was clearly connected with Kramer's arrival there and, presumably, with the old letters Harald was so enchanted with. Thóra was fairly certain that "J.A." stood for Bishop Jón Arason, because 1550 was the year of his execution. On the other hand, she could not figure out why Harald had crossed it out. As far as they could see, this was how Harald imagined the precious object's travels. Matthew had never heard of the visitors' book of the cross—there was no visitors' book in the apartment, nor did he recall the police taking it away during their search. The doorbell disturbed any further speculation.

The students arranged themselves in Harald's living room, sitting close together on the two sofas with Thóra and Matthew facing them on chairs. Thóra had found a few ashtrays and the air was already thick with smoke.

"What do you want from us anyway?" asked the red-haired girl, Marta Mist. Her friends turned to look at her, relieved that a leader had emerged to divert attention from them. They all smoked nonstop.

"We just wanted to talk to you about Harald," said Thóra. "As you know, we've repeatedly tried to meet you but have always received a less than warm response."

Marta Mist was unruffled. "We've been busy at school and we've got better things to do than talk to people we don't know from Adam. Actually, we're under no obligation to talk to you. We've all made statements to the police."

"Yes, quite right," Thóra said, trying to conceal how much the girl got on her nerves, as in fact they all did. "We're very grateful to you for taking the time to come and we promise we won't keep you for long. As you know, we're looking into Harald's murder on behalf of his family in Germany and we understand you were his closest circle of friends."

"Well, I don't know; we went around with him quite a bit but we have no idea what he did on his own, naturally," said Marta Mist, and Bríet nodded solemnly in agreement. The others just stared into their laps.

"You talk like you're one person, not five," said Matthew. "We've spoken to Hugi Thórisson, whom you all know, of course, and according to him it was you, Halldór, who went around with Harald the most—helped him with translations and other things." He addressed his words to Dóri, who sat squashed up against Marta Mist. "Am I correct?"

Dóri looked up. "Er, yeah, we hung around together quite a bit. Harald had trouble with Icelandic documents and stuff that I helped him with. We were good mates." He shrugged to emphasize that their friendship had been fairly ordinary.

"You're a good mate of Hugi's too, aren't you?" Thóra asked.

"Yes. We're childhood friends," Dóri said, and looked down. With a deft jerk of his head he let his hair fall down to avoid further eye contact.

"It must matter to you that we have a clear picture of what happened. One of your friends was murdered and another friend is suspected of killing him. I'd expect you to be eager to help us. Right?" Matthew smiled at Dóri but it failed to penetrate his hair and reach his eyes. He turned to the others. "And the rest of you—the same applies to you, of course?"

They all indicated their agreement by muttering "yes" down into their chests or nodding.

"Good." Matthew slapped his thigh. "So we're all set. Apart from where to start." He looked over at Thóra. "Thóra, would you like to do the honors?"

Thóra smiled at the students. "How about you tell us where you met Harald and explain the nature of this magic society of yours? We find it all very peculiar."

Everyone looked at Marta Mist, hoping that she would take the task on. But she passed the question on to Dóri with a nudge of her elbow, which looked unnecessarily forceful to Thóra. Dóri grimaced, but answered. "How we met? I first met Harald with Hugi last year. They'd met at a bar in town. I thought he was a laugh and we started hanging around together, like you do. We went out to restaurants and bars and concerts and stuff. Then Harald asked if we were interested in joining a society he was thinking about setting up and we just said yes. That's how we met the others."

Marta Mist took over. "I joined the society through Bríet. She'd met

Harald in class and wanted me to see what they were up to." Bríet nodded fervently in agreement.

"What about you?" Thóra directed her words at Andri and Brjánn who sat side by side, smoking.

"Us?" Andri coughed, choking on the smoke he had forgotten to exhale.

"Yes," Thóra replied. "You two." She pointed at them to dispel all doubt.

Brjánn went first. "I'm doing history and I heard about the society the same way as Bríet—I'd chatted to Harald a bit before and he invited me to join. I took Andri along for a laugh." Andri smiled sheepishly.

"And what was the point of this society, if I may ask? We understood from Hugi that it mainly involved orgies—disguised as meetings of people who were interested in sorcery in the historical sense."

The three boys grinned while Marta Mist turned down the corners of her mouth and said in tones of outraged innocence: "Orgies? There were no orgies. We were learning about sorcery and witchcraft culture in ancient times. The old stories really aren't so dull after all, they're really interesting. The fact that we had a bit of fun after the meetings is irrelevant, and Hugi's got the wrong end of the stick as usual. He never had a clue what that society was about." She leaned back and folded her arms. Her frown stayed put. She glared at Matthew and Thóra. "Of course you have no idea what it was about either—I bet you think we were decapitating chickens and sticking pins in homemade dolls."

"Would you be so kind as to explain the world of witchcraft, then?" asked Matthew.

Marta Mist groaned. "I'm not going to play teacher with you. All you need to understand is that magic is just an individual's attempt to influence his own life in unconventional ways—at least, unconventional to the modern mind. In its day it was very common and for those born into poverty at the time it was the only hope they had of possibly changing their circumstances for the better. It mainly involves performing acts that will twist events in your favor—sometimes at someone else's expense, sometimes not. In my view, when you've made the effort to perform the charm you've taken one step toward a specific aim and you can focus on it better afterward, so you're more likely to achieve it than before."

"Can you give me an example?" said Thóra.

"Winning love or success; healing; harming an enemy. There's no limit, really. Most of the old charms are connected with basic needs, though—life wasn't so complicated back then."

After reading *Malleus Maleficarum,* Thóra begged to differ. To her mind at least, it was very complicated to try to defend someone in a judicial system that constantly bent and changed the rules according to the interests of the prosecution. "So what do you use in your spells?" she asked, and to get a rise out of Marta Mist she added: "Apart from headless chickens and homemade dolls?"

"Very funny," said Marta Mist, without a trace of a smile. "In Iceland it was mainly magical symbols—although they often had to do more than carve or draw them to complete the spell. We know of magical symbols from other parts of Europe, too, and the same applied to them—it wasn't always enough just to draw them."

"Such as?" Matthew asked.

"Reciting a charm, collecting animal bones, human bones, the hair of a virgin. That sort of thing. Nothing serious," Marta Mist answered coldly.

"Yes, and sometimes human body parts," Bríet interjected. The group suddenly fell silent. She blushed and clammed up.

"Really?" Matthew said with feigned surprise. "Like what? Hands? Hair?" He paused briefly. "Or maybe eyes?"

No one said anything until Marta Mist spoke up. "I've never read of any spell where eyes are needed—apart from the eyes of animals."

"What about the rest of you? Do you know about any such spells?" asked Matthew.

None of them spoke, but they all shook their heads. "Nope," Brjánn said eventually.

"What about fingers?" Thóra asked quickly. "Have you read about—or performed—a spell that needs a finger?"

"No." Dóri's voice was firm and he swept his hair from his eyes in order to press his point home by looking Thóra and Matthew in the eye. "We want to make it perfectly clear that we haven't been doing spells that use human body parts. I don't know what you're insinuating, but it's ridiculous. We didn't kill Harald—you can rule that out for a start. The cops have our alibis and had them checked out." Dóri leaned forward and took a cigarette from one of the packets on the table. He lit it, took a deep drag, and exhaled slowly.

"So Hugi killed him, then?" Thóra asked. "Are you saying that?"

"No, I didn't say that at all. You ought to listen more carefully," Dóri said heatedly. He leaned forward as if about to say more, but Marta Mist put her arm out and pushed him back against the sofa.

Then she spoke, much calmer than Halldór. "I don't know where your logic is coming from, but just because we didn't kill Harald doesn't automatically mean that Hugi did. Dóri was just pointing out that we didn't kill Harald. *Basta*." Now it was Marta Mist's turn to lean back in the sofa. She plucked the cigarette from between Dóri's fingers, took a drag, and returned it. Bríet's face signaled annoyance; this obvious sign of intimacy seemed to jostle her nerves.

"Hugi didn't kill him. He's not like that," Dóri muttered gruffly. He pushed Marta Mist's arm away and reached across the table to tap the ash from his cigarette.

"What about you? Are you like that? If I remember correctly, you didn't have as good an alibi as your friends." Matthew stared at Dóri and waited for a response.

And it came. Dóri's voice deepened in anger and as soon as he started speaking he shifted to the edge of the sofa—as close to Matthew as he could get without falling off. "Harald was my friend. My good friend. We looked out for each other, did stuff for each other. I would never have killed him. Never. You're even wider off the mark than the cops, and you don't know what the fuck you're going on about." To punctuate his words he stabbed his burning cigarette at Matthew.

"What did you do for him, anyway? Apart from translating for him?" interrupted Thóra.

Dóri took his eyes off Matthew and glared just as vehemently at

Thóra. He opened his mouth as if about to say something, then stopped. After taking a last puff and stubbing out his cigarette, he moved back to his place on the sofa.

Brjánn, the history student, assumed the role of peacemaker. "Er, I don't understand exactly what you're driving at—of course someone killed Harald and if it wasn't Hugi, who was it? But you'll save yourselves a lot of time and effort if you just accept we're telling the truth. None of us killed Harald. We had no reason to—he was fun, always doing crazy things, really generous, and a good friend and companion to us all. Our society's nothing without him, for example. Not to mention the fact that none of us could have killed him—we weren't anywhere nearby and plenty of witnesses can confirm that."

Andri, who was working on a master's degree in chemistry, backed him up. His eyes were glassy and Thóra had a faint suspicion that he was high. Perhaps his interest in chemistry went beyond the realms of academia. "It's completely true. Harald was unique; none of us would ever have wanted to get rid of him. He could be sarcastic and acted weird sometimes, but he was always really decent when it came down to it."

"How lovely," Matthew said witheringly. "But I'd like to know one thing. You were all at the party apart from Halldór. Do you remember Hugi and Harald going into the bathroom together and coming out with bloodstains on their clothes?"

All the students shook their heads, except Halldór. "No one was thinking about clothes in there." Andri shrugged. "That may well have happened but I for one don't remember it." The other three nodded in agreement.

They sat and said nothing for a while. Several cigarettes were stubbed out and more were lit. Matthew broke the silence. "So you don't know who killed Harald?"

In unison, the group said firmly: "No."

"And you've never used body parts, like a finger for example, in your black magic?" he went on.

With less synchronization: "No."

"And you don't recognize this magic symbol?" Matthew threw a drawing of the magic symbol that had been carved into Harald's chest onto the table.

In unison again: "No."

"That would be more convincing if you looked at the paper," Matthew said sarcastically. None had done more than barely glance at the drawing.

"The cops showed us that symbol. We know perfectly well what you're talking about," drawled Marta Mist. She laid her hand casually on Dóri's thigh.

"Fair enough—I understand. But can you tell us what happened to all the money Harald transferred to Iceland shortly before he died?" asked Matthew.

"No, we don't know anything about that. We were Harald's friends, not his accountants."

"Did he buy anything, or talk about buying something?" Thóra asked, directing her words at Bríet, whom she thought most likely to tell the truth.

"He was always buying things," Bríet said, darting her eyes toward Marta Mist and Dóri. Noticing the former's hand on the latter's thigh, she turned back to Thóra and added: "If not for himself, then for Dóri. They were so close." She smiled maliciously.

Thóra noticed a blush fill Dóri's cheeks. "What did he buy for you, and why?" she asked.

Dóri rocked awkwardly on the sofa. "It wasn't like that. Sometimes he gave me this or that in exchange for the help I gave him."

Thóra refused to let him off the hook. "Like what?"

Dóri blushed even more. "Just stuff." He flicked his hair back over his eyes.

Matthew slapped his thigh again—more determined now than before. "Well, folks. I have an idea. Marta Mist, Bríet, Brjánn, and Andri—you don't know anything, so you claim, and there doesn't seem much to be had out of you. How about you going home to study, or to class, or whatever it is you're so busy with—and Thóra and I can have a quiet chat with Dóri?" He addressed Halldór. "Isn't that best? It might be less awkward."

"As if!" Marta Mist shrieked. "Dóri doesn't know any more than the rest of us." She turned to Dóri. "You don't have to stay. Let's all leave."

Dóri said nothing at first, then brushed her hand from his thigh and shrugged. "Okay."

"Okay? Okay what? Are you coming with us?" Marta Mist asked irritably.

"No," replied Dóri. "I want to get this over with. I'm staying."

Marta Mist's expression darkened, but she restrained herself and feigned indifference. She bent over Dóri and whispered something to him before standing up. He nodded vacantly. Thóra watched as Marta Mist planted a soft kiss on Dóri's head and Bríet pretended not to notice. Andri and Brjánn busily put out their cigarettes and got to their feet. There was no mistaking their relief.

CHAPTER 22

Matthew showed the students to the door. Meanwhile, Thóra and Dóri sat in the modern living room with the horrors of the past all around them. Thóra felt sorry for the young man, who obviously wished he was somewhere else. In a way the circumstances reminded her of her own son—a young man locked in a mysterious inner struggle.

"You know we're just looking for the truth, don't you? We're not wondering about anything stupid you may have been up to," she said to break the silence and lighten the oppressive atmosphere. "Really, we agree with you on the basics of the case—that Hugi is innocent, or at least facing more serious charges than he deserves."

Dóri avoided looking at her. "I don't believe Hugi killed him," he said in a low voice. "It's a load of bullshit."

"You're fond of your friend, I can tell," said Thóra. "If you want to help him, by far the best course is not to conceal anything from us. Remember that your friend can't expect help from anyone except us."

Dóri grunted, without indicating whether or not he would help them.

Matthew came back and threw himself down in the chair. He watched Dóri thoughtfully for a while. "A strange circle of friends you've got. The girls didn't exactly look like they'd fall into each other's arms on the way out."

Dóri shrugged. "They're all kind of down at the moment."

"I see. Well, shouldn't we get down to business?" asked Matthew.

"I don't mind," Dóri replied. "Just ask and I'll try to answer." When he reached out for a cigarette, Thóra noticed his hands were shaking.

"Okay, buddy," said Matthew, sounding almost paternal. "We're interested in a number of points you can surely help us with. One is the money that Harald spent and another is the historical research you worked on with him. Let's begin with the money. What can you tell us about his finances?"

"Finances? I knew nothing about that, I swear. But you didn't have to be Einstein to see that he was filthy rich." Dóri gestured around the room, then shrugged. "His car was pretty flashy, too, and he dined out a lot. Unfortunately it wasn't a lifestyle the rest of us could afford."

"Did he dine out by himself?" asked Thóra. "Since you were poor students."

This was clearly an uncomfortable question. "Well, sometimes." He puffed on his cigarette. "Sometimes I went with him. He invited me."

"So he took you along and paid the bill, is that it?" Matthew asked, and Dóri nodded. "More often than he dined alone?" Dóri nodded again. "What else did he treat you to?"

Dóri was seized with a sudden interest in the ashtray and stared at it as if the answer to the question was to be found there. "Well, just stuff."

"That's not an answer," Thóra said calmly. "Just tell us—we haven't come here to pass judgment on you or Harald."

A short pause and then: "He paid for all sorts of stuff for me. My rent, textbooks, clothes, taxis. Dope. Everything really."

"Why?" asked Matthew.

Dóri shrugged. "Harald said the money was his to do with as he pleased—he never denied himself something just because his friends were broke. I found it embarrassing, but I was flat broke and he was such a fun guy. There were never any hassles. I tried to repay him by helping with those translations and other stuff."

"What kind of stuff?" Matthew asked.

"Nothing." Dóri's blushing cheeks grew even redder. "It was nothing sexual, if that's what you think. Neither Harald nor I were, are, on that side of the fence. There have been plenty of girls."

Thóra and Matthew exchanged a look. The spending that Dóri described was peanuts compared with the amount that had disappeared. "Do you know of any large investment Harald made just before the murder?"

Dóri looked up. From his expression it was plain that he was telling the truth. "No, no idea. He never mentioned anything like that. Actually, I hardly saw him the week before—he was busy and I was trying to catch up on my course work."

"You don't know what he was up to, or why he didn't meet you on those days?" Thóra interjected.

"No. I phoned him a few times and he just wasn't in the mood to do anything. I don't know why."

"So you hadn't seen him for several days when he was murdered?" asked Matthew.

"No—just talked to him on the phone."

"Didn't that strike you as odd? Or was he in the habit of locking himself away for days on end?" Matthew persisted.

Dóri thought about it. "I didn't wonder about it then, but now that you mention it, it was a bit unusual. It hadn't happened before, anyway, I don't think it had. I asked him what was going on, but he said he just needed a bit of time by himself. But he was cheerful and all that."

"Didn't you develop a grudge against him over that time?" asked Thóra. It must have been strange for him to lose his best friend for several days with no explanation, considering how much time they spent together.

"No, not like that. I had plenty to do for my classes anyway. And I took shifts and stuff like that. So I had lots of other things to think about."

"You work at the hospital in Fossvogur, don't you?" Thóra asked. Dóri nodded. "How do you manage to work there, study medicine, and do all that partying?"

Dóri shrugged. "It isn't a full-time job, no way. I do the occasional relief shift, that's all. I work there over summer vacations, and if there's a crisis in the winter, I cover if someone's sick or can't come in. As far as my courses go, I'm just incredibly organized about studying. I've always found learning easy."

"What do you do at the hospital?" asked Matthew.

"This and that. I work as an assistant in surgery—clean the instruments after operations, clear up, that sort of thing. Nothing important."

Matthew gave him a meaningful look. "Clear up what? I'm just curious to ask, I know very little about hospitals."

"Just stuff," Dóri replied, reaching for his cigarettes again. "Garbage and things."

"Aha!" Matthew cried. "What's the name of your superior, or someone we could ask about this work—in particular about the night Harald was murdered?"

Dóri picked at one of the studded straps on his left wrist and clearly did not know how to reply. "Gunnur Helgadóttir," he eventually muttered in a sullen voice. "She's the senior surgical nurse."

"I have a question," said Thóra as she scribbled down the name. "Who did Harald's tongue job? It was you, wasn't it?"

Dóri was about to light a cigarette but stopped, startled. "Why? What difference does that make?"

"I want to know. Harald has photos on his computer showing the operation and it was done in someone's house. Presumably someone he knew. The operation isn't the issue—I just want to know."

Hesitantly, Dóri looked at each of them in turn. Thóra thought he was probably weighing whether the operation required professional qualifications or was illegal. After biting his lower lip for a while he finally said: "No. I didn't do it."

"May I see your upper arm?" Thóra asked, smiling as she remembered what Hugi had said about Dóri's regrets over the tattoo he had there.

"Why?" replied Dóri, leaning back in the sofa to put more distance between them.

"We just want to," said Matthew, moving to the edge of his chair. He had no idea where Thóra was taking this. "Be a good boy and roll up your sleeves for the nice lady."

Dóri went red as a beet. Matthew moved even farther forward on the edge of his seat, and Dóri edged farther back in the sofa. Suddenly he lost his nerve. Glowering, he rolled up his sleeves. "Here," he snapped, and held out his arms. Thóra leaned forward and smiled. " 'Crap'?" she read, looking at his right arm just above the wrist.

"So?" Dóri said, rolling his sleeves down again.

"Interesting," Thóra said. "The person who performed the operation on Harald had exactly the same tattoo." She grinned at Dóri as she pointed at his right arm. "So, what's the story?"

"Nothing," Dóri said slowly. He ran his fingers through his hair, then squeezed his eyes shut. "Okay, I did it. We were at Hugi's place. Harald had been pestering me for ages to do it for him and in the end I gave in. I borrowed the instruments from the hospital and stole some anesthetic. Nobody missed it. Hugi helped me. It was pretty disgusting. But it looked cool."

It sure did, Thóra thought. "I wouldn't imagine the hospital would be very pleased to hear that you were stealing drugs—would they?"

"Of course not. That's why I don't want word to get around," replied Dóri. "It's not something most people would understand, and I don't want to get called a freak."

Matthew shook his head, then suddenly changed tack. "I'd like to ask you about one thing that may sound rather strange—or perhaps not; you've presumably been around a bit." After a quick pause in which he caught Dóri's gaze with his own, he continued. "Were you ever aware that Harald practiced sex using asphyxiation to increase the pleasure?"

Dóri's face went bright red again. "I don't want to discuss that," he retorted.

"Why not?" Matthew asked. "Who knows, it may have led to Harald's death."

Dóri's knees bounced up and down as he tapped his feet on the shiny veneered floor. "He didn't die like that," he said in a half whisper.

Thóra spoke. "How would you know that?"

The beat of Dóri's feet grew faster. He remained silent. Neither Thóra nor Matthew said anything—they just stared at the young man and waited. In the end he gave in, took a deep breath, and spoke. "Fuck knows what this has to do with anything, but yes, I knew Harald did that a bit."

"And you know this from whom?" Matthew asked sharply.

Dóri's feet stopped tapping. "He told me. He suggested I try it." He said no more, his eyes flicking from Matthew to Thóra.

"And did you?" she asked.

"No," he answered firmly, and Thóra believed him. "I might do some crazy things but that's the craziest shit I've ever seen."

"Seen?" Matthew repeated.

Dóri's blush grew even deeper. "Not exactly seen—I didn't mean that. Been involved with is more like it." He looked down at the floor. "It was this autumn. I'd passed out on the sofa here after a party and I woke up in the night to this awful gasping noise." He looked up at Matthew. "I don't know how I was lucky enough to come round—normally I'm right out of it when I'm in that state—but anyway, I woke up and went to check it out and saw Harald who was literally in his death throes." Thóra thought she noticed the young man shudder at the recollection. "I undid a belt that was tied really tight around his neck. It wasn't easy, because he'd tied one end to the radiator in his room. Then I managed to bring him around with CPR—only just."

"Are you sure he wasn't trying to commit suicide?" Thóra asked.

Glancing at her, Dóri shook his head. "No, it wasn't a suicide attempt. Believe me. I'd rather not go into details about the state I found him in." Now it was Thóra's turn to blush, which seemed to cheer Dóri up when he noticed. He went on, emboldened. "Then I talked it over with Harald and he freely admitted what he'd been up to. He even suggested that I try it—he said it was far-out. But he'd been in danger and was fully aware of the fact. He was scared to death."

"So you don't think he gave up the habit after that shock?" asked Matthew.

"I bet he didn't," Dóri answered. "Though I don't know for sure—he was scared shitless."

"Do you remember when this was?" Matthew asked.

"The early hours of the eleventh of September," he said without a moment's thought.

Matthew nodded pensively. He looked at Thóra and said in German: "He changed his will ten days later." Thóra nodded too, convinced now that the young man in front of them was the Icelandic heir named in the will. He had just saved Harald's life days before the will was altered; it was unthinkable not to mention him in it.

"I understand German, you know," said Dóri, grinning slyly.

His expression equally malicious, Matthew did not respond. Instead he said: "Hugi told us that Harald was sometimes nasty to you in front of the others—in fact, he humiliated you, if I remember correctly. Didn't that upset you?"

Dóri snorted. "What's he going on about? You know Harald wasn't like normal people. He could wind me up, but he could be a real laugh too. Most of the time he treated me great, especially when there was just the two of us. But when we were with the others he could be a bastard every now and again. It didn't bother me—Hugi can tell you that—and Harald always apologized afterward. It didn't make any difference, just a drag while it lasted."

Thóra didn't think it took much intelligence to see through this statement. Surely he must have found it unbearable. But there was little point in probing him for details. "So what can you tell us about Harald's research?" she asked. "Can you describe what form your help took?"

Dóri answered immediately, happy to change the subject. "It was nothing special. I really only helped him with translations, with a bit of resource work too. He went all over the place—I couldn't see the connections, but I'm not a historian so that's not saying much. He sort of wandered from one thing to the next—in the middle of reading a passage I'd translated from Icelandic into English, he would suddenly ask me to read something else, and so on."

"Can you cite any examples of articles or topics he was interested in?" asked Matthew.

"Er, I can't give you a complete list. When it started I was mainly translating passages from Ólína Thorvardardóttir's Ph.D. dissertation on the era of witch burnings, then he became interested in Skálholt because of a text about sorcery by some of the students at the school there, and a book of witchcraft that was in circulation. He also had an old letter in Danish—I wasn't so great at translating that but I did my best. It was about an emissary and something I didn't understand properly. When he got that he suddenly changed tack, stopped wondering about witch burnings so much and shifted back a century or so.

"I remember translating a passage for him from a description of Iceland by Bishop Oddur Einarsson from around 1590. It was about Hekla and I remember an account in it of a man who went mad after climbing the mountain and looking down into the crater. And he was fascinated by the eruption of Hekla in 1510, and Bishop Jón Arason and his execution in 1550, and Bishop Brynjólfur Sveinsson. Yes, then suddenly he wanted to know everything about the Irish monks. So you could say he was still going back at the time of his murder—to the time before Iceland was properly settled."

From this recitation of dates it was obvious that the young man had a cast-iron memory. Not surprising that he could do his courses in spite of all that partying, Thóra thought. "Irish monks?" she asked.

Dóri nodded. "Yes, the hermits who were here before the Vikings arrived."

"Okay," said Thóra, uncertain what to ask next. Then she remembered poor old Gunnar, who had set up the meeting with Harald's friends. "That old Danish letter—do you know where it came from or where it ended up?"

Dóri shook his head. "I have no idea where he got it—he had other old letters that he was comparing with it. They were in a leather wallet, but the Danish one wasn't. It's bound to be around somewhere."

"Do you recognize the name Mal?" Matthew asked, out of the blue.

Dóri looked at them and shook his head. "No, never heard of him. Why?"

"Oh, no reason," said Matthew.

Dóri was about to say something when his mobile rang. He took it out, looked at the screen, pulled a face, and put it back in his pocket.

"Your mom?" Matthew asked Dóri, grinning.

"Right," he replied bitterly.

A text message alert bleeped in his pocket. Since Dóri made no move for his mobile, Thóra fired her next question. "Do you know anything about a visitors' book that Harald may have owned or talked about? The visitors' book of the cross, or something to that effect?"

Dóri looked baffled. "The visitors' book of the Cross? You mean the religious sect, the Cross?"

"No, not that," replied Thóra. "So you never heard any mention of a visitors' book?"

"Nope."

Matthew clenched his fists. "Tell us about the raven Harald was trying to buy."

Dóri's Adam's apple leaped in his throat. "Raven?" His voice had risen an octave.

"Yes," Thóra chipped in. "We know he was trying to buy a raven. Do you know why?"

Dóri shrugged. "No. But I can appreciate him wanting to own a raven. Interesting birds."

Thóra was convinced that he was lying, but could not work out the best response. Matthew took over before she decided. "Do you know anything about a trip that Harald made to Hólmavík to see the sorcery and witchcraft exhibition?"

"No," said Dóri, clearly lying again.

"What about Hótel Rangá?" Thóra asked.

"No." Another lie.

Matthew looked at Thóra. "Hólmavík, Rangá. Maybe we should do a bit of traveling?" Dóri's expression did not suggest that he approved of this idea.

CHAPTER 23

Dóri was enormously relieved as he hurried away from the house. He looked over his shoulder when he had gone through the gate and onto the sidewalk, but neither Thóra nor Matthew seemed to be watching him from the window. He thought he noticed a curtain twitching on the lower floor and cursed the nosy neighbor. That scraggy old bitch was still up to her tricks, he thought—she never gave Harald a moment's peace, complained about every cough and grunt.

The morning after one of their first parties that summer, Dóri was sent to the door to hear her tirade, and how that woman could nag! He had been so hungover that every word and every wave of sound that came with it felt like the blow of a hammer on his forehead. He shuddered at the recollection, especially at how it had all ended—he had to push the woman out of the way to put his head outside the door and vomit. Understandably she was not impressed, but Harald managed to appease her that evening. For the rest of the summer, Dóri had to keep a low profile whenever he visited. But the other party guests thought the story was hilarious when Dóri finally managed to crawl back up to recount it.

His mobile rang. Dóri took it from his pocket and saw on the screen that it was Marta Mist—again. This time he answered. "What?"

"You done?" Impatient and irritable. "We're waiting for you, come over."

"Where?" Dóri didn't feel like facing anyone at the moment. He just wanted to go home and lie down but knew he wouldn't have the chance. Marta Mist would phone again and again, and she would come by in the end if he did not answer. Best to get it over and done with.

"101—hurry up." She hung up and Dóri quickened his pace even more. It was cold outside and he was exhausted. Before he knew it he was in the hotel lobby, shaking off the drifting snow that had gathered on his hair on the way. He ran his fingers through his hair, then shook his head again. Then he opened the door and went in. Naturally they were sitting in the smoking section—with a few cups of coffee and one glass of beer in front of them. Suddenly, Dóri felt an uncontrollable craving for a beer. He went over to them and sat down in a chair, even though Marta Mist and Bríet had shifted apart to make room for him between them. He could not bear the thought of sitting pressed up against them at the moment.

The girls tried not to look affronted, and Dóri watched them slowly shift back to try to fill the space inconspicuously. Marta Mist was a genius at keeping her cool. She rarely showed any emotions other than outright fury and contempt. Wounded pride was not on her agenda. "Why the fuck didn't you answer the phone?" she snarled. "We've been dying to hear from you."

This infuriated Dóri. "What's wrong with you? I was talking to those lawyers. What was I supposed to say over the phone?" When no one spoke, Dóri repeated the question. "Eh? What was I supposed to say?"

Marta Mist brushed this off. "You could have freakin' texted back. That wouldn't have been too much to ask."

"Oh, of course," said Dóri sarcastically. "That would have looked good. What do you think I am? A thirteen-year-old girl?"

Brjánn chipped in. "What happened—are you okay?" he said calmly while sipping his beer.

It was more than Dóri could take. He waved to the waiter and ordered a large beer. Then he turned back to the group. "It went just fine—you know. They have their little suspicions but don't really know anything." Dóri tapped on the edge of the table with the fingers of his right hand while he searched with his left for the cigarette packet in his coat pocket. He could not find it. "I left my cigarettes there—could you lend me one?"

Bríet tossed her packet at him, and Dóri groaned. They were typical girls' cigarettes, snow-white with menthol, and super slim to top it off. But he snatched up the packet and took one all the same. A shame that Marta Mist was sulking—she smoked real cigarettes, Marlboro. He took a drag, then removed the cigarette from his mouth, looked at it and shook his head. "How can you smoke this crap?"

"Some people say 'thank you,'" grumbled Bríet.

"Sorry. I'm just so wound up." The beer arrived and after a long draught Dóri puffed out his cheeks and exhaled with a sigh. "Ah, that's better."

"You didn't tell them anything, did you?" said Marta Mist. Her rage had subsided.

Dóri took another sip, shaking his head. "No, nothing important. I told them a lot of stuff of course—they grilled me nonstop and I had to answer."

Marta Mist looked thoughtful, then nodded, apparently satisfied. "Absolutely sure?"

Dóri winked. "Absolutely sure—don't worry."

Marta Mist smiled. "My hero."

"What else?" Dóri said casually, waving his chic cigarette in front of his face. "Don't I look cute?"

Andri giggled and tossed his own packet across the table to Dóri. "What do you think they'll do next? Do they want to see us again?"

"No, I doubt it," Dóri replied.

"Good," said Brjánn. "Hopefully they'll run round in circles and give up."

Bríet was the only one not happy. "What about Hugi? Have you completely forgotten him?" She looked round at them all, shocked.

The smile vanished from Dóri's face. "No. Of course not." He took another drink of his beer, which did not taste as good as before.

Marta Mist punched Bríet on the arm, making her yelp. "What's wrong with you anyway? They'll never give up—they'll discover something. The important thing is that we don't get mixed up in it. You and your pessimism."

"People don't get convicted of murders they didn't commit—he'll get off, you wait and see," Andri scoffed.

"What planet are you on?" Bríet asked, undeterred by the pain in her arm. It wasn't often that she dared to confront Marta Mist, but she couldn't help resenting the way she acted with Dóri. "Innocent people get convicted all the time."

"Stop bickering," said Marta Mist, her eyes fixed on Dóri. "It'll be okay, don't worry. Let's go and get something to eat. I'm starving."

They stood and gathered their belongings. When they went to pay for the drinks, Marta Mist pulled Dóri aside. "You got rid of all the—you know?"

Dóri averted his gaze but Marta Mist grabbed him by the chin and forced him to look in her eyes. "Haven't you got rid of it?"

Dóri nodded. "It's all gone. Don't worry."

"I don't even dare keep a joint at home. You'd better be just as careful. If those two start stirring things up, the cops might get ideas and turn up with search warrants all over the place. Are you sure you moved it all?"

Dóri straightened his back and stared into her eyes. He announced firmly: "I swear. It's all gone."

With a smile, Marta Mist let go of his chin. "Come on, let's pay."

Dóri watched her walk away. How amusing that she believed him. She, who always saw through him when he tried to lie to her. He was clearly improving in the dishonesty department. Cool.

Thóra tried not to be distracted by the bushy eyebrows of the man sitting in front of them. She and Matthew were in the office of Thorbjörn

Ólafsson, who had supervised Harald's dissertation. "Thank you very much for seeing us," she said, smiling.

"It's nothing," replied Thorbjörn. "If you ought to thank anyone it should be Gunnar—he arranged the meeting. But I'm impressed that you could come at such short notice." Thorbjörn had phoned shortly after Dóri had left Harald's apartment, and Thóra and Matthew decided to see him at once. Thorbjörn put down the pencil he had been rolling between his fingers. "So what is it you want to know?"

Thóra went first. "I presume Gunnar explained our connection with Harald?" Thorbjörn nodded and she continued. "We wanted to hear your opinion of Harald and also if you could tell us something about his studies, in particular what he was researching."

Thorbjörn laughed. "I can't say I really knew him. I don't make a habit of mixing with my students much—it doesn't tempt me. I'm interested in the progress of their studies but personally they don't appeal to me."

"But you must have formed an opinion about him?" Thóra asked.

"Of course I did. I thought he was a peculiar character, to say the least—and not just because of his appearance. But he didn't bother me in the slightest—unlike Gunnar, for example, who couldn't really stand him. I enjoyed having students who did things their own way. And he was extremely diligent and focused. As a rule I don't make any other demands."

Thóra raised her eyebrows. "Focused? Gunnar gave the impression his research was quite scattered."

Thorbjörn snorted. "Gunnar's from the old school. Harald wasn't. Gunnar wants his students to stick to a prearranged course. Harald was more the type I like—on his journeys he liked to take a look down the side streets, so to speak. That's the way to go about it. You don't know where it will lead and it takes longer, but sometimes it yields windfalls."

"So Harald wasn't going to change his dissertation topic, as Gunnar claims?" Matthew asked.

"Far from it," Thorbjörn replied. "Gunnar's always convinced everything's going to the dogs. I wonder if he was worried that Harald would stay here as a perpetual student. It's happened, you know."

"Would you mind telling us a little about Harald's research?" Thóra asked. "We were wondering if his interest in witchcraft could be linked to the murder."

Now it was Thorbjörn's turn to lift his eyebrows. "Seriously?" Thóra and Matthew nodded their heads. "Well, I never. I'd be very surprised at that. History isn't so exciting that people kill for it very often," he said. "Anyway, Harald was planning to compare witch hunts in Iceland and on the mainland. As you know, it was mainly males who were burned at the stake for sorcery in Iceland, but it was females elsewhere. So that was his starting point. Since he was well acquainted with witch hunts on the mainland, Harald concentrated on acquiring Icelandic resources and studying the history of that period here. In my opinion he had established a good overview when he was murdered."

"So what about those side streets?" asked Matthew.

Thorbjörn paused to think. "Well, he had quite a fascination with Bishop Jón Arason and the printing press he's said to have imported to Iceland. At first I couldn't quite grasp how he intended to link that with witch hunts, but I let him proceed. Then he abandoned that angle for Brynjólfur Sveinsson, the bishop of Skálholt. I thought that was a better approach."

"Was he connected with witch hunts?" Thóra asked.

"Of course," replied Thorbjörn. "He was bishop at the time, but he was generally considered to take a soft line when it came to witches. It is known that he kept some boys at the school in Skálholt from being burned at the stake when a sorcerers' quire was found in their possession. But on closer examination it's an untenable view. For example, he did nothing to restrain his relative, Páll from Selárdalur, who was one of Iceland's most vigorous witch hunters. Seven men were burned at the stake on suspicion of causing an outbreak of illness at Páll's farm."

"This sorcerers' quire that you mentioned, was Harald particularly interested in that?" Matthew asked.

Thorbjörn shook his head slowly. "No, not that I recall. It goes by the name of the Skálholt Quire and Bishop Brynjólfur probably had it destroyed. Though he did make a record of the eighty spells described in it,

I think. Harald was fascinated by Brynjólfur's library, which contained an assortment of manuscripts and books. And his personal history also aroused Harald's interest, of course."

"How?" asked Matthew, adding by way of apology: "I know very little about Icelandic history."

Thorbjörn gave him a pitying smile. "In short, Brynjólfur had seven children, but only two reached adulthood: Ragnheidur and Halldór," he explained. "Ragnheidur gave birth to a son out of wedlock nine months after Brynjólfur had made her publicly swear an oath, on her hands and knees, that she was a virgin. The oath was taken because of rumors that she was having an affair with her father's young assistant, a man by the name of Dadi. Ragnheidur's bastard son was taken from her arms and sent to be brought up by the father's family. She died shortly afterward, when the baby was about one year old.

"Halldór, Brynjólfur's son, died a few years later while studying abroad. Brynjólfur then brought back his only surviving heir, Ragnheidur's son Thórdur, who was six by then. He soon became the apple of the old man's eye. Brynjólfur's wife died three years after the lad moved to Skálholt and to top off the bishop's tragedy Thórdur died of consumption at the young age of twelve. So Brynjólfur, one of the great figures of Icelandic history, was left with no family or heirs. I think Harald was enthralled by the bishop's story and what could be read into it. If Brynjólfur had treated his daughter more fairly at the fateful moment, somehow you feel things would have turned out better for him and his family. Ragnheidur had tricked him, you see. Popular belief has it that she swore an honest oath in the church but allowed herself to be seduced by Dadi the same evening, in vengeance against the old man."

"I'm not surprised that such a story appealed to Harald," said Thóra. *He must have felt sympathy for Ragnheidur,* she thought. "Was Harald still studying Brynjólfur when he was murdered, or had he turned to another topic?"

"If I remember correctly, his interest in Brynjólfur had started to wane—he'd studied him comprehensively. I'm told he took a week off before he was murdered, so I don't know exactly what he was up to then."

"Do you know if Harald had any other business in Iceland apart from studying? Was he trying to buy up antiquities or objects of possible historical value?" asked Matthew.

Thorbjörn laughed. "Do you mean treasure troves? No, we never discussed anything like that. Harald seemed to have both feet firmly on the ground, he was a devoted student and I found him nice to work with. Don't let Gunnar's hysteria deceive you."

Thóra decided to change the subject and asked about the meeting in the faculty building on the fateful night.

"Quite right," said Thorbjörn. The playful glint had vanished from his eyes. "We were here, most of the teachers from the department. Are you implying anything?"

"Not at all," Thóra retorted. "I was just asking in the vague hope that you noticed something that might help us. Something that may have dawned on you since you gave your statement to the police. Memories often take a while to gestate."

"You won't learn anything from those of us who were at the meeting. We left long before the police said the murderer appeared. We were celebrating our application for a grant in cooperation with a university in Norway. We're not exactly party animals, and we don't have much stamina at such gatherings. We'd all left before midnight."

"You're certain?" Matthew asked.

"Absolutely—I was the last to leave and I switched on the security alarm myself. If anyone had been left inside it would have set off every bell in the building. That's happened to me and it's not exactly pleasant." He looked at Matthew, who appeared unconvinced, and added: "The printout from the security system can corroborate that."

"I don't doubt that it can," said Matthew, stone-faced.

CHAPTER 24

The good weather from the previous evening seemed likely to hold. They were at the aviation school office where Thóra and Matthew had hired a plane the day before. While Matthew completed a form for the pilot, Thóra took advantage of the complimentary coffee. The fare had surprised her—the scheduled flight time to Hólmavík was just under an hour either way but it cost less than if they had driven and stayed at a hotel. She had even been offered a lower price if they were willing to accept a trainee pilot. She opted for the higher fare.

"Okay, we're ready." The pilot smiled. He was so young that he must have just been promoted from the lower fare bracket. They followed him to a small plane that accommodated four people including the pilot. Matthew offered Thóra the seat in front, but she declined when she saw how cramped it was in the back. Although tall, she was still smaller than Matthew and therefore less likely to need a shoehorn to get her out at the other end. She climbed in and buckled up.

The pilot took his seat and handed them each a headset. "Put these on. The plane's a bit noisy, so we have to communicate through the mikes on these headphones." Thóra and Matthew put the clunky apparatus over their heads and plugged them in. The pilot turned on the engines, and after a short discussion with the control tower they took off.

They flew over Reykjavík, which looked much larger from the air than on the ground. Matthew looked down, fascinated, but Thóra found it more rewarding to look ahead, a rare opportunity on a plane. "There aren't many tall buildings," observed Matthew, looking back at Thóra. She found it mildly embarrassing to talk over the sound system in case the air traffic controllers were listening in, so she just nodded and averted her gaze downward, watching the low-rise houses zip by. The city and its suburbs were characterized by the Icelandic need to live in a house. Not an apartment, a house. Apartments were mere stepping-stones. Thóra craned her neck to try to see her own home, but could not. They were heading inland, away from the sea. Once they had flown over the boundaries of the residential areas, Matthew turned back to Thóra. "What happened to your trees? There's hardly any vegetation down there," he said in an unnaturally loud voice.

"Oh, most people think the sheep ate them," replied Thóra, now almost certain they were out of earshot of flight control.

"Sheep?" repeated Matthew incredulously. "Since when do sheep eat trees?"

"They don't," said Thóra. "They get the blame, though. I don't think there were ever any trees, to be honest. Maybe some shrubs." She looked down at the barren ground. "I like it this way, actually. Who needs trees?"

Matthew shot her a quizzical glance and then went back to scanning the mountainous landscape up ahead.

The flight to Hólmavík went quickly and the airstrip in the village soon appeared. Thóra saw a gravel runway with a single shed, nothing more. It was just outside the village beside the main road. The pilot flew over the runway and sized it up; then, satisfied with what he saw, he turned the plane and made a soft landing. They unfastened their belts and got out.

Matthew took out his mobile to make a call. "What's the number of the local taxi company?" he asked the pilot.

"Taxi company?" He laughed. "There's not even one taxi here, let alone a whole company. You'll have to walk."

Thóra smiled along with the pilot, pretending she had known this all along. But like Matthew she had expected to be able to take a taxi from the airstrip down to the museum. "Come on, it's not far," she said to Matthew, pulling her shocked companion with her. They crossed the road, which was completely devoid of traffic, and walked to the gas station and shop at the entrance to the village. They went in to ask for directions. The girl working there was very helpful and even went outside with them to point out the museum. It could not have been easier; a walk down the road, along the shore into the village, and there, right next to the harbor, was the museum. A black wooden house with a turfed roof, it was just barely discernible in the distance. It was only a few hundred yards and the weather was good. They set off.

"I recognize this from the photographs on Harald's computer," said Thóra, looking back at Matthew. The pathway was so narrow that they could not walk side by side.

"Were there many shots from here? Anything worthwhile, I mean?"

"Not really," Thóra replied. "Actually just typical tourist shots, apart from a few that he took inside the museum, where photography is prohibited." She cautiously skirted a patch of ice on the path. "Watch out here," she warned Matthew, who strode over it. "You're not exactly wearing the right shoes for walking." She glanced at his black patent leather shoes. They matched Matthew's other clothes: pressed trousers, a shirt, and a half-length woolen coat. She was wearing jeans and outdoor shoes and had put on her goose-down coat as a precaution. Matthew had not yet commented on the coat—making do with a raised eyebrow when he picked her up and she squeezed into his car, the upper part of her body triple its normal size.

"The last thing I expected was to have to go hiking," Matthew said crossly. "He could have warned me, that man." "That man" was the curator of the sorcery and witchcraft exhibition at the museum, whom Matthew had phoned the day before to make sure it would be open.

"It's good for you. It will teach you not to be such a dandy," teased

Thóra. "That doesn't work up here in Iceland. If we don't finish this job soon I'll have to take you into town and buy you a fleece jacket."

"Never!" declared Matthew. "Even if I had to stay here until my dying day."

"If you don't, that day will come sooner than you suspect," she retorted. "Aren't you cold, though—maybe you'd like to borrow my coat?"

"I made a reservation at Hótel Rangá for tonight," he said, swiftly changing the subject. "And I'm going to swap the rental car for a Jeep."

"See, you've gone half-native already."

Finally they made it all the way to the museum—without slipping on the ice. The museum looked old-fashioned from the outside. The yard in front of it, enclosed with a stone-built wall, was covered in beach gravel and a few driftwood logs. The door was deep red, contrasting sharply with the earth-colored hues of the building itself. A portly raven was sitting on a wooden bench outside. It looked skyward when they arrived, opened its beak wide and cawed. Then it spread its wings and soared up to the gable where it watched them go inside. "Appropriate," said Matthew as he opened the door for Thóra.

Inside they found a small service counter on the right with several shelves directly in front of them displaying witchcraft souvenirs. All very unpretentious and tidy. Behind the counter sat a young man, who looked up from his newspaper. "Hello," he said. "Welcome to the sorcery and witchcraft exhibition."

Thóra and Matthew introduced themselves and the young man said he had been expecting them. "I'm just working here temporarily," he said after shaking their hands and introducing himself as Thorgrímur. His handshake was old-fashioned, firm and steady. "The director of the museum is on sabbatical, but I hope that's no problem."

"No, it's fine," said Thóra. "But is it true that you were here this autumn?"

"Yes, that's right. I took over in July." He gave her an inquisitive look and added: "May I ask why you want to know?"

"As Matthew told you yesterday, we're investigating an incident connected with a person interested in witchcraft. He came here this autumn and we thought we ought to drop in for some insight into his world. I presume you remember him."

The man laughed. "You can't be sure. A lot of people come here." Then, realizing that they were the only visitors, he added: "This time of year is nothing to go by—it's packed here in the tourist season."

Matthew gave a faint smile. "You know, this man isn't so easy to forget. He was a German history student with a very unconventional appearance. His name was Harald Guntlieb and he was recently murdered."

Thorgrímur's face lit up. "Oh, yes, he was all—all covered in—how can I describe it—ornamentation?"

"If you can call it ornamentation," said Thóra.

"Yes, sure, I remember him. He came here with another man, a bit younger, who said he felt too hungover to come inside. Soon after that I read in the paper about the German being murdered."

"That fits," Matthew said. "This guy with the hangover—do you know anything about him?"

The man shook his head. "Not exactly—when your friend said goodbye he told me he was a doctor. I think he must have been joking. He had to make an awful noise to wake him up when they left. I was in the doorway watching. I remember thinking how improbable a doctor he was, passed out on the bench outside."

Thóra and Matthew exchanged glances. Halldór.

"Do you remember anything else about their visit?" asked Thóra.

"I remember he was very well informed. It's nice to have visitors who know as much as he did about history and witchcraft. As a rule, people don't know anything; they can't even tell a revenant from a poltergeist." From their expressions he could tell these visitors were two more in that category. "How about taking a walk around the museum and I'll tell you about the main exhibits? Then we can talk about your friend."

Thóra and Matthew exchanged glances, shrugged, and followed the curator inside.

"I don't know how much you know about these matters, but I should maybe give you a little background." Thorgrímur walked up to a wall covered with the skin of an unidentifiable animal. The fur faced the wall, and on the hide facing outward a magic symbol had been drawn, much more complicated than the one carved on Harald's body. Beneath the skin a wooden box was mounted on the wall, resembling an old-fashioned pencil box. It was half-open and full of what looked like hair, along with a silver coin. A simple symbol was carved on the lid and on top of it was a strange creature that could have been mistaken for a mutant hedgehog. "In the age of sorcery, the common people in Iceland lived in appalling conditions. A handful of families owned most of the property while almost everyone else starved. The only way they could see to escape from their poverty was through magic and supernatural powers. In those days this wasn't considered unusual. For example, they thought the devil went around in the company of men, trying to ensnare their souls." He turned to the hide on the wall. "Here's an example of a spell to get rich—the symbol represents a sea mouse or circular helmet. You needed the skin of a black tomcat, then you drew this symbol or circular helmet on it with the menstrual blood of a virgin."

Matthew grimaced and looked out of the corner of his eye to see whether Thorgrímur touched the symbol. Noticing this, the curator told the German dryly: "We used dark red ink." Then he continued. "They had to catch a small vermin that according to folklore lived along the shore and was called a sea mouse. It had to be caught in a net made from a virgin's hair." Thóra felt Matthew running his hand down her long, loose hair. Stifling a giggle, she brushed his hand away inconspicuously. "Then they made a nest for the mouse from a wooden box and the hair and put a stolen coin in it, and then the mouse was supposed to fish a treasure from the sea and into the box. Then you had to put the circular helmet over it to prevent the mouse from escaping and causing a storm at sea."

He turned to them. "So it wasn't just hocus-pocus."

"No," replied Matthew, and pointed to a wall with a glass case containing what looked like the lower half of a human body. "What on earth is that?"

"Ah, that's one of our most popular exhibits. Corpse breeches. They were also supposed to make you rich." Thorgrímur walked over to the showcase. "Of course this is just a replica—obviously." Thóra and Matthew nodded eagerly. Behind the glass was the skin of the lower half of a male body. To Thóra it resembled a pair of gross, pink tights, hairy and with the genitals attached. "To acquire corpse breeches you made a contract with a living man to take the skin off the lower half of his body when he died. When that person died his body was unearthed and the skin removed from the waist down, in one piece. These were the corpse breeches that the other person would wear. Corpse breeches were supposed to graft to the wearer's body and if he put a coin in the scrotum—a coin that he had to steal from a rich widow at Christmas, Easter, or Whitsun—he would never find the scrotum empty, because it would always contain plenty of money."

"Couldn't they have chosen a different place?" Thóra pulled a face. Thorgrímur simply shrugged.

"And what's this?" Matthew asked, as Thorgrímur took them over to a large photograph of a woman in a long, coarse skirt in folk costume style. She was sitting down with her skirt hitched up to expose her bare thigh. On the thigh a wartlike protrusion pointed up in the air.

"You know of course that the majority of sorcerers who were executed in Iceland were male—there were twenty men but only one woman. This is because it was mainly thought to be men who practiced witchcraft in Iceland, unlike in the rest of Europe. This spell—known as a *tilberi*—is remarkable for being the one Icelandic charm that only a woman could perform. To make a tilberi she had to steal a rib from a grave on Whitsun night, wrap it in wool and wear it inside her clothes between her breasts, go to the altar three times and spit the communion wine over the bone, which would bring the tilberi to life. Then it would grow, and to keep it hidden under her clothes the woman had to make an artificial nipple from the skin on her thigh. The tilberi fed there, in between roaming the countryside at night to suck the milk of ewes and cows, which it spat into the woman's butter churn in the morning."

"He wasn't exactly a pinup," Thóra said, pointing at the exhibit. The tilberi was wrapped in wool and barely visible apart from an open tooth-less mouth and two tiny white eyes with no pupils.

Judging from Matthew's expression, he agreed. "Was this one woman who was executed for witchcraft accused of doing that?"

"No, in fact she wasn't. But there was a case in the southwest of Iceland in 1635 when a woman and her mother were suspected of having a tilberi. It was investigated but did not turn out to be true, so they narrowly escaped."

They went on strolling around the museum, looking at the exhibits. Thóra was struck most by a wooden stake standing in the middle of the room surrounded by bushels of straw. As she stood silently contemplating it, Thorgrímur came over and told her that all twenty-one suspected sorcerers had been burned alive. He added that three were known to have tried to break out of the pyre when the stakes to which they were tied burned through. They were thrown back into the flames to die. The first execution took place in 1625, he said, but the proper witch hunts began when three sorcerers were burned at the stake in Trékyllisvík in the northern West Fjords in 1654. Thóra mentally calculated how recent this actually was.

When they had seen enough, Thorgrímur took them to the upper floor. On the way they passed a sign stating that photography was prohibited—the same sign that had appeared in the photo Thóra had seen on Harald's computer. Thorgrímur showed them a large family tree showing the kinship among the most prominent witch hunters in the seventeenth century. He pointed out how members of the ruling class had planted their descendants in the offices of the magistrates and judges. After reading the genealogy, Thóra understood exactly what he was talking about. Matthew paid little attention. He left them and went over to look at a showcase containing replicas of sorcerers' handbooks and other manuscripts. He was bent over the case when Thóra and Thorgrímur came up to him.

"Actually it's incredible that any books of sorcery have been preserved at all," Thorgrímur said, pointing to one of them.

"Do you mean because they're so old?" Thóra asked, leaning forward to take a better look.

"Well, that too, but mainly because it was a capital offense to possess them. Some are handwritten copies of older manuscripts that had presumably suffered damage, so the originals are not all from the sixteenth and seventeenth centuries."

Thóra stood up straight. "Is there any index of all these magic symbols?"

"No, unfortunately there isn't. No one has made the effort to record them as far as I know." With a sweep of his hand he said: "All these symbols on exhibit here represent only a few pages from the manuscripts and old books—a tiny sample. So you can imagine how many symbols there are."

Thóra nodded. Damn it. It would have been marvelous if Thorgrímur could have shown them a list against which they could check the unknown symbol. She moved to look at more manuscripts. The showcase stood in the middle of the room, enabling visitors to walk around it while viewing the pages on display. Matthew, who had been hunched over to get a closer look at one of the panels, suddenly straightened up.

"What's this symbol?" he asked excitedly, tapping on the glass with his finger.

"Which one?" Thorgrímur asked, and took a look at the document.

"This one." Matthew pointed it out to him.

Although Thóra had to lean across the case to see what Matthew was pointing at, she was quicker than Thorgrímur to realize which symbol had caught his attention—simply because it was one of the few symbols that she recognized, the one that had been carved on Harald's body. "Well, I'll be damned," she muttered.

"This one at the bottom of the page?" Thorgrímur asked as he pointed one out.

"No," Matthew said. "This one in the margin. What does it do?"

"Well, I don't know," Thorgrímur replied. "I can't say, unfortunately. The text on the page doesn't refer to it—it's an example of a symbol that the owner of the book added to the margin himself. That wasn't unusual; symbols like this occur in more works than just those specifically describing magic."

"What manuscript is it from?" Thóra asked, peering at the text accompanying the document.

"It's a manuscript from the seventeenth century, owned by the Royal Archive of Antiquities in Stockholm. It goes by the name of the Icelandic Book of Sorcery. Naturally the author is anonymous. It contains fifty spells of various sorts—most are innocent, aimed at personal advancement or defense." He stooped to read the same text Thóra had been peering at. "Some of them are darker, though—for example, one is a death charm, to kill the target. One of the two love spells is also pretty heavy black magic." He looked up from the case. "Funny. Your friend Harald was passionately interested in precisely this section of the exhibition, the old books and manuscripts."

"Did he inquire about this same symbol?" Matthew asked.

"No, not as far as I recall," Thorgrímur replied, then added: "I'm not exactly an expert in this particular field so I couldn't help him much—but I do remember that I put him in touch with Páll, the director I'm standing in for. He knows all about these sorts of things."

"How do we get in touch with him?" Matthew asked excitedly.

"That's the trouble—he's abroad."

"So? Can't we phone him or send him an e-mail?" asked Thóra, no less eager than Matthew. "It's quite important for us to find out what this symbol means."

"Well, I have his number somewhere," Thorgrímur said, much calmer than they were. "I suppose the best thing is if I call him and talk to him first—give him the rundown. He can contact you afterward."

Thorgrímur went behind the counter, produced a notebook and flicked through it. Then he reached for the telephone and dialed a number, taking care not to let them see it. A short while passed before he started speaking—only to leave a voice mail message.

"Sorry. He didn't answer. He's bound to call as soon as he gets the message—maybe tonight, maybe tomorrow, maybe the next day."

Making no attempt to conceal their disappointment, Thóra and Matthew gave Thorgrímur their cards. She asked him to let them know the moment he got in touch with Páll. He gladly agreed and put their cards inside his notebook. "What about that friend of yours—did you want to know why he was here?" he said when he had finished.

"Yes, certainly," Thóra replied. "Did anything besides the manuscripts interest him or did he mention that he was looking for anything?"

"It was mainly the manuscripts, if I recall correctly," Thorgrímur said, thinking back. "Actually he made me an offer to buy the sacrificial bowl in here, but I couldn't tell if he was joking."

"Sacrificial bowl? What sacrificial bowl?" Matthew asked.

"Follow me—it's just inside." They followed him into a small room where a stone bowl was in a display case in the center. "This is a bowl that was used during sacrifices—it was found nearby and the police forensics team has confirmed that there are traces of blood in it. Centuries old as it turns out."

"That's a hell of a lump of rock," exclaimed Thóra. "Couldn't they have made do with a wooden one?" The stone artifact had to weigh at least several pounds. It had been hollowed out to make the middle concave.

"So it's not for sale, then?" Matthew asked.

"No, definitely not. It's the only original exhibit at this museum, and I don't have the authority to sell the objects here anyway."

Thóra peered at the stone. Could this be the object that Harald had coveted? It seemed unlikely, but stranger things had come to light during their investigation. "This is definitely the same stone?"

"What do you mean?" Thorgrímur asked in surprise.

"Well, I was just wondering if the director could have taken Harald at his word, sold him the stone bowl, and had another made to replace it?"

Thorgrímur smiled. "Not a chance. It's the same stone that's always been here. I'd bet my head on it." He turned round and left the room, with them in hot pursuit. "As I said—he just mentioned it casually."

"But was there anything else he said or asked about?" Thóra asked. "Anything out of the ordinary?"

"Well, as I said he was mainly interested in the old sorcery books and manuscripts," Thorgrímur repeated. "He did ask me about *The Witches' Hammer,* if I'd ever heard or seen anything about an old edition of it in Iceland. I'd never heard such a story and told him so. Maybe you don't know what I'm talking about?" He looked at them.

"Oh, yes. We've heard of it," Matthew answered for them both.

"I asked him what he based his claim on and he said that some old letters suggested a copy found its way to Iceland."

CHAPTER 25

The stately approach to the main building of the University of Iceland was in a league of its own when compared with other local buildings. Bríet admired the view as she sat on the steps of the crescent-shaped driveway. For some reason she suddenly wanted to own a car. But that was out of the question on her pittance of a student loan—she'd love to meet the miser who calculated the cost of living it was supposed to meet.

It would be nice to finish her course and start working—not that historians were big earners. If she wanted money she was in the wrong field. So she yearned to sink her claws into a good provider, as her elder sister had done when she married a lawyer. He worked for one of the big banks and was rolling in money. Her sister lived a life of luxury. Now they were building a huge house on the outskirts of the city and her sister, a political science graduate, worked mornings in one of the ministries and could play around shopping for the rest of the day.

Bríet leaned up against Dóri's side; he was sitting next to her. He was so handsome, a great guy really—and, to top it off, doctors generally did very well for themselves.

"What are you thinking about?" he asked as he threw a snowball he had been busy making.

"Oh, I don't know," Bríet answered wearily. "Hugi, mainly."

Dóri followed the snowball's trajectory as it soared high into the air and landed right beside the statue of Saemundur the Wise and the seal. "He was a sorcerer," Dóri said. "Did you know that?"

"Who?" Bríet said in surprise. "Hugi?"

"No, Saemundur the Wise."

"Oh, him. Yes, of course I knew."

Dóri gazed at the statue of the sorcerer beating a seal over the head with a prayer book. According to legend the seal was actually the devil himself, in disguise. It was a strange statue to put in front of a university, and Dóri had long been fascinated with it.

Bríet took a pack of cigarettes out of her bag. "Want one? Your favorite brand." She smirked as she handed him the white packet.

Dóri smiled back at her as he looked up from the packet. "No, thanks. I've got some." He took one of his own and they both lit up. He leaned forward so that Bríet had to take her hand off his shoulder. "What a mess."

"Tell me about it." Unsure of the best reply, Bríet decided to play safe. She did not want him to do anything stupid that would have bad repercussions for her, and of course for him too. But she also wanted to show him that she had more understanding and integrity than Marta Mist.

"I'm sick of this bullshit." He stared straight ahead and thought a moment before continuing. "The other students here are totally different from us."

"I know," Bríet said. "We're not exactly typical university students. I'm fed up with it too." She had no idea what they were talking about.

Dóri went on talking and Bríet had the impression he had not been listening to what she said. "What really strikes me most is that the other students—who aren't always going out and partying—seem just as happy with life as we are. If anything, more satisfied."

Bríet took her chance. She put her arm over Dóri's shoulder and pressed her face toward his. "I've been thinking exactly the same thing. We've gone too far; if Andri and the others want to keep on, they can do it without me. I'm going to get a grip on myself, on my studies and everything really. It's no fun anymore." She had deliberately avoided mentioning Marta Mist by name for fear of giving herself away.

"That's funny—I kind of feel the same way." He turned to her and grinned. "We're not so different, you and me."

Bríet gave him a peck on the cheek. "We're a good team. Forget the others."

"Not Hugi," said Dóri, and his smile vanished as quickly as it had appeared.

"No, of course not him," she hurried to say. "I'm always thinking about him—how do you reckon he feels?"

"Awful. I can't take this anymore."

"What?" Bríet was afraid to ask—she would have preferred to make a guess at what he meant, but she wasn't sure she'd get it right and she didn't want to spoil the way things were going.

Dóri started to get to his feet. "I'll give that lawyer a couple more days—then I'm going to the police. I don't give a shit what happens."

Damn. Bríet desperately tried to think of a way to make Dóri see some sense—she would even have gladly handed him over to Marta Mist, had she been there with them. "Dóri, you didn't kill Harald, did you? You were at Kaffibrennslan, weren't you?"

He stood up and looked down at her, his expression far from pleasant. "Yes, I was at Kaffibrennslan. Where were you?" He walked away.

Bríet was upset. She leaped to her feet and said: "I didn't mean it like that, I'm sorry. I just meant—why go to the police?"

Dóri stopped dead in his tracks and spun round. "You know—I can't understand any longer why you and Marta Mist are so set against it. The day of reckoning always comes. Don't forget that." He strode off.

Bríet had no idea how to react. A few moments later she took out her mobile and punched in a number.

Laura Amaming headed for the lobby of the Manuscript Institute where Gloria was struggling to vacuum the mat. Laura had not had the chance to talk to her alone all morning and she gladly seized the opportunity. "I need to ask you something."

Gloria looked up in surprise. "What? I'm doing exactly what you taught me."

Laura waved her hand dismissively. "I'm not talking about cleaning. I want to know if you noticed anything unusual in the common room over the weekend of the murder. You cleaned it then. Before the body was found."

Gloria's dark eyes widened. "I told you—and the police. There was nothing."

Laura gave her a stern look. She was lying. "Gloria. Tell me the truth. You know lying's a sin. God knows what you saw in there. Are you going to lie to him, too, when the time comes for you to stand in front of him?" Laura took the girl by the shoulder and forced her to look her in the eye. "It's all right. You couldn't know there'd been a murder. No one went into the printer room that weekend. What did you see?"

A tear rolled down Gloria's cheek. Laura was unruffled; this was not the first tear that the girl had shed at work. "Gloria. Pull yourself together. Tell me—I found traces of blood on the window handle of the common room. What was in there?"

The tear became two, then three, then they poured out in a steady flood. Gloria blurted out between sobs: "I didn't know—I didn't know."

"I'm aware of that, Gloria. Everyone is. How could you have known?" She wiped the tears from the girl's cheeks. "What was in there anyway?"

"Blood," the girl said, looking at Laura in terror. "But it wasn't a pool of blood or something like that. It was more like someone had tried to clean up and missed a few spots. I didn't realize until it was up off the floor and on my cloth. I didn't think any more of it then—I didn't know about . . . you know."

Laura heaved a sigh of relief. Traces of blood—nothing more than that. So Gloria was safe, she surely wouldn't land in trouble for concealing it. Laura had kept her own cloth with the blood from the window and could now give it to Tryggvi to pass on to the police. They had methods for tracing the owner of the blood. In her mind Laura had no doubt that the murder was committed in that room. "Gloria—don't worry about it. It's just a trivial matter. You'll just need to make a new statement—just tell the truth, that you didn't realize the importance of this information." She smiled, but the girl was still crying.

"There's something else," she said, still sniveling.

"Something else?" Laura asked, amazed. "Like what?"

"I found something else in there that morning. In the drawer where the knives are kept. I'll show you," Gloria said, and burst into tears again. "I kept it. Come with me."

Laura followed Gloria into one of the cleaning closets on the first floor. Her eyes still shiny with tears, Gloria climbed onto a small set of steps and reached up to the top shelf. Bringing down a small object wrapped in a paper towel, she handed it to Laura. "I kept it because I knew it was rather strange. And when the body was found, I realized what it was, and I got so scared. My fingerprints are on it and I was sure the police would think I killed him. I didn't kill him."

Laura cautiously unwrapped the paper towel. When she saw what was inside, she shrieked and made the sign of the cross. Gloria began to weep again.

Gudrún, or Gurra as her friends called her, repressed the urge to bite her nails with great difficulty. It was such a long time since she had stopped the habit that she could not even remember when—for example, whether it was before or after she married Alli. She looked at her well-manicured hands. Unfortunately she was not wearing nail polish; picking that off was a good way to vent frustration. She wondered whether to paint them for the sole purpose of being able to pick it off again when the polish dried, but she abandoned the idea.

Instead she stood up and went into the kitchen. It was a Saturday and she had planned to make a nice meal. Alli worked every day except Sundays, so Saturday evening was their only time to relax together. Gurra looked at the clock—it was far too early to make dinner yet. She sighed. Everything was clean and tidy—there was no housework left to do. But if she could not find something to keep herself occupied she would go mad. Something to take her mind off her fear. She recalled how scared she'd been when the police knocked on their door with a search warrant for the upstairs apartment. Then nothing had happened. Incredible but true. All her worrying had been unfounded and she had begun to relax again. Until the other day.

Why were those people prying into the case again? Weren't the police satisfied with their findings? So why stir it all up again? She groaned. What had she been thinking? Even though Alli was normally a complete pig and had lost all interest in their marriage, she still didn't want to get rid of him. She even did a thing or two to hold on to him. At forty-three, she was too old to go back out on the market.

How stupid she had been. Sleeping with her lodger. And, the funny thing was, that apartment had often had much more attractive tenants than that freaky German. She could not have been in her right mind— ignoring the fact that it happened more than once, and indeed more than twice. Sex with him had been fun—there was no denying that. There was an air of adventure about it, presumably because she knew she should not be doing it. Harald was also much, much younger than her husband and much more frisky. If only he hadn't been covered in all those awful scars and rings and studs.

Think, think—she took a deep breath. How could they ever find out? No one knew about it; she had never told a soul at least. Common sense alone had stopped her boasting about the affair to her best friend. Harald would hardly have talked about it. He had no need to brag—there was an endless stream of young women through his apartment. He could boast about them if he felt the urge to discuss his sexual conquests. She corrected herself—that "endless stream" had really been only two girls for the most part: a tall redhead and a petite blonde. He would surely never have mentioned his affair with her, and the police certainly had no inkling of it. She had spoken to them briefly a few times and nothing in their words or attitude ever implied that they considered her relationship with Harald to be more than that between a landlady and tenant. Which was actually how it had become toward the end. Harald had told her he couldn't be bothered anymore, he had other fish to fry. She grimaced at the thought.

She would have preferred to be the one who broke it off. To his credit he thanked her very nicely for the memories, but that did not stop her from losing it completely. She blushed at the recollection. How shamefully uncivilized of her. She was really annoyed about his true reason, although he had never actually admitted it to her. He had found himself a steady girlfriend. Gurra had seen them entering and leaving his flat several times during the week before he was murdered. This was a new girl who had not visited Harald before as far as Gurra knew. They spoke German together so she was presumably a compatriot of his—perhaps Icelandic women were not quite good enough for him when it came down to it. She was furious at Harald's hypocrisy; it was fine for her to cheat on her husband but he couldn't cheat on his girlfriend. No, he was too good for that.

So what, it was over and done with and what mattered now was not dwelling on something that might never come to light. She went into the laundry room. It was a long time since she had cleaned it properly. It was located off the corridor and could be reached from her own apartment and the hallway off Harald's. That was one of the few modifications they had made when they decided to buy the house and rent out the upper floor. She put the latch up and went inside.

Yes, there was work to be done here. The floor was still covered with pawprints from the police dogs who had searched everywhere for drugs. Fortunately nothing was found in the laundry—Gurra had no idea whether she and Alli would have been placed on the list of suspects or some sort of narcotics squad register if drugs had been found in the common area. Their presence had been requested during the search, which made no difference, since neither of them had ever touched drugs—at least she hadn't. Who knows what Alli got up to on those endless business trips of his. But it didn't really matter—the police let the dogs sniff all around and when they seemed satisfied they abandoned the room without further ado. One officer had peeked inside the dryer and washing machine, mostly for curiosity's sake. That was it.

She opened the closet and took out a broom and bucket. When she removed the bucket she noticed a box. She stared at it. The last time she had cleaned the laundry room there was no box in the closet. It was usually empty apart from cleaning equipment for both apartments. Carefully she took it out. It must be Harald's. She tried to remember the last time she mopped the floor of the laundry room. Oh, my God—it had been when he dumped her. He had walked in to put some wash in the machine, and when she suggested—with no effort to conceal her real intentions—that she was up for doing it, he announced with a smile that enough was enough.

Since that unpleasant memory was from right before the murder, Harald must have placed the box there just prior to his demise. Why? He had never accepted her offer to use the storage room. The four shelves reserved for the tenant stood empty. Could he have wanted to hide something from his new girlfriend, thrown it into a box and stashed it away there? Judging from his physical appearance and bizarre décor, he was unlikely to have anything to conceal. Her heart skipped a beat. Unless he had secretly filmed his conquests and did not want his girlfriend to find them? There was hardly a more repulsive way to enter a relationship— the thought of becoming an entry in a sexual conquest collection. Gurra clutched her head in both hands. It could even be her on tape or in some photographs. She stood riveted to the spot staring at the box. She had to open it. There was no alternative. She had to open the box and convince herself that nothing in it would reveal her secret.

Gurra bent down and forced up the cardboard flaps. She stared at the contents. No photographs—no tapes. There were dishcloths wrapped around fragile objects, she supposed, and sheets of paper in plastic file holders. It was a massive relief. She reached for one piece of paper and saw that it was a very old letter, presumably valuable. The script and text were undecipherable, so she put it under her arm, planning to take a better look later. She browsed through the rest of the papers and to her great relief saw that they had nothing to do with Harald's private life either. One other sheet caught her attention, though. It appeared to have sloppy scribbles all over it, scrawled in red ink, and the paper—if it was paper—was thick, dark, and waxy. The text was bizarre and a rune or symbol had been drawn at the bottom of the page. It was signed with two names, both illegible although she recognized Harald's as one of them from the tenancy agreement. She put it back in the box. Odd.

Gurra pushed the contents to one side in order to reach the fragile objects wrapped in dishcloths at the bottom. She took hold of one package and carefully lifted it up. It was light—almost as if the cloth was empty. Cautiously she opened it and stared in awe at the contents. She shrieked, clenched her fist around the old letter that she was still holding, and flung the dishcloth to the floor. She ran out of the laundry room and slammed the door.

Gunnar picked up the phone and dialed the extension for María, the director of the Manuscript Institute. She was probably still at work even on a Saturday. A large exhibition was pending, and judging from the commotion surrounding the last major event, the institute would be a hive of activity. "Hello, María, Gunnar here." He made an effort to sound suitably authoritative—the voice of a man of integrity who had no desire to give an exaggerated impression of himself.

"Oh, it's you." Her curt response suggested that his tone had not impressed her. "I was just about to contact you. Any news?"

"Yes and no," Gunnar said slowly. "I'm well on my way to locating the document, I think."

"I feel much better knowing that you *think* you've got it," she said sarcastically.

Gunnar was careful not to get drawn into an argument. "I've looked everywhere in the department and I've contacted the representatives of

Harald's family who are going to search his belongings. The document is there—I'm convinced."

"Don't you mean you *think* you're convinced?"

"Listen, I only called to keep you in the picture—there's no need to be rude," Gunnar said, although what he wanted to do most of all was slam down the phone.

"Quite right, sorry. We're so busy here with the exhibition. I'm all on edge. Don't let it upset you," María said in a much friendlier tone of voice. "But I stand by my word, Gunnar. You have only a few more days to find it. I can't start covering up for your students."

Gunnar wondered how many days "a few" would be. Hardly more than five, probably more like three. He did not want to press her for a more precise answer, from fear that she would shorten the deadline. "I realize that—I'll let you know the moment I hear something."

They exchanged dry good-byes. Leaning forward onto his elbows, Gunnar hid his head in his hands. The letter had to be found. If not, he would probably have to resign. It was unthinkable for the head of department to be implicated in the theft of documents from a foreign institute. Hatred welled up inside him. That bloody Harald Guntlieb. Before he arrived on the scene Gunnar had even toyed with the idea of one day standing for election as vice chancellor. His only dream now was that life would return to normal. That was all. There was a knock at his door.

Gunnar sat up and called out: "Come in."

"Hello, may I disturb you for a moment?" It was Tryggvi, the janitor. He stepped inside and closed the door behind him. With slow steps he walked up to Gunnar's desk and declined the offer of a seat. He held out his hand, palm up. "One of the cleaners found this in the students' common room."

Gunnar picked up a little steel star. After examining it carefully, he looked in surprise at Tryggvi. "What is it? It can't be worth anything."

The caretaker cleared his throat. "I think it's a star from Harald's shoes. She found it the other day but only told me about it just now." Gunnar gave him a blank look. "So what? I don't quite follow."

"There was something else. If I understand her correctly, she also found traces of blood around the window." Tryggvi looked into Gunnar's eyes, waiting for a reply.

"Blood? Wasn't he strangled?" asked Gunnar, incredulous. "Isn't it just an old bloodstain, then?"

Tryggvi shrugged. "I don't know. I just wanted to let you have this— it's up to you what you do with it." He began to turn around, then stopped in his tracks. "Of course, he wasn't just strangled."

Gunnar's stomach churned at the thought of the awful abuse of the body. "Yes, quite right." He stared at the steel star, baffled. Then he looked up when Tryggvi spoke again.

"I'm certain it's from the shoe he was wearing when he was murdered. But of course I have no idea whether the star fell off before then."

"Well, well," muttered Gunnar. Gritting his teeth, he looked sternly at Tryggvi, stood up, and said: "Thank you, it might be irrelevant but you did right to let me know."

The janitor nodded calmly. "Actually there's something else," he said, and produced a folded paper towel from his pocket. "The woman who cleaned the common room over the weekend of the murder found traces of blood on the floor which someone had tried to clean up. And she found this too." He gave the paper towel to Gunnar. "I think we should talk to the police." After thanking the professor, he left the room.

Gunnar sat down again, stared at the star and thought about what to do. Was it important? Would a call to the police be a Pandora's box that would start the questioning all over again? That must not happen. It simply must not happen now that everything was getting back to routine. Apart from that bloody letter, of course. With a groan, Gunnar put the star down. It could surely wait until Monday. He opened the paper towel. It took him a while to realize how the object he was holding was linked to the case. When he realized, he just managed to put his hand over his mouth before letting out a scream. He picked up the telephone and dialed the emergency number for the police, 112. This one could not wait until Monday.

CHAPTER 26

The journey to Rangá went like a dream. The weather had kept up, and although there was snow everywhere, it was calm and bright. Thóra sat happily in the front seat of the new rental Jeep, admiring the view. She had emphasized to Matthew the importance of driving slowly down the winding steep slopes at Kambar and regaled him with endless stories of accidents there, with the result that they ended up driving at a snail's pace. Thóra soon lost count of the cars that overtook them. She used the time to browse through one of the two files returned by the police, which were supposed to contain all the case documents. She paused over the description of the T-shirt that was found in Hugi's closet. "Hey!" she shouted.

Matthew, startled, sent the Jeep into a swerve. "What?"

"The T-shirt," Thóra said excitedly, tapping hard on the open page. "This is the same T-shirt I saw in the photographs of the tongue operation. '100% silicon.' It says that on the front."

"So?" Matthew asked, not following.

"The photographs show a T-shirt with the inscription '100' and 'ilic' or something similar. Here it says that the T-shirt found in Hugi's closet said '100% silicon' in big letters on the front. The blood must have been from the operation." Thóra slammed the folder shut, pleased with herself.

"He must remember it," Matthew said. "It's not every day you have other people's blood splashed all over your clothes."

"Maybe not for you and me," said Thóra. "Don't you remember Hugi saying they didn't let him see the T-shirt? Maybe he didn't remember this one."

"Maybe," Matthew said. They drove on in silence for a while but as they were crossing the bridge over Outer Rangá by Hella he suddenly said: "They're coming tomorrow."

"They who?"

"Amelia Guntlieb and her daughter Elisa," said Matthew, not taking his eyes off the road.

"What? They're coming?" spluttered Thóra. "Why?"

"You were right. His sister was with him just before the murder. She's going to talk to us—I understood from the mother that he told his sister what he was working on. Admittedly not in detail, though."

"Well, well," said Thóra. "I understand about his sister—but what about his mother? Is she coming to stand over us while we talk to his sister?"

"No. She's coming to talk to you. One-on-one. Mother-to-mother—her very words. You knew she was going to talk to you. Did you think she meant over the phone?"

"Actually, I did. Mother-to-mother? Are we supposed to compare notes about child-rearing?" Meeting that woman was the last thing Thóra wanted.

Matthew shrugged. "I don't know, I'm not a mother."

"Christ," Thóra exclaimed, and sank back in her seat. She carefully weighed her words before speaking again. "His sister—could she be involved?"

"No. Out of the question."

"If I may ask: why is it out of the question?"

"Because it is. Elisa's not like that. Also, she says she went home that Friday. She flew from Keflavík to Frankfurt."

"And you're happy to take her word for that?" Thóra asked, surprised at his gullibility.

Matthew glanced at her and then returned his attention to the road. "Not entirely. I had it checked and, believe me, she took the plane."

Thóra did not know what to say. In the end she decided to save further remarks until she had had the chance to meet the girl and talk to her. Perhaps Matthew was right. It might very well be possible to rule her out as the murderer. Thóra spotted a sign saying "Hótel Rangá." "There." She indicated that Matthew should turn right down the drive to the hotel. They headed along the track toward the river and up to a large timber building.

"You know, I don't think I've stayed at a hotel for two years," she said as she carried her flight bag to the hotel. "Not since I got divorced."

"You're joking, of course," Matthew said, taking his own bag.

"No, I swear I'm not," said Thóra, almost enjoying the memory. "We made a final attempt to save our marriage with a weekend in Paris two years ago, and since then I haven't been abroad or had any reason to stay at a hotel. Strange."

"So the trip to Paris didn't work any miracles?" asked Matthew as he opened the door for her.

Thóra snorted. "Not exactly. We were making a final effort to save our relationship, and instead of sitting over a glass of wine and talking things over—finding cracks that we could patch up—he was continually asking me to photograph him in front of tourist sights. That was the death sentence really."

Right inside the door they bumped into a huge stuffed polar bear—standing on its hind legs with glaring eyes, ready to pounce. Matthew walked up to it and posed. "Take a photograph. Please."

Thóra made a face and went up to the reception desk. Behind a computer screen sat a middle-aged woman wearing a dark uniform and white blouse. She smiled at Thóra, who informed her that they had booked two single rooms and gave their names. The woman made an entry in the computer, found two keys, and gave them directions to the rooms. Thóra reached over to pick up her bag and was about to leave when she decided to ask the woman if she remembered Harald as a guest. He might have asked for directions or information that could give her and Matthew a lead. "A friend of ours stayed here this autumn. Harald Guntlieb. You wouldn't happen to remember him?"

The woman looked at Thóra with the patient expression of someone accustomed to all manner of unlikely questions. "No, I don't remember the name," she answered politely.

"Could you check, he was a German with rather unusual facial piercings?" Thóra tried to smile, to pretend this was merely routine.

"I can try. How do you spell the name?" the woman said, looking back at her computer screen.

Thóra recited the letters one by one and waited while she called up the details of Harald's reservation. From where she stood, Thóra could see a succession of menus appearing on the screen. "Here it is," the woman said at last. "Harald Guntlieb, two rooms for two nights. The other guest was a Harry Potter. Does that fit?" If she found the other name odd, she did not show it.

"Yes," said Thóra. "Do you remember them at all?" Peering at the screen, the woman shook her head. "No, sorry. I wasn't even working here then." She looked at Thóra. "I was on holiday abroad. In this line of business it's difficult to get away in the summer," she said apologetically, as if Thóra might reproach her for being a slacker. "Maybe the barman remembers him. Ólafur, or Óli as we call him, must have been here. He'll be on duty tonight."

Thóra thanked the woman and she and Matthew walked off to their rooms. As they turned the corner in the corridor, the woman called after them: "I see here that he borrowed a flashlight from reception."

Thóra turned back. "A flashlight?" she asked. "Does it say what for?"

"No," the woman replied. "It was just noted to make sure he returned it when he checked out. Which he did."

"Can you see whether this was in the middle of the night?" Thóra asked. Maybe Harald wanted to look for something he dropped in the driveway.

"No, the day shift lent him the light," the woman replied. "Excuse my curiosity, but isn't that the name of the foreign student who was murdered at the university?"

Thóra said it was and thanked her again for her help. She and Matthew proceeded to their rooms, which turned out to be side by side.

"Should we rest for half an hour or so?" Thóra asked when she looked inside the nicely furnished room. The big bed was tempting and aroused an urge within her to stretch out for a while—the quilts were big and thick and the linen looked ironed. It was not a sight Thóra saw every day. Her own bed normally greeted her at night in the same state of chaos she left it in when she rushed off to work in the mornings.

"Sure, we're not in any hurry," Matthew replied—clearly with the same idea. "Just knock when you're ready. And remember, you're always welcome to drop in on me." He winked and closed the door before Thóra could respond.

After putting down her belongings and peeping into the bathroom and at the minibar, Thóra flopped back onto the bed. She lay with her arms in a crucifixion position and relished the moment. It didn't last long, however—a ring tone came from her handbag. With a groan she sat up and took out her phone.

"Hi, Mom," said her daughter Sóley cheerfully.

"Hello, sweetie," said Thóra, glad to hear her voice. "What are you up to?"

"Oh," she said, slightly less cheerfully. "We're on our way to the stables." Then she whispered so softly that Thóra had trouble making out the words, especially since her daughter seemed to have pressed her mouth right up against the phone to avoid being heard. Her voice came out muffled. "I don't want to go at all. Those horses are nasty."

"Hey!" said Thóra, trying to pep up her daughter. "They're not nasty; horses are really kind actually. It'll be fun for you—isn't the weather nice?"

"Gylfi doesn't want to either," Sóley whispered. "He says horses are old-fashioned and outdated."

"Tell me something fun: what did you do today?" asked Thóra, well aware that she was not the best advocate for horses.

Her daughter brightened up. "We had ice cream and watched cartoons. It was real fun. Hey, Gylfi wants to talk to you."

Before Thóra managed to say good-bye to Sóley, her son was already on the phone. "Hi," he said glumly.

"Hello, sweetheart," replied Thóra. "How are things?"

"Useless." Gylfi did not even try to whisper—if anything, Thóra thought he raised his voice.

"Oh, is it the horses?" she asked.

"Yes and no. Just everything." After a short pause he added: "I need to have a little talk with you when I get back tomorrow."

"By all means, darling," Thóra replied, not knowing whether to feel happy that he was opening up at last or afraid about what he would say. "I look forward to seeing you both tomorrow night." When the call was over she made another attempt to take a nap—in vain. In the end she got up and took a hot shower.

While she was drying herself with the thick, snow-white towels, Thóra noticed a guide to the local tourist attractions. She browsed for places that might have appealed to Harald. There was plenty to choose from but few possible links with the case. Three places did catch Thóra's attention, however. The see of Skálholt received a two-page spread and had a clear connection with Harald through his interest in the bishops Jón Arason and Brynjólfur Sveinsson. Two other sights were possible candidates, as well: Mount Hekla and some caves from the days of Irish monks at Aegissída on the outskirts of Hella. What surprised her most was that she was fairly sure she had never heard of them before. Thóra wondered whether the name Hella was from the same root as *hellir,* the Icelandic word for "cave." She folded down the corners of the pages describing these three places. Then she dressed, taking care to put on warm clothes—and plenty of them—even though they weren't exactly attractive. If they were going to stroll around some caves, it would help to be dressed for the task. In her mind's eye she saw Matthew clambering over boulders in his dancing shoes. Out of sheer spite she decided not to tell him about the caves until they had left the hotel. Besides, it was going to be dark out soon, and Thóra figured he'd be more likely to give in if she sprang the idea on him last minute. She put her hair in a ponytail, slipped on her coat, and left the room.

No sooner had her knuckles left the door than Matthew opened it. Thóra smirked when she saw his clothes. "That's a nice suit," she said in a jolly tone. "And nice shoes." Judging from the well-polished leather, his shoes must have cost a pretty penny, and Thóra stifled a momentary pang of conscience about not warning him. He was bound to own plenty of other pairs.

"It isn't a suit," Matthew said tetchily. "It's a sports jacket and trousers. There's a difference. Not that you're likely to realize."

"Oh, sorry, Mr. Kate Moss," teased Thóra, now quite at ease with her conscience, and the pending mistreatment of his footwear.

Without answering, Matthew closed the door behind him and jiggled the keys to the Jeep in his hand. "Well, where to?"

Thóra took her phone from her coat pocket to look at the time. "I suppose it's best to start at Skálholt. It's almost four and we'll see from there."

"Fine, Madam Guide," Matthew said, scrutinizing her getup. "You know there's a restaurant at the hotel, don't you? We don't actually have to go out to hunt for our dinner."

"Ha-ha," Thóra said. "I'd rather be warm and cozy than worry about looking cool. Though you might end up cool in more than one sense of the word, dressed like that in this weather."

When they reached Skálholt it was beginning to get dark. The church was open and they hurried inside and began looking for someone to talk to. Soon they found a young man who greeted them and asked if he could help. They explained they were hoping to meet someone who might have spoken to their friend some time before. They described Harald's appearance.

"Hey," the young man said when Thóra was halfway through an account of the studs along Harald's right eyebrow. "Aren't you talking about that student who was murdered? I met him!"

"You wouldn't happen to remember his reason for coming here?" asked Thóra, smiling encouragingly.

"Let's see—if I remember correctly he wanted to talk about Jón Arason and his execution. Yes, and Brynjólfur Sveinsson." He looked at them and hastened to add: "There's nothing unusual about that—a lot of our visitors have heard their stories and want to find out more. They're tragic but do have a macabre attraction. People are particularly interested in the fact that it took seven blows of the axe to behead Jón Arason. His head was literally split from his body."

"Was he just wondering about these bishops in general terms?" Thóra asked. "Or was he interested in anything special connected with them?"

The young man turned to Matthew and switched to English. "I don't know how familiar you are with the story of Jón Arason."

Realizing this remark was intended for him, Matthew answered: "I know as much about him as I do about his mother. In other words: nothing."

"Oh, I see." The man sounded almost shocked. "To cut a long story short, Jón Arason was the last Catholic bishop of Iceland. He was bishop of Hólar from 1524 and controlled Skálholt for a while as well. He was beheaded here in Skálholt in 1550, thirteen years after King Christian III of Denmark abolished Catholicism in Iceland and other parts of his realm. Jón Arason tried to prevent the Reformation and led a revolt against the new Lutheran faith, but he failed and ended up with his head on the block. The execution was a separate story because two weeks before, Jón had been granted immunity until the next parliament convened to discuss his case and that of his two sons. They were executed too."

Matthew wrinkled his brow. "His sons? Wasn't he a Catholic bishop? How could he have sons?"

The young man smiled. "Iceland had won some kind of dispensation—I don't know exactly how—whereby priests, deacons, and bishops could have mistresses. They were even allowed to make formal contracts that were tantamount to marriage vows. If they had children they paid a fine and everyone was happy."

"How convenient!" exclaimed Matthew, taken aback.

"Yes, very," came the jovial reply. "Your friend Harald seemed to know the story well; he'd clearly read up on it. Of course I've only summarized it for you, there's much more to it. But anyway, that's the background to the question you were asking." He looked at Thóra, who tried to conceal the fact that she had forgotten her question long ago. "Your friend was mainly interested in one thing when he talked to me: the printing press that Jón Arason had sent to Iceland in 1534 and set up in Hólar, and what he printed on it."

"And?" prompted Thóra. "What could you tell him?"

"It was a big question," the young man replied. "Very little is known about the first print. Some sources say it was a missal—a sort of manual for priests with a calendar of services, psalms, and the like. The four gospels of the New Testament were also printed at some stage. As far as I can establish nothing else is known about printing in Jón Arason's day. I remember your friend asking some rather curious questions—for instance, if the bishop could have published a certain book that was very popular at that time. I asked if he meant the Bible but he just laughed. I didn't quite see the joke."

"No, I can imagine," said Matthew with a glance at Thóra. *"Malleus?"* She had thought precisely the same. *Malleus Maleficarum* was the most printed book after the Bible in those days. Maybe Harald was trying to unearth whether it had been printed in Iceland. A copy would have been priceless, not to mention its symbolic value to a passionate collector such as him.

"And what did he want to know about Brynjólfur Sveinsson?" Thóra asked.

"That was quite interesting," the young man said. "At first he was only interested in seeing his grave—which is impossible because it hasn't been found yet."

Thóra interrupted him. "Not found yet? Wasn't he buried here?"

"Yes, he was, but he asked to be buried outside the church, beside his wife and children. There's an account of the location, but it still hasn't been excavated. He wanted to rest in an unmarked grave."

"Wasn't that unusual?" Thóra asked.

"Very much so. In fact, the grave was marked later with a wooden fence that stood for thirty years. Then it began to fall down and wasn't maintained, in defiance of the church's orders. No one really knows why he didn't give himself a tomb beneath the nave, as was the custom at that time. It's thought that he found it too cramped when he attended the funeral of one of his clergymen here. Maybe he wanted to put an end to the practice."

"And did it end?" asked Matthew.

"No, not at all. But there may have been another reason. He died a broken man. Understandably—dying alone, that remarkable figure, with all his family dead and no descendants. Most people find his fate very moving."

"But you said Harald was interested in seeing Brynjólfur's grave at first—did he move on to something else?" asked Thóra.

"Yes, he did. I started talking to him about Brynjólfur when I saw how upset he was about the grave. I took him into the crypt and the archaeological exhibition there. Then I showed him the excavations outside. We got onto the subject of Brynjólfur's library—you know that he owned a large collection of Icelandic and foreign manuscripts?" Thóra and Matthew shook their heads—neither had any idea. "And you know that he gave some of Iceland's most remarkable calfskin books to King Frederik of Denmark?" Thóra shook her head again.

"Your friend got very excited when I started telling him about the manuscripts and wanted to know what had happened to them when Brynjólfur died. I couldn't tell him exactly, but I did know that he gave his foreign books to the infant son of the governor of Iceland at the time, who was a Dane named Johann Klein, and that he shared out the Icelandic ones between his cousin Helga and his sister-in-law Sigrídur. As far as I recall, some of the Icelandic books went astray; at least, some were missing when Johann Klein came to collect them. The clergy at Skálholt are suspected of hiding them to stop them from being sent to Denmark. Those books and manuscripts have never been found. No one even knows the titles."

"Where could they have hidden them?" Thóra asked, looking all around.

The young man smiled. "Not in here. This building dates from 1956. The old church that Brynjólfur had built in 1650–51 collapsed in an earthquake in 1784."

"And you haven't looked for them?"

"We still haven't found the graves of Brynjólfur and his family, in spite of the description of the location. He died in 1675. We certainly wouldn't look for books that were only rumored to have been buried here at that time. And the fate of the books he bequeathed is uncertain. Apparently Árni Magnússon came across a few when he began collecting manuscripts. Some of Brynjólfur's books can be recognized from his monogram."

"BS?" Thóra asked, for the sake of contributing something.

"No. LL." The young man smiled.

Thóra repeated in surprise: "LL?"

"*Loricatus lupus*—Latin for 'armored wolf,' which is what the name Brynjólfur means." He smiled at Thóra who could not restrain herself from clicking her fingers. *"Loricatus lupus"* was written on Harald's scrawled map. They were clearly on the right track if his jottings had some connection with the murder.

Their conversation soon came to an end. Matthew and Thóra thanked the young man for his patience. Before starting the car, Matthew turned to Thóra and said: *"Loricatus lupus,* yes. Should we wait until everyone's gone home and dig up everything we can get a shovel through?"

"Definitely," Thóra said with a smile. "Let's start with the cemetery."

"You'll have to do the shoveling, then—you're dressed for the part. I'll sit in the car and light you up with the headlights."

They left Skálholt. "I know where we could go next," Thóra said, with an air of innocence. "There are caves near Hella that were probably dug out by Irish monks. Maybe we can find an explanation there for Harald's interest in the hermits. I have a hunch Harald borrowed the flashlight to take a look around there."

Matthew shrugged. "It's worth looking into—won't we need a flashlight too?"

"Maybe we can pick one up at a gas station."

By the time they reached Hella it was pitch-dark. They began by buy-ing two flashlights at a gas station. The attendant told them they could find information about the caves at Hótel Mosfell. It was only a stone's throw away, so they left the Jeep and walked. At the hotel a friendly el-derly man followed them outside to point out the caves, which were just visible beyond the main road on the other side of the river. He also showed them the best path to take, since the caves could not be approached by car. After thanking him, they returned to the Jeep and drove straight over the bridge to where he had advised them to park. Much to Thóra's delight they had to walk a fair distance over a meadow that appeared to belong to the farm there. Matthew kept stumbling in his slippery shoes but al-ways managed to keep his balance by flapping his arms like he was try-ing to fly. When they reached the edge of the slope down to the caves, Thóra was in excellent spirits.

"There," she said, pointing with her flashlight. She feigned concern. "Do you think you'll make it down there, Fred Astaire?"

Frowning back, Matthew tried to suck it up. He inched his way down the slope like a ninety-year-old man while Thóra bounded down like a spring lamb. She struck a pose in front of him, determined to enjoy the moment, and called out mischievously: "Chop-chop!" Matthew ignored her and finally made it all the way.

"What a rush you're in," he said as he caught up with her. "Are you that excited about having dinner with me afterward?"

Thóra swung her flashlight up and shone it in Matthew's eyes. "Hardly. Come on." She turned round and they entered the first cave. "Wow, how on earth did they think of this?" she said in astonishment, casting the beam of light around the wide space. Unless she had misun-derstood, the caves had been carved into sandstone by Irish monks us-ing primitive tools.

"What do you think they were for?" Matthew asked.

"Shelter, mainly," said a voice from the mouth of the cave.

Thóra let out a piercing shriek and dropped her flashlight. As it rolled along the bumpy floor of the cave, the beam bounced along the facing wall until it stopped. "God, you made me jump out of my skin," she said, bending down to pick up the flashlight. "We didn't know anyone was in here."

"Sorry, I didn't mean to scare you," said the man, whose voice gave the impression that he was quite elderly. "We're even actually," he added. "It's a long time since I've had a shock like the one your scream gave me. They phoned me from the hotel to say some sightseers were on the way to the caves. I thought you might want a guide. My name's Grímur and I own the farm above here. The caves are on my land."

"Oh, yes," said Thóra. Not a bad property to own, she thought. "We'd be delighted to have a guide—we don't really know very much about what we're looking at."

The man walked inside the cave and began explaining what they could see. He spoke Icelandic and Thóra translated the gist for Matthew. Grímur showed them where beds had presumably been arranged by the walls. Then they examined a chimney that had been carved out through the ceiling to let air in, or smoke out. He pointed out an altar and cross that the monks must have chiseled or carved in the wall behind it. "Well, well," Thóra said, surprised and impressed. "This is quite remarkable."

"Yes, it is," the man said feelingly. "This has never been an easy land to live off of—or in, for that matter. Any efforts to acquire shelter would have paid off for the early settlers in the long run."

"I can imagine." Thóra took another look all around with the help of her flashlight. "Have the caves been investigated—I mean, couldn't there be valuables hidden away in here?"

"Valuables?" He looked surprised and then laughed. "It was used as a cattle shed until around 1950. You couldn't really hide anything here. It would have to be very carefully concealed, I can tell you that."

"Ah," Thóra said, disappointed. "So it's all been searched?"

"No, I didn't say that," the man replied. "As far as I know my caves have only been studied once."

"When was that?" asked Thóra. "Recently?"

Grímur laughed again. "No, not recently. I don't remember exactly but it was a good while ago. It didn't yield much, as expected. They found remains of animal bones and a hole that was apparently used for cooking."

He pointed to a hole in the ground near the altar. "No, the little that re-mained to be found has already been found, I assure you."

Thóra's last question was whether the man had noticed Harald visit-ing the caves. He did not recognize the description but added that it didn't necessarily mean he hadn't been there—the caves weren't fenced off and were easy for people to reach without being noticed.

"Go and get changed, then, Crocodile Dundee," Matthew said when they were back at the hotel. "I'm so lucky I can just throw off my jacket and go to the bar—and win back the time I lost on that slope."

Thóra stuck her tongue out at him, but went to her room to change. She put on nice slacks and a plain white blouse, washed her face and put on a little lipstick. There was nothing wrong with a little makeup for a dinner invitation—that didn't necessarily mean you were expecting anything. Yet she paused at the word "necessarily." It wasn't quite con-vincing enough, and worried her slightly. She brushed the thought aside and went up to the bar. Matthew was standing there deep in conversa-tion with the barman—presumably Óli. Matthew smiled at her, clearly pleased with the transformation.

"Nice," he said succinctly. "This is Óli. He was telling me about Harald and Harry Potter—he remembers them well. They drank a lot and stood out a bit from the other guests."

"That's putting it mildly," Óli said, and asked Thóra what she wanted to drink.

"A glass of white wine, please," she replied, then asked him to ex-plain.

"Well," he said. "They drank one shot of tequila after another—played air guitars and did other things you don't see very often around here. Not to mention Harald's appearance. The other guests just gaped at them both. And they smoked like chimneys—I couldn't sell them cigars fast enough."

Thóra looked all around at the cozy bar, which was located under the gabled roof. She agreed—an air guitar did not exactly spring to mind—an air violin at most, if there was such a thing. She turned to Óli again. "Harry Potter—do you happen to know his real name?"

The barman smiled. "His name was Dóri. As the night wore on they were both way too drunk to remember that he called himself Harry Potter. They put on quite a good act for much of the evening, though."

There was nothing else to learn from Óli. They sat down on the big leather couch, drank a toast, and discussed the events of the day. The waiter brought the menu and after ordering, Matthew decided to have another drink. Much to Thóra's surprise she had finished hers as well, so she accepted a second. After dining they went back to the bar, and by her third Cointreau Thóra was on the verge of whipping out her own air guitar solo for Matthew and Óli. But she settled for snuggling up against the former instead.

CHAPTER 27

DECEMBER 11, 2005

Thóra woke up with her head throbbing as if her brain was trying to escape her skull. She clutched her forehead and groaned. Cointreau, of all drinks. She ought to have learned by now that "liqueur" was Latin for "hangover." With a sigh she rolled over onto her side. As she did so her hand knocked something that felt so warm she opened her eyes wide in horror. There was a man in her bed. She looked at Matthew's back. Or was it Óli, the barman? She recalled the previous night and sighed softly at the realization that she had at least opted for the lesser of two evils. The fog in her head obscured her view of a clear exit strategy—how could she slip out unseen without waking Matthew? And an even bigger question: how could she maintain her dignity? Could she pretend nothing had happened? Maybe he couldn't remember anything either. That was the answer—sneak out, meet him afterward, and pray that he had drunk four times as much as she had.

Her plan evaporated when Matthew turned over and smiled at her. "Good morning," he said, his lips parched. "How are you doing?"

Thóra pulled the duvet up to her chin. She was naked under it. If she could be granted one wish, it was to be fully clothed. Her throat produced a strange rattle before her vocal cords kicked in. "Just one thing. To make everything perfectly clear, you know." Matthew looked puzzled but allowed her to continue. "Last night, that wasn't me—it was the alcohol. So you slept with a bottle of Cointreau, not with me."

"Oh, I see," said Matthew, propping himself up on one elbow. "Those bottles of booze never fail to surprise. I didn't know they were capable of *that*. You even praised my shoes. Wanted me to keep them on."

Thóra blushed. She tried to think up a different defense for her virtue but her mind was empty. Gradually the night all flooded back to her and she had to admit to herself that she didn't particularly regret it. "I don't know what came over me," she said, and blushed again.

"You worry too much," Matthew said, putting his hand on her over the duvet.

"It's just not like me at all. I'm the mother of two children and you're a foreigner."

"Well, since you have children you ought to be familiar with the process." He smiled. "It's pretty much the same everywhere, I expect."

Thóra's cheeks grew even redder. And her horror doubled when Amelia Guntlieb suddenly crossed her mind. "Are you going to tell the Guntliebs about this?"

Matthew threw his head back and roared. After laughing his fill he looked at her and said calmly: "Of course. There's a clause in my contract that says I have to submit a sex report to them at the end of each month."

When he realized that Thóra was unsure whether or not he was joking, he relented: "Of course not; how could you think that?"

"I don't know—I just don't want people thinking that I make a habit of sleeping with my colleagues. I've never done anything like this before." Given that she worked with the aging Bragi, Bella from Hell, and the unassuming Thór, that wasn't saying much.

"I didn't take it that way," Matthew said. "I took it as meaning that you wanted to sleep with me at that moment—that you simply found my sex appeal irresistible." He looked at her playfully.

Thóra rolled her eyes. She did not want to answer, because to some extent he was right—at least, she was the one who made the first move, if her memory did not betray her. "My hangover's killing me. I can't think straight at the moment."

Matthew sat up. "I have some Alka-Seltzer. I'll fix you one, you'll feel better straightaway."

Before Thóra could stop him—she realized that he was as naked as she was—Matthew had got to his feet and gone to the bathroom. *What is it that makes men so much less embarrassed about their physique than women?* Thóra wondered. She mused on this a while to keep other thoughts that might have occurred to her at bay, such as how fit and strong he looked. Maybe it had not been so terribly stupid, when all was said and done. She heard the sound of running water from the tap in the bathroom and closed her eyes.

She opened them again only when she was sure Matthew was back under the quilt. He was holding a glass of fizzing water and Thóra braced herself, sat up, and drank it in one draft. Then she threw herself back on the pillow and waited for the nausea to subside. She lay like that for a few minutes until a finger prodded her shoulder through the covers. She opened her eyes.

"Listen." Matthew turned to face her. "I have a suggestion."

"What?" Thóra managed to keep her voice normal. She was almost feeling a little better.

"How would you like to review your opinion that this was a mistake?" He smiled at her. "I can put on my nice shoes, if you want."

Thóra woke up again, this time to the sound of running water from the shower. She leaped out of bed and threw on some clothes, hopping around on the floor. She could not find one of her socks, but gathered up the rest of the clothes in her arms. She called into the bathroom that she would see him at breakfast. It was a huge relief to her when she closed the door to her own room.

A long, hot shower made her feel better in body and mind. Before leaving, she picked up her phone and called her friend Laufey.

"Do you know what time it is?" Laufey grumbled sleepily.

Thóra ignored her, because it was almost ten. "Oh, my God—you'll never guess what!" she cried.

"Well, judging from how excited you sound and the ungodly hour at which you're calling, it must be headline news." A yawn followed.

"I slept with someone!" The reaction was immediate. Laufey had clearly sat bolt upright on hearing the news because no sooner had the words left Thóra's mouth than a mighty creaking was heard.

"Ooh! Tell me, who, who is it?"

"Matthew, that German. I'll have to save the rest for later because I'm off to meet him for breakfast. We're at a hotel."

"A hotel? Well, well, you can't be left by yourself for a second, can you?"

"I'll talk to you later—I'm a bit worried. Somehow I have to get him to understand that it was just a onetime thing, I don't want a relationship."

Braying laughter came down the phone line. "Hello? Where have you been—watching *Teletubbies*? There aren't many single men that age who are looking for a profound relationship. Don't worry about it, girl."

Thóra hung up, slightly irritated at the reaction to news that was supposed to have pleased her friend. She headed off for the breakfast room after taking the time to mess up the sheets so that the hotel staff wouldn't think she was promiscuous. Matthew was sitting at a table for two by a window, drinking coffee. Thóra could not help noticing how handsome he was, which she had always refused to admit to herself. His face had those rough features that appealed to her. Strong jaw, large teeth, well-defined cheekbones, and deep-set eyes. This was doubtless a genetic legacy from her prehistoric ancestors, an attraction to looks that suggested toughness and determination—the perfect hunter. Thóra sat down. "I really think something to eat will do me a heap of good," she said to break the ice.

Matthew poured coffee from the stainless steel pot into her cup. "You left a sock in my room. And it wasn't a woolen sock—incredible but true."

Nothing in the way they acted implied that something had happened since dinner the night before, apart from when Matthew placed his hand over Thóra's with a conspiratorial wink. She smiled back but said nothing. He soon removed his hand and continued his meal. After eating they went to their respective rooms and packed.

While Thóra was waiting for Matthew at reception, her phone rang. It was Gylfi. Before answering, Thóra reminded herself that he had no idea what his mother had been up to the previous night.

"Hello, darling," she said, trying to sound natural.

"Hi." Gylfi's voice was gloomy and a short time passed before he got to the point. "Er, that thing I was going to tell you—where are you?"

"I'm at Hótel Rangá. I was working this weekend. Aren't you home?"

"Yeah." Another pause. "When are you getting back?"

Thóra looked at her watch. It was a few minutes to eleven. "I'll be back around one, I expect."

"Okay. See you then."

"Why aren't you with your dad? Where's your sister?" Thóra said quickly before he rang off.

"She's still with him. I left."

"Left? Why? Did you have an argument?"

"You could say that," he replied. "He started it."

"How?" Thóra gaped in astonishment. Hannes normally had a knack for avoiding quarrels and until now had managed to get along quite nicely with his son, although the latter would hardly consider him a born entertainer.

He sighed. "He acted like he wanted to have a talk with me, and just when I thought he understood me and I told him something, he snapped. I swear he did backward somersaults. I wasn't about to listen to that. I thought he'd understand."

Thóra's thoughts seethed and jostled. She knew that Gylfi's description of his father's behavior must be a huge exaggeration. So what had really happened? She regretted having persuaded Hannes to talk to the boy—obviously it had not helped. "Gylfi, what was it that made your father so mad? Is that what you want to talk to me about afterward?"

"Yeah." No further explanation. She would have to wait until she saw him to find out.

"Listen, I'm on my way. I'm no acrobat so we can surely manage to discuss this calmly. Don't go anywhere."

"You'll have to be back before one. I have to go and see some people."

Some people? Some people? Had he joined a religious cult? Thóra felt a pang in her chest. "Gylfi—don't go anywhere until I'm back. Understand?"

"Be back before one," he said. "Dad'll be there too." He said good-bye and hung up.

Thóra's heart pounded in her rib cage and it took a huge effort not to let out a howl. With trembling hands she dialed Hannes's phone but it was either out of reach or switched off. She stared at her phone. Hannes would never switch off his phone—he slept with it on his bedside table in case anyone needed to contact him in the middle of the night. His riding trips, too, were arranged somewhere his phone worked—she doubted if he had ever been out of signal range since he first bought a cell phone. She tried his home number but there was no reply. What had the boy done? Started smoking? Hardly. Was he a drug addict and on his way to rehab? No, out of the question. She would surely have noticed. Was he coming out of the closet? Off to a gay pride meeting? Hannes would hardly have flipped about that—to give him credit, he was relatively liberal. Besides, she had a feeling that Gylfi had a crush on that girl whose name she could never remember. No, that wasn't the issue. Countless ideas welled up, increasingly absurd. *Que será será.* She stood up and peeped around the corner to see if Matthew was on his way down the corridor. He was standing at the door to his room, dragging out his suitcase.

As soon as Matthew had paid the bill, Thóra took him by the arm and almost dragged him away.

"What's up?" he asked in bewilderment as Thóra pushed him through the door.

"There's a domestic crisis and I have to get home as soon as humanly possible."

He took her at her word, and with no further questions he threw the bags inside the Jeep and climbed behind the wheel. They drove straight to Reykjavík through Hella, Selfoss, and Hveragerdi. Matthew said little on the way. It was not until they reached the Kambar slopes that he asked whether there was anything he could do, but Thóra told him she did not even know what the problem was, let alone how to resolve it. She did tell him that it concerned her son and some news he was going to tell her. They were making good time as they passed the ski lodge, and they were still plugging along when they reached the transport café. But right as they were passing Lake Raudavatn, on the outskirts of the city, they blew a tire.

"What the hell . . . !" shouted Matthew, tightening his grip on the wheel to stop the car from swerving out of control. They slowed down and stopped by the roadside.

"Oh no, oh no," Thóra moaned. She looked at her watch. Twenty-five past twelve. They could still make it to Seltjarnarnes by one if they had no problems changing the tire.

"Stupid cheap tires," muttered Matthew as he struggled to remove the spare from the tailgate. At last it came free and they concentrated together on jacking the car up and changing the tire. Matthew took the burst tire and tossed it through the tailgate where it landed on top of Thóra's flight bag. She couldn't have cared less. It was rapidly approaching one.

They jumped into the car and Matthew roared off. "Wait here," Thóra said as they pulled up outside her house. She ran toward it, taking out her keys on the way so that the doorbell would not delay her. She rang with her left hand to let Gylfi know she was back while putting the key in the lock and opening the door with her right. "Gylfi!" she panted.

"Hi, Mom." Sóley ran out to greet her, all sunny smiles. If something had happened, it had escaped her notice entirely.

"Hello, sweetie. Where's your brother?" Thóra pushed her way past Sóley to look for her son.

"He left. I've got a note for you," she said, pulling a folded scrap of paper out of her pocket.

Thóra snatched the note from her. While she unfolded it she asked: "When did he go? And where?"

"He just left. An hour ago." Sóley had still not figured out the mystery of telling time. Gylfi could have gone a few seconds ago, or two weeks ago for that matter. "He went where it says here." A little finger pointed to the note as if to clear up any confusion with other pieces of paper.

"Come with me." Thóra saw that the address was in Seltjarnarnes, too, so thankfully it was quite close. "Let's go for a drive with the nice man." She threw one of Gylfi's coats over Sóley's shoulders, crammed her into some boots, and pushed her outside. Thóra swung open the rear door of the Jeep and swiftly helped her daughter inside. Then she jumped into the passenger seat and told Matthew to drive away. "Matthew, this is my daughter, Sóley. She speaks only Icelandic. Sóley, this is Matthew. He doesn't speak Icelandic but I'm sure you'll be good friends."

Matthew stole a glance into the back to greet the little girl with a smile. "Pretty, like her mother," he said, turning where Thóra indicated he should. "Same taste in clothes too."

"Here—then first right. I'm looking for number forty-five," Thóra said, still agitated. The house soon came into sight. It was easy to recognize because walking up the drive was Gylfi. "There, there," Thóra gasped, pointing to her son. Matthew sped up a little and pulled up alongside the sidewalk outside the house—the driveway was already full. Thóra recognized Hannes's car. She flung open the door the moment the car stopped. "Sóley, you wait here with nice Mr. Matthew."

Gylfi did not look round until his mother had repeatedly called his name as she ran toward the house. He had reached the front door where he stood slouching after ringing the bell. "Hi," he said morosely.

"I was delayed." Thóra was panting. She put her hand on her son's shoulder. "What's going on, darling? Who lives here?"

Gylfi looked at her with an expression of absolute desperation. "Sigga's pregnant. She's only fifteen. I'm the father. Her parents live here."

The front door opened as he finished speaking. Thóra stood frozen to the spot, her mouth gaping. For some reason her eyes were glued to the iPod her son was wearing round his neck, perhaps because she had been looking at it when the world collapsed around her. If the enraged middle-aged man who opened the door had not been blue in the face, he would surely have laughed at her moronic expression. "Hello," he said to her, then looked at Gylfi, narrowed his eyes contemptuously, and said: "You too." But those two words were obviously not to be mistaken as a welcome. Their implication was more along the lines of: *Get lost, you deflowerer of the young and innocent daughters of worthy citizens.*

Politeness won out from force of habit and Thóra gritted her teeth into a smile. "Hello, I'm Thóra. Gylfi's mother."

The man grunted but invited them in. They took off their shoes under his watchful gaze as he leaned menacingly in the doorway. Thóra had the impression that the man expected Gylfi not to stop at the daughter of the household but to burst in and ravish the mother for good measure.

"Thank you," she said to no one in particular as she walked in past him. She had both arms on her son's shoulders, guiding him along in front of her—in case the man tried to go for his jugular. They walked straight into a large open-plan living room where three people were seated: Hannes, whom Thóra recognized from the nape of his neck; a woman of roughly her own age, who stood up when they approached; and a young girl who was sitting in an armchair with her head bowed in total resignation.

"So, you made it at last," the woman half shrieked. Oh, Lord, may the unborn child inherit my deep alto, Thóra prayed silently. She tried for a second time to squeeze out a smile. Her hands did not leave her son's shoulders.

"Hannes," Thóra said, looking at her ex-husband. She tried to signal that he should do his duty now and allow her to join him where he was seated. But instead of signaling back "message received," he glared back furiously. "Hello, Sigga," she said in the friendliest voice she could manage to the young girl, who then looked up. Her eyes were puffy, with heavy tears glittering in each corner.

Gylfi finally shook off Thóra's grip and ran over to her. "Sigga!" he moaned, clearly moved at the sorry state of his beloved.

"Oh, great!" snarled the mother. "Romeo and Juliet. I'm going to throw up."

Thóra swung round to face her. She was seething with rage. Two youngsters had made a terrible mistake and this woman had the nerve to mock their fate, even though one of them was her own daughter. Thóra rarely lost her temper, but it happened now. "Excuse me, but this is difficult enough as it is—don't go spicing it up with sarcasm." Hannes leaped to his feet and Thóra felt him push her down onto the sofa before she could even begin to resist. Sigga's mother gasped—anger blazed from her eyes.

"I see where your son gets his manners from," she said, and sat down, too, her back straighter than a ballerina's. Her husband chose to remain standing, towering over them from the middle of the floor.

"Mom!" Sigga wept. "Shut up!" Thóra took an immediate liking to the girl—her prospective daughter-in-law.

"What's all this bitching about?" said Sigga's father. "If we can't discuss this like civilized human beings, we might as well forget it. We're here to face up to this terrible news and let's do just that." The word "terrible" was stressed with great drama.

Hannes sat up. "Agreed, let's try to keep calm—this isn't easy for any of us."

The woman snorted again.

"Well, anyway," Hannes continued solemnly. "Maybe I should begin by saying how saddened I am and on behalf of my family I want to apologize for our son's behavior and the pain he's caused you."

Thóra took a deep breath, wanting to digest Hannes's words before killing him. She turned to him, perfectly calm. "For a start, just to set the record straight, we're not a family. My son and daughter and I are a family. You're a cheap excuse for a weekend father, but unlike most of them you can't even take your own son's side when you need to." When she looked away from Hannes she noticed the others were staring at her. Her son was watching her proudly. She repeated for emphasis: "Just to set the record straight."

Hannes took a sharp breath, but Sigga's mother beat him to a reply. "How appropriate. I want to take this opportunity to point out that your darling prince—that son of yours"—this family's talent for drama knew no bounds. She gave a grandiose emphasis to her words with an exaggerated sweep of the hand—"will soon be the same 'cheap excuse for a weekend father' as your ex-husband."

"No!" The shout came from Gylfi. Proudly he went on: "I . . . I mean we. We. We're going to stay together. We'll rent an apartment and look after the baby."

Thóra suddenly wanted to laugh out loud. Gylfi renting an apartment! He didn't even realize that everything he took for granted—heating, electricity, television, water, garbage collection—all cost money. But she kept her thoughts to herself for fear of discouraging her son. If he believed he was going to rent an apartment, so be it.

"Yes!" cried Sigga. "We can do it—I'm almost sixteen."

"Rape!" shouted her mother. "Of course. She's not even sixteen! It's rape!" She glared at Gylfi and shrieked: "Rapist!"

Thóra did not quite understand how this was supposed to improve the situation. She turned to Sigga. "How many months, dear?"

"I don't know. Maybe three. I haven't had a period for three months anyway." Her father blushed to the roots of his hair.

Gylfi had turned sixteen a month and a half before. Not that it made any difference. "Let me point out that the age of consent in such a case is fourteen, not sixteen. Besides, my son wasn't sixteen himself when the child was conceived and the law makes no exemption for either gender in cases of sexual harassment, as it's called."

"Nonsense." The father snorted. "As if a woman could rape a man? To say nothing of a child, as in my daughter's case."

"And my son's," replied Thóra with a victorious smirk.

"May I point out that your son's at secondary grammar school while my daughter's still in basic school. That must carry some weight with the law," the man said arrogantly.

"None whatsoever," Thóra replied. "There's no mention of educational level, I can assure you."

He frowned. "Those fucking queers in parliament."

"You're crazy!" yelled Sigga. "It's my child. I'm the one who has to carry it around and get a huge belly and ugly breasts and can't ever go to the prom." A fresh bout of tears prevented her from continuing.

Gylfi tried to offer what he must have felt was romantic consolation. In an emotional voice he declared to all present: "I don't care—you can get a really fat belly and horrible breasts. I won't leave you and I won't invite anyone else to the prom. I'll just go by myself. You're the girl I love."

Sigga cried even harder while the adults all stared at Gylfi, open-mouthed. Somehow this ridiculous confession of love drove home the truth that Mother Nature had made an appalling error of judgment—these were children having a child, and identifying the culprit was not necessarily the point.

Only Hannes spoke after this collective realization. He turned to Thóra, his features distorted by rage. "It's all your fault. You live a wild life and sleep with anyone who shows you the slightest interest. The boy did nothing like that while I lived there—he's imitating the only role model he knows."

Thóra was too taken aback to answer. Wild life? One session of sex—admittedly two, if you counted the replay—in two years. That was hardly a wild life. Even her eighty-eight-year-old grandfather had urged her to go out and have more fun—to say nothing of her girlfriend Laufey, although she could hardly be called a preacher of morals.

"I knew it, you're a slut!" the mother screeched, piercing all their eardrums. "A sex addict—and it runs in the family." She stared at Thóra triumphantly.

Thóra found an unexpected ally when Sigga's father joined the fray. "Well, honey, rejoice in the fact that at least your daughter's not frigid like her mother!"

Suddenly Thóra could take it no longer. She had heard more about her son's prospective in-laws than she cared to know. Ahead of them lay a baptism, a string of birthdays, confirmation, and God knows what else. Thóra had no desire to recall these people's most intimate secrets on such occasions. She stood up. "You know what—I don't know whose bright idea it was to meet here in the first place." She pointed at Hannes. "Feel free to talk to Gylfi's father, all night if need be. But I've had enough." She spun around to leave but was forced to return to the gathering when she realized she wanted to take her son with her. "Gylfi, come on." Her departing words were for poor Sigga, who was still weeping with bowed head. "Sigga, the baby will always be welcome in my house—as will both of you if you want to live there together. Good-bye to you all."

She walked out with Gylfi at her heels. She was completely drained. They slammed the front door behind them and went over to Matthew's Jeep, which fortunately was still in its place. Without saying a word, Thóra sat in the passenger seat and Gylfi in the rear beside his sister. "Hannes-ar-dóttir," Sóley said emphatically, teaching Matthew to pronounce her last name.

"Let's go," said Thóra, clutching her head in her hands. She looked at Matthew—relieved that her son had only a fleeting grasp of German and her daughter none at all. "Guess what? I've been devalued. You've just slept with a granny."

To her surprise, Matthew roared with laughter. "I must say that Icelandic grannies are rather different from German ones." He darted a glance toward the backseat, where Gylfi sat immersed in doubts about his future. The only straw he could clutch at now was his mother, who had flown into a rage, largely because she was still half hungover. "Hello, son of Thóra. I'm Matthew." He winked at Thóra. She looked back at him, too, ready to repay his honesty. Now she would tell her son that Matthew was more than a friend and colleague. Noticing the iPod still dangling from the lad's neck, she decided not to.

"Gylfi. This is Matthew, who's working with me. I invited him round for dinner. We'll talk things over quietly together when he's gone." She swallowed a lump that suddenly appeared in her throat. She was going to be a grandmother, thirty-six years old. Jesus, Mary, the Holy Ghost, and the other one from the Trinity whose name escaped her—may the child be healthy and its parents' lives a bed of roses in spite of this mistake. She fought back the tears that pressed forth uninvited. She was swamped with old signals she should have figured out. *It's no fun being alone with Gylfi—he's always jumping on the bed and howling* . . .

"Thóra." Matthew pulled her out of her thoughts. "I had a phone call from the museum of sorcery just now. It seems there's an explanation for the state Harald's body was in."

CHAPTER 28

Thóra was determined not to cancel the dinner invitation. As if in a trance she threw some food from the refrigerator and freezer into a pot, not paying much attention to the outcome.

"Dinner is served," she called, trying to sound cheerful. Matthew sat down at the kitchen table straightaway and watched wide-eyed as a succession of bowls appeared. When the table was set, the meal consisted of peas, chips, rice, couscous, soup, jam, and traditional Icelandic flatbread.

"Looks delicious," he said politely when they were all seated. He reached for some canned peas.

Thóra surveyed the table and groaned. "I forgot the main course," she said resignedly. "I knew there was something wrong." She began to stand up to look for something to make the best of a bad job: frozen lasagna, pasta, meat, or fish. But she knew she had nothing—she had planned to go shopping but had been swept along by events. Matthew grabbed her by the arm and pulled her back to her seat.

"It's fine. It's an unconventional dinner but so is the timing, so it's all right." He smiled at the children poking at the mixture on their plates.

Thóra looked at the clock and saw it was only three—she had certainly gone off the rails. She forced a smile. "I'm still in a state of shock. I'll invite you for dinner again next year if I've recovered by then."

"No, there's no need. I'd rather invite you out," Matthew said, taking a bite of plain Icelandic flatbread. "Exquisite." He grinned.

None of them cleared their plates, and the trash can was filled with leftovers at the end of the meal. Sóley asked to go round to see her friend Kristín, and Thóra agreed without a word. Gylfi disappeared into his room, said he was going on the Internet. Thóra hoped he would not visit any sites about baby care. He would give up in despair if he saw in black-and-white what that entailed. When they were left by themselves, Thóra and Matthew sat down in the living room. She had made coffee that they took with them.

"Well, well," he said awkwardly. "I won't stay long, given the circumstances. Don't grannies need to take a nap after every meal?"

Thóra snorted. "This granny fancies a gin and tonic," she said as she sipped her coffee. "But we both know the consequences so I'll pass for now." She smiled at him and blushed a little. "Anyway, I'm ready to hear what the man from the sorcery museum said." She leaned back in the sofa and curled up her legs.

Matthew took out a piece of paper and unfolded it on the coffee table. "Thorgrímur phoned. He got in touch with that walking encyclopedia called Páll. He could reel straight off all that's known about that magic symbol—do you know why?"

Thóra shook her head. Matthew had clearly expected a more active response, so she ventured: "I don't know—because he's a walking encyclopedia?"

"No. Or yes, he may well be. But he knew all about the symbol because he remembered how incredibly excited Harald was to hear about it."

"So Harald talked to him about that particular symbol?" asked Thóra.

"Yes and no. Harald originally contacted Páll in connection with magic symbols in general and asked him about some that weren't in the standard reference books. Then he asked about the Icelandic book of spells we saw at the exhibition. Páll described the main spells in it and said one in particular had aroused Harald's interest—a fairly nasty spell, although it belongs to the cycle of love charms. Apparently Páll asked Thorgrímur if we'd noticed it. The leaf we saw at the exhibition is the opening passage—there's a lot more on the next page which is not on show. Guess what the spell involved."

"You take a dead man's eyes and do something with them?" Thóra guessed.

"No, but that's still important. If I understood it right, this charm is supposed to make a woman fall in love with you. You have to dig a hole in the floor that the woman walks over, put snake's blood in the hole, and write her name with some magic symbols. Finally you recite a charm— the very charm that was sent to Harald's mother." Matthew gave a proud smile.

"You mean the poem?" asked Thóra.

"You got it," Matthew replied. "That's not all. Páll said Harald was profoundly interested in the charm and they discussed it in depth— whether it only worked on a lover or could apply to a different form of love, whether the hole had to be in the floor, and so on. Then they discussed the symbol scrawled in the margin of the charm." Matthew paused.

"And?" Thóra asked impatiently.

"It turns out that the symbol in the margin is unknown, but resembles a Nordic symbol for a revenge charm. The only difference is one branch missing from the arm at the top. The Nordic spell is found in one manuscript fragment without the poem. All that has been preserved is a description of how to perform the spell and the first line of the charm, which is 'I look at you'—the same opening as the love charm. Páll infers that the owner of the book drew the symbol beside the spell because he either knew for sure or just assumed that the same poem applied to both. The book was apparently the work of four different people, three Icelanders and a Dane, and the last scribe could well have drawn the symbol beside the charm for the same reason. He said this Nordic spell was much darker than the others and of uncertain origin, although the text with it in the manuscript was in Danish. The manuscript is privately owned and has been dated to the late sixteenth century, while the Icelandic book of spells is thought to have been written around 1650."

"What do you mean, a darker spell?" Thóra asked.

"'Blacker magic' may be a better term. Shadier. What he meant was that it was specifically designed to cause harm. A person who has it carved on his body after death can haunt someone who failed him in life—as in watch from the grave and make them regret the way they treated him. And in the end that regret brings doom. And wait for this— to perform the spell you need a certain body part, and you can guess what that is."

"Eyes," Thóra said with conviction.

Matthew nodded. "But hold your horses. When Páll described the spell to Harald he became incredibly excited and demanded to hear in detail how to perform it. Páll gave him a full account over the phone, then sent him scanned copies of the book and the manuscript."

"Yes. And?" muttered Thóra eagerly.

"Well, the way it works is that the seeker of revenge makes an agreement with someone else to perform the spell after his death. Not unlike the corpse breeches. They draw the symbol together on a patch of animal skin using their own blood and raven's blood. It takes a lot more than a few drops, because under the symbol they are supposed to write that X promises to perform the spell for Y, then X and Y confirm this by signing their names." Matthew sipped his coffee before continuing. "Here comes the punch line. When Y is dead, X carves the symbol on the body, lets out enough blood to write with, and—thank you very much—removes the eyes from the body."

"Jesus." Thóra shuddered. "Why on earth—isn't it enough to write in blood and carve up the body?"

Matthew smiled. "Clearly not. Páll said the symbol should be carved into the body to remind the dead person that his eyes were removed at his own request. Otherwise he would rise from the grave and search for his eyes—and presumably kill the friend who took them. But the blood is used to write the now forgotten curse that goes with the symbol. It has to be mixed with raven's blood too."

"Which explains the passerine DNA found when the blood was analyzed!" exclaimed Thóra. "The raven is the largest passerine bird native to Iceland." Her school biology never failed her when she really needed it.

"Anyway, the survivor does not need to add his blood. The eyes are wrapped in the skin with the curse on it and both are then presented to the one who failed the dead person, the object of his revenge. After that the victim is never safe; the dead person will haunt him and constantly remind him of his misdeeds until he cracks and dies a terrible death."

"And the curse that was sent to Harald's mother . . ." Thóra said sadly. Her voice trailed off as her thoughts took over. *How appalling. What could have caused Harald to feel such deep-rooted hatred toward his mother? What on earth had she done to him? Perhaps it was merely a figment of his imagination; he could just have been mad and blamed his mother for it.*

A sudden idea pulled her out of her reverie. "Wait a minute—were the eyes sent to her?"

"No," Matthew said. "They weren't included. I have no idea why. Maybe they got lost or damaged; I simply don't know."

Thóra sat in thought for a while. "Halldór, the medical student. It must have been him who took care of the body," Thóra said. "So he killed Harald."

"It looks that way," Matthew replied. "Unless Harald caused his own death and Halldór took over."

"How?" Thóra asked. "He was strangled."

"Maybe doing his erotic asphyxiation? We have to consider that possibility at least. Or that one of the others killed Harald or made the contract with him. They all looked equally sheepish when we showed them the magic symbol. So Hugi could just as easily have been involved."

"We have to talk to Halldór again—that's for sure. All of them if we can. Good luck arranging that."

Matthew smiled. "So we're not total idiots. We've made a lot of progress. All that's missing from the picture is the money. What happened to that?"

Thóra shrugged. "Maybe Harald managed to buy that repulsive sorcery manuscript. It would be in character."

Matthew mulled the idea. "Maybe. But I doubt it because Páll said it was in the national library of Norway. That's also why the police couldn't identify the symbol—it's very unfamiliar, there's really no one in Iceland who knows it apart from Páll, who's studying abroad. He was never consulted about its origin."

"Maybe Harald transferred the money here to pay Páll for the information and then buy the manuscript from the library, but then he was killed for it by one of his so-called friends. They could have taken the money, couldn't they? People have killed for less."

Matthew agreed. He looked at the clock and then at Thóra, thoughtfully. "The plane from Frankfurt landed at half past three."

"Damn it!" Thóra swore. "I can't talk to his mother now—I simply can't. What if she asks me about my children? What am I supposed to say? 'Yes, Frau, my son is a precocious boy—didn't I tell you, he's going to be a father?'"

"Believe me, she won't have much interest in your children," Matthew said calmly.

"It won't be any better discussing her own son. How can I look her in the face and tell her that Harald struck a bargain with the devil, or as good as, to make her life sheer hell and eventually kill her?" Thóra looked at Matthew, hoping for a constructive answer.

"I'll tell her the news, don't you worry. But you can't get out of talking to her. If you don't do it today, it will have to be tomorrow. She's come all this way for the express purpose of talking to you, remember. When she told me she wanted to meet you in person and alone, she sounded more relaxed than I've ever heard her. You have nothing to fear."

Matthew did not sound quite convincing enough for Thóra. "Will they phone, or what are the arrangements?"

"They'll phone when they get to the hotel." He looked at the clock. "Very soon, I expect. I could call them, if you want."

Ow. Catch–22. Thóra could not decide. "Yes, call them," she said suddenly, then immediately shouted: "No, don't!"

Before she could change her mind again, Matthew's phone rang. Thóra groaned when he took it out, checked the display, and said: "It's them." He pressed the talk button and said: "Hello, Matthew here."

Thóra heard only one side of the conversation but could vaguely discern the voice on the other end while Matthew listened. The conversation seemed very superficial: "Did you have a good trip?" "What a pity." "You know the name of the hotel, don't you?" and so on. The conversation ended when he said: "Auf Wiedersehen. Good-bye." He looked at Thóra and smiled. "You're in luck, Granny."

"What?" Thóra asked excitedly. "Didn't she come?"

"Oh, yes, she came. But she has a migraine and wants to postpone meeting you until tomorrow. It was Elisa who called—they're in a taxi on their way down to Hótel Borg. She wants to meet us there in half an hour."

CHAPTER 29

The young woman bore no resemblance to her mother, but was good-looking nonetheless. She was dark like her father and seemed to take after him, judging from the family photographs Thóra had seen. Her whole air was unpretentious; her long, straight hair kept away from her face in a ponytail, and she wore nice black slacks and a black shirt that looked like silk. The only visible jewelry was a diamond ring on the ring finger of her right hand, the one Thóra had seen on the photograph from the kitchen. Thóra was struck by how slim she was, and when she shook her hand she thought the girl was probably even skinnier than these clothes made her look. Matthew received a much warmer welcome—Elisa hugged him and they kissed each other on both cheeks.

"How are you doing?" he asked after releasing his grip on Elisa's shoulder. Thóra noticed that he did not address her formally, as she would have expected from an employee of the family. Matthew was clearly close to these people, or ranked higher in the firm than she had presumed.

Elisa shrugged and forced a faint smile. "Not too good," she said. "It's been difficult." She turned to Thóra. "I would have come much sooner if I'd known you wanted to talk to me. I had no idea my visit to Harald would matter."

Thóra found this strange, given that the girl had been with her brother immediately prior to his murder, but said only: "Well, you're here now and that's what matters."

"Yes, I bought a ticket as soon as Matthew phoned. I want to help," she said, apparently sincere. Then she added: "And so does Mother."

"Good," said Matthew in an uncharacteristically loud voice. Thóra wondered whether he did so from a fear that she would say something inappropriate.

"Yes, good," Thóra parroted, to convince him she had no such intention.

"Shouldn't we sit down?" asked Elisa. "Can I get you a coffee or a glass of wine?" Thóra had quit drinking for life so she ordered a cup of coffee. The others ordered glasses of white wine.

"Well," Matthew said, settling back in the armchair. "What can you tell us about your visit, then?"

"Shouldn't we wait for the wine? I think I need that first," Elisa said with a pleading look at Matthew.

"Of course," he answered, and leaned forward to pat her hand where it rested on the arm of the sofa.

Elisa looked at Thóra apologetically. "I can't quite explain it but I find that visit so uncomfortable to recall. My feelings are still in a tangle; in retrospect it's as if I was really self-absorbed and only talked to him about myself. If only I'd known it was the last time I'd ever see him I would have told him so much about my feelings for him." She bit her lower lip. "But I didn't, and now I never can."

The waiter brought the drinks and they toasted nothing in particular. Thóra regretted having given up drinking when she sipped her coffee and watched them take their first swallows of wine. She decided to fall off the wagon at the earliest opportunity—but was embarrassed to ask for a glass after making her choice.

"Maybe I should tell you why I came to see Harald," Elisa said, putting down her glass. Thóra and Matthew nodded. "As you know, Matthew, I'm going through a bit of a crisis with Mother and Father. They want me to study business and join the bank, as do most people I know, in fact. Harald was the only one who told me always to do what I wanted—play the cello. Everyone thinks I should do business and keep the cello as a hobby. But Harald knew it's not like that, although he was not a musician. He understood that once you've achieved a certain level of skill and potential, it's either/or."

"I understand," Thóra said, not really understanding.

"That's why we mainly talked about me when I came," Elisa continued. "I went to him for encouragement and that's exactly what I got. He told me to defy them and keep on playing. He said faceless suits who could run a bank were a dime a dozen but brilliant musicians were so much rarer." She hastened to add: " 'Faceless suits' were his words—that's what he said."

"If I may ask, what did you decide to do?" Thóra said, out of curiosity.

"To keep playing," Elisa said with a bitter smile. "But I've enrolled in business studies now and the course starts soon. You decide one thing and do something else, that's the way it goes."

"Isn't your father pleased?" Matthew asked.

"Yes, but mostly he's relieved. It's hard to be happy in this family. Especially now."

"Elisa, I know it's difficult to discuss your own family affairs, but we saw some of the e-mails between Harald and your father. They didn't seem to be particularly close, as father and son." Thóra paused, then added: "Just as we have reason to believe he didn't exactly have a model relationship with your mother."

Elisa took a sip of wine before answering. She looked Thóra straight in the eye. "Harald was the best brother you could imagine. He may well have been unconventional, especially recently." She stuck out the tip of her tongue and pinched it, alluding to Harald's cleft tongue. "But I would still have stood by his side anywhere. He had a noble character, and not just toward me—he championed our sister; I never saw anyone treat a disabled person so kindly." She contemplated her wineglass on the table. "Mother and Father, they just . . . I really don't know what to say . . . They never gave Harald his due. My first memories of them are endless hugs, love, and care, but I never saw Harald get much attention. They just . . . well, they just didn't seem to like him." In a flurry of words she interrupted her own train of thought. "They were never exactly bad to him. They just didn't love him. I don't know why, if there is any particular reason."

Thóra tried to conceal her low opinion of the Guntliebs. She itched to find the person who killed that poor boy. She could not conceive of a more wretched fate than a loveless upbringing. Children have a tangible need for affection and it was downright criminal to deprive them of it. No wonder Harald was strange. Suddenly she looked forward to meeting his mother the next day. "Yes," she said to break the silence. "This doesn't sound good, I must say. It might not have anything to do with our speculations, but I do feel it explains a lot about his character. I'm sure you'd prefer not to discuss it with a stranger, though, so maybe we should turn to what happened between you."

Elisa smiled, relieved. "As I said, we mostly talked about me and my problems. Harald was great and we didn't do anything in particular really. He took me to the Blue Lagoon and to see a geyser. Otherwise we just strolled around town or stayed at home watching DVDs, cooking, and chilling out."

Thóra tried to visualize Harald swimming at the Blue Lagoon geothermal spa, but could not conjure up a sufficiently convincing image. "What did you watch?" she asked curiously.

Elisa grinned. "*The Lion King,* strange as it may sound."

Matthew winked at Thóra. So he hadn't been lying about the disk in the player. "Did he tell you anything about what he was up to?"

Elisa thought. "Not much. Actually he was in incredibly good spirits and was clearly doing well here. I'd rarely seen him so cheerful. Maybe it was getting away from Mother and Father. Maybe because of a book he found."

"A book?" asked Thóra and Matthew in unison. "What book?" said Matthew.

Their reaction clearly startled Elisa. "That old book. *Malleus Malefi-carum.* Isn't it at his apartment?"

"I don't know, I don't even know what book you're talking about exactly," said Matthew. "Did he show it to you?"

Elisa shook her head. "No, he hadn't got it yet." She paused. "Maybe he didn't manage to get it before he was murdered. It was just before then."

"Do you know if he was going to pick it up from someone?" asked Matthew. "Did he mention that?"

"No," replied Elisa. "Actually I didn't ask about it—maybe I should have."

"That doesn't make any difference," Matthew said. "But did he tell you anything about this book?"

Elisa's face lit up. "Yes. It was quite an awesome story. Let's see, how did it go again?" She thought for a moment before going on. "You remember his grandfather's old letters, don't you?" She addressed Matthew, who nodded in agreement. Thóra did not want to interrupt by asking what letters they were talking about, but assumed she meant the letters from Innsbruck in the leather wallet. "Harald was like Grandfather," Elisa went on. "Fascinated by them, reading them over and over. He was convinced that the author had done something awful to Kramer in revenge for the way he treated his wife." She looked at Thóra. "You know who Kramer was, don't you?"

It was Thóra's turn to nod. "Yes, I've even had the misfortune to read his masterpiece, if that's the right word for *The Witches' Hammer.*"

"I've never bothered, but I know all about it—you can't avoid it in my family. Harald became obsessed with finding out what had happened. I tried to point out to him that it happened five hundred years ago and there was no chance of unearthing it now. But he always maintained that you could never rule anything out. The Church was involved and most of its documents have been preserved. He didn't give up, anyway—he enrolled in history to gain access to archives. Then he chose witch hunts to give the theme of his dissertation more credibility. Of course that was plain sailing, with his grandfather's collection in front of him and the old man's passion in his blood."

"So your grandfather was kind to him?" Thóra asked, knowing the answer would be positive but nonetheless wanting it confirmed.

"Oh, yes," Elisa said. "They spent a lot of time together. Harald always sought his company, even when Grandfather was in the hospital on his deathbed. Understandably, Grandfather was much fonder of him than he was of the rest of us. Maybe because he felt Harald was the odd one out with our parents. Harald inherited his interest in history. They seemed able to pore over it endlessly."

"And did his research lead anywhere?" asked Thóra. "Did he find anything out from all this?"

"Yes," replied Elisa. "So Harald claimed, at least. Through the university in Berlin he gained access to the Vatican archives and went to Rome after his second year. He spent a long time there, probably most of the summer. He said he'd found a document from Kramer demanding permission for a second witch hunt—he claimed they'd stolen a copy of a book he had written. Kramer apparently said the book was invaluable to him, a manual on how to uproot sorcery and prosecute witches. He was worried they could use the book to curse him and wanted to reclaim it whatever the cost. Harald couldn't find the Vatican's answer to his request, but because Kramer apparently didn't go back to Innsbruck, it was probably rejected.

"Anyway, Harald became incredibly excited and thought he had discovered what was stolen from Kramer and sent all the way to hell: Kramer's draft of *The Witches' Hammer,* the oldest known version of that famous book. It wasn't identical to the edition published a year later, Harald said; presumably it was illustrated and handwritten. Kramer's coauthor, Springer, still had to make his contribution, and this was one of the main reasons for Harald's interest. Kramer's original manuscript would dispel all doubt as to who wrote what. Some people claim Springer had no hand in it at all."

"But didn't the thief send the manuscript straight to hell? Wasn't

that the phrase?" asked Thóra. "The obvious conclusion is that it was
burned."

Elisa smiled. "The last letter to the Bishop of Brixen mentioned an emissary who was bound on a journey to hell and asked the Church to assist
him on his way. So the book wasn't burned, at least not immediately."

Thóra raised her eyebrows. "An emissary on a journey to hell, yes.
Sounds like the most natural thing in the world."

Matthew smiled. "Quite." He took a sip of his wine.

"In those days it wasn't so absurd," Elisa said seriously. "Hell was considered to be a real place—in the bowels of the earth. There was even
supposed to be a hole down to it in Iceland. On some volcano whose
name I can't remember."

"Hekla." Thóra helped her out before Matthew tried to pronounce it.
So that was it—Harald's motive for coming to Iceland. He was looking
for hell, just as Hugi claimed he had whispered to him.

"Yes, right," said Elisa. "That was where the manuscript was supposed to be sent. Or so Harald claimed, at least."

"Then what? Did it ever get there?" asked Thóra.

"Harald told me he'd been looking for information on this emissary's
journey and had found a reference to it in a church chronicle from Kiel
from 1486—at least he thought it was the same man. The chronicle men-
tions a man on his way to Iceland with a letter from the Bishop of Brixen
asking for him to be given lodgings and provisions on his journey. He
arrived on horseback carrying something that he guarded jealously. He
could not even accept the sacrament because the package couldn't be
taken into church, and he never let it out of his sight. It says he stayed for
two nights, then continued on his way north."

"Did Harald find any clues about how the journey ended?" asked
Matthew.

"No," responded Elisa. "Not immediately, at any rate. Harald came
here to Iceland after he gave up trying to trace it on the mainland. At
first he made little headway, then he got hold of an old letter from Denmark that mentioned a young man who had died of measles at a bishop's see whose name escapes me—he was on his way to Iceland. He

staggered into the see at night, desperately ill, and died a few days later. But before he died he managed to entrust to the bishop a package that he was supposed to take to Iceland and throw into Hekla—with the blessing of the Bishop of Brixen. Some years later the Danish bishop wrote to ask the Catholic authorities in Iceland to finish the task. The bishop said he would hand over the package to a man who was on his way to Iceland, if I remember correctly, to sell pardons for the pope to finance the building of St. Peter's Church in Rome."

"When was this?" Thóra asked.

"I think Harald said it was quite a while later, probably around 1505. The bishop was old by then and wanted to clear up unfinished business—he'd kept the package for almost twenty years without passing it on."

"So the package came to Iceland?" mused Thóra.

"Harald was adamant that it did," Elisa replied. She ran her right index finger in circles around the rim of her wineglass.

"Didn't they throw the manuscript into the volcano then?" Matthew asked.

"Harald said that couldn't be right, because no one would have dared climb the mountain then. The first recorded ascent is much closer to our day. Then it erupted a few years later. Harald thought any potential candidate for the job would have been put off once and for all by that."

"So where did the manuscript end up?" asked Matthew.

"At a bishop's see, something beginning with s, Harald thought."

"Skálholt?" Thóra guessed.

"Yes, that sounds right," replied Elisa. "At least, that was where the pardoner went with the money he'd collected."

"Then what? No manuscript of *The Witches' Hammer* has ever been found in Skálholt," said Thóra, pouring herself more coffee.

"Harald claimed it was kept there until the first printing press arrived in Iceland, when it was sent to another see. This one began with *p*, I think."

"Hólar," declared Thóra, even though there was no *p* in the name. Iceland only had two sees, so it was an easy guess.

"I don't remember," said Elisa. "But it could well be."

"Did Harald think they were going to print it there?"

"Yes, I had that impression. It was the most widely published book in Europe at the time, apart from the Bible, so they probably considered it at least."

"Presumably someone opened the package then and saw what it contained. Surely they were tempted to take a peek," said Matthew. "But what happened to the book? It was never published here, was it?" he asked Thóra.

"No," she said. "Not as far as I know."

"Harald said he had traced it," said Elisa. "He said he'd gone on a wild-goose chase looking for the printing press and that place beginning with *p*—"

"Hólar," Thóra interjected.

"Yes, right," said Elisa. "He thought the bishop had sent the book somewhere else before he was executed, but then he became convinced that it was never removed from the other see—that S-place."

"Skálholt," said Thóra.

"Whatever," Elisa replied. "Anyway, he located the book when he started investigating that angle—he said it had been hidden away to save it from being sent out of Iceland."

"And where was it?" asked Thóra.

Elisa took a sip of wine before answering. "I don't know. He wouldn't tell me. He said he'd save the rest of the story until he could show me the trophy."

Thóra and Matthew made no attempt to conceal their frustration. "Didn't you ask any more about it? Didn't he imply anything?" Thóra asked impatiently.

"No, it was late by then and he was so delighted about the whole business that I didn't want to ruin his pleasure by nagging on about it." Elisa smiled apologetically. "The next day we talked about completely different things. Do you think it's linked to the murder?"

"I honestly don't know," Thóra said in disappointment. Suddenly Mal crossed her mind. Maybe Elisa knew Harald's friends. They seemed to have been close, judging by everything she said. This Mal might have the missing information. "Elisa, do you know who Mal is? Harald had an e-mail from him suggesting that Mal knew something about his search for the book."

Elisa smiled. "Mal, oh, yes. I know Mal. His full name's Malcolm and they met in Rome. He's a historian too. He phoned me the other day— said he'd got a strange e-mail about Harald from Iceland. I told him he'd been murdered."

"Do you think he knows more about it?" asked Matthew. "Could you put us in touch with him?"

"No, he knows nothing," said Elisa. "He's been asking me about the book; he said Harald told him he'd found it but gave no details. Malcolm had always thought Harald was chasing a red herring, so he was interested to find out what had happened."

Thóra's mobile rang. It was the police.

Thóra exchanged a few words with the officer, put down the phone, and looked at Matthew. "Halldór, that medical student, has been arrested in connection with Harald's murder. He wants me to act as his legal counsel."

CHAPTER 30

Thóra felt uncomfortable sitting at the police station. She was wondering whether she could be disbarred for serious abuse of her position and a flagrant conflict of interest. In fact she was unsure whether the law made such a provision; if not, it needed to be amended. The position was this: she was working for the family of a murdered man and was about to become the lawyer of the alleged killer. It was an on-the-spot decision and she had rushed out to hail a taxi. Matthew stayed behind with Elisa and took it upon himself to tell Frau Guntlieb the news and the rationale behind their sudden decision. Presumably he would argue that it gave Thóra a chance to talk to the murderer in person and get answers to the remaining questions. *Good luck to him,* Thóra thought, not envying him the task. Migraine sufferers were not usually very understanding.

"Hello. He's ready." The police officer had walked up to Thóra without her noticing him.

"Yes, thank you," Thóra said, and stood up. "Can I see him alone or am I supposed to be present when he's interrogated?"

"He's made a statement. He refused counsel then. It was a rather awkward situation—we're not used to questioning people without counsel on such serious charges. But he insisted, and in the end we had to leave it to him. It was only when he'd given his statement that he asked to see his lawyer. You."

"Is Markús Helgason in?" asked Thóra. "I was wondering if I could have a word with him before I see Halldór," she added as meekly as she could.

The officer showed her into his colleague's office.

Thóra greeted Markús, who was sitting with his Manchester United coffee cup in front of him. "I don't want to bother you for long, I just wanted to see you for a moment before I go in to Halldór."

"Of course," Markús said, but his tone suggested that he was none too excited.

"I expect you remember that I'm working for Harald Guntlieb's family, don't you?" The officer nodded thoughtfully. "I'm in a rather uncomfortable position, sitting on both sides of the table, so to speak."

"Yes, you certainly are. You ought to be aware that we strongly advised Halldór against choosing you, for precisely that reason. But he wouldn't listen. In his mind you're a kind of Robin Hood figure. He hasn't confessed to the murder. I suppose he thinks you can get him out of this mess." Markús grinned spitefully. "Which you can't."

Thóra brushed aside the slight. "So you believe he's guilty?"

"Oh, yes," said Markús. "Further evidence has come to light that proves his involvement. Watertight—absolutely. They did it together, the two childhood friends. The funny thing, if you can call it that, is that the evidence came from two different sources on the very same day. I've always liked coincidences." He smiled.

"And this has just happened?"

"Yesterday afternoon. We received phone calls connected with the dead man from two people. Both had acquired information that demonstrated not only Halldór's guilt but also the probable scene of the murder."

"Who were these people, if I may ask?"

"It doesn't make any difference if you find out now or later." Thóra shrugged. "A box of gruesome objects was found where Harald lived—in the space he shared with the other tenants. This box contained a strip of skin with a contr—"

"A contract about removing his eyes," interrupted Thóra calmly. "I knew about it."

The officer's face reddened. "And it didn't occur to you to contact me? Do you know anything else that you've been concealing from us?"

Thóra dodged the second question by answering only the first. "To tell you the truth, Matthew and I just discovered this today, and it was only a suspicion. We didn't have the proof you seem to have."

"But you still would have been legally required to let us know," said Markús, still annoyed.

"Which we would have done, of course," Thóra said, quite irritated herself. "It's Sunday today—we would hardly drag you out on your day off because of a hunch. We were going to try to see you tomorrow." She turned on the sweetest smile she could manage.

"All right. I hope that's true." He gave her a skeptical look.

"What other 'gruesome objects' did you find?" Thóra asked.

"Two fingers, a whole hand, a foot, and an ear." He stared at her, half expecting her to say she knew about them too. Her expression told him that she didn't. "From different owners, we think." He waited for her reaction.

"What?" Thóra was taken aback. She knew only about the finger that Gunnar had mentioned—the finger that was found at the faculty building but could not be linked to Harald. What was going on? "Are you talking mass murder? Collecting body parts from the victims?"

"At the moment we don't know. Your client says he knows nothing about it. But he's lying. I can tell when people are lying."

"So what evidence do you have—only the contract, presumably signed by Halldór?"

"Yes," replied Markús. "And a steel star from the shoes Harald was wearing the night of his murder—found under the doorsill in the students' common room. That suggests the body was dragged through the door, and it's worth noting that Halldór had access to that room. So the murder was surely committed there. What's more, a teaspoon was found at the same location. A bloodstained teaspoon. It's been dusted and Halldór's fingerprints were on it. The blood is from Harald; at least, that's what the initial tests suggest."

"A teaspoon," repeated Thóra, surprised. "A bloodstained teaspoon. How do you link that to the case?"

Markús evaded a direct answer. "The janitor, who's also the head of maintenance, handed it over to a professor who brought it straight here." Markús looked reproachfully at Thóra. "Unlike some people, he didn't decide to wait until Monday."

"But a bloodstained teaspoon? I don't quite see how that fits in, nor why it's just now being discovered. Didn't you search the whole building after the body was found?"

"The teaspoon is thought to have been used to remove the eyes from the body. As far as the janitor goes . . ." Markús hesitated and Thóra realized she had hit a sore spot. "Of course a search was made. How we missed the spoon is unclear at the moment. We'll find out why."

"So you have a contract and a bloodstained teaspoon," Thóra said, watching Markús rock back and forth on his chair. There was something else. "I don't think that necessarily proves Halldór's guilt, to tell you the truth. As far as I remember he has an alibi."

"That barman?" Markús scoffed. "We need to talk to him again. Don't faint if his testimony starts to crack under pressure." He looked at her down his nose. "Also, we have more evidence against your client. Two pieces of evidence, actually."

Thóra raised her eyebrows. "Two?"

"Yes—or one pair, to be more accurate. They turned up in a search of Halldór's place this morning. I have no doubt they'll be enough to convince even his own mother of his guilt." Markús's expression was so smug that Thóra thought about yawning and leaving without asking any more questions just to put him in his place. But her curiosity got the better of her.

"So what did you find?"

"Harald's eyes."

CHAPTER 31

Thóra regarded Halldór silently. He was sitting directly opposite her with his head down on his chest—he had not spoken a single word since she entered the interrogation room. After glancing up when she sat down, he immediately resumed laser-beaming a hole in the floor with his eyes. "Halldór," Thóra said with a hint of impatience. "I can't stay very long. If you don't want to talk to me, I have other things to do with my time."

He looked up. "I want a cigarette."

"You can't," Thóra said. "Smoking's not allowed in here. You're ten years too late if you've come here to smoke."

"That doesn't stop me wanting a cigarette."

"Maybe the police will let you have one somewhere else afterward. You're not allowed to smoke in here, though, so let's get to the point. Agreed?" He nodded wearily. "You know why you're in here, don't you?"

"Yes. More or less."

"And presumably you realize that you're in trouble. Big trouble."

"I didn't kill him," Halldór said, looking her straight in the eye without flinching. When she ignored this he began fiddling with a hole on the knee of his jeans—which was certainly there when he bought them and had doubled their price.

"Let's get one thing straight before we say anything else." Thóra waited for his full attention and did not continue until he looked up. "I'm working for Harald's family. That means that your interests and theirs are not necessarily the same. Especially now. I advise you to get another lawyer immediately. Meeting you here right now is all I'm going to do. I can give you the names of some good people who can provide you with all the assistance you need."

Halldór screwed up his eyes and thought for a moment. "Don't go. I want to talk to you. None of those cops believe me."

"Have you wondered whether that might be because you're lying to them?" Thóra asked dryly.

"I'm not lying. Not about the main points."

"And I assume it's up to you to decide which are the main points and the minor ones?"

Anger flashed across his face. "You know perfectly well what I mean. The main point is that I didn't kill him."

"And the minor points? What are they?" asked Thóra.

"This and that," he said, bowing his head.

"If I'm supposed to be of any use to you I want you to do one thing for me," said Thóra, leaning across the sturdy table separating them. "Don't lie to me. I can tell when people are lying." She hoped she had managed to convey the same conviction as the police officer.

Halldór nodded, his expression still peevish. "Right—but what I tell you is in confidence. Okay?"

"More or less," Thóra said. "I've told you I won't act as your defense if you go to court, so you can tell me pretty much anything—except of course the crimes you're going to commit later in life. Don't mention those to me." She smiled at him.

"I'm not going to commit any crimes," he said gloomily. "You promise nothing else goes further?"

"I promise it won't go to the police—even though it can only improve your standing with them. You're already in the doghouse; it won't get much worse than this. But if it makes you feel better, we can agree that we're only speculating about extenuating circumstances. Happy with that? Then you get help without actually saying anything."

"Okay," he said, but with a hint of doubt in his voice. Then he added huffily: "Ask me, then."

"Harald's eyes were found in your flat. How can you explain that?"

Halldór's arms twitched. Nervously he scratched the back of his left hand. Thóra waited calmly while he decided whether to tell her the truth or deny having anything to do with them. She was determined to walk out if he chose the latter option.

"I . . . I . . ."

"We both know who you are," Thóra said impatiently. "Answer me or I'm leaving."

"I couldn't send them," he suddenly blurted out. "I didn't dare. The body had been found and I was afraid they'd be discovered in the mail. I was going to do that later when it had all died down. I used the blood to write the curse, and I put the letter in an envelope that Sunday. Then I dropped it in a box in town." After his confession he took a deep breath, then squeezed his lips tightly together as if he intended to say nothing else.

"Was it because of the contract?" asked Thóra. "Were you really trying to honor that ridiculous contract about the revenge curse?"

Halldór glared at her, furious. "Yes. I swore I'd do it and I wanted to keep my word for Harald. It meant so much to him," he answered, red in the face. "His mother was a total scumbag."

"You realize that this is absolute madness?" Thóra asked in amazement. "How could you even entertain the idea?"

"I just did," came the sheepish reply. "But I didn't kill him."

"Hang on, we haven't got that far yet," said Thóra. He was getting on her nerves. "You removed his eyes—have I understood that correctly?"

Halldór nodded reluctantly.

"And you took them home?"

He nodded again.

"Where, if I may ask, did you keep them?"

"In the freezer. Inside a loaf of bread. I stuffed them inside the bread and put it in the freezer."

Thóra leaned back. "Of course. Inside a loaf of bread. Where else?" With considerable effort she tried to erase the image from her mind. "How could you do it? The operation itself, I mean."

Halldór shrugged. "It was no big deal. I used a teaspoon. Carving the symbol was harder. It didn't go too well. I was really stoned—I had to keep going over to the window for fresh air."

"No big deal," echoed Thóra, perplexed. "Pardon me for doubting that."

He glared at her. "I've seen much more revolting things. And done much more revolting things. What do you think it's like, slicing your friend's tongue in half? Or watching surgical operations?"

Thóra could not imagine, but she still doubted that it was as repulsive as plucking out someone's eyes with a teaspoon. From now on she would stir her coffee with a tablespoon. "Be that as it may, it can't have been pleasant."

"Of course not," Halldór shouted. "We were stoned out of our minds. I told you."

"We?" Thóra asked, startled. "So you weren't alone?"

Halldór paused before answering. He picked at the hole in his jeans and started scratching the back of his hand again. Thóra had to repeat her question before he answered. "No, I wasn't alone. We were all there: me, Marta Mist, Bríet, Andri, and Brjánn. We were on our way back from town. We were going back to the party—Marta wanted some dope and Bríet said Harald had some Es hidden away in the common room."

"What about Hugi, wasn't he with you?"

"No. I didn't see Hugi that night. He left the party with Harald and we didn't see him again. Him or Harald. Alive, I mean."

"So you went up to the faculty building?" Thóra marveled. "How did you get in? The security system didn't record any movements."

"It was out of order—I think it always is. And do you really think somebody marches around the whole building making sure no one else is in there? Not likely."

"Thorbjörn Ólafsson, Harald's supervisor, insists that he switched the system on," said Thóra. "He says that's definite."

"It wasn't on when we arrived. Harald's killer must have switched it off."

"But the building was still locked and you need an access code to get in," Thóra said. "It all goes through a computer and the records show that no one went through the door." A printout from the security system had been among the evidence the police had sent to her, and she had seen it with her own eyes.

"We got in through an open window at the back of the building. It's always open, actually—there's some moron with a room there who never remembers to shut it. That's what Bríet says, anyway. We left through it too. She didn't have her key; neither did Brjánn."

"And?" Thóra said. "Was Harald there? Passed out? Dead? What?"

"I told you I didn't kill him. He wasn't crashed out when we got there. He was in the common room. On the floor. Dead. Fucking dead. Blue in the face with his tongue out. You didn't have to be a pathologist to see that he'd been choked." The tremor in Halldór's voice suggested he was not quite as cool as he pretended to be.

"Could he have choked while performing some sex act? Did you remove anything that could have implied that?"

"No. Nothing. There was nothing around his neck—just a nasty bruise."

Thóra thought about it. Of course, he could be telling her a pack of lies, but if so he was certainly a damn good liar. "What time was this?"

"About five. Maybe half past. Or six. I don't know. I remember leaving the bar around four. How long we hung around, I can't say. We didn't care what the time was."

Thóra took a deep breath. "And then what—you just started removing his eyes and carving him up right there? And how did he end up inside the printer room?"

"Of course it wasn't the first thing I did. We stood there like a bunch of idiots. Didn't know what to do. Even Marta Mist was hysterical, and she's always supercool. We were desperate, off our heads, stoned and drunk. Then all of a sudden Bríet started talking about the contract, latched onto me and said I had to honor it, otherwise Harald would haunt me. We'd signed it at one of our meetings in front of the others—just for show, really, but Harald was serious about it. Hugi was the only one who didn't know about the contract. Harald always said he didn't take sorcery seriously."

"Was the contract only about the revenge curse?" asked Thóra.

"Yes—the written one," Halldór replied. "Actually we made a second one. It was a love charm to enhance the effect of the first one by arousing Harald's mother's belated love for him, to make her mourning even tougher. That contract was verbal. I was supposed to make a hole at the end of Harald's grave and draw some symbols in it and write his mother's name. Then I'd put some snake's blood in the hole. Harald even bought a snake for the purpose. A week before he died he asked me to look after it and I've still got the bloody thing. It's driving me nuts. You have to feed it live hamsters and stuff. It makes me sick."

So Harald had bought the hamsters to feed the snake. Of course. "So he expected to die?" Thóra asked.

Halldór shrugged and left the question open. "I just did what I had to do. I remember Marta Mist and Brjánn puked their guts out while I got to work on the body. Then Andri said we had to get Harald out of the room or we'd be suspects. We used the common room a lot. We thought that was a good idea so we dragged him to that little room. We had to prop him up inside because there wasn't space on the floor to stretch him out. It took a lot of shuffling around and it was a real hassle. Then we got out—went back to Andri's, who lives quite close by. Marta Mist threw up in his bathroom the whole morning. The rest of us just sat paralyzed in the living room until we all crashed out."

"Where did you get the raven's blood to write with?"

Shame clouded Halldór's face. "We shot it. By the sea at Grótta. There was no other way. We'd been to the children's zoo to see if anyone there would give us or sell us a raven, and we'd talked to all the pet shops. But that didn't work. We had to write the contract in blood."

"Where did you get a gun?"

"I stole my dad's rifle. He goes hunting. He didn't notice, though."

Thóra was lost for words. Then she remembered the box with the body parts. "Halldór," she said calmly. "What about the body parts at Harald's flat? Did you two have any use for them or did they just happen to belong to Harald?" It was not exactly appropriate to say "belong" in this context, but it would simply have to do.

Halldór coughed, then wiped his nose with the back of his hand. "Um, yes, those," he said sheepishly. "They're not from corpses, if that's what you think."

"Think? I don't *think* anything," Thóra snapped back. "Right now I'd expect you to say absolutely anything. You could tell me that you'd dug up coffins and I'd take it in stride—"

Halldór cut her off. "That's just stuff from work. Stuff that was supposed to be thrown away."

Thóra laughed mockingly. "I've been giving you the benefit of the doubt, but come on! Stuff that was supposed to be thrown away!" She pretended to lift something up and examine it with a sour face. "What's this foot? Bloody stuff everywhere. Just throw it out." She tossed aside the imaginary foot. "Don't be stupid. Where did it come from?"

Halldór stared at Thóra, blushing furiously. "I'm not stupid. It was stuff that was supposed to be thrown away—not literally thrown away, but incinerated. If the police investigate it, they'll find out it's all damaged body parts that had to be removed surgically. Part of my job is sending those things off to the incinerator. I took them home instead."

"I think it would be more correct to say it *was* your job, pal. I doubt that you'll be doing any more shifts there." Thóra tried to get a grip on the countless thoughts and questions whizzing through her mind. "How can you keep a foot and a finger for—how long was it again? Doesn't human flesh get moldy if it's not preserved? Maybe you kept them in the freezer too?"

"No, I baked them," Halldór answered, as if nothing could have been more natural.

Thóra gave another nervous laugh. "You baked body parts. Who do you think you are, Sweeney Todd? Jesus Christ, all I can say is I pity your lawyer."

"Ha-ha. Very funny. I didn't literally bake them." Halldór scowled. "I dried them over low heat in the oven. That way they don't rot. Or at least they rot a whole lot slower. By the way, decomposing flesh is said to rot, not 'get moldy.'" He flung himself back angrily in his chair. "We needed it for our spells—it made them much more fun."

"And the finger that was found in the faculty building—was that from your cooking sessions too?"

"It was the first one. I wanted to tease Bríet with it and I put it in the hood of her coat. I expected it to slide down her face to freak her out, but it dropped out without her noticing. But fortunately they couldn't link it with us. I didn't play practical jokes with body parts after that, because we came very close to getting into big trouble."

Thóra sat absorbing all this. She decided to change tack a little—she'd had enough blood and guts for the time being. "Why did you lie to us about your trips to Strandir and Rangá? We know you went there with Harald."

Halldór looked down. "I didn't want anyone to connect me with the sorcery exhibition. It was there that Harald found the spells for our contract. Nothing much happened there. I waited outside on a bench while Harald talked to the curator. They got on well, I know that much, and they shook hands heartily when we left. I was incredibly hungover and felt like shit so I didn't want to go inside. A friendly raven stayed and kept me company."

"He didn't discuss it on the way home?" asked Thóra.

"No, the pilot was with us."

"What about Rangá? What did he do there? I know you were with him there too."

Halldór blushed. "I don't know what he did. One thing's for certain, he didn't go hunting. I don't really know anything else. We stayed at the hotel and Harald went somewhere while I stayed in my room and read."

"Why didn't you go with him?" asked Thóra.

"He didn't want me to," said Halldór. "He took me along because I'd told him I was up shit creek with one of my courses—he said he knew a place where there was nothing else to do and he'd lock me up with my books for the whole weekend. He kept his word—not literally, but he refused to let me join him on his excursions. I don't know exactly what he did, but Skálholt's close by."

"You must have spent some time together then too—didn't you talk about it?" asked Thóra.

"Of course we met up in the evening—had dinner, then went to the bar," Halldór said, smiling at her. "We were discussing completely different things, though, you see."

"So why did you deny going there?" Thóra asked in surprise. "And why on earth were you booked in under the name Harry Potter?"

"For a laugh," Halldór said in an irritated tone. "Harald booked me under that name. Nicknames amused him and that time I was the butt of his little joke." He paused. "And why didn't I tell you about it? I don't know—I just lied for the sake of lying. Okay?"

"Unfortunately I don't think the police were wrong. I think Hugi killed Harald and you took over, possibly without realizing. Maybe he had gone home, that could very well be true. But you're clearly a warped personality—and presumably he's just as crazy as you, so he killed Harald on account of some stupid thing that no one but him understands."

"No!" Halldór's anger had given way to desperation. "Hugi didn't kill Harald—there's no way."

"A T-shirt with Harald's blood on it was found in his closet. Hugi hasn't managed to explain how it got there. The police think it was used to mop up Harald's blood." Thóra looked at Halldór. "The T-shirt in question is the same one that someone was wearing when Harald's tongue job was done. It says '100% silicon' on it. Does that ring a bell?"

Halldór nodded eagerly. "That's the T-shirt Hugi was wearing. Some blood splashed onto it and he took it off. I used it to mop the floor after the operation." Sheepishly he added: "I didn't want to tell Hugi about it. I just threw the T-shirt in his closet. Hugi didn't kill Harald."

"Who, then, pal?" asked Thóra. "Someone did, and I predict that Hugi will be found guilty of it, not to mention what's going to happen to you and your friends for abusing a dead body."

"Bríet," Halldór said suddenly. "I think Bríet killed him."

Thóra pondered. Bríet. That was the little blonde with the big breasts. "What makes you think that?" she asked calmly.

"I just do," Halldór answered in a weak voice.

"No, tell me. You must have some grounds for naming her in particular. Why her?" Thóra asked firmly.

"Because. She slipped out of the bar when we were in town. She said she lost us, but we didn't leave the place—some of us anyway."

"That's not enough," Thóra said. She couldn't be bothered to ask why he had not told the police about this. According to their testimonies, they all stayed more or less together.

"The teaspoon," Halldór said quietly. "She was supposed to get rid of the teaspoon but didn't. She can't have been so stupid as to put it in the drawer where the police claim they found it—I can't believe that. Marta Mist disposed of the knife and that's gone. But now all of a sudden the teaspoon materializes. I don't think that fits."

"Why would she sneak it back in there? That doesn't exactly sound logical."

"She wanted to get me into trouble. She never held the spoon with her bare hands like I did. She was wearing mittens. She's mad at me for dumping her. I don't know." Halldór rocked in his chair. "She was acting a bit strange that night. When we found the body she was the only one who didn't howl and scream. She kept her cool. She just looked at it without saying a word while the rest of us completely freaked out. Not a word until she reminded me of the contract. She was going to set me up. Just ask the others if you don't believe me." He leaned forward and grabbed Thóra's arm across the table. "She knew about the window—maybe she climbed out of it earlier that evening, how should I know? She was mad at Harald for not talking to her the previous week—he didn't talk to any of us, but that's beside the point. Maybe she got mad or something; she had a date with him and he stood her up. Whatever. Believe me, I've thought about this a lot and I know what I'm saying. Check it out—talk to her for my sake, if nothing else."

Thóra freed her arm. "People react to shock in different ways—maybe she's the type that goes into a trance. I don't want to talk to her. Leave that to the police."

"If you don't believe she's crazy, ask around at the university. She did some project with Harald and fucked it up completely. Ask them." He fixed his eyes on her imploringly.

"What project, and what went wrong with it?" Thóra asked slowly.

"Something to do with collecting and documenting all the contemporary accounts of Brynjólfur Sveinsson from different archives. She got this idea into her head that some documents had been stolen. It caused a hell of a scene. Then it turned out to be crap. She's such a nutter, I couldn't see it until now. Talk to the university—if nothing else."

"Who supervised this project?" Thóra asked, and regretted her question immediately. She was sounding as though she was starting to accept this theory of his, which couldn't have any foundation.

"I don't know—it must have been that Thorbjörn guy—they know at the university. Go and ask. Please, I promise you won't regret it."

She stood up. "See you later, baker boy. I'll find you a lawyer if you want."

He shook his head and stared into his lap. "I thought you'd understand—you wanted to help Hugi and I thought I could get you to help me too."

All at once, Thóra began to pity him. Her maternal instinct kicked in. Or was it her grandmotherly instinct? "Who said I wasn't going to help you?" she said. "Let's see what I can find out. I wouldn't touch your defense with a ten-foot pole, but I'll be in court. I wouldn't miss the trial for all the tea in China."

He looked up with a faint smile. Thóra knocked on the door and the police let her out. It was drawing to a close. She could tell.

CHAPTER 32

DECEMBER 12, 2005

Thóra sat drumming on the edge of her desk with a pencil. Matthew watched her in silence. "I hear the Rolling Stones are looking for a drummer. Your newfound grandmother status should qualify you immediately," he said.

Thóra stopped tapping and put the pencil down. "Very funny. That sure helps me think."

"Think? Why do you need to think now?" The day before, Thóra had told Matthew about Halldór's desperate attempt to turn the focus on Bríet, and he had scoffed at the theory. Thóra found it far-fetched, too, but after lying awake all night tossing and turning she was not so certain. Matthew continued: "It seems to be falling into place apart from a few loose ends. Believe me, when the police investigate Halldór the money will turn up; the manuscript, too, if it exists."

He looked out the window. "Let's go to a restaurant and have a late breakfast." Matthew had just arrived at Thóra's office after oversleeping.

"We can't. It's the catering union's anniversary today," Thóra lied.

"They don't open until noon." Matthew groaned. "You'll survive—there are some biscuits in the kitchen," she said. She reached for the phone and called Bella. "Bella, could you bring in the packet of biscuits that's by the coffee machine?" Sensing the "no" that hung in the air she quickly added: "It's for Matthew, not me. Thanks." She turned to Matthew. "Don't you think there are grounds for checking what he said about Bríet? There may be something to it."

Matthew leaned his head back and stared at the ceiling before answering. "You realize that Halldór's cornered, of course?" Thóra nodded. "Nothing we've seen or heard suggests Bríet's implicated apart from being a little crazy and taking part in strange rituals involving baked body parts."

"Maybe we've simply overlooked something," said Thóra without much conviction.

"Such as?" Matthew asked. "Unfortunately, Thóra, it looks like Hugi killed Harald after all and then his friend took over. All that remains to be established is whether they were working together and pocketed the money. There are overwhelming odds that they told Harald a pack of lies about the manuscript and pretended to know where to find it. You must admit Halldór was in a key position to invent a story when he helped Harald with his translations. They could have pretended to arrange the deal and then swiped the money. When the time came to hand over the manuscript they had to take measures to keep Harald quiet. Halldór's explanation for the T-shirt has to be made up."

"But . . ." At that moment Bella stormed in with the biscuits, without knocking. She had arranged them neatly on a plate and poured a cup of coffee. One cup of coffee. Thóra had a hunch that if the biscuits had been for her, Bella would have lobbed the unopened packet from the doorway, aiming straight for her head.

"Thank you very much," Matthew said, taking the refreshments. "Some people don't understand the importance of breakfast." He nodded toward Thóra and winked at Bella. Bella frowned at Thóra, then gave Matthew a wide smile and walked out.

"You winked at her," Thóra said, astonished.

Matthew winked twice at Thóra. "Two for you. Happy?" He put a biscuit in his mouth with a dramatic gesture.

Thóra rolled her eyes. "Watch it, she's unattached and I might just tell her what hotel you're staying at." Her mobile rang.

"Hello, is that Thóra Gudmundsdóttir?" asked a woman's voice that Thóra vaguely recognized.

"Yes, hello."

"This is Gudrún, Harald's landlady."

"Ah, yes, hello." Thóra scribbled down her name and who she was and showed it to Matthew. She added a double question mark to indicate that the purpose of the call was unclear.

"I don't know if I'm phoning the right person but I had your card and . . . anyway, I found a box belonging to Harald here this weekend, with all sorts of things in it." She fell silent.

"Yes, I know what was found," Thóra said to spare the woman from describing the baked body parts.

"You do?" The relief in her voice was tangible. "I was terribly shocked as you can imagine, but I just now realized that I took a piece of paper with me when I ran out of the laundry room."

"Which you still have?" Thóra felt she had to help the woman stay focused.

"Yes, right. I took it with me when I went to phone the police and just found it in the kitchen by the telephone."

"Did this piece of paper belong to Harald?"

"Well, I honestly don't know. It's an old letter. Ancient really. I remembered that you were looking for something like that, and thought it might be better to let you have it rather than the police." Thóra heard the woman take a deep breath before continuing. "They've got enough on their plate. I can't imagine this has anything to do with the case."

Thóra wrote on the piece of paper: "Old letter??" Matthew raised his eyebrows and took another biscuit. To Gudrún, Thóra said: "We'd like to take a look at it at least. Can we come to see you now?"

"Um, yes. I'm at home. There's just one thing." She paused.

"What?" Thóra asked cautiously.

"I'm afraid the letter got quite crumpled in my rush. I was in total shock. It's not ruined, though." She hurried to add: "That was really why I didn't tell the police about it. I didn't want them fussing about me damaging it. I hope you understand how it happened."

"No problem. We're on our way." Thóra put the phone down and stood up. "You'll have to take the biscuits with you, we're leaving. We may have found the lost letter from Denmark."

Matthew grabbed two biscuits and had a last sip of coffee. "The letter the professor was looking for?"

"Yes, hopefully." Thóra swung her bag over her arm and went to the door. "If it is, we can return it to Gunnar and maybe try to get some more details out of him about the story Halldór told me about Bríet." She smiled triumphantly, pleased at her good fortune. "Even if it's not the letter, we can pretend to think it is."

"Are you going to trick the old fellow?" Matthew asked. "That's not a very nice thing to do—given what the poor guy's been through."

Thóra looked over her shoulder on her way down the corridor and smiled at him. "The only way to find out if this is the letter is to take it to Gunnar. He'll be so delighted when he sees it that he'll do anything for us. Two or three questions about Bríet can hardly hurt."

Thóra's smile had faded by the time they found themselves sitting in Gudrún's kitchen with the letter on the table in front of them. Gunnar would hardly be pleased to retrieve it in such bad condition. He'd probably wish it had never been found. "You're sure it wasn't torn when you took it out of the box?" asked Thóra, carefully trying to smooth out the thick sheet without ripping the part that had almost been torn off.

Gudrún cast a guilty look at the letter. "I'm quite certain. It was intact. I must have ripped it in my agitation." She smiled apologetically. "They can stick it back together—can't they? Maybe iron it out a bit?"

"Oh, yes. I'm sure they can," said Thóra, although she suspected that a repair would be a rather complicated procedure, if it was possible at all. "Thank you very much for contacting us. You did the right thing—this is probably the document we were looking for and it really has nothing to do with the police investigation. We'll return it to its rightful owners."

"Good. The sooner I get rid of everything to do with Harald and leave all this mess behind, the better. It hasn't been pleasant for my husband and me since the murder. And I'd like you to tell his family I really want the apartment cleared soon. The sooner I can forget all this, the sooner I can start to get over it." She placed her slender hands down flat on the table and stared at her fingers, adorned with rings. "Not that I didn't like Harald himself. Don't misunderstand me."

"Oh, no," Thóra said in a friendly voice. "I can't imagine it's been at all pleasant." After a short pause she asked: "One final question. I'd like to ask if you got to know Harald's friends—saw them or heard them?"

"Are you trying to be funny?" the woman asked, her tone suddenly turning dry. "Did I hear them? At times they might as well have been in *my* apartment, there was so much noise."

"What kind of noise?" Thóra asked cautiously. "Quarreling? Shouting?"

Gudrún snorted. "It was mostly loud music. If music's the word. And terrible thuds, like they were stamping their feet or jumping. The odd howl, shouting and hooting—I often thought I'd have done better renting the place to animal keepers."

"Why did you go on renting it to him?" asked Matthew, who had kept himself out of their conversation up to that point. "If I remember correctly, there was a clause about conduct in the tenancy agreement and the right to terminate it in the event of noncompliance."

Gudrún blushed. "I liked him despite everything. I suppose that's the explanation. He paid the rent promptly and was a good tenant himself."

"So was it mainly his friends who made all the noise?" asked Thóra.

"Yes, you could say that," said Gudrún. "At least, it intensified when they were around. Harald played loud music and stomped around sometimes—but when his friends were with him it was so much louder."

"Did you ever witness arguments or disagreements between Harald and his friends?" Thóra asked.

"No, I can't say I did. The police asked me the same question. All I remember was one very heated exchange between Harald and some girl in the laundry room. I didn't get involved, I was busy baking. I wasn't in there or anything, I just happened to hear it when I walked past." The blush returned to her cheeks. Previously, Gudrún had shown them the laundry room to explain how she found the box. The room was off the hallway and it was impossible for her to have walked *past* unless she had just come in through the front door. She had obviously been eavesdropping and Thóra tried to think of a way to let her say what she heard without admitting that she had had her ear against the door.

"Oh." She sighed, full of sympathy. "I once lived in an apartment where the door to the laundry room was next to mine, and the things I had to put up with. You could hear almost every single word. I found it awfully uncomfortable."

"Yes," Gudrún said hesitantly. "Harald was generally in the laundry room by himself—fortunately. I don't know if this girl was helping him with the washing or was just there to keep him company, but they were very worked up. It had to do with a missing letter if I recall. This one, I guess." She gestured with her chin toward the table. "Harald kept asking her to forget about something; calmly at first, but he got very worked up when she demanded to know why he refused to back her up. She kept saying it would give her such awesome leverage—whatever that means. That was all I heard because I was just walking past, as I said."

"Did you recognize the girl's voice—could it have been that little blond friend of his?" Thóra asked hopefully.

"I couldn't really say," said Gudrún, sarcasm creeping back into her tone. "There were mainly two who came here: a tall redhead and that blond one. They both looked like hookers who'd suddenly been drafted into the army—covered in war paint and wearing those baggy camouflage trousers. Awfully unattractive and rude, both of them. We often bumped into each other but I don't think they ever said hello to me. There was no way for me to tell who it was without actually seeing her."

While Thóra agreed that Bríet and Marta Mist were rude, they could hardly be called unattractive. She was beginning to suspect that the woman fancied Harald and had a grudge against his girlfriends. Stranger things happened. She tried to conceal her hunch. "Well, that doesn't matter anyway. I'm sure it has nothing to do with the case." She stood up and took the letter. "Thank you very much again, and I'll pass on your request about clearing out the apartment."

Matthew stood up, too, and shook the woman's hand. She smiled at him and he gave a meaningful smile back. "Why don't you just take the apartment instead?" she said, putting her left hand warmly over his.

"Yes, no, I won't be in Iceland for too much longer," he stammered as he tried to think of a way to retrieve his hand.

"Anyway, you could always move in with Bella." Thóra smiled. Matthew gave her a dirty look, but his expression softened slightly when Gudrún released his hand.

"You give him the document," said Thóra, trying to get Matthew to take hold of the large envelope. Gudrún had found it for them as they were leaving, placing the old letter inside to prevent further damage. As if there was any point.

"Out of the question," said Matthew, crossing his arms tight. "It was your idea, so I'm just going to sit and watch—I might hand him a handkerchief if he bursts into tears when he realizes it's in tatters."

"I haven't felt like this since the time I came back from my driving test and reversed straight into our neighbor's car," Thóra said while they sat waiting. They had been offered a seat and told that Gunnar would see them after his class ended. Since no one seemed to be around, Thóra took the opportunity to stretch out in the chair. "It's not as if it was me who ripped the letter."

"But you're the one who gets to break the news," Matthew said, looking at the clock. "Is he coming? I have to have a proper meal before you go meet Amelia. Are you sure this caterers' holiday is only until noon?"

"We'll be quick, don't worry. You'll be eating before you know it." Hearing footsteps from the other end of the corridor, she looked up. It was Gunnar. He had a pile of papers and books in his arms and seemed surprised to see them.

"Hello," he said, trying to fish the key to his office out of his pocket. "Have you come to see me?"

Matthew and Thóra stood up. "Yes, hello," said Thóra. She waved the envelope in front of her. "We wanted to ask you whether a letter that was found over the weekend might be the one you're looking for."

Gunnar's face lit up. "Really?" he said, opening the door. "Do come in. What marvelous news." He went over to his desk and put down the books and papers. Then he sat down and gestured to them to take a seat. "Where was it found?"

Thóra sat down and put the envelope on the table. "At Harald's flat, in a box of odd stuff. I must warn you that the letter's not in good condition." She gave an apologetic smile. "The person who found it had a little fit."

"A little fit?" Gunnar repeated vaguely. He took the envelope and opened it carefully. He slowly removed the letter, and as its condition became clear he grew more and more distressed. "What on earth happened?" He put the letter down on the desk and stared at it.

"Um, the woman found all kinds of other things that upset her," said Thóra. "With very good reason, I can assure you. She asked us to return it because she was very sorry and hoped it could be repaired." She smiled even more apologetically than before.

Gunnar said nothing. He stared at the letter as if frozen. Suddenly he began to laugh. Disturbing laughter—not at all like amusement. "My God." He sighed when the bout of hysteria had ended. "María will be furious." A little spasm passed through his body when he said the name. He stroked the document, lifted it up, and examined it. "But this is the letter; we should be pleased about that, at least." He giggled.

"María?" said Thóra. "Who's María?"

"The director of the Manuscript Institute," Gunnar replied weakly. "She's the one who's worried about this letter."

"Maybe you could pass the message on from the finder," said Thóra, "that she's very sorry."

Gunnar looked up from the letter. His expression implied that this would have little effect. "Yes, I will."

"I want to use this opportunity, Gunnar, to ask you about a student in your department—Bríet, Harald's friend."

Gunnar narrowed his eyes. "What about her?"

"We were told that they had an argument. Something to do with their joint project on Brynjólfur Sveinsson. They had a fight about a lost document. Do you know anything about it?" Thóra noticed a painting on the wall behind Gunnar which, as far as she could tell, showed the bishop. "Isn't that him?" She pointed to the picture.

Gunnar said nothing. He was deep in thought. He did not look around, since he was well aware what was hanging on the wall. "That's not Brynjólfur Sveinsson, it's my great-grandfather, whom I'm named after. The Reverend Gunnar Hardarson. He's wearing clergyman's vestments, not the robes of a seventeenth-century bishop."

Thóra blushed a little and decided not to ask about another of the numerous photographs she noticed on the wall—one which appeared to show Gunnar and the farmer from Hella she and Matthew had met when they went to the caves. Her embarrassment cheered Gunnar up a little and he leaned forward to hiss: "You two are the least welcome visitors I've ever had."

Thóra was taken aback. "I'm sorry. But I'd still like to ask you to show a little patience—we're just trying to tie up a few loose ends, and Bríet is one of them. If you'd prefer not to discuss it, you might be able to give us the name of the teacher or professor who was in charge of the project."

"No, no. I can tell you all about it—that shouldn't be too hard for me. I only meant that you have a knack for unearthing very sensitive in-house matters, which you seem to have done again."

"Really?" Thóra said in surprise. "I thought it would be most sensitive for Bríet. We understand she behaved rather strangely, that's why we're asking."

"Bríet, yes. Quite right, her behavior was most odd. It was really thanks to Harald that we managed to stop her before the department ended up in a very embarrassing position." Gunnar loosened his tie.

"So what did this involve exactly?" she asked as she noticed Gunnar's tiepin for the first time. It reminded her of something that she could not quite place.

Gunnar's eyes darted down to his tie as he sensed Thóra staring at it. He stroked it with his palm just in case he had spilled some food on it. He scratched himself on the pin and pulled his hand back quickly. "What did it involve, you say—let's see. If I remember correctly, Harald and Bríet decided to compile a register of all known records about Brynjólfur Sveinsson as part of a course they attended. I think Harald proposed it, not Bríet. She just tagged along; she was in the habit of latching onto others for projects."

"Was it connected with his dissertation?" asked Thóra; she expected he had really been investigating whether the bishop had had a copy of *Malleus Maleficarum*.

"No, not at all," Gunnar replied. "We found him rather lacking in focus, as I believe I told you. Instead of using his course projects to prepare his dissertation, he roamed far and wide—absorbed himself in topics that sometimes had nothing to do with the history of sorcery. That was particularly true in Brynjólfur Sveinsson's case—he was around in the seventeenth century, as you know."

"Were you his supervisor on this project?" asked Thóra.

"No, I think it was Thorbjörn Ólafsson. I can check if you want." Gunnar gestured at the computer screen on his desk.

Thóra declined the offer. "No, that probably won't be necessary. If you could just tell us what happened we'd be perfectly happy. This is all we need to know at the moment. We're rather pushed for time."

Gunnar looked at his watch. "So am I, actually—I have to hand over the letter to María." Judging from his expression, he did not relish the task. "Anyway, they went to the main archives in Reykjavík, the national archives, the manuscript department of the national library, and such places to compile a record of all the documents and letters mentioning Bishop Brynjólfur Sveinsson. They made good progress, I understand, until Bríet claimed to have discovered that some letters were missing from the national archives."

"Isn't that conceivable?" Thóra asked, with a glance at the ripped letter on the desk. "I mean, such things happen."

"That may well be, but in this case it was a simple administrative error. Admittedly the whereabouts of the letters are uncertain, but she blamed the theft on a certain man who is above suspicion in this instance."

"Who?" Thóra asked.

"Yours truly," said Gunnar, then fell silent. He looked at them, his eyes daring them to challenge his innocence.

"I see," Thóra said, looking Gunnar firmly in the eye, then added: "Excuse me for asking, but why should she have suspected you?"

"As I said, there was an administrative error. According to the records I was the last person to have examined the letter, but I never touched it. Either someone used my name, or the entry numbers were mixed up. Brynjólfur Sveinsson does not interest me and it never occurred to me to look for documents related to him. What made the matter even more unfortunate was that the girl tried to take advantage of this to make me help her through her course. She said straight out that she'd keep quiet if I gave her a helping hand, as she so tastefully put it. I discussed it with Harald and he promised to talk her out of this nonsense. I contacted my friends at the archives and demanded an inquiry. I didn't want some silly girl thinking she could blackmail me. But they found nothing because it was such a long time ago, a decade or so. In the end they admitted that it must have been a mistake on their part, the letter had presumably been filed away with another and would eventually come to light. Bríet had the sense not to mention it to me again."

"What was this letter anyway?" asked Thóra. "What was it about, I mean?"

"The letter was written in 1702 from one of the clergymen at Skálholt, to Árni Magnússon. It appears to be a reply to his inquiry about what had happened to part of the foreign manuscript collection owned by Bishop Brynjólfur, who had died some time before, in 1675. So there's no doubt the letter was in the archive. Many people remember it. It was old news."

"Nothing else?" Thóra persisted. "Nothing about hidden manuscripts or attempts to spirit them away from Skálholt?"

Gunnar studied her face. "Why do you ask if you already know the answer?"

"What do you mean?" Thóra exclaimed. "All I know about that letter is what you've just told me." Her eyes returned to Gunnar's tiepin. Why the hell was it bothering her? And what was the man driving at?

"It's a remarkable coincidence," said Gunnar dryly. He clearly believed she and Matthew knew more than they actually did. "We can go on beating about the bush if you want. The letter contains a cryptic passage about safeguarding valuables from Danish colonial officials and storing them beside the ancient cross. This is generally agreed to be a reference to the holy cross in the church at Kadlanes, which was removed during the Reformation when places of worship were stripped of their icons."

"You seem to know an awful lot about this letter," said Matthew, chipping in for the first time. "Considering that you've never seen it."

"Of course I acquainted myself with it when the accusations were made against me," Gunnar snapped. "The letter is well known among historians, and several fine papers have been written about it."

Thóra stared at his tie as if in a trance. The pin was unusual, quite irregular in shape and apparently made of silver. "Where did you get that tiepin?" she asked suddenly, pointing to his chest.

Gunnar and Matthew both looked at her, dumbfounded. Gunnar grasped his tie and examined the pin. He released it and looked again at Thóra. "I must admit I don't understand the direction this conversation is taking. But since you seem so interested, it was a fiftieth-birthday present." He stood up. "I don't think there's any point in talking further—I have no particular interest in discussing my appearance. I have a less than pleasant meeting awaiting me with the director of the Manuscript Institute and I can't waste any more time on such nonsense. I sincerely wish you all the best with your investigation but I suggest that you stick to the present, because the past has nothing to do with Harald's murder."

He accompanied them to the door.

CHAPTER 33

Matthew looked at Thóra and shook his head. They were standing in the lobby of the faculty building. "That went well."

"Didn't you notice his tiepin?" Thóra hissed. "It was a sword. The pin had a silver base with a silver sword on it, lying across the tie. Didn't you notice it?"

"Yes. So?" replied Matthew.

"Don't you remember the pictures of Harald's neck? The mark that looked like a dagger or a cross? What was it the doctor said? 'If you look closely you can see it resembles a little dagger.'"

"Oh, yes," Matthew responded. "I see what you're driving at. But I'm not sure it's the same object. The photos weren't that clear, Thóra." He sighed. "The man's a historian. The Viking sword on his tiepin is obviously connected with his specialist field, the settlement of Iceland. I wouldn't read too much into it. The mark on Harald's neck looked more like a cross to me." He smiled. "Maybe he was killed by a mad vicar."

Thóra hesitated. She reached for her mobile. "I want to talk to Bríet. There's something funny about all this."

Matthew shook his head, but Thóra went ahead undeterred. Bríet answered on the fourth ring, grumpily. When Thóra told her the news of Halldór's arrest, the girl relaxed a little and agreed to meet them at the student bookshop in a quarter of an hour. Matthew mumbled a protest, but when Thóra told him he could buy something to eat there, he gave in. He was busy devouring a pizza when Bríet appeared.

"What's Dóri told the police?" she asked in a quavering voice the moment she sat down at the table.

"Nothing," replied Thóra. "But he's told me bits and pieces about that night and your part in what went on. I wouldn't be terribly surprised if he tells more people before long. He thinks you killed Harald."

All the color drained from Bríet's face. "Me?" she squeaked. "I had nothing to do with his death."

"He said that you vanished from the group that night and acted strange when you all found the body—not like your usual self."

Bríet's jaw dropped and she sat gaping for a while before she spoke. "I nipped out for twenty minutes—max. And I was in total shock when we found the body. I couldn't even think, let alone string a sentence together."

"Where did you go?" asked Matthew.

Bríet gave him a suggestive smile. "Me? I went to the bathroom with an old friend of mine. He can vouch for that."

"For twenty minutes?" Matthew asked doubtfully.

"Yes. So? You want to know what we were doing?"

"No, thanks," interrupted Thóra. "We can guess."

"What do you want from me, anyway? I didn't kill Harald. I just stood beside Dóri while he fixed the body. Andri's the only one in deep shit if Dóri tells the cops. He helped. I didn't even touch Harald." Bríet was trying to reassure herself, without much success.

"I'd like to ask you about a project you did with Harald on Bishop Brynjólfur Sveinsson, and the missing letter," said Thóra. "Dóri told me you and Harald quarreled over it. Is that right?"

Bríet looked blank. "That crap? What's that got to do with this?"

"I don't know, that's why I'm asking," Thóra replied.

"Harald was pathetic," said Bríet suddenly. "I had Gunnar by the balls. He got nervous when I went to him and told him I knew he'd stolen a letter from the national archives. He definitely did it, whatever anyone says."

"In what way was Harald pathetic?" Matthew asked.

"At first he thought it was funny and dared me to have a go at Gunnar. We even sneaked into his office to look for it after the old bastard threw me out. It was really weird. We were inside and then Harald suddenly changed his mind. He found some old article about Irish monks and flipped like I've never seen before."

"How do you mean?" asked Thóra.

Bríet shrugged. "It was some research paper by Gunnar in one of the cabinets. Harald found it and got me to tell him what the captions said. He was incredibly excited about two of them. One was a cross and the other some fucking hole. Then he wanted to know all about another drawing. I was shitting bricks because I was afraid Gunnar would come. I didn't want to hang around there translating for Harald. In the end he stuffed the article in his pocket and we stopped searching. We just ran."

"What did he say exactly? Can you remember?" asked Thóra.

"Not exactly. We went to the common room and he insisted I tell him what the hole in the photograph was. It was a fireplace in some cave. The cross too. It was carved into the wall there. Some kind of altar."

"And the drawing?" asked Matthew. "What did it show?"

"It was a plan of the cave with symbols showing what was what. If I remember right, one was beside the cross, another by a hole in the roof— I think that was a chimney—and the third was by a hole that was supposed to be a fireplace." Bríet looked at Matthew. "I remember him pointing excitedly at the third symbol and asking me if I thought the monks would have cooked on the altar. I said I had no idea. Then he asked if I thought they would have put the fireplace under the chimney. It wasn't like that at all on the drawing. The fireplace was beside the altar but the chimney was by the entrance. It was so boring, and it wasn't like Harald to get worked up about that kind of nonsense."

"Then what happened?" Matthew asked.

"He went and talked to Gunnar. Afterward he ordered me not to do anything else about the letter." She looked at them angrily. "But he was the one who'd been egging me on to torment Gunnar in the first place—fucking Gastbucht, as he called him."

"Gastbucht?" exclaimed Thóra. What did it say on Harald's sketch? Gastbucht? So it wasn't the visitors' book of the cross, as she had imagined—it wasn't a cross but the letter *t,* and Gastbucht was the nickname Harald had made up from Gunnar's last name, Gestvík: Guest's bay.

Thóra and Matthew went straight back to the faculty building. As they hurried along, she called Markús at the police station and told him the idea she and Matthew had had about Gunnar, which he immediately scoffed at. After a little persuasion, however, he agreed to check the professor's bank account transactions.

Gunnar's office was empty when they arrived. Instead of waiting, they took the liberty of sitting down inside, assuming that Gunnar had gone to meet the director of the Manuscript Institute to hand back the letter.

Matthew looked at the clock. "Surely he'll be back soon."

At that moment the door opened and Gunnar walked in.

He was flabbergasted to see them. "Who let you in?"

"No one. It was open," Thóra said calmly.

Gunnar strode over to his desk. "I thought we'd said good-bye earlier." He sat down at his desk and glared at them. "I'm not in the best of moods. María wasn't exactly overjoyed at getting the letter back in that state."

"We won't keep you for long," said Matthew. "We didn't quite manage to conclude our business with you."

"Really?" snapped Gunnar. "I don't think I have anything left to say to you."

"We just want to ask you about a few outstanding details," Thóra said.

Gunnar tipped his head back and stared at the ceiling. He groaned before looking back at them. "Fair enough. What would you like to know?"

Thóra looked at Matthew first, then at Gunnar. "The ancient cross mentioned in the letter to Árni Magnússon—could it be the cross in the Irish monks' cave near Hella?" she asked. "You're supposed to be an expert on that period—aren't you? At least, the cross was in Iceland before the settlement proper began."

Gunnar turned beet red. "What would I know about that?" he stammered.

Thóra shrugged. "Actually, I think you know all about it. Isn't that a photograph of you and the farmer who owns the land where the caves are?" She pointed to the framed photograph on the wall. "The monks' caves?"

"As it happens, it is. But I don't see the connection," Gunnar said. "I find your questions irrelevant and I can't understand your interest in history. If you want to enroll in the department, there are application forms in the office."

Thóra went on, unruffled. "I think you understand the connection perfectly. You were at the celebration that lasted until midnight on the night of Harald's murder." When Gunnar said nothing she added: "Could it be that you met Harald that night?"

"What nonsense is this? I've made countless statements to the police about Harald's untimely death. I had the misfortune to find the body but in other respects it has nothing to do with me. You should get out of here." He pointed a shaking finger at the door.

"I'm certain the police will recheck all their statements from you now that it's clear how the marks on Harald's body were made," Thóra said, smiling nastily.

"What do you mean?" asked Gunnar, agitated.

"They've found the person who removed the eyes and carved the symbol on the body. Your reaction on seeing the body is no guarantee that the police will treat you with silk gloves. Everything appears in a completely different light now."

Gunnar seemed to be having difficulty breathing. "You're busy people. So am I. I'd hate to delay you. Let's call this a day."

"You strangled him with your tie," Thóra continued. "Your tiepin will confirm that." She stood up. "The motive has yet to be revealed but it's unimportant at the moment. You killed him. Not Hugi, not Halldór, and not Bríet. You." She looked him in the eye, torn between revulsion and pity. Gunnar shuddered and Matthew stood up slowly, using one hand to edge Thóra gently back toward the door. It was as if he feared Gunnar would jump over the desk with his tie held aloft to strangle her too.

"Are you mad?" shouted Gunnar, staring at Thóra. He leaped clumsily to his feet. "How could you imagine such a thing? I advise you to seek help immediately."

"I'm not mad—you killed him." Thóra stood her ground. "We have several pieces of evidence to prove your guilt. Believe me. When the police get it and look into your case you'll have trouble coming up with a defense."

"This is ludicrous, I didn't kill him." Gunnar looked at Matthew pleadingly, hoping for support.

"The police may be interested in hearing you deny it—but we're not." Matthew was stone-faced. "Perhaps the department can assist with an investigation into your private affairs. And perhaps a search will reveal more clues if the tiepin isn't enough."

Thóra's phone rang. She kept her eyes on Gunnar for the short duration of the call. He nervously listened to her conversation without a clue about the context. Thóra put her phone back in her pocket. "That was the police, Gunnar."

"So?" he blustered. His Adam's apple bobbed.

"They asked me to go down to the station. They've discovered some interesting transactions from your bank account and want Matthew and me to explain our case more fully. As far as I can see, the police are closing in on you." She stopped talking and stared at him.

Gunnar looked back at them, confused. Then he lifted his tie and stared at the pin. He opened his mouth twice to say something, then thought better of it. In the end he bowed his head in resignation. "Are you looking for the money?" he slurred. "I haven't spent much of it." He watched them, but got no response. "I have the book, too, but I'd rather not hand it over. It's mine. I found it." He clutched his forehead in a gesture of desperation. "I have nothing else valuable or unique. Harald seemed to have everything, plenty of money at least. Why couldn't he covet something else?"

"Gunnar, I think we ought to call the police," said Thóra gently. "You don't need to tell us any more—save your strength." She saw Matthew take out his phone, ready to dial. "One-one-two," she said quietly to him. Gunnar didn't notice. Matthew stepped outside to make the call.

"I always expected the police to accuse me of murder when they questioned me about finding the body. I was convinced they were just playing a game with me, pretending not to know I killed him. Then it turned out I wasn't even under suspicion." He looked up, smiling faintly. "It would have been impossible for me to feign the horror I felt when the corpse fell on me. The last time I'd seen it was on the floor of the common room. For a moment I thought he had risen from the dead to take revenge. You must believe that I did nothing to his eyes. I just strangled him."

"In itself that's quite enough," said Thóra. "But why? Because he wanted to buy the manuscript of *The Witches' Hammer* from you? Did you have it?"

Gunnar nodded. "I found it in the cave. Twenty years ago. I was on sabbatical, absorbed in the Irish monks. I got permission from the farmer to excavate there in the hope of finding relics of human habitation to prove whether the caves had been dug by them. They hadn't been studied before. Mine was the first shovel to break the earth there, although a few other caves in the area had been investigated much earlier. Cattle were kept in them until the middle of the last century, so they were largely unexplored. But instead of finding relics of presettlement habitation I found a little chest which was completely hidden in a hole beside the altar. It contained that manuscript and a few other works. A handwritten Bible in Danish, a hymnal, and two beautiful books on the natural sciences in Norwegian." He looked deep into Thóra's eyes. "I couldn't resist.

I rushed off to hide the chest in my car before the farmer caught me, and I never told a soul about it. Gradually it dawned on me what treasures I had in my possession: the lost bounty from Skálholt. Two of the books were marked with Brynjólfur Sveinsson's initials—LL. But it was not until Harald turned up that I received an explanation for what this bizarre edition of *The Witches' Hammer* was doing there."

"But how did he figure it out?" Thóra asked, adding: "You don't have to tell me if you don't want to."

Gunnar ignored the latter remark and answered her. "Beginner's luck," he said. "Actually, I wouldn't call it luck, but rather misfortune. Harald came here specifically to look for that manuscript, as I'm sure you know. He turned all the sources inside out until he got on the right track, or so he thought. He was convinced that Bishop Jón Arason had taken the manuscript to be printed but hid it when his power base began to collapse upon the conversion to Lutheranism. At that time I didn't realize what he was up to and did nothing to obstruct him. He went to Skálholt to examine the site of Jón Arason's execution. There he got on the trail of the manuscript by sheer chance—someone told him about Brynjólfur's collection of manuscripts and he studied all the records in the hope of identifying what had gone missing. It was only when he came to see me after Bríet had found out about the letter that disappeared from the national archive . . ."

He lowered his gaze, then looked back up at Thóra. "Of course I kept the letter after I realized what I'd discovered. I was scared it would lead other people to the caves—that someone would reach the same conclusion as you about the holy cross. That was a costly mistake. Bríet was easy to deal with, but then Harald appeared. He had studied the content of the letter. He got straight to the point, said he knew I'd found Kramer's *Witches' Hammer* and he wanted it. He had stolen an article about the Irish monks and the caves from my office—an old paper I was forced to write at the end of my sabbatical. I had to report on what I'd done and I published the article in an obscure journal that has since gone under. I made the mistake of including a photograph of the hole where I dug up the chest. I said it was an ancient fireplace. No one countered that finding—in fact I don't think anyone ever bothered to read the paper at all. Harald simply put two and two together. And I thought the cleaner had stolen the article."

Gunnar paused for a moment. "He wanted *The Witches' Hammer.* Said he didn't care what else had been there, but he had to have the book. Then he offered to buy it from me. He named an incredible sum, much more than I could have got for it on the black market even if I had the faintest idea where that market is. Instead of refusing and throwing him out, I lowered my defenses. The money tempted me. At the time I still didn't know how remarkable the manuscript was. Harald didn't tell me the whole story until he gave me the money. And that made me change my mind. But of course I couldn't tell him that." Gunnar sighed. "Naturally you can't understand, but when you spend your whole life working with history, you instinctively become enchanted by what's survived. I had my hands on a remarkable treasure. Absolutely unique."

"So you killed Harald to keep the manuscript—without trying to return the money or find out if he was prepared to back down?" asked Thóra. "Maybe he would have chosen to live without it, rather than to die."

Gunnar laughed weakly. "Of course I tried. He just laughed in my face and said I'd be better off dealing with him than with the authorities, because he wouldn't hesitate to inform on me if I double-crossed him." He sighed. "I saw him. He was cycling up to the campus when I was driving home. I turned back and caught up with him at the entrance. He threw his bike aside and we entered the building together. One of his hands was covered in blood from a nosebleed he had. Disgusting." Gunnar closed his eyes.

"He used his key and PIN number to open the door. He was drunk and high. I tried to talk to him again, asked him to show a little understanding. He just laughed at me. I followed him into the common room where he rummaged around in a cupboard and found a white tablet that he swallowed. That made him even weirder. He slumped down in an armchair, turned his back to me, and asked me to massage his shoulders. I thought he'd gone mad, but I later learned that he'd taken ecstasy, which apparently heightens the need for physical contact. I went up to him and at first I thought of indulging him in the hope that he would agree to my request. Suddenly I was seized with such fury that before I knew it I'd taken off my tie and wrapped it round his throat. I tightened it. He struggled. But there was no fight. Then he died. He slowly slipped out of the chair onto the floor. And I left." Gunnar looked at Thóra, gauging her reaction. He seemed to have completely forgotten Matthew.

The sound of sirens could be heard through the window, growing louder. "They're here to collect you," said Thóra.

Gunnar looked away from her and stared out of the window. "I was going to run for vice chancellor," he said sadly.

"I think you can forget that now."

EPILOGUE

DECEMBER 13, 2005

Amelia Guntlieb stared at the tabletop, silent as the grave. Thóra suspected she did not feel up to talking. In her position, Thóra would doubtless have had little to say. Matthew had just given an account of the events as they understood them. Any more important details were unlikely to surface now. Thóra admired how he played down the parts of the story that must have hurt Harald's mother. It was still a repulsive tale and difficult to listen to—even for Thóra, who already knew it inside and out.

"They've located *The Witches' Hammer* and other things that Gunnar dug up in the cave," said Matthew calmly. "The money too. He had spent only a fraction of it. It was all in the bank."

After the police had arrested Gunnar the previous day, Thóra and Matthew's plans to dine out were nixed by the interrogation. Thóra had not felt up to meeting Amelia Guntlieb after they left the police station. Instead she went home. Before sitting down with Gylfi to talk about Sigga and the baby she had a long chat with Laufey. She advised Thóra to make the situation clear to Gylfi by doing something to personalize the baby for him. That would help him realize what was going on. For example, she should encourage him to think of names for the child.

They were sitting in the deserted cafeteria in city hall. Elisa had shed a few tears while Matthew was telling the story, but her mother sat in stunned silence. She looked from her lap to the tabletop and back. Now she raised her head and took a deep breath. No one said a word. They half waited for her to say something, weep or show her feelings in some other way. It did not happen. Instead of looking at any of them she fixed her gaze on the large glass wall overlooking the lake and watched the ducks swimming there with a few geese. The wind ruffled the surface of the water and the birds gently bobbed with the waves. A seagull suddenly swept down into the midst of the dispersed group. "Should we take a look at the map of Iceland?" Matthew said suddenly to Elisa. "It's out front." Elisa nodded distractedly and they stood up and went over to the hall next to the cafeteria. Thóra and Harald's mother were left sitting together.

The woman gave no sign of noticing that anyone had left the table. Thóra politely cleared her throat, without the intended result. She waited for a while but saw that more direct action was needed to capture the woman's attention. "I don't have much experience with this sort of thing so I find it difficult to express how sorry I am. I just want you to know that you and your family have my deepest sympathy."

The woman snorted. "I don't deserve sympathy—neither from you nor anyone else." She turned away from the window and looked at Thóra. Her face was full of anger, then she seemed to soften up. "Sorry. I'm not my usual self." She put her hands on the table and began fiddling with her rings. "I don't know why I feel compelled to talk to you." She looked up at Thóra from her jewelry. "Maybe because I'll never see you again. Maybe because I need to have the chance to justify my actions, now that my behavior has had these terrible consequences."

Thóra could only guess that "these terrible consequences" was a reference to Harald's death. "You don't have to explain it to me," she said. "I wasn't born yesterday, and I know there's often more to things than meets the eye."

The woman smiled vaguely. Thóra noticed how well she'd looked after herself. Admittedly she was beginning to show her age, but she was still stunning even as her beauty was beginning to fade into elegance. Her clothing did little to dispel that impression. Thóra imagined her dark dress suit and coat probably cost more than she herself spent on clothes in a whole year. "Harald was such a wonderful child," the woman said dreamily. "When he was born we were immensely happy. We already had Bernd, he'd just passed two, and then came that lovely baby boy. My memories of the years after that, until Amelia was born, are how you would imagine paradise. Not a shadow fell on any moment of it."

"She was ill, wasn't she?" asked Thóra. "Didn't she have a congenital disease?"

Amelia Guntlieb's smile vanished as quickly as it had appeared. "No. She wasn't born like that. She was perfectly healthy. She was the spitting image of me, judging from the photos I had of myself as a toddler. She was wonderful, as all my children have been—slept well and only cried now and again. None of them had stomach trouble or earaches. Lovely babies." Thóra made do with nodding because she was unsure of the appropriate response. She saw a tear appear in the corner of the woman's eye. "Harald . . ." Her voice cracked. She paused to collect herself before proceeding and swept away the tear with a deft movement of her hand. "I haven't discussed this with a soul, apart from my husband and our doctors. My husband mentioned it to his parents but never to anyone else. We're not an open family and we find it difficult to discuss things— accepting other people's sympathy isn't our greatest strength. I think that's the reason anyway."

"It can be difficult," said Thóra, who had no idea how it must have been. Fortunately she had not needed much sympathy up to now.

"Harald was extremely fond of his little sister but jealous too. He had been my little baby for more than three years and sometimes found it hard to accept the new member of the family. We didn't take it seriously, expected it to pass." The tears rolled down her cheeks. "He dropped her, threw her on the floor." She stopped talking and went back to watching the birds.

"He dropped the baby on the floor?" asked Thóra, taking care to remain calm. A shiver ran down her spine.

"She was four months old, asleep in a car seat. We'd just come back from shopping. I went to take off my coat, and when I got back, Harald was standing holding her in his arms. Not exactly in his arms, actually. He was holding her by the legs like a rag doll. Of course she woke up and started to whimper. He yelled at her and shook her. I ran over to him but I was too late. He just looked at me and smiled. Then he dropped her. Straight onto the tiled floor." Her tears poured in single file, leaving glittering marks down her face. "I could never erase that memory. Whenever I looked at Harald I saw his expression when he dropped her." The woman paused to gather her strength. "Her skull was fractured," she continued, "she went into a coma at the hospital and developed encephalopathy as a result. She never woke up the same again. My little angel."

"Surely you must have been suspected of child abuse? Here they would have removed the baby from your care while they investigated the circumstances."

Amelia's expression implied that Thóra was rather naïve. "We didn't need to go through all that. The family doctor helped us, and the other doctors who looked after her showed nothing but total understanding. Harald was sent to a psychiatrist, but that had no effect. He showed no signs of psychological disorder. He was just a jealous little child who made a terrible mistake."

Thóra did not reveal her doubts that this incident could be classified as the behavior of a normal child. What would she know about that? "Did Harald remember this or did he forget it over time?" she asked instead.

"I honestly don't know. We didn't talk much together, the two of us. I think he probably knew—at least, he was especially kind to Amelia Maria until she finally found peace and died. My impression was that he was constantly trying to make up for what he did."

"So this tainted your relationship all these years?" asked Thóra.

"There was no relationship. I found it hard to look at him, let alone be in his company. I simply avoided my son whenever I could. His father did the same, really. Harald found it difficult to take at first, he didn't understand why his mother didn't want him around any longer. Then he grew accustomed to it." She had stopped weeping and her face had hardened. "Of course I should have forgiven him—but I just couldn't. Perhaps I should have seen a psychiatrist myself, it might all have been different then. Harald would have been something other than what he became."

"Wasn't he a good boy?" Thóra asked, remembering what his surviving sister had said. "Elisa seems to remember him as a good person."

"He was the inquisitive type," the woman said. "Let's put it that way. He was constantly trying to earn his father's affection—which he never won. He soon gave up on me. What saved him was how kind his grandfather was to him. But when he died, Harald lost his bearings. He was a student in Berlin and soon began using drugs and playing at cheating death. One of his friends did die. That was how we found out."

"You didn't back down and try to repair your relationship?" Thóra asked, although she knew the answer in advance.

"No," said Amelia curtly. "Subsequently he developed this ghastly interest in black magic; his grandfather had got him into it. When Amelia Maria died he joined the army. We did nothing to stop him. It didn't turn out to be the best decision—I won't go into details, but he was sent home after less than a year. He had plenty of money which he had inherited from his grandfather and we didn't see much of him. But he did contact us when he decided to come here; he phoned to let us know."

Thóra looked at the woman thoughtfully. "If you're asking me to understand, I can't. But I do sympathize. I don't know how I would have reacted myself—perhaps exactly the same. But I hope not."

"I so wish I had been the type of person who could rebuild my relationship with Harald. Now it's too late and I have to come to terms with it."

Thóra found this ironic. Perhaps the revenge curse had worked after all? "Don't think that I want to make your suffering any worse, but I must point out that it has affected other people too. Now, for example, a young man is in prison, a medical student who was a friend of Harald's. He won't have a chance of being reaccepted by society after making friends with your son."

Amelia looked out of the window. "What will happen to him?"

Thóra shrugged. "He'll probably be convicted of failing to report a dead body and mutilating a corpse, and he'll do some time in prison. Presumably they won't let him back into the faculty of medicine at the university. I have a hunch that he'll take the rap to spare his other friends from being implicated—but you never can tell. In fact I think Harald mentioned him in his will. That's some compensation."

"Did he prove to be a good friend to Harald, in your opinion?" the other woman asked, looking at Thóra.

"Yes, I think so. At least, he kept his promise to Harald—however repellent and stupid it may have been. Your son didn't exactly choose his friends on the basis of how normal they were."

"I'll take care of him," whispered Amelia. "That's the least I can do. He can enroll in medicine abroad. We would have no problems arranging that, even if he does get sentenced for what he did." She stretched out her fingers and then clenched her fists as if feeling a twinge of arthritis. "It would make me feel better to be able to do something. It would ease my suffering a little."

"Matthew can arrange that, if the offer's sincere." Thóra got ready to stand up. "I suppose there's nothing else," she said, sincerely hoping that there wasn't. She had had enough.

Amelia took her handbag from the back of the chair and put it over her shoulder. She stood up and buttoned her coat, then shook Thora's hand. "Thank you," she said, and seemed to mean it. "Send us the bill—it will be paid the moment it arrives." They exchanged farewells and Thóra walked rapidly toward the exit. She could not wait to get out into the fresh air.

On her way she walked past the hall where the map of Iceland was on display. She stopped and watched Matthew and Elisa strolling around the horizontal relief map. When he saw her out of the corner of his eye, Matthew looked up, took Elisa lightly by the arm and pointed at Thóra. They exchanged a few words and Matthew hurried up the steps to her.

"How did it go?" he asked as they walked past the foyer window with the poem etched into the glass.

"Fine—badly," replied Thóra. "I honestly don't know."

"You owe me lunch," he said, opening the door for her. "But since I'm a fair person and not at all hungry I'm quite prepared to accept it in kind."

"How do you mean?" Thóra asked, although she was well aware of the scenario that was unfolding.

They walked off in the direction of Hótel Borg.

Thóra slipped out of the bed two hours later and got dressed. Matthew did not stir. She found paper and a pen on the desk, wrote a brief note to him and placed it on the bedside table.

She left the room without waking him, hurried out to the street and walked toward Skólavördustígur to fetch the car marked "Bibbi's Garage." She deserved the rest of the day off.

Her phone rang in her coat pocket and she answered it.

"Hello, Mom," her son said cheerfully.

"Hello, darling," replied Thóra. "How are you doing? Are you back home?"

"Yes, I'm here with Sigga," he answered awkwardly. "We're discussing names, like you told me to. Is Pepsi a girl's name or a boy's name?"

If you enjoyed *Last Rituals*, don't miss

MY SOUL TO TAKE

the next Thóra Gudmundsdóttir mystery from
Yrsa Sigurdardóttir.

Available in hardcover April 2009 from

wm

WILLIAM MORROW
An Imprint of HarperCollins*Publishers*

BIRNA LOOKED AROUND HER AND TOOK A DEEP BREATH. SHE PEERED through the thin fog hovering above the water and watched a pair of seagulls plunging to compete for food. Neither bird won and they rose back up with a great fluttering of wings. Then they vanished into the denser bank of fog that hung a little farther out. It was low tide and wet seaweed lay spread across the rocky expanse. This was an unusual beach: no sand, only boulders of all shapes and sizes, their surface smoothed by the passage of a million tides. The position of the beach was unique, as well: a small cove surrounded by high cliffs of columnar basalt, which could have been custom-designed by the Creator as a high-rise dwelling for seabirds. Every ledge was occupied, with a corresponding volume of noise. Birna walked over to where the cliffs formed another cove, leading on from the one she was in now. The tide flowed in through a stone arch, and the cove was completely enclosed by cliffs. It could only be seen through the narrow gap between the high walls of rock, but the squawking of the birds inside nonetheless resounded along the whole of the beach.

Birna stopped. The fog had suddenly thickened, reducing her visibility to just a few meters. She inhaled deeply again, this time through her nose, savoring the scent of the sea. If she could, she would sleep out here in the open, wreathed in fog. She had absolutely no desire to go back to the hotel. It should not have been that way. She had loved that building and swelled with childlike pride every time she saw it, even while it was still under construction, the barest bones of what it would become. She had even liked the hole that had been dug for the foundation. The site of the hotel had somehow captured her imagination the first time she visited. The land overlooked the open sea on the southern shore of Snæfellsnes. In this it was like most other farms in the district, although slightly more remote; the farmhouse only came into view when one had walked almost right up to it. It had been built on a grassy patch in a rough field of lava that reached almost to the water's edge. The dramatic scenery inspired her. So did the old house. She had been commissioned to design a gigantic annex, which must not overwhelm or smother the main house. This had caused her a lot of worry—modesty was often the greatest challenge; grandeur, that was a piece of cake.

The sensations that the project aroused were unfamiliar to her. Much as she loved architecture, the other buildings she had designed had not made her feel this way, but she knew exactly why. This hotel was far and away her most successful project. From the moment she began sketching the first draft at her studio in Reykjavík, she had realized that she was on the right track. The building was so much better than all her previous efforts. She realized that she would make a name for herself at last. She would become sought after.

She had often wondered why this project had seized her imagination so immediately and why the outcome had been such a success. There was nothing remarkable about the old house or the land, although the house was unusually grand for its age. It had also been exceptionally well maintained, considering no one had lived in it for about fifty years. She soon realized that someone had looked after the house over the years, perhaps intending to use it as a holiday home or to get away from the city, but those plans had never materialized. Inside the building, there was nothing to indicate that the twenty-first century had begun. A thick layer of dust had covered everything, but mousetraps here and there showed that someone had made sure that the interior and furnishings escaped unnecessary damage. The first time Birna went there, she had found it difficult to look at the tiny skeletons in some of the traps, but otherwise the house had impressed her, inside and out.

Birna looked at her watch. What was wrong with the man? Had he been delayed at that stupid séance? The message had been clear enough. She took out her mobile and scrolled through the texts. Yes, perfectly straightforward: "Meet me @ cave @ 9 2nite." What a load of shit. Before putting her mobile back in her pocket, she double-checked that the cove was out of range. It was. That was one of the most annoying things about this area, she thought, bad mobile reception.

She decided to walk back to the cave. Maybe he was there. Although the cave was high up on the shore, visibility was so poor that she could have missed him. Also, the screeching of the birds drowned out everything else, so she wouldn't have heard him arrive. She set off, taking care to look down because it was easy to lose one's footing on the stones. They crunched together beneath the weight of her feet. Hopefully he had finally come around to her way of thinking. She had expended enough energy on this whole business. She didn't really think he'd changed his mind, as he'd been so adamantly opposed. If by any chance he had, she knew she had herself to thank for his change of heart. She had given in and slept with him. The sex was intended to influence Jónas's deciston in her favor; she had certainly not done it for her own pleasure. It was important to have several projects on the go when the competition came around. Although she had the prize pretty much in the bag, she needed to be sure, so she had to take on that burden. What did one quick shag matter, compared with winning the competition? She would be the talk of the town and, more importantly, her peers. Birna smiled to herself at the thought.

An unusually loud squawking from the cliff pulled her out of her reverie. It was as if all the birds of the heavens were calling out in unison. Perhaps they wanted to remind the world beyond the fog that they existed. Birna sighed. It had turned cold and she wrapped her anorak more tightly around her. What sort of summer was this, anyway? She reached the cave but could see no one. On the off chance that he was there she called out, but no one answered. Ten minutes. She would give him ten minutes and then leave. This was just plain rude. Anger flared inside her, warming her slightly. How dare he make her wait like this? It wasn't like being late for a meeting at a café in Reykjavík. There she could flick through magazines to kill the time, but here there was nothing to do. And beautiful as the area was, right now there was nothing to see but fog.

Five minutes. She would give him just five minutes. She wanted to get back and she was dying for a piss. An odd thought struck her, nothing to do with the beach or being made to wait alone in the freezing fog. She felt suddenly sad that she had not learned more about the geology of this area and other parts of Snæfellsnes. For example, how was Kirkjufell, the mountain that fascinated her, formed? It stood alone in the sea on the northern shore of the peninsula, and she knew enough geology to tell that it was not volcanic. She wished she had taken more interest in her studies when she was at school. When she got back home, she was going to look it up, just as she had planned to do the first time she had seen the mountain.

Birna jumped as the noise of the birds got louder again, raucous cries from farther up the cliff she was leaning against. She took two steps away from the wall of rock. She shuddered, gripped by a feeling of unease, not for the first time. There was something about this place. Not just the obvious, those weirdos who worked at the hotel and claimed to be spiritual assistants to the guests. The guests too. All nutcases, but not quite as bad as the staff. No, there was something else wrong here. Something that had slowly but surely intensified, making its presence known on her first inspection and beginning with goose bumps on her upper arms when she saw the skeletons of the mice. It had now transformed into a persistent unease that Birna found difficult to identify. It wasn't the rubbish about ghosts that scared her—she was pretty sure the hotel staff made those stories up, although only God knew why.

Birna tried to smile as she recalled the behavior of Eiríkur, the resort's aura expert, when she had arrived a week before. He had grasped her upper arm and whispered that her aura was black. She should watch out. Death was after her. She frowned at the memory of his foul breath.

Five minutes had passed. He'd be getting a piece of her mind for this. She could have been working: there was a lot to do and her time was precious. If she had not received the text message, she would have spent this time working on the plans for the new building, and maybe she'd have reached a conclusion by now. It was supposed to stand by itself, a short way from the main building. For some reason she had still not been able to decide on the exact location. There was something about the place she had chosen that disturbed her. That wasn't quite it: there was something about the spot that struck her, something that did not quite fit, although she had no idea what it was. She had asked several of the hotel employees whether they could see anything odd about that patch of land, but in vain. Most of them had answered the question with a more obvious one: "Why don't you choose another place if this one disturbs you? There's plenty of land here." But they didn't understand her. They understood the relative configurations of the constellations. Birna, on the other hand, understood the relative configurations of buildings. This was the location; any other was out of the question.

The birds' squawking intensified again, but Birna was too deep in thought to notice properly. She threaded her way carefully along the rocks toward the gravel path above the beach. Suddenly she stopped in her tracks and listened. She could hear crunching in the pebbles behind her. She began to turn, looking forward to venting the anger that had been building up inside her since she got there. About fucking time.

Birna did not manage to turn around completely. Even over the noise of the birds on the cliff she clearly heard the rock swishing through the still sea air toward her head, and caught a glimpse of it as it struck her forehead with terrible force. She did not see anything more in this life, but she felt many things. In a vague and dreamlike state, she felt herself being dragged along the rough terrain. She felt the goose bumps that the cold fog brought out on her bare flesh as her clothes were removed, and she felt nauseous as she tasted the ferrous tang of blood in her mouth. Her socks were pulled off and she felt a terrible pain on the soles of her feet. What was happening? It was all like a dream. A voice she knew well was ringing in her ears, but given what was happening, that couldn't be right. Birna tried to speak, but couldn't produce the words. A strange groan came out of her throat, but she had not groaned. How very strange all this was.

Before everything turned black, it occurred to her that she would never read about the origin of Mount Kirkjufell. Oddly enough, this hurt the worst of all.

The same pair of gulls that Birna had watched plunging into the sea for food were waiting farther along the beach, watching what was done to her through the mist. Patiently they waited for calm to return. The beach and the sea look after their own. No one here has to starve.

CHAPTER 3

FRIDAY, 9 JUNE 2006

I CAN'T UNDERSTAND what's become of Birna," muttered Jónas, reaching for a floral-patterned cup containing the elixir whose praises he had just been singing to Thóra. This was a special brew of tea from local herbs that, according to Jónas, cured all manner of ailments and ills. Thóra had accepted a cup and taken a sip, and judging from the taste, the tea must have been exceptionally wholesome.

"I would have liked the two of you to meet," he added, after taking a mouthful and placing the cup down carefully on the saucer. There was something quite ridiculous about this, for the cup and saucer were so oddly delicate, bone china with a slender handle that looked even smaller in Jónas's big hands. He was far from delicately built—big-boned without being fat, weather-beaten and with an air of one who would rather swig strong coffee from a mug onboard a trawler than sip un-drinkable herbal tea from a ladylike cup following a yoga class.

Thóra smiled and made herself comfortable in her chair. They were in Jónas's office at the hotel, and her back ached after driving up west. The Friday traffic had been heavy, and it didn't help that she had had to drive her children to their father's house in Gardabær on her way out of town. The traffic had crawled along as if every single resident of the capital were on exactly the same route. Although this was not officially his weekend to have the children, Hannes had offered to swap because he would be abroad at a medical conference the following weekend. Consequently Thóra had decided to take Jónas up on his offer and spend the weekend at the New Age spa hotel on Snæfellsnes. She was going to use the opportunity to relax, have a massage and unwind, as Jónas had suggested, but the main purpose of her trip was of course to dissuade him from claiming compensation for the supposed haunting. Thóra wanted to end the conversation as quickly as possible and go to her room for a nap.

"She'll turn up," Thóra said, just for the sake of saying something. She knew nothing about the architect; the woman could easily be a raving alcoholic who had fallen off the wagon and would not be seen for weeks.

Jónas huffed. "It's not like her. We were meant to go over the draft plans for the new building this morning." He flicked through some papers on his desk, clearly annoyed with the architect.

"Couldn't she just have popped back to Reykjavík to fetch something?" Thóra asked, hoping he would stop talking about this woman. The ache in her back was beginning to spread to her shoulders.

Jónas shook his head. "Her car's outside." He slammed down both hands on the edge of the desk. "Anyway. You're here at least." He smiled. "I'm dying to tell you about the ghost, but that will have to wait until we have more time." Glancing at his watch, he stood up. "I have to do my rounds. I make it a rule to talk to my staff at the end of every day. I have a better sense of the operations and the situation if I know about any problems from the very start. That makes it easier to intervene."

Thóra stood up, delighted to be free. "Yes, by all means. We'll talk about it tomorrow. Don't worry about me. I'll be here all weekend and there's plenty of time to discuss it." As Thóra slung her bag over her shoulder, she noticed an awful smell and wrinkled her nose. "What's that stink?" she asked Jónas. "I smelled it out in the car park too. Is there a fish-oil factory near here?"

Jónas took a few deep breaths. Then he looked at Thóra with a blank expression. "I can't smell anything. I suppose I've got used to the goddamn stench," he said. "A whale has washed up just down the beach from here. When the wind's in a certain direction, the smell wafts over the grounds."

"What?" Thóra said. "Do you just have to wait for the carcass to rot away?" She pulled a face when another wave of the stench swept in. If only the problem she was here to deal with was something like this, it would be a cinch.

"You get used to it," Jónas said. He picked up the telephone and dialed a number. "Hi. I'm sending Thóra over. Have someone show her to her room and fix a massage for her this evening." He said goodbye and put the receiver down. "If you go to reception, I've reserved you the best room, with a lovely view. You won't be disappointed."

A young girl accompanied Thóra from the reception to the much-praised room. She was so small that she barely reached up to Thóra's shoulder. Thóra disliked letting such a slip of a girl carry her bag for her, but had no say in the matter. She was glad that her luggage was not that heavy, even though, as always, she had brought far too much with her. Thóra was convinced that different laws applied on holiday from everyday life, that she would wear clothes that she normally neglected in her wardrobe, but she always ended up in the same clothes as usual. She followed the girl down a long corridor that appeared wider than it was because of the skylight that ran its length. The evening sun shone on the thin, fair hair of the girl in front of her.

"Is this a fun place to work?" Thóra asked, making small talk.

"No," replied the girl without turning around. "I'm looking for another job. There's just nothing going."

"Oh," said Thóra. She had not expected such a frank answer. "Are the people you work with boring?"

The girl looked back over her shoulder without slowing her pace. "Yes and no. Most of them are all right. Some are real idiots." The girl stopped by one of the doors, fished a plastic card out of her pocket, and opened it. "But I'm probably not the best judge. I'm not too keen on the bullshit they try to feed the guests."

For the hotel's sake, Thóra hoped that this girl did not have much contact with the customers. She wasn't exactly the world's best saleswoman. "And is that why you want to quit?" she asked.

"No. Not exactly," the girl answered, showing Thóra into the room. "It's something else. I can't explain exactly. This is a bad place."

Thóra had entered the room first and couldn't see the girl's face as she said this. She couldn't tell if she was serious, but the tone of her voice suggested that she was. Thóra looked around the beautiful room and walked over to a wall of glass overlooking the ocean. Outside was a small terrace.

"Bad in what way?" she asked, turning to look at the girl. The view implied quite the opposite; the waves glistened beyond an empty, peaceful beach.

The girl shrugged. "Just bad. This has always been a bad place. Everyone knows that."

Thóra raised her eyebrows. "Does everyone know that? Who's 'everyone?'" If the place had a bad reputation that the sellers knew about but had neglected to mention, it might provide some flimsy grounds for a compensation case.

The girl looked at her with the scorn only a teenager can muster. "*Everyone,* of course. Everyone here, anyway."

Thóra smiled to herself. She didn't know the population of the southern coast of Snæfellsnes, but knew that the word 'everyone' could not cover many people. "And what is it that everyone knows?"

Suddenly the girl became evasive. She thrust her hands into the pockets of her far-too-large jeans and looked down at her toes. "I've got to go. I shouldn't be talking to you about this." She spun around and walked out into the corridor. "Maybe later." In the doorway she stopped and looked imploringly at Thóra. "Don't tell Jónas I've been gossiping about this. He doesn't like me talking to the guests too much." She rubbed her left hand between the thumb and index finger. "If I want to be able to find work, I need a reference. I want to work at a hotel in Reykjavík."

"Don't worry. I'm not an ordinary guest. I'll tell Jónas that you've been particularly helpful and ask his permission to talk to you properly when things are quieter. Jónas asked me to come here to investigate various matters. I think you can help me, and that would help him too." Thóra looked at the girl, who glared at her suspiciously. "What's your name, anyway?"

"Sóldís," the girl replied. She stood in the doorway for a moment, as if unsure what to do, then smiled weakly, said goodbye and left.

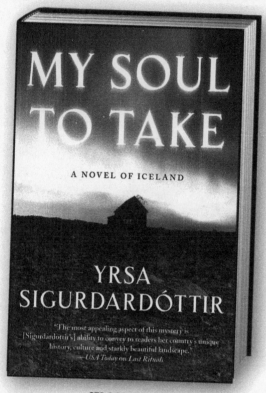